Frank Zafiro channels Ed McBain and Joseph Wambaugh in this taut and frightening thriller.

Simon Wood, author of *Terminated*

Frank Zafiro's *River City* series succeeds where so many fail of late, in not only delivering whipcrack plotlines, but characters as real as the breath in your lungs. You feel with them, rage with them, and bleed alongside these cops. Mr. Zafiro's writing deserves more than comparison with the greats of the police procedural sect, it holds it's own amongst them.

Todd Robinson, editor of Thuglit

With *Beneath A Weeping Sky*, Frank Zafiro lays the whammo on us. Once again, Zafiro brings us back to the River City police force as we follow the lives of these officers as they try to catch the Rainy Day Rapist, whose crimes are becoming increasingly more violent. With straightforward and highly readable prose, Zafiro sucks us into this compelling story, offering psychological insight into both the crazy as hell rapist and the cops chasing him, particularly the damage that the job does to them. This is great stuff, and any fan of Ed McBain or realistic police procedurals should be looking for this book, because no one is writing this stuff better than Zafiro.

Dave Zeltserman author of *Bad Thoughts*

BENEATH A WEEPING SKY

A River City Crime Novel

Frank Zafiro

Gray Dog Press
Spokane, Washington
www.GrayDogPress.com

Publisher's Cataloging-in-Publication Data

Zafiro, Frank
    Beneath A Weeping Sky
    p 483
1. Crime—Fiction. 2. Detective—Fiction.
3. Contemporary fiction. I. Title
Library of Congress Control Number: 2010920762

ISBN: 978-1-936178-12-4

Cover photos: Matt Rose, Matt Rose Photography

PRINTED IN THE UNITED STATES OF AMERICA

Dedication

*This is for the love of my life—my Kristi May,
who knows and believes.*

Acknowledgments

The writer spends many lonely, thrilling hours alone in front of the computer, plying his trade, crafting his world, writing his novel. But making a novel come to fruition is far more involved than simply putting words down on virtual paper. At the risk of using a tired cliché, each novel is like a new child. Any writer will tell you that many a novel is conceived in discussions over coffee with other writers or trusted confidants. That moment of conception is exciting and sexy and glowing. Once so conceived, it grows in the womb, often due to the encouragement of those other supportive people. And when it finally slides out of the womb of the author's mind, that newborn novel is not a pretty sight. It's covered in blood and goo and a host of mistakes and imperfections. Those other writers and readers and editors are like nurses and midwives, lifting the disgusting little creature up and cleaning it off. They treat it for some ailments, inoculate it against others. So when the proud author is finally allowed to leave the hospital with that completed novel in his arms, it is as close to beautiful as it is ever going to get.

So...the point of all that is this: I might technically write these books alone, but I don't finish them alone. I get life-saving help from a number of people—too many to mention, if the truth be told. But I'd like to acknowledge just a few that were pivotal to this one making it through, warts and all.

Every reader who thought to give me feedback on the first two books—you know who you are. You'll see your hands at work in this one.

T. Dawn Richard, whose enthusiasm as a fellow writer is infectious and whose coffee conversations have fed my fire...not to mention her divine editing.

Carly Cortright, for insights into characters and plot problems.

Jill Maser. My dear Tosh, queen of the line edit. What would I do without you? I'd publish significantly poorer stories, that's what for starters. Thank you for your deep crits, deeper insight and your willingness to always call things as they truly lie.

My fellow officers at my home agency. Thank you for all you do every single day.

Julie Shiflett, who over time has helped me understand even just a little bit of what an assault victim goes through.

And lastly, they say that every writer has a particular reader in mind when s/he puts those words on the page. I never really did, to be honest with you. I've been writing since I was ten or eleven, but my "reader" was always a vague, inexact personage that I hoped would dig what I had to say. Since reuniting with my best childhood friend (and marrying her), I've found my "first reader" (as the venerable Mr. King puts it). So my last thank you is to you, Kristi…my gracious, brilliant wife, who reads everything I write as if it were bound for best-sellerdom, criticizes it with a kind, insightful heart and who believes in me more than anyone else, including myself.

Affectionately and gratefully,
Frank
September 2009

Rain falls into the open eyes of the dead
Again again with its pointless sound
When the moon finds them they are the color of everything.
William Stanley Merwin

Part I

Life being what it is, one dreams of revenge.
Paul Gauguin,
French Post-Impressionist painter (1848 - 1903)

ONE

Heather Torin never intended to be a victim.

No one ever does.

She ran the same route every day except Sunday, when she didn't jog at all. It was two and eight-tenths miles long according to the odometer in her Honda Accord. She would have preferred to jog a three-mile course, but the route was just too perfect and so she sacrificed the two-tenths in the interest of aesthetics.

Running was the one thing she did entirely for herself. She enjoyed the firmness it gave her legs and buttocks, but it was the mental benefits that kept her going out day after day. After her three miles, almost every frustration from her day was flushed out, pouring out of her with the sweat on her forehead.

Wednesday's run was usually the hardest run of the week for some reason. Saturday morning runs were her favorite. She left before anything in her day had happened and with no frustrations to burn off, she experienced a calm that she imagined was similar to meditation.

Her breathing was deep and fluid as she padded along through the damp streets of River City's north side. It had been a mild winter, even though traces of snow still littered the ground where it had been piled high during the winter months. March began as a very wet month, but it had none of the iciness of January and February. Heather enjoyed the coolness of the air as she drew it in and released it, trying to keep her breathing as slow as possible. Trees lined the street beneath an obscured, gray sky above.

She passed the two-mile mark. *It's all on the way home now*, she told herself. Good thing, too, since her legs felt a little weak today for some reason. She forced herself to keep up the pace as she approached the park.

Heather liked zigging and zagging along the trail of the small, heavily-wooded park. The coolness in the air was palpable. She could almost taste the wetness and the bark on the pine trees. The damp earth muffled her footfalls. She skipped over a root that protruded from a massive pine.

She sensed the movement rather than saw it. The blow struck her in the rib cage, sending a shock wave of pain through her chest. She felt a pair of arms wrapping around her waist, grasping at her. Those arms slid downward until they clutched at her legs. Like a running back caught in open field, she took two stumbling steps to her left and she fell to the ground. The bulk of her attacker's weight was not on her. She tried to squirm loose.

"Don't move," a man's cold, angry voice growled at her.

Fear lanced through her belly. She opened her mouth to scream but he clamped a hand over her mouth and chin. His fingers mashed her lips into her teeth.

Oh, God. He's going to kill me.

Heather thought of her parents and her sister. She saw her funeral in a flash of light.

The attacker kept one hand firmly sealed over her mouth and the other arm around her waist as he half-carried, half-dragged her off the small trail and into the wooded brush. She kicked and struggled gamely, but his grip was strong and she could not break it.

Heather sobbed once underneath his strong, smooth hand. She didn't want to die.

"Shut up, bitch," the man whispered. "Shut up or I'll lay the whammo on you."

Heather's breath raced in and out of her nose. She couldn't get enough air.

The attacker flung her to the ground. She landed on her back with a dull thud. She felt a curious pain in her chest and realized that her wind had been knocked out of her. *Funny,* she thought. *That hasn't happened since I was about eleven and fell out of the tree in Grandma's—*

The attacker fell on top of her, forcing her legs open.

He pulled her running shorts down her hips and tore at her panties. The action registered slowly with Heather.

He's going to rape me.

Heather shuddered.

My God. He's going to kill me after he rapes me.

She struggled to get air into her lungs as she swam in darkness.

I should open my eyes. In case he doesn't kill me, I can identify him.

She forced her eyes wide open and stared up into her attacker's face. It was covered with a ski mask. The impersonal wool scared her even more. She tried harder to inhale so that she could scream.

Still no breath came.

The attacker fumbled with his pants, his hips still pressed against her thighs. She felt him shudder momentarily. His breath came in ragged gasps. Then he stopped.

For a moment, all was still. There were no human voices, only the distant sound of automobiles and closer, the evening sounds of birds. Heather stared into the man's eyes and searched for mercy. She could find nothing behind the impenetrable gaze.

He rolled her over onto her stomach.

"Don't move, bitch or I'll lay the whammo on you."

Her lungs ached.

"Please," she tried to say, but there was no breath to propel the words out her mouth.

She waited for the pain, expecting him to force himself into her and terrified at not knowing when the attack would come. She felt her fingers and toes twitching.

Will he kill me afterwards?

After an eternity, the smell of wet earth and leaves filled her nostrils.

Smell. She could smell. And breathe.

She took two short breaths.

No attack came.

Still breathing in short breaths, she twisted her neck and looked behind her.

He was gone.

She rose to a sitting position, full of disbelief. She hadn't heard him leave. But he was definitely gone.

Heather stood shakily, pulling her running shorts up and brushing the dirt and leaves from her hair. She stood perfectly still for what seemed like an hour or a lifetime, afraid he would come back and kill her for moving. But no one came. She stood alone in that small wooded area, where she first cursed God, then thanked him.

She eventually walked home on rubbery legs, her mind dazed and racing.

What had she done to cause this?

Who was going to know?

Her mother?

She drew in a deep, wavering breath.

Oh, God, her *father*?

What was everyone going to think?

Right then, Heather Torin decided not to tell anyone about what happened to her. But she stopped jogging that very day.

1722 hours

The dank smell of the laundry room sickened him, but not as much as his own weakness. Cursing, he ripped the pieces of clothing from his body and slapped them into the empty washer. The sweatshirt and pants were soaked in sweat, as was the woolen ski mask. His underwear was soaked in semen, which he wiped away from his body. The rubbing caused him to twitch half-erect.

Don't touch that! Dirty little boy!

His erection faded.

He hurled the wet, sticky underwear into the washer. Then he quickly added soap and turned on the machine.

Dead.

Dead.

She was dead.

He shook his head. He needed a shower.

Trudging upstairs, a sense of great failure enveloped him. He'd failed.

Failed to lay the whammo on that bitch in the park because he'd been too excited.

More than that, he'd failed to show his mother who was stronger. And now, she was forever gone from his grasp. He'd stood in his dark suit just yesterday as they lowered her into the ground. His girlfriend held onto his arm and cried for him because he didn't let a single tear fall.

He couldn't cry.

He didn't want to cry.

He'd wanted to scream.

He'd wanted to laugh.

He'd wanted to rip her from the casket and lay the whammo on her.

But he only stood at the graveside, solemn. Letting no one know. Not any of the mourners. Not the priest. Not the faking bitch at his side. No one knew his mind. No one knew his plan.

But now his plan had failed.

He had failed.

The warm water that pulsed from the showerhead did little to wash that feeling away. He turned the water on hotter yet, but the scalding heat did not make a difference. It didn't burn away his shame. He stood under it as long as he could stand it, then twisted the dial back down to a comfortable level.

"I really should have laid the whammo on her," he told the flowered tile of the shower stall.

Things were going to change.

This was an inauspicious beginning.

He would have to do better the next time.

Part II

April 1996
RIVER CITY, WASHINGTON

[The rain] descends with the enthusiasm of
someone breaking bad news.
H. V. Morton

TWO

Katie MacLeod turned off the engine of her Jeep Cherokee and rubbed her tired eyes. Some mornings, she came home full of energy and too jacked up to sleep. Other mornings, like this one, she returned home almost a zombie and couldn't wait to fall into bed.

The wet, crisp air smelled fresh to her as she trudged up the walkway to the front door of her small house. Living in a house instead of an apartment for the first time as an adult took some getting used to. For example, even through her sleepy senses, she noticed that the grass needed to be mowed. She promised herself to do that during the coming weekend.

Not for the first time, she wondered if the 9-to-5ers had an easier time of it when it came to taking care of their household chores. Still, she wouldn't trade her job for anything.

Most of the time.

Inside, the house was silent except for the light hum of the refrigerator and the tick of the old-fashioned clock on the wall. She listened for Putter, but the cat was either too busy sleeping or out adventuring to be bothered with greeting her.

I should've gotten a dog instead, she mused. *At least a dog would be happy to see me.*

She knew she wasn't home enough to take care of a dog, though. Cats were more self-sufficient, if aloof at times.

Katie hung her jacket. She debated a shower before bed but quickly decided against it. She was just too tired.

The heavy weight of her off-duty gun on her hip was the first thing to go. She set it on her nightstand and dropped her badge next to it. Years ago, when she first came on the job, she would carry a pair of handcuffs and her radio with her, too. Now she didn't bother. If anything ever happened off-duty, the gun would be for dealing with the bad guys and the badge would be for dealing with the good guys when they arrived.

Katie finished undressing and put on her robe. She wandered into the kitchen for a glass of orange juice. She drank it standing next to the sink and rinsed the glass when she had finished.

To bed.

On her way to the bedroom, she saw the blinking light on her answering machine. She considered letting it sit until she woke up that afternoon, but knew she couldn't do that. The call might be from work. Or her mother. Neither party would be happy about a return call at four in the afternoon.

Katie pressed the PLAY button. There was a beep and a male voice came on.

"Katie? Are you there? It's Stef." There was a pause. Katie could hear the sound of vehicle traffic in the background. "If you're there, will you pick up? I...I want to talk to you."

Anger flared in Katie. After what he'd said and done to her, there was no way—

"Katie, please? Pick up."

She detected the slight slur in his voice then. He'd been drinking and probably made the call after the bars closed. She knew that was how he'd been spending his time since he took a medical retirement from the police department. Drinking and feeling sorry for himself. And now he wanted to drag her into it.

No way.

The message ended and the machine beeped. Katie pressed the DELETE button.

He was a coward. That was the conclusion she'd reached in the year or so since his departure. Sure, he'd been shot up physically. And sure, he made a tragic mistake that cost a little girl her life. But he acted as if he were the only one on the job who experienced pain or who ever failed. In doing so, he belittled everyone else's experiences.

She flashed to the Post Street Bridge and the image of a mentally unstable man dangling his infant son over the edge of the bridge. The rush of impending doom flooded her chest. She saw herself standing helpless, pleading with the man.

Katie bit her lip.

"Goddamn you, Stef," she whispered. "Don't call me any more."

She walked into the bathroom and turned on the hot water. Maybe she needed a shower after all.

0721 hours

Officer Thomas Chisolm tried to sprint the final block of his run, but his tired legs and aching lungs wouldn't cooperate. He managed to work up to a long-striding lope as he finished off his five miles, then slowed to a walk in front of his home. Hands on his hips, he walked in large circles around the front yard, slowing his breathing and letting his legs cool down.

Mornings were melancholy times for him. Sometimes he had thoughts of Scarface, the robber he'd killed. Other times, memories of Vietnam crept back in to his consciousness, forcing their way out of the shallow graves in his mind.

Like Bobby Ramirez.

Or Mai.

He needed sleep. That's all it was. Some water, a hot shower and sleep.

As his breath slowed, he turned on the water in his front yard and drank from the hose. The city water had a slight metallic tang to it, but he took a deep draught before turning the spigot off.

Chisolm made his way up the short, concrete steps and removed his house key from his sock. Unlocking the door, he went inside, tossing the key on the kitchen table. A hot shower was calling to him.

As he walked past the refrigerator, a picture taped to the front caught his attention. An attractive, dark-haired woman stared out of the photograph at him. She had a smile on her face but her eyes were slightly sad. They'd always had that hint of sadness, as long as he'd known her.

Sylvia.

He'd intended to remove the photo over two years ago, but never remembered to do it. He didn't bother with it now, reasoning that the shower was more pressing. He almost fooled himself into believing that as he walked out of the kitchen and toward the bathroom.

Thomas Chisolm refused to think of her, concentrating instead on what he had to accomplish after he woke up and before going to work tonight. If he opened up the door to memories, far too many would come unbidden. Especially in the mornings.

"Regret is a luxury you can't afford," he told his reflection.

We live in a world of broken promises, he added silently. *And life is full of failure.*

Chisolm undressed and took his shower. He turned the hot water up until the searing heat was as hot as he could stand. Despite admonishing himself to forget about Sylvia, he allowed himself to brood a little more as the water cascaded down on his head. He knew that if he stopped thinking about her, there was another memory standing in line behind her.

Stop chasing ghosts. Just stop.

0938 hours

Lieutenant Alan Hart drummed his fingers on the desktop. The rhythmic thud echoed through the empty office.

He stared down at the file in front of him, his eyes skipping over the words in the report that he'd already read three times and nearly had memorized.

According to the report, Officer James Kahn drove through the Life's Bean Good coffee stand several times a night. He bought coffee each time, tipped generously, and asked the nineteen-year-old barista out on a date. She reported being flattered at first, then uncomfortable with his advances. When she told her boyfriend about it, he made her call in a complaint.

Identifying Kahn had been no problem. Skirt chasers were common enough, but Kahn gave the barista his business card with his cell phone number on the back. He insisted she call him by his first name. Besides that, when she came into the office, Hart directed her to the picture wall that held every officer's photo but no names. She immediately pointed right at Kahn's picture.

Hart flipped the page and read the transcript.

```
Question: How often did the officer
    visit your place of business?
Answer: Two or three times a day, at
    least.
Question: Did he buy something each
    time?
Answer: Yes.
Question: Did he ask you out on a date
    each time?
Answer: No, but more than once. And he
    flirted with me a lot.
Question: Did you ever feel afraid of
    him?
Answer: No.
Question: Threatened? Unsafe?
Answer: No. I just didn't want to go out
    with him.
Question: Did his demeanor ever change
    when you turned him down?
Answer: Not really. He just smiled and
    kept trying.
```

Hart sighed and closed the file. He'd been assigned to Internal Affairs for almost a year and here he was, reduced to investigating some patrol cop trying to get laid. That wasn't why he took the job.

He glanced around the empty office and smirked. When the Chief decided to assign a lieutenant to Internal Affairs, he pulled out all four of the previously assigned detectives. Hart had no support staff and even had to type his own reports. He knew the Chief did it as a form of punishment, but he refused to let it get to him. He might be banished from patrol and investigations, but he still intended to have an impact on the department.

Kahn' file stared up at him. He snatched it up and replaced it in his active cases drawer. What a waste of time. The worst the guy would get is a verbal reprimand from his sergeant and told to stay away from Life's Bean Good. He'd just go find another barista. There was a coffee stand on every corner in River City.

Besides, these cases were a smokescreen. They had to be. Hart knew there were things happening out there that he needed to find. Cops stealing. Faking evidence. Beating people. Just because River City was nestled in Eastern Washington, right in the center of the Pacific Northwest, didn't mean there wasn't corruption. Maybe not New York or Los Angeles level corruption, but Hart knew it was out there. The cops were covering for each other, that was all.

They thought they were so smart.

But Hart knew they weren't as smart as him.

1122 hours

Patricia Reno wished there were an easier way to get thin. Jogging was too painful.

She'd started jogging almost a month before, finally tired of the weight that never came off after Joshua, her second son, was born. Sit-ups, she discovered, did not burn fat and she couldn't afford a gym membership, so she took up jogging.

As her feet thudded heavily on the pavement, she felt her thighs and belly jiggle. Her breasts flopped uncomfortably. She vowed for the tenth time to buy a sports bra. At least she was starting to notice a little difference in her body. She was now able to just squeeze into clothes she'd worn early in her pregnancy.

If only her husband, Roger, would notice.

Patricia's breath labored in and out of her lungs, but she no longer experienced the ragged throat sensation that she had for the first week. Her wind had improved quickly. That made it easier for her to avoid smoking again. She'd quit the day she learned she was pregnant and hadn't started back up yet, but it was hard. Especially since Roger smoked like a chimney.

She spotted the small park less than a block away. As soon as she ran through that, she would only be five blocks from home. That meant four blocks of running, one block of walking to cool down.

Despite the discomfort, Patricia found that she was beginning to enjoy her daily run. She still struggled with it too much to have a chance to think while running, but with two kids to worry about, the solitude was nice. So was the sense of accomplishment. She hadn't stopped during a run since that first week.

The air became cooler as she entered the park and ran along the twisting trail that led into the small wooded area. The tree roots and turns of the trail forced her to adjust her gait. That nearly killed her three weeks ago, but now she did so much more fluidly and deliberately. She watched the ground, not wanting to trip on the damp earth.

She caught a flash of movement, but before her mind could register and identify it, someone forced a towel into her face. A strong arm encircled her waist and carried her several yards before she felt herself hurled to the ground. A hard heavy body fell on top of her. She lay on her back with her right forearm pinned under the small of her back.

The towel restricted her air. She panicked and flailed frantically with her free left hand, struggling to breathe. The cloth slid up, exposing her mouth. She took a deep, ragged breath. An iron hand clamped over her mouth.

"If you scream, I'll lay the whammo on you." A male voice rasped in her ear. "Understand?"

Patricia lay still, stunned.

He jerked her head powerfully. "I said, do you understand?"

Patricia nodded, whimpering beneath his hand.

"Good."

The hand came away from her mouth and Patricia sucked in a grateful breath. He tugged at her waistband, sliding her sweats and panties down over her knees.

Should I resist?

She gulped more air.

Will he kill me?

He pulled her clothing over her running shoes and tossed them aside. She heard them land on a bush, a moment's rustle, then still.

There was a long pause. She heard paper tearing.

Should I beg? Or just be quiet and let him do it?

How could this be happening to me?

She gasped in pain as he thrust inside her forcefully.

"Oh, my sweet little bitch," he moaned in her ear, thrusting slowly.

Patricia began to cry softly.

"Unnnnh, Unnnnh," he moaned, pulling the towel more tightly across her face.

Patricia tried to stop crying, but instead she broke into a sob.

He stopped.

She thought for a moment that it had been her crying that made him stop, that it touched him or even enraged him. She stopped crying, quivering as she waited. He lay across her with the dead weight of a spent man. That was when she realized he was done.

After a few moments, he pulled out of her and rolled her onto her stomach. Panic surged through her again. When he pulled the towel from her head, she sighed in relief.

"Don't look up," he told her gruffly.

She wouldn't. She never wanted to see his face. If she did she would be dreaming of it every night for the rest of her life.

"Don't tell anyone," he growled at her. "Or I will find you again and I will lay the whammo on you."

"I won't," she whimpered.

He gave her a shove in the back of the head to reinforce his warning. She took it with a small cry. Then she lay still, breathing in the humid, earthy smell of the damp soil and pine needles.

What is Roger going to say?

When she was sure he was gone, she fumbled with her clothing, lifting them from the damp earth. Numbly, she pulled her panties and sweats over her running shoes. Then she rose on wobbly legs and stumbled home to call the police.

1314 hours

"Adam-254?" Janice Koslowski's dispatch voice was pleasantly female.

Officer Anthony Giovanni reached for the mike. "Go ahead. I'm at Wellesley and Division."

"Deaconess Hospital for a rape report. Contact Charge Nurse for victim info. Deaconess for a rape report."

Gio keyed the mike. "Copy." Then he muttered, "Thanks a lot, Janice."

A rape report. That meant a long interview, a long report and then he had to put the rape kit on property. The rape kit was a real pain in the ass, too, requiring some swabs to be placed in the drying room, some blood vials in the refrigerator and some property in the property bins. Gio looked at his watch. It was 1314 hours. This would definitely take him into overtime.

He drove past Franklin Park, wondering for a moment why a south side unit hadn't been dispatched. Deaconess Hospital was clear on the other side of downtown. The answer came to him almost immediately, though. The rape must have happened on the north side, so a north side unit got sent.

As he dropped down the Division Hill and headed downtown, he did a little bit of quick figuring. Even with the rape kit, he should be done with the call before it got to be too late. Besides, the girl he was seeing that afternoon didn't get off until three or so. That'd leave him plenty of time to get home, shower and change, rape report or not. And if he didn't, he figured the girl would wait.

The girl, he thought. Melanie. Or Mallory. Whatever it was. She'd wait.

Six minutes later, he pulled into Deaconess, parking in a slot marked for emergency vehicles only. Before exiting the patrol car, he gathered up his face sheet for the report and a steno pad from his bag. Rape reports needed to be detailed and details were easier to write in a steno pad than the small pocket notepad all officers carried in their breast pocket.

The white-shirted security guard gave him a professional nod as he walked through the sliding doors to the emergency room. Gio nodded back with a small grin, ignoring the metal detector that loomed over fully half the entryway. He could hear the creak of his leather equipment as he walked up to the front desk.

"Charge nurse?" he asked the frumpy, gray-haired R.N. that sat behind the admissions desk doing paperwork. When she looked up, he gave her his best Giovanni hello smile.

The R.N. was unmoved. "No, I'm the Admissions nurse," she said in a clipped tone. "Are you here for the rape victim?"

Gio nodded.

The R.N. pointed at an open door with a number three hanging above it. "She just finished the exam. Should be about thirty or forty minutes before they have the kit ready for you."

"Thanks," Gio said, still smiling.

The nurse gave him a curt nod and returned to her paperwork.

Gio walked to the room. Past the open door was a drawn curtain, providing privacy to the patient in the bed. He paused just inside the entryway. "Uh, ma'am?"

"Yes?" Her voice sounded small.

"Police officer, ma'am. Are you dressed?"

"Yes."

Gio pushed the light curtain aside and stepped in. He saw a woman about thirty seated on the small bed. Her sandy brown hair was tousled and she wore a pale blue hospital gown. She watched Gio with a hint of shame in her expression.

He felt a flash of guilt for his earlier reaction to getting this call. Yeah, he might be a little late for a date that he wasn't even going remember a month from now, but that was nothing compared to what this woman had just gone through.

"I'm Officer Giovanni, ma'am."

She gave him a shaky nod.

Gio smiled softly. "If you want, you can call me Gio."

The woman took a wavering breath. "Okay. Gio." She said the word tentatively, as if she were trying it out. "Gio."

"Can I get your name, ma'am?"

"I'm Patricia," she answered, her voice still soft. "Patricia Reno."

Gio noticed the tremor in her voice despite its soft tone. He moved slowly towards the bedside, then stopped. "Do you mind if I stand next to you?" he asked her.

Patricia looked at him for a moment, then nodded. "That'd be fine."

"Thanks," Gio said. He moved next to her bedside. Aware that a rape victim had experienced the ultimate loss of control during the assault, he always tried to find ways to restore some measure of control to their lives as quickly as possible. "Do you like to be called Patricia?" he asked. "Or Pat? Or is Mrs. Reno best?"

"Patricia," she answered. "I go by Patricia."

Gio still made no effort to open his steno pad. "Is it all right if I call you that?"

"Sure," she said. "Of course."

"Thank you," Gio said. After a short pause, he continued. "Ma'am, I understand you were assaulted."

Patricia nodded slowly, looking away. Her lip quivered. "He... I was raped."

"Do you know who did this?"

She shook her head.

"When did this happen?"

"About forty minutes before I came up here, I guess."

Gio opened his pad and noted the time frame.

"Where did this happen, ma'am?"

She let out a long, wavering sigh. "In a park, about five blocks from my house. I don't know the name."

"That's all right. Where do you live?"

She told him her address. Gio wrote it down.

"Was it possibly Corbin Park?" he asked.

"No," she said. "I know that one. It's a little park. With some trees..."

Gio nodded. He knew which park she meant. It was about three blocks north of Corbin, just below the hill. He'd have to look up the name on his map.

"That's good. That will help a lot," Gio said in an encouraging voice. "Now, do you remember where in the park this happened?"

She took another wavering breath. "There's a spot on the trail where there's a break in the bushes. About in the middle of the park. I was running towards my house. It happened there."

"Okay." Gio smiled warmly. "Patricia, I am going to call the detectives and send them down there to see if they can find any evidence. Then I'll be right back to talk with you about the rest of what happened. Will it be all right with you if I take some notes?"

"That's fine. Could I call my husband, though?"

Gio nodded. "Of course. Or I can call him for you, if you like."

She thought about it for a moment, then nodded her head. "Yes. That would be better." She gave Gio the phone number.

"All right," he said. "I'm going to call the detective, then your husband, then I will be back in about five minutes. Do you need anything? Would you like me to get the nurse?"

She shook her head. "No, I'll... be okay."

Gio turned to go.

"Officer?"

He stopped and faced her again. "Yes, Patricia?"

She swallowed nervously and gave him a plaintive look. "Tell me honestly. Is there any chance of catching this man?"

Gio returned her questioning stare with a frank, even gaze. "At this point, I don't know yet, Patricia. I really don't. But we are going to try. I promise you that."

Patricia's eyes teared up. "It's just that...he said he'd come back and find me..."

"The most important thing," Gio said, "is that you're safe now. You're here and you're safe."

Tears flowed down her cheeks. Her breath caught as she spoke. "I didn't... I didn't fight back... I should have done... I could have..."

Gio returned to her bedside. Carefully, he let his hand rest lightly on her shoulder. "Patricia, this wasn't your fault. You didn't cause this to happen. There's nothing you could have done."

"I could have...I should have fought or..."

Gio shook his head gently. "You did what you needed to do in order to survive. That took guts. Just like telling me about this takes guts."

Patricia thought about his reply, meeting his gaze.

"This is *not* your fault," Gio whispered to her.

Slowly, she gave him a small nod in return.

Gio nodded back and gave her a warm smile. Then he left the curtained room to call the Sex Crimes Unit of the Investigative Division. He didn't bother to glance at his watch.

1428 hours

Detective John Tower replaced the phone receiver with a muttered, "shit." A rape report. He was in the middle of a nasty date rape case and didn't need another case dropped on him. But he was up next in the rotation and that was the reason Lieutenant Crawford transferred the call to him.

Unfortunately, this one didn't sound like much of a workable case, either, Tower reflected as he slid his jacket on and adjusted it around his shoulder holster. The victim didn't know the suspect. Usually, they did.

Tower shrugged. Well, maybe she'd be able to give a good suspect description. He could check the Department of Corrections records for registered sex criminals and have her look through some photos. He might get lucky.

He picked up the phone and dialed police dispatch. He spoke briefly with the supervisor, Carrie Anne, and asked her to send a patrol unit to the park to secure the crime scene.

Lieutenant Crawford strode into the Sex Crime Unit bullpen. "You headed out on that stranger-to-stranger?"

"Yeah," Tower replied shortly, hanging up the phone.

"Where's the vic at?"

"Deaconess."

Crawford's unlit cigar poked out of his mouth around his dark, drooping mustache. No matter how hard Tower tried, he couldn't shake the image that Crawford was actually the actor from the TV show *Cannon*. He had the balding hair, the heavy stomach and fat cheeks, everything. All he was missing was the bad 1970s suit. He even had the cigar, which he chewed on but dared not light despite his long tenure on the department.

"Keep me updated," Crawford ordered.

"Yes, sir," Tower said on his way out the bullpen.

Come to think of it, he thought as he walked down the hall, *that was a pretty damn bad suit. Maybe not 1970s bad, but pretty close.*

He smiled.

Outside, the clouds were full of gathering blackness and he expected it would rain again before quitting time. Tower started up his car and drove directly to the small park that Officer Giovanni had described on the phone. As he pulled up, he saw that there was only one marked car on scene. He recognized Jack Stone standing near the car, but didn't know the civilian woman seated in the front seat.

"Hey, Jack," he greeted the gruff veteran.

"John."

"Citizen ride-along?" he asked, gesturing toward the woman in the car.

"Yeah," Stone said with a nod. "She just went through the Citizen's Academy. Real pro-police. Block Watch captain and everything."

"Good," Tower said. "We need all the support we can get."

Tower turned his attention to the small wooded area just to his north. The park was small by park standards, less than one square block, but it was huge by crime scene standards. He chewed on his lip, considering his best course of action.

"You want some help?" Stone asked.

Tower nodded, still thinking. She had used the trail, so he would start there.

"Let's do this," he instructed. "The trail is the center of the park. The victim was pulled from the trail. Let's start on each side of the trail and walk through the park. We'll start on the south side and work north. If we find anything, we'll stop and section it off. Hopefully, we can at least pin down where this occurred."

Stone nodded. "Okay. Are you going to call out Forensics?"

Tower considered. The Crime Scene Forensic Unit was much better equipped to photograph and collect evidence. But they needed something to work with first. "If we pin down where it happened, we'll cordon it off and have them come down here and work it."

"What about bringing the victim down here?"

"If I have to. But I'd rather not, at least not right away."

Stone shrugged. "What about my rider? Can she help at all?"

Tower considered for a moment, then shook his head. "No. But she can stand at the curb and observe, if she wants to. I don't want her to accidentally trample evidence."

Stone grunted. "You mean like patrol officers usually do?"

Tower shrugged, unsure if Stone were joking or if the veteran officer had taken offense. "Hey," he answered with a grin, "if the crime scene is going to get trashed, I want it done professionally."

Stone put his back to the woman in the car, brought his hand up to the center of his own chest and extended his middle finger.

Tower raised his eyebrows. "Never on a first date."

Stone laughed.

Together they walked to opposite sides of the trail and began their modified line search. Tower's eyes scanned the ground and the low bushes for anything that could be construed as evidence. He glanced up periodically to make sure he didn't miss the forest for the trees. To his left, he heard Stone shuffling along.

Ten minutes into his line search, Tower was sweating profusely despite the overcast weather. He removed his jacket and folded it over the crook of his arm. He felt sorry for Stone, who wore a wool uniform shirt over a bullet-resistant vest.

As minutes dragged by, his patience wore thin. He'd never been a particularly patient man and because of that, the job of detective often frustrated him. He used to hope that the years of experience would increase his patience level, but all it seemed to do was teach him to cope with the impatience that inevitably rose up. It didn't take away the tickle of frustration from his gut.

Tower forced himself to concentrate as he came into a small opening of brush that fit the victim's description of where the rape took place. He searched high and low, then low and high but saw nothing. The grass did not even appear disturbed.

"I think this is it," he told Stone.

"You found something?"

Tower shook his head. "No. But this is the only place that fits what she told the officer at the hospital."

Stone grunted noncommittally.

Tower marked the area in his mind and moved on.

After forty minutes of searching, he reached the north side of the park, which was bordered by a paved street. He waited there, wiping sweat from his brow until Stone completed his sweep.

"Anything else?" the veteran asked him.

"*Nada.* I think that spot I mentioned is where it happened, but the scene looks clean."

"Too bad." Stone wiped the sweat from his forehead and cheek. "It's muggy out here. I need something cold to drink."

"Me, too. Guess I'll grab something up at Deaconess."

"That where the victim went?"

Tower nodded.

"This a stranger-stranger or what?"

"Sounds like a stranger. Did radio put out any calls that might be related to this area? Screaming, suspicious persons, anything?"

"Nope, not that I heard." Stone keyed his mike and asked radio if they had received any such calls.

"Negative," came the terse reply.

Stone gave him a shrug. "You think the victim's making it up?"

Tower shrugged. "I don't know. It wouldn't be the first time."

"Won't be the last," Stone added.

"Can you throw up some crime scene tape around that area for me?" Tower asked.

Stone nodded. "How big an area you want roped off?"

Tower thought about it, then answered. "Make it about twenty by twenty. Center on the break in the bushes by the trail."

"Okay. Outer perimeter?"

Tower waved his hand around the park. "Take the whole park. You don't have to run tape, though. Not unless you get serious foot traffic. Just keep people out of the park."

"I'll call another unit," Stone said.

Tower nodded his thanks and made his way to his car. Once en route to Deaconess Hospital, he plugged his department issued cellular phone into the cigarette lighter and called Forensics.

Diane answered on the second ring. "CSFU, Diane."

"Diane, it's John Tower. I need you to process a rape scene."

"Address?"

Tower told her where the park was and described the crime scene area. "I don't know if you'll find any evidence or not, but at least get some good photographs."

"I will."

"I'm on my way to the hospital now," Tower said. "I'll let you know if I need anything besides the scene processed."

"I'll call if we get anything," Diane said.

"Thanks," Tower replied and broke the connection.

As he drove, large drops of rain began plopping intermittently onto his windshield. After a few moments, the plops became a steady pour of heavy drops slapping against the glass.

"Goddamnit," he muttered. Rain wreaked havoc with any outdoor crime scenes. He sincerely doubted that CSFU would get anything out of their search now.

He took a deep breath and forced himself to stop worrying about the crime scene that he could do nothing about. Instead, he considered the rape itself. Stone had asked if he thought the victim might be lying, but even without meeting her, he doubted it. A daylight, stranger-to-stranger attack was bold. It wasn't an opportunity rape or a rejection rape. Something like this had to be carefully planned.

That worried him.

Tower pulled into the hospital parking lot. He'd been to Deaconess more times than he could count and almost felt like he should have his own parking spot. He settled for the emergency vehicle slot next to a marked patrol car that he imagined belonged to Gio.

The white-shirted security guard at the emergency room entrance did not know him and started to ask him to step through the metal detector. Tower showed his badge and was waved through. He wondered briefly what the guard would do if a bad guy came to the hospital with a gun and refused to step through the metal detector. After all, the guard himself was not armed.

He recognized Roberta, the grey-haired, pudgy admissions nurse who pretended to be grumpy at everyone. He'd known her since he first came on the job, back when both of them worked nights. Now, years later, they were both working day tours. Circle of life, he figured.

He smiled at her. She didn't smile back, but instead pointed to number three.

"Is the officer in there?"

"No. He's in our break room." Her tone of voice suggested that in her opinion, Gio was trespassing there. Tower was surprised that Giovanni's legendary charm hadn't softened her up.

"Thanks, Bertie," Tower said, smiling again. "Did you lose some weight?"

She gave him a flat gaze. "Hardly," she answered. He noticed the corner of her mouth twitch upward before she caught herself.

Almost got ya, Tower thought to himself.

Officer Giovanni was sipping coffee from a small Styrofoam cup and staring down at his report when Tower entered. He greeted the detective.

"Anything at the scene?" Gio asked.

Tower shook his head. "Can you give me a thumbnail sketch of her account? I'll read your report later."

Gio nodded. He took another sip of his coffee and set down his pen. "It's pretty straightforward. Basically, she was jogging southbound through Clemons Park when a male attacked her. He blindsided her and knocked her down. Then he put a towel or something over her face and pulled her a little ways off the trail. He raped her vaginally, turned her onto her stomach, removed the towel and left."

"Any suspect description?"

"She never saw his face."

Tower cursed. Gio sipped his coffee.

"Did he say anything to her?" Tower asked.

"Uh, yeah. I wrote it down. Called her a bitch and threatened her. I've got the exact quote in my notes."

"Did he ejaculate?"

"She thinks so."

"Did the doctor find any semen or anything?"

Gio shook his head. "No. She told him that the last sexual encounter with her husband had been two weeks ago. Doc said there was trauma and small tears but no fluids."

"She a Forty-eight?" Tower asked, using the code for a mentally unstable person.

"No, not at all. Nice lady. Just shaken up."

"Understandable. Anything else?"

"She did say that once he had her pinned, there was a few seconds where he paused and she heard some paper ripping."

"Paper?"

Gio nodded. "I'm thinking maybe he gloved up."

"A rapist that uses a condom?" Tower asked, skeptical.

Gio shrugged. "Safety first."

Tower scratched his head. "Or he didn't want to leave any evidence."

"Could be," Gio agreed. "Maybe he didn't want to pull an O.J."

Tower considered. With DNA technology making leaps and bounds, identifying someone from their semen was a distinct probability. Thanks to the O.J. Simpson trial, pretty much everyone was aware of that. The use of a condom was the obvious preventative. It also indicated greater preparation and planning.

Tower cursed under his breath. Then he said, "She's in number three, right?"

Gio nodded.

"You can take off," Tower told him, "if you're done."

"Nah. I promised to take her home afterwards. Her husband couldn't be reached."

Tower thought about offering to drive the woman home so Gio could leave, but supposed that the officer had established a good rapport with her. It was best not to shuffle the victim around from person to person. "Does she have an advocate with her?"

"No, she wanted a friend instead. Her name's Sally. She's been helpful."

"Good. You want to introduce us, then?"

"Happy to." Gio rose and led him toward room number three.

On the way, Tower asked, "Clemons Park is the name of that little park there, huh?"

"Yeah. I had to look it up myself," Gio said. He stopped at the door and knocked softly. Someone said "come in," so he opened the door and entered.

Patricia Reno sat on the bed, crying softly. Another woman stood at her bedside, consoling her.

"Patricia?" Gio asked. "Are you ready to talk to the detective? Because if you want to wait—"

Patricia Reno nodded, wiping at her eyes. "No, I'm ready. I'm sorry. I was fine until Sally got here."

"No need to be sorry," Gio said. "You didn't do anything wrong." He pointed at Tower. "This is Detective John Tower. He might have a few questions for you. John, this is Patricia Reno. The other woman is her friend, Sally."

Tower nodded at Sally and stepped up next to Patricia. "Mrs. Reno, I really don't have too many questions for you right now. I'll read the officer's report and be in contact with you after that. Probably in a couple of days. But I have been to the scene already."

He described the small opening and she nodded emphatically. "Yes, that's it. That is exactly where it happened."

Tower nodded. "I searched the area. Unfortunately, there was no physical evidence there that I could see. Our forensics unit will photograph it and search it again." Tower leaned forward slightly. "Ma'am, would you recognize the man's voice if you heard it again?"

Patricia's eyes widened. She nodded slowly. "Oh, yes. I'll never forget that voice."

"Good." Tower knew they would never get a conviction off a voice identification, but every little bit helped. "That's really all for now, Ma'am. I wanted to meet you and let you know who I am. This way, when I call you in a day or two, you can put a face with a name."

"Thank you."

He handed her his business card. "Do you have any questions for me?"

Patricia clutched the card, looked down at it for a moment, thinking. Then she shook her head. "No, I think that the officer...that Gio already answered them."

"All right. And he gave you a card with some resources available to you? Counselors and such?"

She dipped her chin again.

"Okay. Is Sally driving you home?"

Sally nodded. Patricia looked up at Gio. "Sorry," she said in an apologetic tone.

"Don't be sorry," Gio told her kindly. "I can see you're in good hands."

"Well, you've been so nice and you've been waiting here so long just to give me a ride..."

Gio smiled. "Patricia, I have to write this report and it doesn't matter where I am when I do it. You haven't put me out at all. Sally can take you home and help you settle in, if that's what you want. It's no problem."

"Thank you," she said again, looking at each of them.

"I'll be in touch," Tower said as they left the small room.

Gio pulled the door shut carefully.

"Nice woman," Tower observed as the two men turned and walked down the hall.

Gio nodded. When they reached the break room, he gathered up his belongings. "It's too bad nothing will ever happen on this."

Tower fought off a sigh. Gio was probably right. Without something more, this investigation was most likely a dead end.

"Maybe something will turn up," Tower said, not really believing it. "Forensics might get lucky."

"Maybe," Gio said, half sighing. "And maybe I'll cure cancer on my way back to the station."

"Stranger things have happened," Tower said.

As they walked out into the rain together, one thought kept bothering Tower. It was a thought he hated to acknowledge, even though his impatient gut told him it was the truth.

This isn't done. He isn't finished.

1633 hours

She comes to him.

She wants him.

He is so strong. Such a man.

"I want you deep inside me with your hugeness," she coos at him, crossing her arms under her breasts and pushing them up at him. "Only you can satisfy me, baby. No one else ever has."

He is so strong. Such a man.

She is dancing now, though there is no music. Swaying lightly, her small black panties shifting on her hips as she moves from side to side. "Do you want me?" she asks him seductively.

"I want you," he breathes.

"Not as bad as I want you, you big, glorious man," she answers and drops down onto him, her lips searching for his, her tongue alive with warm action. Her hands find his erect member and stroke it gently in counterpoint to her hard, deep kisses. He can feel her breasts press firmly against his chest. He squeezes her buttock, hard. She moans in pleasure.

He is such a man.

"Rip them off," she gushes hotly in his ear, biting the lobe.

He tears the panties from her. She cries out, part pain, part pleasure. She guides him into her hot wetness. "Deep inside me with your beautiful self," she whispers, her hands running all over his back.

He thrusts deep. Each thrust is met with a yelp of pleasure from the buxom blonde.

Over her shoulder, he can see his father's face, with an approving leer.

"Fuck her hard, son. And if she doesn't want it, lay the whammo on her!"

"Fuck me hard!" she squeals.

He is truly a man.

He reaches for the white towel.

He knows that she is unaware...

"Unnnnnnhhh, Unnnnnnh," he grunted, arching his hips into the air, his hand moving feverishly up and down. Semen spurted, arching in the air onto his stomach and chest. He let a small moan escape his lips. A few more strokes, then he stopped, collapsing back onto the mattress.

He lay on the bed, bare except for a sheet and a thin blanket. His girlfriend had taken the comforter when she moved out. He pushed thoughts of her away. Instead, he tried to enjoy the afterglow, which always gave him the sense of honey dripping from a broken jar. The constant patter of rainfall outside added to the experience.

After a few moments, though, his thoughts turned to more practical matters.

He had been a fool to attempt two rapes so close to his home. He needed to move farther away for the next one. Police weren't brilliant, but they weren't all stupid, either. Every true crime book he'd read told him that. If rapes kept happening in the same park or the same neighborhood, the police would get a clue. Especially when the victims could tell them that the rapist left on foot.

He needed to stay more random, vary his methods. Don't want to make it too easy for the cops.

Slowly, he roused himself and walked into the bathroom, where he wiped himself off. His thoughts strayed to his ex-girlfriend. He tried to tell himself that he was glad she was gone, but he knew it wasn't true. He didn't love her, nor had he hated her. For a while, she'd been a good woman, but some time after she'd moved in, things started to go south. She became demanding. She wanted this, she wanted that. Most importantly, she started to make him feel like he was small and insignificant.

Just like all the others, he thought.

Just like my mother.

They're all sisters, he figured. Some hid it better than others, but they were all sisters in the end.

Another thing that bothered him was inconsistency. It was simply another form of hypocrisy, really. If a person can't be counted on to behave a certain way for a reasonable percentage of the time, what was that? An integrity issue? An insanity issue?

An old, hard face flashed before his mind's eye.

No! He threw the tissue into the toilet and clenched his fist. *She* was dead and that was fine with him. The only regret he had was that he hadn't shown her who was stronger in the end. Simply outliving the bitch wasn't good enough. He'd have preferred more.

Much more.

He flushed the toilet.

Truth was, he realized, that bitches ruin everything.

He smiled slightly.

"Yes, they do," he whispered. Then, more powerfully, he repeated, "Bitches ruin everything."

That sentiment calmed him. He unclenched his fists and turned on the shower. As he stepped under the hot water, his thoughts strayed to his next victim. He had come up with a good idea. An excellent variation on his plan. It just had a few things that needed working on, that was all. As the soap cleansed him, his mind buffed out those rough edges.

THREE

Monday, April 15th
Graveyard Shift
2101 hours

The clock on the wall in the roll-call room read 2101 hrs when Lieutenant Robert Saylor stepped up to the lectern and said, "Okay, listen up."

Katie MacLeod had been making notes in her notebook from the crime analysis daily flyer. She finished scrawling the last bit of information on a wanted burglar before closing the flyer.

"Psssttt," Connor O'Sullivan said to her and pointed at the flyer. He mouthed "gimmee." Katie played confused for a few seconds, then smiled and slid it to him.

"Several stolen vehicles," Saylor said, reading off a half-dozen license plates with descriptions. Katie made notes, as did most of the officers in the room.

"Detective Finch has probable cause to arrest Kelly Carepi on first degree assault charges," Saylor said. "He'll have a warrant sometime tomorrow, but if you come across him before then, book him on Finch's probable cause." He read for a moment, then continued, "I guess this stems from the incident up on Dalke about a few nights ago. Who had that?"

"I wrote the report," said Officer Westboard from his seat next to Katie. "Just about everybody in Adam sector did additional reports, though."

"This is the thing with the golf club, Matt?"

Westboard nodded. "Yep."

"It was actually a nine-iron, El-Tee," said Thomas Chisolm. The veteran grinned at the lieutenant. His thin, white scar which ran from his temple to jaw melted into his laugh-lines. "I was clearing Holy Family when the call came out, so I went over there."

"A nine-iron, huh?" Saylor asked, willingly playing the role of straight man.

Chisolm nodded. "Yeah. And you should've seen the divots all over the victim's face. The guy must be a terrible golfer."

The roll call room rumbled with laughter as Saylor added, "That's what handicaps are for, Tom."

When laughter subsided, Saylor asked Westboard, "Is this Cannon Street address any good for Carepi?"

Westboard shook his head no. "It's over a year old."

"Okay. Next item. It seems that the Chief and the Sheriff are in a pissing match about parking. So, until further notice, do not park your personal vehicles in the county lot." He raised his hands to quell the uproar. "Hold on, hold on. I think this will blow over in a few days. Just park on Adams for now and walk the half-block."

Katie nodded to herself. She did that anyway. The police station was located right next to the county jail and there were windows in the jail that looked right out onto the county parking lot. She wasn't too comfortable with the idea of inmates looking down at her as she parked her personal car and walked into the station. Or going home, for that matter.

Saylor read the information on two escapees. Katie jotted down their information.

"Detective Tower is working a stranger-to-stranger rape that happened in Clemons Park," Saylor read from the clipboard. "No suspect description, but the victim was a jogger. So stop and do a field interview on any suspicious males in that area. Give Tower a heads up if you do."

He looked up at the assembled shift. "Anyone have anything for the shift?"

No answer.

"All right, then." He stepped away from the lectern. The sergeants began the sector table meetings. Saylor strode to the Adam sector table and leaned down toward Katie.

"MacLeod, stop by and see me before you head out, okay?"

"Yes, sir." She wondered what for, but didn't ask.

Saylor half-smiled, half-nodded at her, turned on his heel and left the room.

"That's it, MacLeod," O'Sullivan said. "All your nefarious deeds have caught up with you."

Katie rolled her eyes. "Whatever. You know, you talk like a bad novel, Sully."

"He's right, though," Officer Anthony Battaglia said. "Why else would the lieutenant call you in there if it wasn't to let you go?"

"Maybe he wants to know how I put up with all your bullshit."

Battaglia shook his head. "Nah, he's firing you."

"It's the axe fer ya, lass," Sully said in exaggerated Irish brogue.

"What size shirt do you wear, Katie?" Battaglia asked, hammering on the age-old cop joke. "I'll buy it from you when they let you go."

"Gee, thanks, Batts," Katie shot back. "You want to buy my bra, too? It's about your size."

There was a rumble of laughter at the table.

"All right, that's enough," Sergeant Miyamoto Shen said, shaking his head and smiling. "This crew is way too loose. You're going to get *me* in trouble with the lieutenant."

The platoon quieted down. Shen ran through a few administrative items and released them.

Katie stood and walked to the lieutenant's office. At the door, she hesitated before knocking. She wondered what he could want, but drew a blank. Never one to avoid confronting issues, she raised her hand and rapped on the door.

"Come in," Saylor called.

Katie opened the door and stepped into the small office. Saylor finished signing some paperwork and looked up.

"Please, sit down," he said, gesturing toward the chair in front of his desk.

Uh-oh. Sitting down is usually a bad thing.

Katie took a seat and said nothing.

Saylor folded his hands and smiled at her. "How're you doing, MacLeod?"

"I'm fine, sir."

Saylor watched her for a moment, nodding slowly. She wondered what he was thinking about. She'd been in some serious situations over the last couple of years, including being shot at by the Scarface robber. That hadn't been nearly as bad as the incident on the Post Street Bridge when the mentally disturbed father dangled his own infant son over the edge. Katie pressed her lips together and tried to force the image from her mind before she saw him release his grip, letting the child tumble into the Looking Glass River hundreds of feet below.

Did Saylor think she hadn't rebounded from those events?

A momentary anger flared in the pit of Katie's stomach. If she were a man, would he be worried about—

"Good," Saylor said. "You seem fine. I know you've been through some traumatic experiences in the last couple of years. Some cops have trouble with that. You seem to be coping well."

"I am."

"Good," Saylor repeated. "That's good."

Katie waited, watching him cautiously.

Saylor smiled again and reached for a file. "You put your application in for a Field Training Officer position last month. All the applications were reviewed by shift lieutenants and the captain has made his selections."

And I didn't get it because you think I'm a basket case?

Saylor extended his hand. "Congratulations, MacLeod. You were selected. You'll get the two percent pay raise as soon as your first recruit is assigned to you."

Katie's mouth fell open. "I got it!"

Saylor nodded. "You got it. Shen gave you a great recommendation and your work speaks for itself. Congratulations."

A huge smile spread across Katie's face. She reached out, took Saylor's proffered hand and shook it. "Thank you. I...thank you, sir."

"Officer Ken Travis will be assigned to you in his third rotation," Saylor told her. "He's with Bates now."

"Travis? He's the one that used to be a reserve?"

"Yes."

Katie nodded. Travis had ridden with her on a couple of occasions. He was a solid troop and would be a good first recruit for her. It occurred to her that this was likely the reason Saylor made the assignment.

"I won't let you down, sir," Katie said.

"I know," Saylor said.

Katie left his office, gathered her patrol bag and seemingly floated down to the basement sally-port to get a car from swing shift. Sergeant Shen looked up at her from his clipboard.

"How'd it go?" he asked, suppressing a grin.

"I got the FTO spot," Katie answered. "But you already knew that, didn't you?"

Shen nodded. "I founded out when I came in tonight. But the lieutenant wanted to tell you himself."

"Well, thanks for whatever you said to him to make it happen, sergeant."

Shen shook his head. "All I did was tell the truth. You're a good troop, MacLeod. You deserve it."

Katie felt a small surge of pride. Her cheeks warmed slightly. "Thanks," she managed.

"Hey, Sarge!" Battaglia interrupted from across the sally port. "Okay if Sully and I ride together?"

Shen regarded him. "Didn't you two ride together last night?"

"Yeah."

"And the night before?"

"Yeah. So? We're a good team."

Shen pretended to sigh. "Fine, fine. Ride together. But this is the last time." He made a notation on the markup.

"Last time until tomorrow, you mean," Katie joked.

Shen shrugged. "They do good work together. I'd like to see more two-officer cars out there, if we had the staffing for it."

"Hey, MacLeod!" Battaglia called. "How much for that shirt?"

Katie waited until Shen glanced down at the clipboard and shot Battaglia the bird.

"Promises, promises," Battaglia said with a grin.

"Nice comeback, Potsie," Sully told him. He popped open the trunk and inventoried the contents.

Katie shook her head and headed to an empty car near the end of the line. She passed Westboard, who was busy inspecting the outside of the car with his flashlight for any damage.

"Forget Battaglia. I've got dibs on that shirt," he kidded her. "What did the El-Tee want, anyway?"

"Nothing much," Katie said, before breaking into a huge smile. "He just wanted to tell me I got that vacant FTO position."

Westboard grinned and gave her a thumbs up. "Way to go! That's great."

"Thanks."

"I'll buy you coffee later to celebrate," he said.

"Sounds good."

"See you then," Westboard said and returned to inspecting the car.

Katie continued down the line of cars. The last in line turned out to be one of the newest ones in operation. The faintest hint of new car smell still hovered inside. Katie strapped her patrol bag into the passenger seat and checked the car into service. After a quick check in the trunk and the exterior for damage, she opened the back door and searched the back seat where the prisoners were transported. She found nothing and that was a good thing. Sometimes prisoners dumped items back there.

Katie cleared and reloaded the shotgun, tested the lights and then waited in line for her chance to head out the sally port. One by one, the police cars zipped out of the basement and onto the street. Their exit was punctuated by the chirp of tires and a quick siren test at the top of the sally port.

The cool night air streamed through the windows, the clean smell of earlier rainfall riding on it. Katie turned the heater on low. She took a deep breath of the fresh air and prepared for whatever River City had to throw at her.

2316 hours

"*Adam-122?*"

Officer Anthony Battaglia reached for the mike. "Twenty-two, go ahead."

"*Respond to the area of 400 West Cleveland. Complainant states she saw a man in dark clothing acting suspicious in the alley. Requested police response. 400 block of West Cleveland.*"

"Copy," Battaglia answered. "Is the complainant requesting contact?"

"*Negative.*"

Battaglia clicked the mike and hung it back on the holder.

"That's right near Corbin Park," Sully said, flipping a U-turn and heading that direction.

"Duh. So what?"

"So, Corbin Park is just a little south of Clemons Park."

Battaglia clapped his hands together in slow, exaggerated applause. "Your orientation skills are impressive."

Sully shook his head. "Clemons Park is where that rape happened."

"What rape?"

"Tower's rape. The one the lieutenant mentioned at roll call."

"The lieutenant talks at roll call?"

Sully sighed. "Yeah. You probably missed it, dreaming about linguini or something."

"Just like an Irishman," Battaglia said. "Jealous because Italian food is good food."

Sully turned onto Post and headed north. "What are you talking about? Irish food is good food."

"Right."

"It is."

"Sure it is. That's why there's an Italian restaurant on every corner and there isn't a single Irish restaurant in this city."

"Just because Americans don't go ga-ga over Irish food doesn't mean it isn't good."

Battaglia began ticking off on his fingers. "Spaghetti, lasagna, chicken parmesan, baked ziti, pizza—"

"Shut up." Sully took a right onto Cleveland.

Battaglia shrugged, looking out the window. "You're just pissed because all you can offer up is haggis."

"Haggis is Scottish," Sully corrected.

"Same thing."

"Not even close. The two countries are separated by the Irish Sea. That's like me saying Italy and Greece are the same even though the Adriatic Sea—"

"Right there!" Battaglia said, pointing south.

Sully braked. "Where?"

"The alley there! Back up, quick!"

Sully threw the patrol car into reverse and backed up into the intersection. As he cranked the wheel, Battaglia grabbed the microphone.

"Adam-122 on scene," he said. "Also."

Sully goosed the accelerator and the patrol car leapt forward.

"The alley eastbound," Battaglia said, pointing. "I saw a guy duck back into the darkness there."

"Okay."

"Adam-122, copy. Go ahead your also."

Battaglia pressed the mike button. "We might have that suspicious male here in the south alley on the six hundred block of Cleveland."

"Copy. Adam-112 to back?"

"Copy." Chisolm's steady voice came through the radio.

Sully rolled slowly down the alley, activating the overhead lights, bright takedown lights and the alley lights on the sides of the light bar. He turned on the spotlight and used his left hand to search with it between the houses as the car crawled forward.

"What was he wearing?" Sully asked.

"I didn't get much of a look. Just dark clothing."

"White guy? Black?"

"Coulda been purple for all I know," Battaglia answered. "I didn't get a good look."

Sully swung the spotlight past a parked car next to a chain link fence. The fence door stood open. He stopped and both officers exited the car.

"Adam-122," Battaglia reported, "we've got an open back gate about mid-block on the north side of the alley."

"Copy. The address?"

"I don't know," he answered and rolled his eyes at Sully. "The house numbers are usually on the front."

There was a moment of radio silence while both officers approached the open gate. Then the dispatcher, Irina, came back.

"Adam-122, what is the color and description of the house?"

Battaglia glanced at the home. "Single-story, yellow with white trim. Mid-block."

Radio copied.

Sully stepped through the gate and shone his powerful flashlight around the backyard. The well-maintained grass was wet from the recent rain. A few pinecones littered the yard, but it was otherwise clean.

Battaglia joined him in sweeping the back yard with beams of light.

"Hey," Battaglia whispered.

Sully followed the beam of light from Battaglia's Mag-Lite. It illuminated a doghouse in the corner of the yard. The tips of a pair of tennis shoes protruded from the doorway.

"You've got to be kidding," Sully whispered back. He drew his gun and covered the doghouse.

Battaglia grinned at him, then turned his attention back to the shoe tips.

"Attention in the doghouse!" he bellowed. "River City Police Department! Come out with your hands where we can see them!"

The shoes did not move.

"We can see your shoes," Battaglia told him. "Now come out of there or we'll have the K-9 come in and get you out."

After a moment, the shoes moved outward, exposing a leg. Then the rest of a man's body slid out, dressed in black jeans and a dark blue sweater.

"Hands where I can see them!" Sully ordered him, shining his light directly into the man's face.

The suspect stood slowly, holding his hands above his shoulders, squinting and blinking into the bright flashlight beam.

"Turn around," Sully barked. "Hands on your head. Don't move."

The suspect obeyed. Battaglia moved in and handcuffed him.

A window slid open from the house. "What's going on?" a woman's voice asked.

Sully held the flashlight up and directed the light down onto his own face and badge. "Police, ma'am. Everything all right in there?"

"Sure, but—"

Sully illuminated the suspect again. "Do you know this man?" he asked the homeowner.

"No. Who is he?"

"A fine question," Sully quipped with a hint of brogue. "I assume he was trespassing then?"

"I guess so," the woman answered. "I mean, I don't know him, so..."

"Thanks, ma'am. We'll figure it out and let you know if we need anything from you."

"Okay," she said, her voice still sounding confused by sleep.

"Where's the dog?" Battaglia asked suddenly.

"Huh?"

"The doghouse," he said, flashing his light on the suspect's former hiding place. "Where's the dog that goes with it?"

"Oh," the woman said. "He died last summer."

"I'm sorry," Battaglia said.

"He was fourteen," the woman told him.

Battaglia nodded. "Well, you might want to lock your gate. Or get a motion sensor light out here."

"Or a new dog," Sully suggested.

"Oh," the woman said, still blinking sleepily. "Yes, that might be a good idea."

"Thanks for your help tonight, ma'am."

"Okay," she said and slid the window shut.

"She'll think this was all a dream in the morning," Sully chuckled. He squatted down and flashed his own light into the interior of the doghouse. "Empty," he reported.

Battaglia nodded and took the suspect by the shoulder. "Let's go, Rover." They lead him back to the car, where Battaglia removed the man's wallet.

"Hey," he said. "What are you doing?"

"Finding out who you are." Battaglia removed the man's driver's license and dropped the wallet on the hood of the car. Then he reached for his shoulder mike. "Adam-122 to Adam-112."

"Twelve, go ahead."

"Tom, can you contact the complainant and ask her if she knows a guy by the name of Victor Preissing."

"Affirm."

Battaglia switched to the data channel and gave the dispatcher Preissing's information for a warrant check.

"What's your story?" Sully asked Preissing.

"No story," Preissing told him. "I'm, uh, just out for a walk."

"Just out for a walk?"

"Yeah."

"That's why you ducked back in the alley when you saw our car, huh?"

"I didn't duck into the alley. I was already headed this way."

"Headed on your way to go hide in a dog house, were ya? I could probably work up a burglary charge on that."

Preissing's shoulders slumped. "I got scared when I saw the lights."

"Why?"

He licked his lips. "I'm from L.A. The cops used to beat me up all the time for no reason. So I got scared."

Sully snorted in disbelief.

"No shit," Preissing said.

"No," Sully answered. "Just shit. Where are you walking to tonight?"

"Just around. Taking a walk."

Sully's radio crackled as Chisolm checked out on scene at the complainant's residence.

Battaglia read Sully the address on Preissing's license.

"That's clear on the other side of town," Sully said. "Why are you way over here taking a walk?"

"It's a free country."

"That," Sully told him, "is known in police parlance as a non-answer. It indicates deception."

Preissing shrugged and swallowed nervously.

"I'll ask again. Why are you taking a walk at eleven-thirty at night clear across town from where you live?"

Preissing's eyes darted back and forth between the two officers. "I like Corbin Park. It's a nice place to walk."

"Oh, that's believable," Sully said. "Do you have any warrants, Mr. Preissing?"

"I've never been arrested."

"Guess what?" Sully said. "That wasn't my question. You can still have a warrant out for your arrest whether or not you've ever been arrested before."

"So what?"

Sully turned toward Battaglia. "He's starting to sound like you. I'm definitely arresting him."

Before Battaglia could answer, Chisolm's voice came over the radio. *"Adam-112, that would be a negative on the complainant knowing Preissing."*

Sully copied.

"Put him the car," he said to Battaglia. "Then we'll figure this out."

Battaglia patted down Preissing, checking for any weapons.

"You can't hold me," Preissing said.

"Sure we can."

"On what probable cause?"

"You're acting suspicious."

"That's not a crime. I want my lawyer."

"Trespassing is a crime," Sully told him. "Just because Rover's dead doesn't mean you can move into his dog house."

Preissing stared at Sully. "Is everything funny to you?"

Sully grinned at him. "No, but your situation here sure is."

"What's your badge number?" he demanded.

"Get in the car," Battaglia said and slid Preissing into the back seat of the patrol car.

"Why do you have to fuzz them up like that?" he asked after he'd slammed the back door and stepped away from the car.

"That's my job. Just like it's *your* job when *I'm* searching them. It's called cooperation. You know, teamwork?"

"Whatever. What do you think about this guy?"

"Data channel come back yet?"

Battaglia shook his head. "Not yet. You think he's a peeping tom?"

Sully frowned. "Sorta feels a little like that, don't it?"

"Sorta. But not quite. He's too confident."

"I agree. Not milquetoast enough. But definitely suspicious."

"Definitely."

"No question the guy was up to something."

"Definitely."

"He looks too old to be out prowling cars," Sully observed.

"No backpack, either."

"And no burglar tools of any kind."

"Nope."

"Big goddamn mystery." Sully sighed. "So we'll do a field interview report for Tower on him."

"Definitely."

"Who knows? Maybe he's the rapist."

Battaglia shrugged. "And maybe I'm Vito Corleone."

"You wish."

Thomas Chisolm pulled into the alley. He parked behind their patrol car and got out. On his way past their car, he peered into the back seat at Preissing.

"You recognize him, Tom?" Sully asked.

Chisolm shook his head. "What's this guy's story?" he asked them.

"We were just discussing that."

"You come up with any answers?"

"Not really," Sully said. "He almost acts like a peeping tom, but not quite. He's got no backpack for prowling cars or burglar tools on him."

"Maybe he dumped them after he spotted you guys," Chisolm suggested.

Sully and Battaglia both raised their eyebrows and looked at each other.

"Why didn't you think of that?" Battaglia asked.

"Because I'm Irish," Sully told him.

Chisolm chuckled. "I'll check." He turned and walked westward down the alley, shining his light and looking in trash cans.

"Adam-122?"

"This better be good," Battaglia muttered and keyed the mike. "Go ahead."

"Preissing is in locally with a clear driver's license. His only entry is a domestic order of protection."

Both men smiled at each other in triumph.

"Why didn't you think of that?" Sully asked.

"Because I'm Italian," Battaglia answered.

Halfway down the alley, Chisolm stopped searching and strolled back toward the patrol cars.

Battaglia asked the dispatcher, "Who is the protected party?"

"Lorraine Kingston," Irina advised them.

"That's not the complainant," Chisolm told them as he approached. "Her name was Sandy something."

"What's Lorraine's address?" Battaglia asked into his shoulder microphone.

"405 West Cleveland."

Sully smiled. "Sandy the Neighbor spotted Victor the Stalker and called it in."

"Probably," Battaglia agreed. He keyed his mike. "Pull a copy of the protection order and give me the terms, please."

"Already done," Irina replied. *"He is restricted from being within two city blocks of Lorraine Kingston's home or business, as well as being restricted from contacting her in any fashion."*

"Copy," Battaglia said and turned to Sully and Chisolm. "Well, it doesn't get much easier than that, does it?"

"Should we do a show-up?" Sully asked. "Get Sandy the Neighbor over here to ID Preissing?"

"On a misdemeanor?"

"It's a domestic violence. You know how they are about DVs."

"They who?"

"Sergeants, prosecutors," Sully smiled. "Italians. You name it."

Battaglia sighed, not taking the bait. "Look, we caught him within the two blocks. Let's just book him."

Sully shrugged. "Fine. What about the trespass?"

Battaglia frowned. Sully raised his hands in apology.

"I'll go back and get the rest of the neighbor's information," Chisolm said.

"Thanks, Tom."

Battaglia popped the back door. "Get out," he told Preissing.

"About time," Preissing said, stepping out of the car awkwardly. "Now take off these cuffs before I call my lawyer."

"How about you call him from jail, smart-ass?" Battaglia said.

"Huh?"

"What were you doing over at Lorraine's house?" Battaglia asked. He began to search Preissing, removing items as he came across them.

"Lorraine who? What are you doing?"

Sully shook his head and clucked his tongue while Battaglia searched. "The stupid routine isn't going to impress the judge."

"Maybe it's not a routine," Battaglia said.

"I want my lawyer," Preissing said. "Joel Harrity. Right now."

Battaglia finished his search. "Like I said, call him from jail. Now get back in the car." He guided Preissing into the back seat and closed the door.

"Lorraine who," Sully muttered. "What an idiot."

Battaglia gathered Preissing's property. "No way is this guy Tower's rapist," he told Sully. "He's just a loser stalking his girlfriend."

Sully shrugged. "Still worth an FI."

"Waste of paper."

The two got into the patrol car. Sully reset the mileage on the odometer and put the car in gear. Battaglia advised dispatch, "Adam-122, we're en route to jail with a male for a protection order violation. Mileage is reset."

"Copy."

Battaglia reached for the stereo. "Country, you figure?"

Sully shook his head. "Heavy metal."

"Forget that. That shit hurts my head." Battaglia turned on the stereo and channel surfed. When he landed on the oldies station, a familiar tune came through the speakers. He grinned broadly and turned it up, fading the volume to the rear.

"Classic," Sully said.

"Fitting, too," Battaglia answered, laughing at his own joke. He sang along with the chorus. *"Well if you feel like loving me...if you got the notion...I second that emotion."*

"Turn that shit down!" Preissing yelled from the back seat, his voice muffled by the music.

Both officers grinned. Sully took over. *"Hey!"* he sang, *"So if you feel like giving Lorraine a lifetime of devotion...I second that emotion!*

"That's fucking harassment!"

"Hey!" Sully and Battaglia crooned together. *"I second that emotion!"*

"You guys are assholes," Preissing hollered.

Sully looked at Battaglia and shrugged. Battaglia shrugged back.

"He's probably right," Sully said.

"Screw him," said Battaglia. "He's going to jail."

FOUR

Tuesday, April 16th
Day shift
0911 hours

Detective Tower tapped his pen against the open file folder. His left hand curled around a cup of coffee. He'd read and re-read the contents in the hope that something new would jump out at him, but all he'd succeeded in doing was giving himself a headache.

He took a sip of coffee and reviewed Giovanni's report again. Although the use of the unique term "whammo" was interesting, he didn't see any plausible avenues for investigative follow-up. He'd conduct a follow-up interview with Patricia Reno in a day or two, as well as review the medical evidence, but he was skeptical that anything new would come up.

He pulled out the FI written by Officer O'Sullivan the previous night. Victor Preissing sounded promising at first, but as soon as he read about the old girlfriend, his heart sank. The guy was stalking his ex-girlfriend, that was all.

Tower pursed his lips. Maybe. But maybe he was striking back at his ex-girlfriend through another woman. Psychological transference or whatever the textbooks called it. It happened.

Tower frowned. He doubted it. Still, it was worth checking out. Hell, everything was at this stage, since he didn't have anything else to go on. Any minute now, the Crawfish would be—

As if on cue, Lieutenant Crawford strode into the Sexual Assault unit office. Tower tried to hide his disappointment.

"Where are we?" Crawford asked gruffly.

Several smart alec answers occurred to Tower, but he suppressed them. "On the Reno rape, you mean?"

Crawford narrowed his eyes. "No. On the JFK assassination, Tower. What do you think?"

Tower couldn't resist. "I think Oswald did it, but there's no way he acted alone."

A few cubicles down, someone tittered. Georgina, the unit secretary, lowered her eyes and seemed to be concentrating on her keyboard.

"Very funny," Crawford answered, dismissing the joke. He gave Tower an impatient wave. "Spill."

Tower leaned back in his chair and sighed. "It isn't good."

Crawford shrugged and motioned for him to continue.

"Well, for starters, the lab is backed up two weeks," Tower said, "so I don't know if we got anything at all on forensics."

"Order a rush," Crawford said. "Anything short of homicide, this should get precedence."

"It won't do any good. Diane is in court for the next week on a murder case from last year. One of Browning's cases, I think. I was lucky she was able to come out to the scene of the Reno rape. Anyway, with her in court, that leaves Cameron alone except for the intern."

"We need to hire another forensics person," Crawford muttered. "Okay, what else have you turned up?"

"Nothing. No witnesses in the area, despite a canvass. I've checked with Renee in Crime Analysis for registered sex offenders on file, especially any recently released, that showed anything close this M.O."

"What'd ya get there?"

Tower shook his head. "If you sort the by 'blitz attack,' you get half the database. If you sort any more specifically, you get almost no one."

"Almost?" Crawford raised his eyebrows hopefully.

"Yeah, almost. A few names popped up, but all were either dead, incarcerated or living out of state."

Crawford grunted.

Tower continued. "There's no similar instances city-wide in the last ninety days and none in that immediate area. If we expand the area a little bit, there are some incidents, but all of them are date rape scenarios with known suspects."

"And there's nothing in her background to look at?"

"No. She's clean."

"I don't mean just criminal," Crawford said. "I mean situational."

Tower clenched his jaw. *Don't tell me how to do my job, Lieutenant-never-was-a-detective Crawfish!*

Crawford was still eyeing him, so he forced his jaw to relax and answered. "Nothing there, either. She's married, has a couple of kids and stays at home with them."

"No guy on the side?"

Tower turned up his palms. "How am I supposed to know that?"

"You ask her, that's how," Crawford snapped back. "Maybe she had a boyfriend or some Good Time Charlie on the side. If she dumped him, he might have decided to get some revenge on her."

Tower ground his teeth. "I don't think that's it."

"Have you got something better to run down?"

He glanced down at the case file. "Uh, actually, yeah."

"What?"

Tower snatched up O'Sullivan's FI. "A couple of patrol cops caught a guy slinking around last night in the same neighborhood as the rape. I figured I'd interview him."

Crawford regarded him for a moment, then nodded. "That sounds promising. Do it."

"Yes, sir."

Crawford pointed at him. "But then check into that other angle. And anything else that comes up, too, no matter how small."

Tower nodded that he understood. Crawford turned on his heels and headed back to his office in the Major Crimes division.

Georgina glanced up at Tower and raised her eyebrows a bit. Tower shrugged, as if to say, "What a jerk, huh?"

It wasn't like he didn't know how to investigate a rape. He'd been in the Sex Crimes Unit for six years. In that time, he'd handled all kinds of rapes and molestation cases. Why was Crawford so intense about this one?

But Tower knew why. Most rapes were committed by someone known to the victim. The bulk of the case involved proving what happened and whether there was consent, not discovering the suspect. True stranger-to-stranger rapes were rare.

And, Tower figured, that type of rape was a little unsettling. Some unknown man out in the community committed a violent sexual assault and no one knew who he was. That's why Crawford was so keen on Tower's progress on the case.

Still, Tower groused, *does he have to be such a hard ass about it?*

He picked up the telephone and called over to jail. He had to schedule an interview with Victor Preissing.

1109 hours

The prostitutes were thick on East Sprague even though it was the middle of the day. He'd noticed that the prostitute population went in cycles. During the summer, it was like high tide. The whores flooded the streets, some of them from out of town and not bad looking. They wore revealing clothing, sauntering up and down the sidewalk just like the movies. Winter was more like low tide. The hotter-looking ones moved on, leaving behind the fat ones wrapped in long winter coats and the crack heads who didn't know enough to wear coats.

Aside from that, though, there were mini-cycles in which they went from thick to thin to thick again. He didn't know for sure, but he suspected that the cycles were a direct result of police enforcement action. When undercover cops busted the hookers, they tended to move on for a while or take it indoors. When they did stings on the johns, business slowed to a trickle, so they moved on.

He wasn't stupid. He knew how things worked.

She was attractive, he thought, as he watched her walk slowly along the sidewalk. Her blond hair was teased up in a mid-eighties poof and a black one piece skirt hugged her too-thin body. Probably one of the crack addicts, he reasoned. Which meant she worked for cheap. Still, he thought she was attractive, for a fucking whore.

He glided up next to her in his respectable four-door compact. She glanced over at him, glanced around, then approached the car.

"Hi, baby," she said.

"Hello."

"You lookin' for a date?"

He nodded. He doubted she was an under-cover police officer, but he was not taking any chances. He would make her say everything just to be sure.

The prostitute got into his car and directed him where to drive. He drove silently, mostly in circles as she watched to see if they were being followed. He noticed she was unable to sit still, another characteristic of crack addicts. He was almost certain she wasn't a police officer now.

She directed him to a dead-end street. He parked next to an abandoned house. As he put the car into park, he felt her hand snake out and squeeze his crotch. He became erect immediately. She grinned at that and removed her hand.

"So what are you looking for?" she asked, leaning back against the door.

"A good time," he said.

She frowned slightly. He could tell she was still trying to decide if he was a police officer or not.

"A *very* good time," he added.

She chewed on her lip, remaining cautious, but he could see the desperation in her eyes. He waited.

Finally she said, "So you want head or straight sex or what?"

"Straight would be good," he told her and waited.

She paused again, chewing her lip. The pause was not as long as the first one when she said, "Fifty."

"Okay," he said. He slid his seat back. She reached out and began to unbuckle his belt with one hand. She held out her other hand. He put two twenties and a ten in her hand and watched her slip it into her bra.

With both hands free, she slipped his pants down around his knees in a matter of seconds. She reached into her purse and removed a condom.

"Can't be too careful," she explained with a wink. She tore open the wrapper and slid the condom expertly onto him.

"I agree," he said. To his disgust, he realized his left leg was twitching uncontrollably. That'd happened to him the first time he was with a woman, too. He cursed his weakness.

This is just a dirty little whore, he told himself. *Nothing to be nervous about. It's not like you haven't had a whore before. My father fucked one every time the ship docked in the Philippines. So what's the problem? Get tough.*

She climbed on top of him, being careful not to bump the horn on the steering wheel. Guiding him into her, she settled onto his lap.

"How's that feel?" she asked him.

He avoided her gaze, running his hands up her arms to her shoulders, where he grabbed hard and pulled her into him. She grunted in pain.

"Hey, watch it—"

"Shut up," he growled and began thrusting hard. "Just shut up, you dirty little whore."

"Easy on my goddamn arms," she complained.

He released her arms and grabbed her around the throat with both hands, squeezing hard.

"Do you like this, you little bitch?" he asked her as her face flooded red. Her hands flew to her throat and she tried to pry his fingers loose.

He continued to thrust into her, watching panic enter her eyes. "Yeah, you like it, don't you? Oh, I am going to lay the whammo on you, my sweet little bitch."

He closed his eyes as he came, arching his hips up and forcing the small of her back into the bottom of the steering wheel. Her fingers pulled weakly at his hands as his orgasm caused him to squeeze harder. He finally relaxed his grip as he collapsed back onto the seat.

He sat still for a moment, surprised both at how fast he'd climaxed and how quickly his choking had affected her. He released his grip on her throat. She breathed raggedly and in gasps, her hands massaging her throat.

"Stupid little whore," he muttered. He opened the car door. With his hips and right arm, pushed her from his lap, out the door and onto the ground. He grabbed her small purse from his passenger seat and hurled it at her. She sat blinking stupidly at him as the purse bounced off her forehead and fell onto her lap.

"You're lucky," he told her. "I let you live because you're beautiful."

Women are vain, he thought as he pulled up his pants. Compliment them and nothing else matters.

Then he drove away quickly, leaving her to sit along the side of the road in front of the abandoned house.

Ten blocks away, he pulled in behind a convenience store. A large fence blocked the view from two directions and the store from a third. Quickly, he unzipped his pants and cleaned up. He threw everything into the dumpster. Then he changed his license plates back to the proper ones, backed out and drove away. The entire process had taken him less than three minutes. The car-clock told him he still had twenty minutes of his lunch hour left.

I wish I could have gone to the Philippines, he thought as he drove towards his workplace. But the military wasn't right for him. He was certain that if his father had stuck around long enough to know that his son hadn't followed in his footsteps, the old man's disappointment would have been even greater than it already was.

He frowned at that. Still, he'd done a number on that last bitch, hadn't he? She got a taste of what it was like to have a real man lay the whammo on her.

As he drove back to work, he whistled tunelessly to himself. But already, the gnawing desire within him began to grow again.

F Ī V E

Tuesday, April 16th
Graveyard shift
2014 hours

The ring of the telephone stopped Katie MacLeod at her door.

She paused, considering whether to answer it or not. As it was, she was going to have a difficult enough time getting her patrol uniform and gear on before roll call. Depending on who it was on the phone, she might not make it. And if it was her mother...well, forget it. She'd be on the phone for an hour.

I'll wait to see who it is, she decided. *In case it's an emergency.*

After the fifth ring, the answering machine kicked on. Her own voice sounded strange to her as it pleasantly asked the caller to leave a message at the beep.

The machine beeped.

"Katie?"

It was Stef.

Katie clenched her jaw.

"Are you there?" he asked, his words slurred. "If you're there, pick up."

Katie considered it for a moment. She thought very seriously about picking up the phone and telling Stefan Kopriva that he could go straight to hell. Which was where he seemed bent on going anyway, with the drinking and the pills.

"Katie, please. I... I have to... talka someone..."

The anger brewed in the pit of her stomach. Who did he think he was, calling her now? A year later? A goddamn *year*?

After what they shared together? What he threw away?

"Everythins' so fucked up," he slurred. *"I'm so fucked up."*

She thought of Amy Dugger, the six year old girl that had died because of Kopriva's mistake. A stab of pity cut through some of the anger in her belly. She took a step toward the telephone, letting the door swing closed.

"Jus' the whole world," he said.

She reached for the receiver. When her fingers touched the plastic, she paused.

Remember what he said to you? After what happened to you on the bridge, do you remember what that selfish bastard said?

She stood stock-still, struggling with her own thoughts. The cool plastic of the phone vibrated slightly with every word that came through the tiny speaker of the answering machine.

"Are you even there?" Kopriva asked, a tinge of anger settling into his voice.

"I'm here," she whispered, but kept her hand still.

"Oh, fuck it," he said. "Like you even give a shit."

The line disconnected. A pair of clicks came through the speaker, then a dial tone. The answering machine stopped recording.

Katie stood at the phone, surprised that no more anger welled up inside her after his parting shot. Instead, she felt a deep sadness overcome her. She choked back the tears that rose in her throat.

"I did give a shit," she whispered at the flashing red light on her answering machine. "Once. I really did."

The light blinked in steady cadence.

"But not anymore," Katie said.

She knew it was a lie as soon as she said it.

"Oh, Stef," she said in a hoarse whisper. She reached out and pressed the delete button. The long beep that sounded when she pressed the button took on an almost accusatory tone. "Please don't call me again."

She'd considered changing her telephone number when she moved out of her apartment, but hadn't. It was the same number she'd had since she moved to River City after graduating from WSU. She'd felt sentimental about it somehow. It was the first telephone number that belonged to her. Not her mother in Seattle.

Not the entire dorm floor. Not her and three roommates that final year at college. Just her. So each time she moved, she kept the number. Now, she questioned that decision. The silence of her small house seemed to throb around her while she stood next to the telephone. She wiped away the beginnings of a tear from her eye and glanced up at the clock.

Great.

Now she was going to be late.

Katie turned and walked away.

2237 hours

"Adam-122?"

Battaglia reached for the mike. "Twenty-two, go ahead."

"Respond on a vehicle theft report."

"Great," Battaglia said sarcastically, ignoring the dispatcher's description of the call. "A real challenge."

O'Sullivan didn't reply.

The dispatcher relayed the address and Battaglia copied the call. Then he turned to Sully. "So I guess there's no RPW to be done tonight."

Sully made a U-turn. "Since when are stolen cars not real police work?"

"Stolen cars *are* real police work. They can even lead to pursuits. Which is fun." Battaglia replaced the radio mike on the hook. "But stolen vehicle reports *suck*. There's no challenge to them."

"A call is a call."

"*A call is a call*," Battaglia mimicked. "Well, these calls suck. Every one is the same. And that's if it is even actually a real stolen." Battaglia mimed removing his notepad and flipping it open. He poised an invisible pen above his open palm. "Do you own the car? When did you see it last? Do you know who took it? What color is it? What do you want us to do with when we find it? Blah, blah, blah, boring."

"Sometimes life is not all about every call being exciting," Sully said.

"Oh, aren't we just the philosopher tonight?" Battaglia observed. He paused to look through the windshield, then left and right. "What the hell?"

"What the hell what? That there's actually a world out there?"

"Screw you, Soh-crayts."

"Soh-crayts?" Sully shook his head. "It's Socrates, you idiot. Sock-Ruh-Tease."

"Like you know," Battaglia said, waving his hand. "And the what the hell is, where are you going?"

"To the call."

"Not the way you're headed. Take Wall. It's quicker."

Sully snorted. "I'm driving, Guido. So don't worry about it."

"I'm telling you, Wall is quicker than Monroe."

"It's the same."

"It's quicker."

"Shut up. Like you know this town."

Battaglia raised his eyebrows in indignation. "I know this town like the back of my hand."

"Bullshit. You can barely find the station on a good day. That's why you always ride with me and that's why I always drive."

"I ride with you because no one else will and Sarge wants me to keep an eye on you." Battaglia sniffed dramatically and rubbed his nose. "And I let you drive so I don't offend your Irish sensibilities."

"*My* sensibilities? Coming from Captain Sensitivo over here, that really hurts."

"I know this town," Battaglia insisted.

"Not only do you not know this town, you don't even know anything *about* this town. You're ignorant of your own city's history."

"Oh really? And what are you? The River City History Channel?"

"No," Sully said, "but I know a few things."

"So do I."

"Like what?"

"Like it's called River City because it was founded by a river."

"Oh, that's good. Don't stretch your brain."

Battaglia shrugged. "It's true. Deal with it."

"So why's Mount Joseph called by that name?" Sully asked.

"It's named after some guy named Joseph."

Sully slapped the steering wheel. "Another brilliant insight. Okay, Mensa boy, who was Joseph?"

Battaglia paused. "Some Indian, right?"

"Good guess. Yeah, some Indian. A chief, actually."

Battaglia snapped his fingers and pointed. "That's it. Mount Joseph was named after Chief Joseph."

Sully sighed. "No kidding. So what tribe did he belong to?"

"Sioux?"

"No."

"Pawnee?"

Sully shook his head. "Uh-uh."

"Apache?"

"Oh, come on. The Apache live down in the desert."

"We've got deserts around here. You ever been to Yakima?"

"*Real* deserts," Sully said. "As in New Mexico and Arizona?"

Battaglia shrugged. "A desert's a desert."

"It's Nez Perce," Sully told him. "Chief Joseph was a Nez Perce Chief. *From where the sun now stands, I will fight no more forever.* You didn't learn this stuff in school?"

"Hey, I went to Rogers. We learned *From where the sun now stands, I will kick your ass forever.* And so what? At least I got that he was an Indian Chief."

Sully stopped for a red light and looked over at Battaglia. "Fine. How about the river, smart guy? Why is it called The Looking Glass River?"

"Easy. It's named after that Alice in Wonderland movie."

Sully gaped at him. "You're kidding me, right? I mean, you're totally screwing with me here?"

Battaglia shook his head. "No." He pointed at the stoplight. "Light's green."

Sully glanced up at the light and goosed the accelerator. "Unbelievable," he muttered.

"What? You gonna tell me it's not named after that Disney cartoon, then?"

"News flash. That cartoon was made back in the forties. The river was named about a hundred years ago. Do the math."

Battaglia scrunched his eyebrows. "You sure?"

"Yes."

Battaglia considered a moment. Then he said, "Well, wasn't there a book or something that they based the cartoon on? It coulda been named after that."

"Yes, there was a book. But—"

"See?"

"No, no, no, *no*," Sully said with an emphatic head shake. "The river was named after one of Joseph's sub-chiefs, Chief Looking Glass. It was named after a man, not a cartoon."

Battaglia shrugged. "I didn't know that."

"I know!" Sully said, nodding repeatedly. "You could fill a large museum with what you don't know, Batts."

"Bullshit."

"No, you could." Sully raised his hand from the steering wheel and mimed a headline in the air. "The Official 'Stuff That Anthony Battaglia Doesn't Know' Museum. It'd be a huge building, too. Bigger than the Louvre."

"The what?"

"The Lou—never mind. It'd be a big building and it would be full of shit. Just like you. That's my point."

"Whatever, dude. The only point I'm seeing is the one on top of your head."

"Oh, har-dee-freaking-har." Sully picked up the radio mike and held it out toward Battaglia. "Hey, 1972 called. They want their joke book back."

Battaglia clapped his hands together slowly. "Ha. Ha. *Ha*."

Sully re-hung the microphone, turned onto Dalke and killed the headlights.

Battaglia shook his head. "It still woulda been quicker to take Wall."

Sully pulled to the curb two houses from the complainant's address. "Guess we'll never know, will we?"

The two clambered out of the car, shutting the doors quietly.

The home was a small yellow rancher with a well kept yard. A pair of lawn gnomes stood as stoic guards on either side of the concrete steps up to the front door. The officers climbed the stairs. Without discussion, each took up a position on opposite sides of the doorway. Battaglia rapped on the door.

After a few moments, a short pudgy man in his forties answered. He wore khakis and an unbuttoned Hawaiian shirt over a white tee. Sully glanced at the man's thinning hair, which was plastered tight to his skull with gel and drawn together into a nub of a ponytail.

Ooh, he thought. *A hipster.*

"Good evening," Battaglia said. "You called about a stolen car?"

"Yeah, yeah," the man said, opening the screen door and waving them in. The officers filed past him and into a living room furnished with post-modern furniture. Several stark, nude line drawings of Marilyn Monroe encased in neon frames dotted the walls.

Battaglia removed his notebook and flipped it open. "Tell me about this stolen car."

The man sank into an armless futon. "It's my Beemer," he sighed grandly.

Battaglia's eyes flicked to Sully's, then back to the complainant. Sully knew what the glance meant.

I'm supposed to be impressed?

"And?" Battaglia's tone held the barest hint of his unspoken sarcasm.

The man seemed to sense Battaglia's subtext. "Well, it's stolen."

Battaglia nodded his head. The man pointed to his notebook. "Are you going to write that down?"

Battaglia's head stopped moving up and down and shifted seamlessly to a left to right head shake.

The man looked to Sully for help.

Sully suppressed a sigh. "What's your name, sir?"

"Tad."

"Last name?"

"Elway. Like the quarterback. You know, John Elway?"

Sully nodded. "I've heard of him."

"I'd hope so. He's only been to the Super Bowl three times and —"

Never won yet, Sully finished silently. "What happened to your car, Mr. Elway?" he said aloud.

Tad stopped. "I told you. It was stolen."

"Right. How exactly?"

Tad bit his lip in contemplation. "Well, I loaned it to a friend and it hasn't been returned."

"You loaned it?"

Tad nodded. "Yes."

"To a friend?"

"Yes."

Sully glanced at Battaglia, knowing his partner probably shared his thoughts.

This isn't going to be a stolen car. It'll be civil. An ex-girlfriend, probably. A drug buddy, maybe. Or a hooker.

"What's with all the looks?" Tad asked, irritation plain in his voice.

"I'm not sure what you mean," Sully said.

"You two keep looking at each other like I'm lying or something."

Sully shook his head. "No, sir. We don't think that at all."

"Then what's the deal?"

"Why don't you just go ahead and tell us about your car so that we can take your stolen vehicle report?" Sully suggested.

"No," Tad said, his tone indignant. "Not if you're both going to stand there and treat me like some kind of criminal. I'm the *victim* here."

"That's why I need to get this information from you," Sully said.

Tad would not be so easily assuaged. "It's totally unprofessional," he continued. "The way you two are acting. Interrupting people and having all these sarcastic little looks back and forth."

Sully took a deep breath and let it out.

"Don't sigh at me," Tad snapped.

"I didn't sigh."

"You did. You did just a second ago."

Sully sighed.

"There! You did it again," Tad said. "What is *with* you two assholes?"

Sully felt the heat of frustration creep up the back of his neck.

"So sorry to take time out of your busy day," Tad sneered. "I mean, it's only your *job*."

The heat flowered into outright anger and flooded his limbs. He knew that if he was feeling it, Battaglia was probably about to explode.

"Is this how you treat every victim?" Tad shook his head. "No wonder people hate cops. You guys are so–"

"Who took your goddamn car?" Battaglia snapped.

Tad's eyes flew open at the profanity. "What?"

"Your precious BMW. Who took it?"

Tad stood up. "You can't talk to me like this."

"Was it an ex-girlfriend? Is this a domestic issue?"

"No, it's not. And I want to talk to your–"

"Was it a male or a female?" Battaglia's question was cold and forceful.

Tad paused. "Female," he admitted.

Battaglia nodded and gave Sully a purposeful glance.

Sully couldn't resist. He sighed loudly.

"Was she a doper or just a hooker?" Battaglia asked Tad.

Tad's jaw dropped.

"Our practice is not to take stolen reports if you what you did was let a prostitute 'borrow' your car," Battaglia mimed a pair of air quotes and continued, "to go get dope or in exchange for sexual favors."

Tad's mouth snapped shut. "She was–she–" he stammered, his face turning red.

"Which is illegal, by the way," Battaglia finished.

Tad stopped trying to speak. He glared at Battaglia, who stared back dispassionately, though Sully knew from experience that he was furious inside.

"So what was her name?"

"Jade," Tad answered through gritted teeth.

"Is that her real name? Do you even know her last name?"

Tad gave his head one slow, short shake.

"Your relationship to her was what, exactly?"

Tad didn't answer.

Battaglia waited, returning Tad's hot glare with flat coolness.

Thirty seconds passed. Sully listened to the sound of Tad's breathing and the slight hum of the neon picture frames.

Finally, Tad growled, "I'd like you to leave now."

Battaglia raised his eyebrows. "You don't want to make a report?"

"Get the hell out of my house," Tad snapped.

Without a word, the officers filed out. As they reached the bottom of the front steps, Tad slammed the door behind them.

Battaglia didn't even look back. Neither did Sully. They walked without a word until they reached the car. Sully unlocked his door and hit the door unlock button for Battaglia on the passenger side. The two men got inside the car. Small flecks of rain started pattering against the windshield.

"Little arrogant *prick!*" Battaglia roared, once the doors were safely shut.

Sully's anger at Tad's attitude had already subsided. Now he was more worried about a complaint.

"You believe this guy?" Battaglia shouted.

"I'm right here," Sully said. "You don't have to yell."

"Don't tell me that didn't piss you off, Sully. That little prick didn't get your Irish up at all?"

"Already up and down," Sully said, slipping the key into the ignition and starting the engine. "Now I figure we're getting a complaint."

"For what? Not taking a report?" He snorted. "Whatever. Ten to one, that Jade he mentioned is a hooker."

"I know."

"And we don't take those reports."

"I know."

"So we're within policy."

"I know."

"So where's the goddamn complaint?"

Sully pointed at him. "Right there."

"Me?"

"Your mouth."

"What did I say?"

"Does *goddamn* ring a bell?"

"*What?*" Battaglia asked, surprised. "Are you the fucking language police now, Sully?"

"I'm not. But Lieutenant Hart is."

Battaglia opened his mouth to reply, then fell silent.

Sully rubbed his eyes. The sound of the rain falling against the outside of the car grew to a dull roar.

"Goddamn," whispered Battaglia. "You're right."

"I know."

Both men were silent again for several moments. Then Battaglia broke the silence with a shrug. "Fuck it. What's done is done. That guy is an asshole who loaned his car to a hooker."

"Maybe."

"Maybe? You're taking his side?"

"No. *Definitely* he's an asshole. *Maybe* the woman who took his car is a hooker."

"I like my odds," Battaglia said.

"Either way, he's the kind of guy who calls and complains."

"Yeah," Battaglia agreed. "He's also the kind of guy who is probably living in the house his mother left him."

"Probably."

"Probably lived in her basement until she died and he inherited the place."

Sully nodded. "Good chance of it. That's why the inside is decorated like an uncool bachelor trying to impress women but the outside is still all Mom."

"Yeah, he's impressive all right."

"He's something." Sully pulled away from the curb. He drove past Tad's house. Both officers eyed the front again.

As they drove on, Battaglia shook his head and grunted. "Maybe not."

"Maybe not what?"

"I don't think he inherited the house from his mom. I don't think he's the son at all," Battaglia said. "In fact, I'm a little concerned."

"Huh?"

"You saw those yard gnomes out front, right?"

"Sure."

"There were two of them."

"So?"

Battaglia sighed. "Sully, everyone knows those things travel in packs of three."

"What are you talking about?"

"Listen," Battaglia said with mock patience. "My theory is this. The guy calling himself Tad inside that house is actually the third yard gnome."

A smile spread across Sully's face.

Battaglia continued, "I'm thinking he probably came to life one night, murdered the occupants of the house and assumed the identity of the son. Now he's got his two buddy gnomes guarding the front door – you saw them there, standing like sentries, right?"

Sully nodded, chuckling.

"So he's got his guard gnomes standing post while he is out living the high life. Driving the Beemer, doing some dope, fooling around with some hookers, you name it."

Sully laughed. "Yeah, you're probably right. So should we call it in to Major Crimes? Get Lieutenant Crawford and some detectives out here to investigate?"

"I think it definitely warrants some looking into," Battaglia said. "But I think we've got even bigger problems than that, you and I."

"What?"

"Well, the thing is, if dipshit does file a complaint, you know his gnome friends are going to buddy him up. I'm positive that they'll be witnesses for him."

Sully laughed out loud.

"And those gnomes, they'll say anything," Battaglia said, his voice changing pitch as he held back his laughter. "Those little fuckers."

Sully laughed louder and slapped the steering wheel. Battaglia finally broke down and joined him.

Maybe a complaint is coming, Sully thought. But Battaglia sure knew how to keep him from worrying.

"Lying, murdering, Beemer-driving yard gnomes," muttered Battaglia through his laughter.

The two officers drove down Wall Street, howling.

"Well, at least this was one stolen vehicle report call that didn't suck," Battaglia said. "That's something."

2319 hours

Katie MacLeod sipped her coffee, looking out at the rain that ran down the window outside the café booth. Across from her, Matt Westboard blew wordlessly on his own coffee. The easy silence between them comforted Katie somehow. Westboard, sometimes a goof and other times sensitive, seemed to intuit her moods almost better than she did herself. The respite from Sully and Battaglia's constant banter and James Kahn's grouchiness was always welcome.

The coffee's aroma filled her nostrils. She sipped again. All around them, Mary's Café bustled with activity. Conversation buzzed, dishes clattered. Linda, the waitress, flitted from table to table, topping off coffee cups and smiling.

From across the table, Westboard slurped his coffee loudly.

Katie shot him a glance, momentarily irritated. He knew she hated that. Then she saw the coy smile playing on his lips.

"Matt—"

He slurped again.

"Knock it off."

Westboard answered with a long slurp.

"Don't be a jerk," Katie said, but with the beginnings of a smile.

Westboard shrugged and put the coffee cup down. "So you going to talk to me or what?"

Katie sighed. "I was kind of enjoying the silence."

Westboard nodded. "Yeah, silence is good."

Katie returned his nod and sipped her coffee.

"The other nice thing about silence," Westboard continued, "is that it solves *so* many problems."

Katie swung her gaze back to the straw-haired officer. "Are you being sarcastic?"

"Nooooooo," Westboard answered. "Not at all. I completely believe that if you have a problem, the best thing to do is to remain absolutely silent about it. If you ignore the problem, it will almost always go away."

"Shut up."

"It also works for ostriches, I hear."

"Asshole," Katie muttered without much conviction.

Westboard smiled tightly, picked up his coffee and slurped loudly.

Katie groaned. "You're worse than those two juveniles at roll call."

"Everyone copes in different ways," Westboard said, motioning to Linda for more coffee.

"Maybe I cope by being silent," Katie suggested.

Linda appeared at the table and refilled both cups, disappearing without a word.

Westboard picked up his cup, paused, then slurped.

"Fine," Katie said, exasperated. "I'll spill. Will that make you happy?"

Westboard leaned forward. "Yeah. But I think it will make you happy, too."

"You really *are* an asshole," Katie said with a grin.

Westboard grinned back. "And you've got a potty mouth, Officer MacLeod, as well as an apparently limited vocabulary. Now what's up?"

Katie shrugged. "I just keep getting these calls."

"Calls?"

"From Stef."

Westboard's eyes narrowed with confusion. "Kopriva's calling you?"

Katie nodded, looking away. She figured the relationship she'd had with Kopriva was probably common knowledge in the undercurrent of department gossip. Still, she didn't care to talk about it out in the open, even with Westboard.

He gave a low whistle. "How long has this been going on?"

"It started a couple of months ago," Katie answered. "It's nothing regular, just every now and then."

"What's he say?"

"Just that he wants to talk."

"What do you two talk about?"

Katie shook her head. "It's usually a message on my machine. Even if I'm home, I don't answer the phone."

"Why?"

Katie gaped at him. "Why? Matt, what do we have to talk about?"

Westboard didn't answer. He turned to his coffee for a moment. Katie stared at him, feeling a tickle of anger in her stomach.

After a short silence, Westboard asked, "How does he sound?"

"Drunk," Katie snapped.

"Yeah?"

"Yeah," Katie answered.

Westboard nodded. "That's all?"

"No."

Westboard waited.

Katie sighed. "Fine. He sounded like he was hurting, too."

"That's probably why the drinking," Westboard observed.

"So what? He acts like he's the only one who ever felt any pain in this world. Like he's the only one who –" She broke off, biting back tears. She stared down at her hands and realized that she was twisting the napkin in her fingers.

"Everyone copes in different ways," Westboard said quietly.

The phrase seemed to have a decidedly different meaning to her the second time around. She gave the napkin a final twist and dropped it in next to her cup. She wondered why Westboard was being so sympathetic toward Kopriva. Maybe the next time the sonofabitch calls, she should just give him Westboard's number.

"Yeah," she answered instead, her voice thick with sarcasm. "Especially cowards."

Westboard's eyes widened slightly. He opened his mouth to reply.

"Adam-116, Adam-114," crackled both radios.

Westboard lifted his radio to his mouth, his eyes remaining on Katie's. "Fourteen, go ahead for both."

"Northgate shopping center parking lot, near the battery store." Dispatcher Janice Koslowski's voice remained stoic, but Katie could sense the gravity in it. *"I have a female at the pay phone stating she has just been raped."*

Katie and Westboard rose as one, pushing back from the table and bolting for the door. She heard Westboard copy the call for both of them as she swung open the door of her patrol car. A moment later, she fired the engine to life, punched her overhead lights and headed toward Northgate shopping center.

2326 hours

Thomas Chisolm looked up from the theft report he was writing in the car. His radio had been turned low, but the words "Northgate" and then "rape" caught his ear. He turned up the volume.

"Continuing for Adam-116," Janice's voice filled the car, *"the victim is not very responsive, but says the assault took place within the last five minutes."*

"Copy," Katie replied over the air.

Chisolm heard the deep-throated roar of her engine and the yelp of her siren in the background.

"Victim has now hung up the phone," Janice reported.

Chisolm tossed his half-written report into the passenger seat atop his patrol equipment bag. Without pause, he dropped the car into gear and punched the gas.

Northgate was a ways off, but he figured he'd start that way just in case they decided to set a perimeter and do a K-9 track. Or there was always the chance that someone saw the suspect and got a good description and direction of travel. Plus, there was no telling if the victim had hung up the phone on her own or if the suspect had returned and interrupted her call for help.

As he zipped up Nevada, he listened for further radio traffic. In his rearview mirror, he noticed a blue truck keeping pace with him. He glanced down at his speedometer. Forty miles an hour. The speed limit was thirty.

What the hell was this guy doing?

Chisolm nudged the accelerator up to forty-five. The truck fell back, but kept following him.

"Adam-116 on scene," Katie transmitted.

"Copy."

Chisolm turned left on Francis, a wide arterial. He accelerated again, this time up to fifty miles an hour. He hoped there was a chance that the rapist was still in the area. He'd like to get his hands on a guy like that.

Behind him, the headlights of the blue truck kept pace.

Who was this guy?

Chisolm recalled the vendetta that a gang member named Isaiah Morris had developed against Kopriva a couple of years before. The gangster stalked Kopriva on duty before ambushing him at the Circle K at Market and Euclid. The resulting "Shootout at the Circle K" was now department legend, despite Kopriva's fall from grace last year.

I've made a lot more enemies out here than Stef ever did, Chisolm thought. Could this guy be stalking him?

"Adam-116, I'm not seeing the victim yet," Katie informed Radio.

Chisolm momentarily considered stopping the truck, but rejected the idea almost immediately. Katie might need his help. The blue truck mystery would have to wait.

2328 hours

Katie cruised through the parking lot, searching for the rape victim. The battery store was closed and there were no cars in front of it, so she rolled slowly through the lot. Her eyes scanned for dark figures in the poorly lit area. The short burst of rain had slackened to a slight, spitting mist, so she shut off her wiper blades.

She wondered briefly if this were a false report. That happened sometimes, especially if a certain crime gained any notoriety. She hadn't seen any media coverage of Tower's rapist cases yet, but she didn't watch the news too often, either. When the Scarface robberies were going on, though, the media covered it extensively. Day shift patrol officers even caught an imposter before the real Scarface was captured.

Killed, you mean. Thomas Chisolm killed him.

Katie shrugged off that thought. Instead, she remembered the media feeding frenzy that had occurred during the Amy Dugger kidnapping last year. And when Kopriva's mistake came to light–

There!

Katie slammed on her brakes. Off to her left, a woman huddled near the front wheel well of a Chevy Blazer. Katie turned her spotlight on the shivering figure. She was met with the woman's frantic stare. Katie snapped off the light and reached for her mike.

"Adam-116, I have her over near The Onion restaurant."

"Copy, near the Onion."

Katie activated her flashers and stepped out of her patrol car. The woman stared in her direction. Katie thought she should smile, but then stopped herself. Instead, she let what she hoped was a warm, open expression fill her features as she stepped over toward the crouched woman.

"Police officer, ma'am," she said in a soft voice. Even so, the terrified woman jumped at her words.

Memories echoed across the years inside Katie's head.

Don't be a goddamn tease.

"Easy," Katie said, pushing the thoughts away. "I'm here to help."

The woman began to sob.

You liked it. The male voice in Katie's head was full of drunken confidence. *Don't forget that.*

She crouched next to the victim. "Do you need a doctor?"

The woman didn't answer.

"I know you're hurt," Katie said, "but do you need medics right now? I can call them for you."

Still sobbing, the woman shook her head.

Ma, I have to tell you something.

"Okay," Katie said. She reached out and touched the woman on the shoulder, causing her to start. "I'm here to help you. You're going to be all right."

Well, at least you weren't a virgin.

Katie took a deep breath. She hated to push victims for information too quickly, but she knew that every moment was precious. The man who did this to her was moving further away every second.

"What's your name?" she asked the woman.

"M-M-Maureen," she sobbed.

Katie gave her shoulder a gentle, reassuring squeeze. "Maureen, I want to help you. But I need to know how long ago this happened to you."

2330 hours

Chisolm braked, slowing slightly before turning onto Division Street. Northgate was only a couple blocks away. He cast a quick glance into his rear-view mirror to see if his tail was still there. The twin headlights beamed back at him.

He ignored the following vehicle and pulled into the parking lot, looking for Katie. He spotted her flashing lights near The Onion Restaurant. Katie's door and trunk lid stood open. She was nowhere to be seen.

Chisolm goosed the accelerator and cut through the lot quickly. As he approached Katie's car, he spotted her kneeling next to a nearby vehicle. She wrapped a blanket around the shoulders of a huddled woman.

He stopped the car near hers and exited. Light drops of cold rain bit into his face, but he ignored them. As he approached, he saw that Katie was speaking in quiet tones with the victim. She glanced up at him briefly and nodded, so he held up and stood a cautious distance away. His experience with rape victims told him that every woman reacted differently. Some wanted the immediate comfort and safety of a man near them. Others wanted nothing to do with a man. He always tried to gauge the individual's response as best he could, but it was an imperfect art.

After a few moments, Katie helped the woman to her feet and walked her toward the patrol car. Chisolm hustled ahead of them and removed Katie's patrol bag and gear from the front seat of her cruiser. If there was one thing he knew, it was that it was a bad idea to put a woman who had just been sexually assaulted into the back seat of a patrol car. Prisoners went in the back seat. Bad guys. Not victims.

As he put Katie's patrol bag into the trunk for her, Chisolm looked up to see the blue truck park a short distance away. The driver focused a camera on Chisolm. Chisolm stared back at him, seething.

Who the hell was this guy? A reporter? If he was a stalker, he sure wasn't very good at it.

Chisolm closed the trunk and started walking toward the truck. The driver hurriedly put the camera aside, gave an almost playful wave and drove away, chirping his tires in the process. Chisolm tried to read the front plate of the truck, but it was too late.

Back at the car, Katie asked, "What was up with that?"

Chisolm shrugged. "Some lookie-lou." He motioned with his head toward the front seat of her car. "More importantly, what's up with that?"

Katie sighed. "She was raped. It sounds a little bit like the other one that the El-Tee mentioned at roll call."

"The one over at the park?"

Katie nodded. "Yeah. The suspect did a blitz attack while she was out for a walk, not jogging. But still..."

"Hooker?"

Katie frowned. "I don't think so. They don't usually work this far north. Plus, she's dressed in workout clothes. I think she's just a citizen out for a walk."

Chisolm nodded. "Okay. Who's working the other rape case?"

"Detective Tower, I think."

"I'd have radio give him a page, in case he wants to come out. You never know."

"Right," Katie agreed.

Chisolm glanced toward the front seat and shook his head sadly. "Terrible crime, rape." Visions of his two tours in Vietnam pushed their way forward. He remembered the pleading eyes of a young Vietnamese girl, barely fifteen. Saw her accusing eyes. He clenched his jaw as the images blasted into his mind's eye.

Mai. Her name was Mai.

"A guy who rapes should be castrated," Katie said. "Simple as that."

"Ouch."

Katie grinned, but the expression had a grim undertone to it. "Hey, I never claimed to be Mother Teresa."

"Not with that attitude." Chisolm forced his own smile, but unbidden, the face of Mai flashed behind his eyes.

A North Vietnamese uniform on top of her, tearing at her clothing.

Then, later, an American uniform.

Her unforgiving eyes.

A sense of shame washed over him. He looked away from the woman in the front seat.

"I'll take her to the hospital," Katie said.

Chisolm nodded, hoping that his memories weren't showing on his face. "Good. That's good."

SIX

Wednesday, April 17th
DAY SHIFT
0818 hours

Detective Tower tapped his pen slowly on the case report as he read it. The steady rhythm helped the flow of his reading. He imagined it bothered anyone around him, but he couldn't help it. When he read, he tapped. If someone called him on it, he made an effort to stop. Otherwise...tap, tap, tap.

The report belonged to Officer Katie MacLeod. Tower knew her only in passing and mostly by reputation. By all accounts, she was a solid troop. He pretty much ignored the bits of gossip about her sex life or orientation. When it came to the River City PD, the rumor mill never stopped. He was relatively certain that it was even worse for the women of RCPD than for the guys, at least on average. As a result, he tried not to get drawn into the gossip. The secretary in his unit, Georgina, was the queen of department gossip, but Tower wasn't kidding himself. He knew patrol cops and detectives that were three times as bad.

Tower forced himself back to Katie's report. It was well-written, describing her encounter with the victim, Maureen Hite. He wished he could have come out to investigate the rape himself, but he never received the call. The battery in his pager died and he'd stayed the night at Stephanie's house, so calls to his house had gone unanswered.

According to the report, Maureen Hite had been out walking along a path through Friendship Park. Tower was familiar with the park. Mostly open field, the park was lightly wooded along the west side.

Tower read from Katie's report, his pen tapping a steady rhythm.

The victim stated that she was northbound along the path when she heard a shuffling noise behind her. Before she could react, she was struck on the head. She thinks that it was with a fist or possibly an open hand but she was not sure. The blow stunned her. The suspect pulled her into the treed area near the sidewalk. He covered her face with some sort of towel or rag. He ordered the victim not to look at him or he would "lay the whammo on" her. He also called her several derogatory names such as "little whore" and "bitch."

Tower shook his head, reading forward.

The suspect removed the victim's sweat pants and underwear. He then sexually assaulted her vaginally from behind. During the act, he struck her several times on the back of the head, leaving her further stunned. She was not sure if he ejaculated or not. When he was finished, he told her that he knew who she was and that he would kill her if she reported the rape to police.

When the victim realized that the suspect had left the scene, she stood and began walking again. Due to her dazed state, she didn't think to knock on one of the doors in the neighborhood. It wasn't until she reached the parking

lot five blocks away that she found a
pay phone to call 911.

    I transported the victim to the
hospital. On the way, we drove to the
park where the assault occurred. She was
able to point out the approximate area
where she was attacked. Officer Chisolm
searched the area for any evidence. See
his report for further.

    The victim was unable to describe the
suspect, other than to say he "sounded
white."

Tower sighed. This had to be the same guy. The M.O. was too similar and the phrase about "the whammo" was too unique. So he had been right about the guy. Whoever he was, he wasn't finished.

Tower cursed. Most of the rapes he investigated involved suspects that were somehow known to the victim. Even if the connection was tenuous, there was usually something that linked the two. Dating, working together, even just a one-time social connection. The point was, a rape was usually not a *who*dunit. Usually, his biggest obstacles were proving that sexual intercourse occurred and that it involved forcible compulsion. In other words, most of the time it was a *DidHe*dunit. More directly, it typically ended up being, from an investigative standpoint, a case *CanIProveHe*dunit.

Stranger rapes were much rarer.

That presented a number of problems for him as the investigator. For one, he didn't even have a suspect.

Sure you do, John. About forty thousand of them.

Plus, if this guy really was a serial, he might get better and better with his technique as he went along, making each successive case even harder to solve. Tower had to figure out how to catch the guy before he attacked another victim.

But how?

He shook his head. He could definitely use someone to bounce some ideas off of.

Tower looked around the unit. A pair of empty desks sat behind him. He had no idea where the detectives that sat in those desks might be and didn't much care. Prather and Carlisle were thick as thieves. Neither one of them spoke to him much and that suited him just fine. Both specialized in child molestation cases, anyway.

The third empty desk belonged to Ted Billings. Sex Crimes was a demotion from Major Crimes for him. Crawford had busted him back before Tower even came to the unit. The way Billings worked, Tower could see why. As detectives went, Billings made an excellent paper weight. It was pretty obvious to Tower that Billings was R.O.D. – Retired On Duty.

So who did that leave?

No one in his unit.

Tower reached into his desk drawer and removed the Patricia Reno file. Then he scooped up the newest file on Maureen Hite and took both with him as he made his way to the Major Crimes unit. Once there, he found Detective Ray Browning sitting at his desk, reviewing a file of his own.

"Ray?"

Browning, a black man with compact features, looked up from his file. His warm, brown eyes regarded Tower calmly. "John. What's up?"

Tower motioned toward the file on Browning's desk. "You deep into that?"

Browning shook his head. "No, just some housekeeping. It's already gone to the prosecutor. I'm going on vacation after tomorrow, so I wanted to get all the little odds and ends tidied up. Why?"

Tower held out his two files. "I'm looking for suggestions. I want to catch this prick."

Ray smiled graciously. "You want to run it for me?"

Tower shook his head. He knew Browning preferred to read the reports himself rather than hear a synopsis. He held out the files and Browning accepted them. Tower settled into the empty desk across from him. Browning opened the files and read carefully, stroking his graying goatee as he scanned the pages.

Tower tapped his pen and waited.

Browning glanced up. "You're not going to sit there and tap the entire time, are you?"

Tower stopped. "Sorry."

Browning smiled at him. "Get yourself some coffee, John."

Tower nodded. "Good idea." He rose and left the bullpen, making his way past Glenda, the Major Crimes secretary. The smell of good coffee wafted toward him. He grabbed a Styrofoam cup and poured some.

"That's a quarter," Glenda told him, her tone mock-scolding.

Tower fished a dollar out of his pocket and stuffed it into the jar near the coffee pot. "It's worth it. The coffee over in Sex Crimes sucks."

Glenda shrugged. "What can I say? This is Major Crimes. The varsity team."

Tower smiled. "Don't be humble or anything."

"Humility is an affectation that I don't have time for," Glenda said, a smile playing on her lips. "It tends to get in the way of accomplishing anything great."

"And greatness courses through the veins of every member of the Major Crimes unit," Tower said.

Glenda narrowed her eyes. "Drink your coffee, serf."

Tower turned his empty palm up. "You got me. I have no response for that."

Glenda raised her eyebrows in mock haughtiness. "I thought not."

Tower chuckled and sipped his coffee.

"Tower!" Lieutenant Crawford bellowed from his office.

Tower suppressed a sigh. "Yeah?"

"Don't 'yeah' me," Crawford barked. "Stop flirting with my secretary and come in here!"

Tower tipped Glenda a wink and made his way into the Lieutenant's office. He stood in front of Crawford's desk, ignoring the open chair.

Crawford eyed him for a moment, then lifted a clipboard. "I've got a stranger-to-stranger rape on my report list."

"I know. I've already got the file."

Crawford glanced down at the clipboard. "Maureen Hite?"

Tower nodded.

"Is it a good rape?"

Tower cringed at the question. He knew that a percentage of rape reports that came through were false. Most of the time, alcohol and the wrong partner were involved. It was a reality he'd come to understand as a sex crimes investigator – sometimes women lied about rape. Of course, at the same time, they often didn't report it at all. He'd investigated a number of false claims, so he knew they happened. Still, Crawford's word choice bothered him. He wasn't a screaming liberal about the issue, but—

"Tower? I asked you a question."

He nodded. "Yeah, it is. It's a good rape."

Crawford reached for his cigar box. "Anything like the last one?"

"A lot like it, actually."

"Did you get called out on it?" Crawford lifted a thick cigar from the box and slipped it between his lips.

Tower had a passing thought about Freud and suppressed a grin.

Crawford's brow furrowed in a scowl. "Something funny, Tower?"

"No, sir."

"Then answer my question. Did you get called out?"

"No. My pager battery died on me."

Crawford fixed him with a dark stare. "Your pager died?" he repeated.

Tower nodded.

"Pretty rookie mistake, Tower."

Tower didn't reply.

"You know where we keep the batteries, right?"

"I do."

"And you can install them?"

Tower clenched his jaw. "Of course I can."

Crawford removed the unlit cigar and waved out toward the bullpen. "Because I can have one of these guys tutor you on that battery thing, if you need it."

Tower sighed. "It just went dead. Okay?"

Crawford grunted. He slid the cigar back into the corner of his mouth, gripping it with his teeth. "So your pager died. Did your phone die, too?"

Tower shook his head. "I wasn't at home last night."

Crawford raised his eyebrows. "Oh? Do I need to start calling you Giovanni Junior now?"

Tower ignored the jibe. "I don't know that there's much I could've done last night, anyway," he told Crawford. "MacLeod did a great interview and a great report. Chisolm and Westboard searched the crime scene and didn't find anything. They took photos anyway."

"Those are patrol officers," Crawford said, "not detectives."

Tower shrugged. "It was good police work."

Crawford grunted again. "So where are you at with this case, then? If the police work was so good."

"I think this guy might be a serial."

"And?"

"And I'm trying to figure out how to work it. None of the lab work is back or will be anytime soon. The victims didn't get a look at the guy. I've got no witnesses. I'm looking for an angle to play. Maybe Renee in Crime Analysis—"

"You're looking for a magic bullet."

"Huh?"

Crawford shifted the cigar to the other side of his mouth. "You're looking for a magic bullet to solve this case. It ain't gonna happen. You think you'll go down to Crime Analysis and flirt with Renee like you're flirting with Glenda in there. Then her computer will spit out some guy's name. But it doesn't happen that way."

Tower shrugged. "Sometimes it does."

"Bah." Crawford waved his hand. "You need to get out there and wear out some shoe leather. Canvass the area where the assault occurred. Somebody saw something."

"This isn't the 1940s," Tower said. "It's the nineties. I agree on the canvass, but –"

"Stop looking for a magic bullet, Tower. Wear out some shoe leather, like I said."

Tower clenched his jaw and nodded. "Fine."

"You want help on this?"

"Ray's looking at the files."

"Ray's going on vacation. I mean, you want me to reassign Prather and Carlisle to help you on this?"

Tower shook his head. "They've got their own cases. If I need help with anything, I'll grab somebody in patrol. Or, if it's in the office, I'll get Billings to help."

"Billings?" Crawford snorted. "Good luck with that."

Tower didn't reply, mostly because he knew the lieutenant was right.

Crawford gave Tower an appraising look. "How sure are you this is a serial?"

"Pretty sure. The M.O. is identical and he used a key phrase both times."

"The whammo thing?"

"Yeah."

Crawford chewed slowly on the cigar. "This is two rapes in two days, right?"

Tower nodded.

"Pretty short turnaround, isn't it?"

Tower nodded again.

"You figure he'll hit again soon?"

Tower shrugged. "I don't know. Maybe whatever is driving him has been satisfied for a little while. But who knows?"

"I'm sure the FBI knows," Crawford said sarcastically.

"The FBI knows everything," Tower agreed, deadpanning.

Crawford didn't smile, but Tower spotted laughter in his eyes. "All right, Tower. Do what you can. Get Browning's input. Check with Renee in Crime Analysis. But get out there and find a witness."

"Yes, sir."

"And get me copies of both files. I'm going to have to alert the media on this."

"I understand."

"I figure you want the whammo thing as a keep back?"

Tower nodded. "Yeah. Just in case the false confessions start rolling in."

"All right." Crawford looked down at the paperwork on his desk, signaling a dismissal.

Tower turned and left the office.

0837 hours

"Yes, sir, I understand," Lieutenant Alan Hart said to the man on the telephone. "From what you're telling me, the officers behaved quite inappropriately."

"I pay their wages," the man on the other end said. "I don't need them coming to my house and being smart-asses. Or cussing at me. Especially when I'm the victim."

"I agree," Hart replied. "Mr. Elway, would you be willing to come down to the police station and sign a formal complaint?"

"Well..."

"You needn't worry about any repercussions. If an officer were to retaliate in any way against a citizen who files a complaint..."

"It's not that. It's just that I don't have my Beemer back yet. And you guys aren't even looking for it."

Hart cleared his throat. "I can come to you with the complaint form, Mr. Elway."

"Fine. But what about my stolen car?"

"I'll have an officer dispatched right away."

"Good."

"Thanks for calling, Mr. Elway," Hart said. "It's citizens like you that make this department a better one."

"I just want my car back," Elway said. "But what's going to happen to those two clowns you guys sent up here?"

"They'll be dealt with," Hart assured him.

"I hope so. Guys like that shouldn't be cops."

"I agree."

Elway hung up without a word.

Hart replaced the receiver. He finished scratching out the nature of the complaint on his notepad. He'd transfer it later to an official form, but he liked to get it all down while the call was still fresh.

O'Sullivan and Battaglia. A couple of hot-shot, graveyard jokers. He used to come across the two of them as they were getting off of graveyard shift and he was coming on day shift, back when he was the lieutenant for day shift patrol. He still recalled the arrogant, condescending looks they'd cast toward him as they bit off the words, "Good morning, Lieutenant."

Well, he had them cold now. From Tad Elway's statement, they'd get charged for Officer Demeanor and Inadequate Response. The demeanor charge was iffy on O'Sullivan, but when Battaglia cursed and was directly rude to Elway, that sealed things. While that charge might only result in a written reprimand, the inadequate response had some teeth. A citizen reported a stolen vehicle and officers failed to take a report. That was serious. There might even be a suspension on the horizon for both officers.

Hart smiled. He wondered how funny those two jokers – no, Elway had called them 'clowns' and he liked that better. He wondered how funny those two *clowns* thought a suspension would be.

When he'd finished making his notes, he fired up his computer. He typed in his password – INTEGRITY, something a lot of River City officers could improve upon – and opened a new, official complaint form.

He assigned a case number. When the previous investigators ran IA, they investigated about fifty complaints a year. Most, even

Hart had to admit, were frivolous. But he felt that those investigators had been lazy. Either that, or they were overly sympathetic to the officers.

Hart didn't have that problem. It was only April, and he'd investigated fifty-three already.

Correction, he thought as he typed in the narrative of Tad Elway's complaint.

Fifty-four.

His phone rang.

He snatched the receiver off the hook eagerly. "River City Police Internal Affairs. Lieutenant Hart speaking."

"Is this where I'm supposed to call to complain about an officer's driving?"

Hart nodded, even though the caller couldn't see him. "Yes, it is."

"Good. Because this guy was flying. And he wasn't even using his siren."

"Really?" Hart raised his eyebrows. If that were true, that was a clear policy violation. Another slam-dunk complaint.

"Yeah. And if you ask me, that's bullshit."

"When was this, sir?"

"Last night," the caller said. "Look, I've been in trouble before and I've been hassled by the police. So if I have to obey the law, then so does he."

"That's true." Hart agreed. He often felt that police officers believed themselves to be above the law.

"And if it was such an emergency, why didn't he turn on his siren. Or at least his lights?"

"I don't know," Hart answered. "But I'll find out."

"Good."

"What's your name, sir?"

"Marty Heath."

"And did you get a car number on the patrol vehicle you saw speeding last night, Mr. Heath?"

"Oh, I did more than that," Heath gloated. "I've got *pictures.*"

Hart smiled.

Pictures? Well, that was like Christmas.

0903 hours

"What do you think, Ray?"

Ray Browning leaned back in his chair and stroked his goatee. "Well, I think you've definitely got a serial. The M.O., the 'whammo' thing..."

Tower nodded. "I agree."

"I'm worried, too," Browning said. "For a guy to strike twice in two days? That's uncommon, especially early on. Usually there's a longer break, at least until the subject is further along in his series."

"Sure," Tower said. "After he's been doing it for a while, the thrill wears off sooner each time."

"Right. So either he hasn't hit for a while...or he didn't use the catchphrase..." Browning shook his head. "I don't know. But it worries me."

"You're worried he's going to escalate?"

Browning nodded. "Yeah, I am a little bit. He's already become more violent in the second rape than the first. But that doesn't surprise me as much as the quick turnaround."

"Maybe it's been building up for a while," Tower suggested.

Browning shrugged.

"Maybe he just got out of prison?"

"Could be."

"I'll have Renee check that."

"You should check Maureen Hite's relatives and associates, too," Browning said. "The subject said that he knew her. That might just be a threat. But then again, he just might."

"I'll see if there are any links between Hite and the first rape, Reno."

"Renee can help you with that, too."

"Okay."

"And you're going to canvass, right?"

"In just a little bit, yeah."

"Good." Browning rubbed his eyes. "Beyond that? I guess you could hope something comes up on the lab results."

"I don't put a lot of faith in that."

"Why not?"

"I think the guy used a condom. And the victims didn't get much of a chance to fight back, so I don't think the fingernail scrapings are going to be any help, either."

"That's troublesome," Browning said.

"What?"

"The condom."

Tower nodded. "I know. It means we've got a thinking rapist."

"One who plans ahead," Browning said.

"Who isn't leaving behind DNA."

"And who appears to be getting more violent," Browning added.

"And," Tower finished, "to top it off, no one has seen the guy's face."

"Something set him off." Browning said, nodding in agreement. "Don't forget about that."

Tower sighed. "It's a bitch of a case, Ray."

"Just keep working it. Something will break."

1104 hours

The camera equipment bathed Shawna Matheson in a bright wash of light. She held her microphone below her chin and stared into the lens. At this close range, she could see her perfectly coiffed hair and heavy television makeup reflecting back at her in the thick glass. Above the lens, the red light was dim.

Her camera man, an idiot named Ike, held up his hand. "Five, four, three," he said, dropping his fingers as he counted. Shawna was frankly surprised the troglodyte could count.

At 'two,' he went silent. The red light came on.

She affected a solemn expression.

On 'one,' he pointed at her.

"Good afternoon," Shawna said in her perfectly drilled television voice. "I'm Shawna Matheson, here at the River City Public Safety Building with breaking news. Earlier this morning, Lieutenant Crawford of the Major Crimes unit confirmed that police are investigating a potential serial rapist."

She paused a half beat, letting the gravity of her words sink in.

"Police are not releasing many details at this point and the investigation is continuing, but here's what we know so far. Two women have been assaulted in the past two days. One was assaulted while jogging, the other while out for a walk. Both attacks occurred near city parks."

Shawna continued, though she knew the techies back at the station were likely throwing up a graphic on the screen instead of showing her. "The first assault occurred near Clemons Park, in the north central section of the city. The second occurred at Friendship Park, which is on the far north part of town. I spoke to Lieutenant Crawford about these assaults, and this is what he had to say."

Shawna paused. The red light went dim.

"We're on cutaway," Ike told her.

No kidding, she thought to herself.

She replayed the interview with the bombastic Crawford in her mind. The man was egotistical and always sparse with information, but she had learned how to flirt with him just subtly enough to get something good out of him. Although his statement contained stock police responses about ongoing investigations and safety tips, she'd managed to get something from him off camera that she thought was singularly wonderful.

When she asked him if the rapist was being called by any nicknames, he'd scoffed at her.

"What, like the Park Rapist or something?"

"Something like that," Shawna had answered, though she was looking for something not quite so banal. "Does he have any peculiarities?" She'd given Crawford that slight smile she'd perfected over time—the one that said she was flirting but no one else could tell except him.

Crawford had cleared his throat, looking just a little off-balance from her tactics. "Nothing I can share at this time," he'd answered her.

"Nothing?"

Crawford had shrugged. "What can I tell you? There are some things we have to keep back. I mean, what do you want? That the guy has only raped on rainy days?"

After that, Shawna had only smiled and thanked him.

"Coming back in five, four, three," Ike said, walking through his countdown with her again.

Shawna opened and closed her mouth, stretching her jaw.

At 'two,' the red light kicked on.

Shawna put on her solemn face.

At 'one,' Ike fired his pointer finger at her.

"Police are cautioning women to travel in pairs or small groups and to be aware of their surroundings," she said, leading up to her big finish. "Although they are not certain if and when he'll strike again, there is one thing that people may be able to watch for. In both instances, the rapist attacked women on rainy days, thus earning him the nickname, 'the Rainy Day Rapist.'"

She paused a full beat.

"For Channel 5 Action News," she finished gravely, "I'm Shawna Matheson."

She held her pose until the red light went dim.

"And we're out," Ike told her.

Shawna let herself smile. This was good. In fact, it might just be enough to be her ticket out of River City and to a larger, more important market. Seattle or Denver, perhaps. Or maybe somewhere in California.

After all, it wasn't every day you got to name a serial rapist.

1248 hours

The rain came back just before noon. It fell in light sheets while Detective Tower and Officers Ridgeway and Giovanni canvassed the neighborhood around the second rape. In the hour they knocked on doors, neither officer found anyone who had seen anything. Wet and discouraged, the officers stood near the light post they had agreed upon as a rally point.

Ridgeway glanced up at the gray sky and felt the drizzle on his face.

"This rain sucks," Gio said, standing beside him and shaking the water from his jacket.

"I like it," Ridgeway said.

"That figures," Gio muttered back.

Ridgeway shrugged. "A brave man likes the feel of rain on his face."

Gio smirked. "And a wise man has the sense to get out of the rain."

Ridgeway flashed Gio an uncharacteristic grin. "Saw that movie, huh?"

Gio nodded. "Kurt Russell was great."

Ridgeway glanced back up into the sky. "Still, I like the rain."

Gio didn't answer. While he waited, he found himself wondering if his date last night with Mallory would be his last. She'd started using little code phrases that he'd come to recognize as attachment words. It might be time to jet.

Detective Tower strode toward them, his sport coat drenched. As he drew close, Ridgeway saw that the detective's hair was matted against his head.

"Any luck?" Tower asked them.

Both officers shook their heads.

Tower muttered a curse. "Well, hopefully someone that wasn't home right now saw something and will call it in. I left my card in about ten doors."

"Most witnesses don't even know when they see something," Gio said. "I doubt anyone will call."

Tower shot him a scowl. "Don't mess with my mojo."

"It's true," Gio said. "And on top of that, most witnesses who think they saw something important didn't see a thing at all or what they saw really doesn't matter for much."

Tower looked at Ridgeway. "What is this, Instruct The Detective Day?"

Ridgeway shrugged. "Not like you dicks don't need it, right?"

"Ha, ha." Tower hunched his shoulders and looked up. "I hate the rain."

"I kinda like it," Ridgeway said.

Tower looked at him flatly. "That figures."

"What's that supposed to mean?"

Tower snorted. "Gee, I don't know. I'm only a detective." He thumbed toward Gio. "Why don't you ask Casanova over here?"

"Let's just hope it stops soon," Gio said. "Because I'm sick of it already."

"It messes up your perfect gigolo hair, Giovanni?" Tower asked.

Gio reached up and touched his wet mop. "Nah. Let's just hope the wet look is in." He glanced over at Ridgeway. "It doesn't work for you, though, Mark."

Ridgeway shrugged. "Let's just hope it doesn't make your boy go out and rape again, huh, Tower?"

Tower's eyes narrowed. "My boy?"

"This rapist."

"Oh." Tower eyed him suspiciously. "Why would the rain make him do this again? What's that supposed to mean?"

Ridgeway glanced at Gio, who laughed.

"You don't listen to the news?" Gio asked Tower.

Tower shook his head. "Not if I can help it. Why?"

"They're calling this guy the Rainy Day Rapist."

"Who they?"

"The media. All of them."

Tower stared at him for a long moment, then dropped his eyes. "Fuck," he muttered. After another moment, he lifted his jacket upward and gave it a shake. "Let's get out of here."

The three men turned and made their way toward the street where Tower's unmarked detective's vehicle sat behind the officers' marked cruiser. On the way, Ridgeway could hear Tower muttering but couldn't make out the words. Once at his car, the detective got in without so much as a thank you and pulled away.

"What's up with that?" Ridgeway complained. "We just walked around in the rain for an hour knocking on doors and he can't even say thanks?"

"He's probably under the gun over this. I imagine Crawford is all over him." Gio opened the car door and slid into the driver's seat.

Ridgeway slid into the passenger seat. "I'm sure it helped that you brought up the Rainy Day Rapist thing."

"I didn't bring it up." Gio fired up the engine. "The media brought it up. I just passed it on."

"Whatever," Ridgeway said. Although he knew Gio was right. "My guess is that it was that fluff head from Channel Five."

"Shawna Matheson?" Gio dropped the car into gear. "She's hot."

"She's an idiot," Ridgeway answered, but he knew it didn't matter which of the newscasters actually said something first. Once one of them has it, they were all like a bunch of parakeets anyway, with no sign of an original thought.

Gio turned onto Lincoln Road. "Whatever pressure he's under now, it's nothing like what he'll be facing now that the media is hyping this story."

Ridgeway didn't answer, but he knew Gio was right.

1301 hours

He cruised through the East Sprague corridor, eyeing the prostitutes that posed in the doorways. None so far had been willing to venture out from protective cover when he slowed down to examine them. The drizzle of cold rain kept them huddled like drowned cats in the doorways, staring bleakly out at him.

He decided it was too much work today. Perhaps he could save it up and spring it on some other bitch later tonight or tomorrow.

He reached for the car radio, turning to the news station for the top of the hour coverage.

"Police continue to search for clues," the polished male newsman's voice intoned, "in the brutal rape of a woman on River City's north side last night. This is the second such rape by the man now dubbed The Rainy Day Rapist."

His jaw dropped.

The Rainy Day Rapist?

He shook his head in disbelief.

How could they call him that? It was a stupid name. It made him sound like some wimp in a musical or something. There was nothing powerful about a name like that.

He pulled into a convenience store parking lot, where he stopped the car and took a deep breath. He knew that part of what he was doing was compulsion. He couldn't stop it, even if he wanted to. He'd read about it in college, at least in the couple courses he managed to take at the community college. He understood the concept intellectually. But it was a different story when it became a reality. When the urge to dominate came over him. When these bitches need him to put the whammo down –

He stopped. What good had it done him, though? To end up with a name like this?

He gripped the steering wheel and took stock of his career. He'd raped three women already, not counting whores. Well, okay, maybe the first one didn't count, either, since he didn't exactly seal the deal. And the cops must not be counting it, since the media didn't report it. Or maybe the stupid bitch didn't even call the cops. But number two and three called the cops. They definitely counted. And the last one got the whammo good. She figured out exactly what kind of man she was dealing with.

And yet, when his crimes finally go public, they saddle him with a ridiculous nickname like this? What level of respect was that?

He wondered if he should respond. There was a payphone across the parking lot. He could call in and muffle his voice. Or better yet, maybe he should send a letter into the newspaper, like the Zodiac Killer.

That thought stopped him cold.

The Zodiac...*Killer.*

No one ever called a killer by some stupid name. They respected a killer because they feared him. Only women feared a rapist. *Everyone* feared a killer.

A sudden calm washed over him. He realized he had found his answer.

His purpose.

His destiny.

1317 hours

Tower shook the rain off his jacket as soon as he entered the police station. Without pause, he made his way straight toward the Crime Analysis unit. He intentionally chose his route to avoid the door to the Major Crimes bullpen, just in case Lieutenant Crawford was watching out for him.

"Hey, girl," Tower said as he stepped through the door to the cramped Crime Analysis office.

Renee looked up from a stack of reports with bleary eyes. "Hey back," she said. "Did you find anything on your canvass?"

Tower shook his head. "*Nada.* I need your help."

Renee yawned and rubbed her eyes. "All right," she murmured.

"Don't get too excited," Tower said.

"I won't," she assured him.

"Am I pulling you off something big?"

Renee shrugged. "Just trying to figure out this Rainy Day Rapist."

Tower frowned. "That's a stupid name. Where'd it come from?"

"I don't know. If I had to guess, I'd say good old Channel Five." Renee stood and walked to the nearby coffee pot. She filled her cup and held the pot out toward Tower, offering.

Tower considered, then shook his head. "Naw, I'm coffeed out."

"Suit yourself." Renee shuffled back to her seat and sat down lightly. She curled her legs to one side in the giant, black chair and sipped from her cup.

Tower let his head dropped forward toward her expectantly. "So?"

Renee acted surprised. "Oh, you want a report?"

Tower cast a baleful look at her.

Renee cocked an eyebrow back. "Careful, cowboy. You throw around looks like that and you will find yourself in a shootout."

"I can take you," Tower said.

"Not with that shoulder rig, you won't."

"Newsflash," Tower said to her. "You don't even carry a gun."

Renee smiled mysteriously. "Not that you can see."

Tower held up both palms. "I surrender."

"Wise move." Renee returned to her coffee, sipping and staring at the wall.

Tower waited patiently. Renee was, in his estimation, an odd duck at times. He wasn't sure how the neurons in her brain fired exactly, but he was usually pleased with the result. All it seemed to take was some banter and a little patience.

"I don't think it's about rain for him," Renee told him.

"How's that again?"

"The Rainy Day Rapist," Renee said. "I don't think it fits. I think the rain is a coincidence."

Tower shrugged. "Okay."

"Though," she added, "now that he has this name in the media, that may just change."

"May?"

"Yes. It *may*. Then again, it may *not*. You never know, at least until there's a more detailed profile of the suspect. And that's something we really don't have just yet."

"That's helpful," Tower said. "Thank you, Nostradamus."

Renee cocked her eyebrow again. "I'm just letting you know what I *think*. That's because there isn't much for me to say that I *know*."

Tower walked wordlessly to the coffee pot. He grabbed a small white Styrofoam cup and filled it halfway.

"I thought you were coffeed out," Renee said.

Tower turned back to her and did his best to cock an eyebrow. "I'm getting the feeling I'm going to need it."

Renee chuckled. "Touché."

Tower stepped over to her desk. "You've read the reports?"

Renee nodded. "MacLeod's was especially good."

"She's a good troop."

"She covered everything you could ask for. The one before that – Giovanni, I think – was pretty solid, too. That's the good news." Renee sipped her coffee and continued. "The bad news is that when I run his M.O. as a distinct, specific M.O., I get no hits."

"So run the basic M.O. Blitz attack, and so forth."

"That's too general. I get a phone book of rapists."

Tower sighed. "Same as the first rape, then."

"Exactly. There's really no difference in the M.O., other than the location. Even that's similar." Renee held up one hand, then the other. "Park, park."

"Yeah," Tower agreed. He sipped his coffee thoughtfully, then said, "Odds are it's one of those guys that popped up when you got the phone book."

"Maybe," she conceded. "I'm running all of them to see who's incarcerated, who's out of state and who's still a possible suspect. The problem is that while we have a distinct M.O. in both cases, the victims don't really provide much information. Neither one saw him. He didn't say much."

"He said 'whammo.'"

"Yes, he did."

"That's pretty unique."

"Too unique." Renee leaned forward and fished a computer printout from the stack of paperwork on her desk. "I ran that term through our system. I came up with zero exact hits. Here's a list of close matches."

Tower took the paper from her hand and scanned the list. There were seventeen entries.

"Most of those," Renee explained, "aren't used in anywhere near the same context."

"Context how?"

Renee lifted a finger. "Not the same type of crime, for starters. There wasn't a single use of anything similar to 'whammo' in any rapes. Same story with any assault by a male subject on a female victim. Also, even in the instances where some form of the phrase pops up in a couple of male-on-male assaults, the usage is completely different."

"How different?" Tower asked.

Renee s closed her eyes for a moment. Then she said, "I think one guy said something about getting blindsided in a fight. He said that he was dealing with one issue and then *wham!* He was hit from behind."

"That's not even close."

"Nope. My point exactly."

Tower waved his Styrofoam cup at the computer. "I figured you could do better with all this."

Renee sighed. "I've told you this before, John. It is better. We may have come up empty on the search, but we came up empty that much sooner."

"Oh, great," Tower said. "Because I hate to wait for disappointment."

"Don't be sarcastic," Renee said calmly. "It doesn't solve anything."

"It isn't supposed to," Tower grumbled.

Renee reached into her stack of papers and removed a yellow sheet of legal paper. She extended it toward Tower. "Take a look at this."

Tower reached out and took the paper. "What is it?"

"Questions."

"I've already got plenty of those."

"Still."

Tower looked down at the legal sheet. Renee's measured writing stood out against the yellow paper. She'd written three questions.

Why does he rape?
Who does he hate?
Is he evolving?

Tower looked up at her. "Are you serious?"

"Why would you ask that?"

"Because," Tower answered, "how in the hell am I supposed to know the answer to these questions?"

"That's the point."

Tower stared at Renee. She stared calmly back. Tower took a sip of coffee and considered her words. After a full thirty seconds had passed, he shrugged, "You win. Explain this to me before my head explodes."

Renee smiled graciously. "Your head won't explode."

"I can feel it pulsing already."

Renee waved his words away. "Look, John. You're a detective. You follow the clues, right?"

"Sure."

"But in this case, you don't have any witnesses. Not even the victims are truly witnesses to anything other than some bare facts."

"Yeah."

"Forensics hasn't come through at all."

"No. I think he was wearing a condom."

Renee nodded. "And probably gloves and a hat."

"Probably."

"So the conventional clues are a dead-end."

"So far, yeah."

"Then it's time to get unconventional."

"Unconventional? How?"

Renee pointed at the paper in Tower's hands. "You ask yourself those questions. You try to answer them."

"With the puny evidence we have?"

Renee shrugged. "With the evidence. And with your own mind."

Tower rolled his eyes. "You want me to profile him. Like those FBI guys."

"Not exactly."

"That's exactly what it sounds like," Tower said. "And that shit is just theory and voodoo."

Renee stared at him with a flat expression, saying nothing.

After a minute, Tower began to squirm. "What?"

She shook her head slightly at him. "John, I don't appreciate the attitude. I'm trying to help you here."

"I realize that. But—"

"There is no *but*," Renee cut him off. "And on top of that, I'm not asking you to dance with bloody chickens or something. I'm asking you to perform a little bit of a Victimology exercise, that's all. Major Crimes does it all the time in homicide cases."

Tower snorted. "Sure, in homicide it makes sense. Most people are killed by someone who knows them. But they can't tell the detective who killed them. So if you get to know the victim, you have a better shot at figuring out who the killer is."

"This is no different," Renee insisted.

"A rape victim is different than a homicide victim. She's still alive. If she knows her attacker, she can name him. This is a stranger rape. It is *very* different."

"No, it's not. You're just looking at the suspect instead of the victim."

"An *unknown* suspect," Tower corrected.

"That's the point, isn't it?"

"Yeah," Tower said, frustrated. "That is the point. With a known homicide victim, you can try to fill in gaps about her." He tapped the notepad Renee had written on. "But I don't know who this guy is, so there's no way I can answer these questions."

"You have to use your imagination," Renee said, her face tightening into a scowl.

"Two things, Renee." Tower held up one finger. "One, I can't present my imagination as evidence in court."

"I know that," Renee answered quietly. "I'm not suggesting –"

"And two," Tower raised his voice to override hers. "Just run the list of suspects that match the basic M.O. and let me know who is still a viable suspect. I'll run down each lead."

"I'm not against the shoe leather approach," Renee said, "but if you want to get an edge on this guy –"

"Sounds like you and Crawford both like the same method," Tower interrupted. He drank the last of his coffee and crumpled the small cup. "Just get me the names, Renee."

Renee's eyes narrowed. "Fine."

Tower tossed the crumpled Styrofoam into the trash. Then he set the yellow paper on her desk next to her. "And if I want any voodoo, I'll call the F.B.I."

Renee didn't answer.

Tower left the room without a word.

1900 hours

"Do you have any objection to this interview being taped, Officer Chisolm?"

Chisolm shook his head coldly.

"Can you verbalize that response, please?" Lieutenant Hart asked.

Chisolm waited a full fifteen seconds before enunciating clearly, "No, sir, Lieutenant. I have no objection to this interview being recorded on audio tape."

Hart pursed his lips in irritation at Chisolm's mock politeness. The reaction warmed the veteran officer's heart. Then Hart continued, "And would you like to have Union representation present?"

"Do I need my Union rep?"

"That's your decision, Officer. I can't advise you either way."

"Am I accused of something or am I a witness?"

Hart smiled coolly. "You are the accused."

Chisolm nodded his understanding. "And who is the investigator?"

"I am," Hart replied.

Chisolm allowed a slow, confident smile to spread across his face. "I don't think I'll need any Union representation here tonight," he said.

Hart didn't seem to know whether to scowl at the inference Chisolm was making or revel in the even playing field. Both reactions flashed on his face before he appeared to settle for assuming a neutral expression. "That's fine," he said officiously. "Then we'll get right to business."

"Let's," Chisolm said stiffly, folding his hands in front of him.

Hart was staring down at his notes and didn't notice. "What is your current assignment, Officer?"

"Patrol."

"Were you working last night?"

"I was."

"Did you respond to assist Officer MacLeod on a call?"

"Probably more than one," Chisolm replied evenly.

"This would have been at 2325 hours."

"That's a very precise time."

Hart looked up. "It is, Officer. Do you recall responding to assist Officer MacLeod at that time?"

"No," said Chisolm. "Why don't you refresh my memory?"

"It was at Northgate."

Chisolm raised his eyebrows in recognition. "Ah. Then yes."

"You remember now?"

"Yes."

"Did you respond Code-3?"

"We don't tend to call it Code-3 anymore, Lieutenant."

"What?"

"Lights and siren?" Chisolm answered. "We don't usually call it Code-3 anymore. We're moving to plain language on the radio. We just say 'responding code' now."

"Well—"

"That's probably changed since they moved you out of patrol," Chisolm added.

"What?" Hart's jaw clenched. He glared at Chisolm.

The veteran officer kept his face impassive, despite the howling laughter he felt inside. "I'm just letting you know. I think it's a recent change."

"Fine," Hart said, biting off the word. "Thank you. Now—"

"Since you were moved out of patrol, I mean," Chisolm said.

Hart stopped and stared daggers at Chisolm. Chisolm maintained a calm exterior.

You got nothing, Hart, he thought. *And you never will.*

Hart cleared his throat. "Did you have on your lights and siren, Officer?"

"No, Lieutenant, I did not."

"Why?"

"I didn't need to."

"Why not?"

"Traffic was light to non-existent. I was able to respond safely without activating my emergency equipment."

"So you sped."

Chisolm shrugged. "I don't know. I responded quickly and effectively, though."

"What if I told you that a citizen saw you driving recklessly?"

"I wasn't driving recklessly."

Hart ignored him. "What if this citizen paced you at almost fifty miles an hour?"

"What if worms had .45s?"

"Huh?" Hart cocked his head at Chisolm.

"I said, what if worms had .45s?" Chisolm allowed himself a slight grin.

Hart shook his head slowly in confusion.

"Well," Chisolm said, "if worms had .45s, then birds wouldn't fuck with them."

The blood left Hart's face. Chisolm had seen this before. It usually presaged an outburst. He waited patiently for the storm to hit.

But the lieutenant seemed to bite back whatever had been rising up inside of him. Instead, he said in clipped tones, "That's very unprofessional, Officer. And it doesn't answer my question."

Chisolm considered. "Well, if what the citizen said is true, then I'd say he was driving recklessly to keep up with me."

"That's not the point."

"I'd say it's pretty important, since he had no reason whatsoever to be speeding. If I was speeding, it was to assist an officer. What's his excuse?"

Hart shook his head. "No. He's the citizen. We serve the citizenry. You don't get to question him. He was monitoring your poor behavior."

Chisolm snorted. "Did you bother to look up the call that MacLeod was on?"

"Of course I did."

"It was a rape," Chisolm said, ignoring him. "And the second one that was stranger-to-stranger this week."

"So?"

"*So?*" Chisolm's eyes flew open. "So I figured that I was best serving the public to get to the call quickly."

"Without using your lights," Hart stated.

"There was no need."

"And speeding."

Chisolm shrugged. "If you say so."

"I don't say so," Hart said. "A citizen is saying so. Someone who pays our wages, Officer Chisolm."

Chisolm nodded slowly. "I see. And who is this stand-up citizen?"

"That's not important."

"*I* think it's important."

"What you think isn't—"

"I have a right to know who my accuser is," Chisolm insisted. "In fact, I'm pretty sure that's policy."

Hart paused, then shrugged. "Fine. But understand that any retaliation on your part will be actionable."

Chisolm held up his hands, palms up.

"Just so we're clear, then," Hart said. He turned a page in his notes. "The complainant's name is Marty Heath."

Chisolm sat still for a moment, then his jaw dropped. "Marty *Heath*?"

Hart nodded.

"The same Marty Heath that lives in the apartments off of Euclid?"

Hart glanced down at this notes. "Yes. How did you know that?"

Chisolm shook his head in disgust. "He's a child molester. I served registration papers on him about six months ago."

Hart stared back at Chisolm, disbelieving.

"He raped a little girl in his basement after he kidnapped her," Chisolm said.

"Raped?" Hart asked, his voice faltering.

"Yeah," Chisolm snarled. "He snatched her and raped her. Then he went to prison. Now he lives just a few feet beyond the legal distance he is required to be away from an elementary school."

"I didn't—"

"You didn't check his record?"

Hart held up the snapshots of Chisolm's vehicle. "He had pictures. He said—"

"He's a scumbag rapist piece of shit," Chisolm said.

"Officer, that's not—"

"We're done here," Chisolm said, standing up. "If you want to rip me for supposedly speeding based on the word of this lowlife, go for it."

Hart swallowed, unable to reply.

Chisolm turned and stalked from the room.

What an asshole, he thought. That thought was quickly followed by, *Seems like old times.*

Chisolm smiled slightly as he left the Internal Affairs office.

2043 hours

"You want a beer, hon?"

Tower looked up from his hands. Stephanie stood at the glass slider door with a pair of Kokanee bottles in her hand.

"Sure," he said.

She stepped outside onto the small patio and slid the door closed. When she settled into the chair next to him, she proffered one of the beers. He took it wordlessly.

The two sat in silence for several minutes. Tower sipped his beer and listened as Stephanie sipped hers. After a while, he became aware of her shivering, despite wearing his bulky sweater.

"You can go inside," he said.

"I'm fine."

"You're shivering."

"It's the beer, that's all."

"Steph, you're cold. Go inside."

"I want to sit with you."

Tower glanced over. "It's okay. You can go inside."

Stephanie responded by pulling the large sweater close to her and drawing her knees to her chest. "Not until you tell me what's wrong."

"Nothing's wrong."

Stephanie sighed. "You're such a guy, John."

"Should I say thank you?"

"If you had a hole in your chest, you'd deny it was bleeding."

"Only if it wasn't."

"It is," Stephanie said. "Now what's the matter?"

Tower shrugged. "Just work."

"I figured that. What specifically?"

It was Tower's turn to sigh. "I caught a couple of rapes."

"That's your job, isn't it?"

"Yeah."

"So what's the big deal—wait! Do you mean that one on the news? The Rainy Rapist or whatever?"

Tower nodded glumly. "That's the one."

"Oh, John," Stephanie said. "That's scary. Some strange guy out there raping women? It makes every woman worry."

"I know. Believe me, I know."

"Are you going to catch him soon?"

"I'm trying."

"Are you close?"

"No."

"Why?"

"Jesus!" Tower stood suddenly and drained the beer. He fixed Stephanie with a tight, cold smile. "Well, I'm fucking trying, all right?"

He strode to the sliding door and flung it open. Once inside, he didn't know where to go, so he stalked into the kitchen and then stomped down the hall to the bedroom. The stalking and the stomping didn't make him feel any better, so he slammed the door.

The slamming felt good. He took a few deep breaths.

What the hell?

The thought floated through his mind as he stood next to the bed. His pulse pounded in his neck. He sat on the edge of the bed and stared down at his feet. Why was he so stressed? He'd had tough cases before. Hell, the Dugger case last year had been a huge burden. Missing child? That brought some serious pressure. So why was this getting to him?

He knew the answer, of course. This one was all his. No partner. And the guy was still out there, planning his next attack. That is, if he planned. Either way, he was a ticking time bomb. And all he could do at this point was sit and wait for that bomb to go off.

Tower took another deep breath through his nose and let it out slowly through his mouth.

Relax.

Nothing more you can do tonight.

He took another breath.

I want to catch this son of a bitch.

Another breath.

Stephanie didn't deserve that outburst, he realized. For that matter, neither did Renee earlier in the day. Both of them were trying to help him. He shouldn't have treated them so poorly.

He drifted into the facts of the case again. He ran through the facts that he did know, the precious few things he could say he knew for sure. What did they reveal? Nothing of value. So what were his options? He could wear out shoe leather, a la Crawford. Or he could hope that Renee got lucky with her computer searches. But if one of those approaches didn't yield some results quickly, he knew his next step was going to be to simply wait for this guy to strike again.

Great police work, John.

He drove his fist into his palm. He hated this feeling of impotence that coursed through him. There had to be something he could do.

Renee's words came back to him. She wanted him to use his imagination. That meant trying to climb inside the mind of this sick fuck. He didn't relish the prospect of doing that. Still, maybe she had a point.

The sound of the door opening caused him to look up. Stephanie stood in the doorway. Her eyes were wet with tears, but her mouth formed a tight, angry line.

"John, I know you're under stress, but –"

He stood and stepped toward her.

"—there's no reason for you to take it out on me."

He reached out to her and pulled her into his arms. "You're right, Steph. I'm sorry."

"I was only trying to help," she said, her voice dissolving into a squeak. He felt her shoulders hitch.

"I'm sorry, baby," he whispered. "I'm sorry."

Stephanie cried into his chest.

They stood in the bedroom, finding each other in the silence.

SEVEN

Wednesday, April 17th
GRAVEYARD SHIFT
2119 hours

"If I knew anything more about it," Sergeant Shen told Sully and Battaglia, "I'd tell you. All I know is that Lieutenant Hart wants to see you both at 0600 hours tomorrow morning. He didn't say what it was about."

"Both of us?" Sully asked.

Shen nodded. "Both."

"Do we need Union representation?"

Shen shrugged. "Your call. You're entitled if you want it."

Sully glanced over at Battaglia. "Who's the Graveyard Union rep?"

Battaglia shrugged his shoulders. "I don't know."

Sully looked back at Shen. "Did he say if we were a witness or an accused?"

Shen shook his head. "I told you everything I know. Zero six hundred tomorrow. That's it. Anything you want to tell me?"

"No," Sully said.

"No," Battaglia said.

Shen looked from one officer to the other. "Then you're dismissed."

Sully and Battaglia turned in unison and left the office.

"It's that fucking gnome," Battaglia whispered as they headed down the hallway outside the sergeant's office.

Sully shushed him.

"I'm telling you—"

"Shhhh."

Battaglia reluctantly stopped talking.

When they reached the basement, Sully finally spoke. "I told you that guy would complain."

Battaglia opened up the trunk and tossed in his patrol bag. "So?"

"So, now we're in hot water."

"That guy was an asshole."

"So were we."

Battaglia shrugged. "It's small time, Sully."

"That's why Hart wants to see us?"

Battaglia snorted. "Hart will make a mountain out of a mole-hill."

"True," Sully agreed. "But he'll make sure you get suspended for that mole-hill, too."

Battaglia nodded. "You're right. Now let's go work."

Sully stared at him in surprise. "How can you shrug it off like that?"

Battaglia removed his side handle baton and slid it into the holder on the passenger side of the patrol car. Then he looked up at Sully. "I figure, what the hell can I do about it now? So let's go work."

Sully met his gaze, his mind processing Battaglia's words. Then he shrugged, too. "You're right."

"I know."

"Let's go."

Battaglia nodded. "Now you're talking. And you know what?"

"What?"

"Screw Hart," Battaglia said.

Sully smiled. "Yeah. You're right. Screw him."

Battaglia nodded again and dropped into the passenger seat. While Sully checked the exterior of the vehicle, Battaglia loaded the shotgun and racked a round into the chamber. Between the two of them, the car was ready for service in less than two minutes.

Without a word, Sully fired up the engine. As they zipped out of the basement and up the ramp, Battaglia cycled the lights, sirens and the air horn.

They headed out into the night.

Thursday, April 18th
0129 hours

Katie MacLeod cruised slowly toward the call without any urgency. According to Radio, some mental guy was breaking up his house, talking with Mental Health, and then the line went dead. Katie was cautious when dealing with mentals, or Forty-eights, as they were called in police jargon. It seemed like they were always doing some whacked-out thing or another. In most cases, it was impossible to reason with them. But the majority of them were too smart to be manipulated, too. She just hoped that this one hadn't cut himself or done something foolish like that.

The worst of it was, it was her call. That meant that she would likely be the one taking a trip up to Sacred Heart Hospital where the Mental Health wing was located. It also meant a marginally long report justifying why she committed the guy for mental evaluation.

Maybe she was getting ahead of herself. Maybe this guy wasn't too bad. It was always possible they could check on him, work things out and then clear the call without a report.

Katie arrived on scene and parked one house away. As she exited the car, she saw Matt Westboard whip around the corner and cruise to a stop one house away in the other direction. As he approached, he said, "Good. Now we have him surrounded."

Katie nodded, smiling. "The question is, is this one going to be a run-of-the-mill forty-eight, or is this one going to excel and be a ninety-six?"

"Let's hope for low numbers," Westboard said as they walked up to the porch.

At the door, Westboard knocked, but there was no answer. Both officers waited for almost a minute, listening intently. Katie looked at Westboard, who shrugged. Katie reached for the doorknob and turned it. It was unlocked.

Katie hesitated. She always did in a situation like this. For one, it was a big issue for an officer to make a warrant-less entry into someone's house. Were the circumstances exigent? Did an emergency exist? Would the officer do more harm from walking away than from making an entry? Such issues were always gray to the street officer who had the responsibility of solving the problems in the field. To an administrator, they were easily defined from the comfort of his office at the police station the following day. They were even clearer yet to the lawyer in a courtroom. And, she thought, the issue was crystal clear to the journalist slamming the cops for making the 'wrong' choice...which was whatever choice the officer made, regardless.

Westboard watched her, waiting. Katie knew what he was thinking. Since it was unlocked and entry did not have to be forced, they should go in. If the door had been locked and no noise came from inside the house indicating an emergency, they would probably search for an alternate way in without breaking anything. They did have an obligation to make sure the forty-eight inside hadn't cut his wrists open or something.

Of course, forty-eight or not, the man had a constitutional right against unreasonable entry into his home.

Hell.

"What do you think?" Westboard asked.

Katie sighed. "I can't walk away. This guy called for help. If he's hurt…"

Westboard nodded. "I'm with you."

"Okay, then." Katie pushed the door open slowly. "River City Police!" she announced loudly, hoping the neighbors could hear and would make good witnesses. "We received a 911 call. Is everyone all right?"

There was no answer.

Katie caught Westboard's eyes. The veteran gave her a nod. They made entry to the house quickly. Katie's hand rested on her pistol, just in case.

"Anybody home?" She called out.

No answer.

The house had been torn apart. She saw broken glass all over the small living room. A typewriter sat on the coffee table. Plates and glasses, some broken, were scattered throughout the house. Katie could detect the unmistakable pungent smell of body odor.

"Bathroom and bedroom are clear," called Westboard from the others side of the tiny house. He was back at her side in a few moments. "Bathroom mirror is smashed. A little blood in the sink, nothing major."

Katie nodded and moved into the kitchen. A phone with no receiver hung on the wall. In the far corner of the kitchen sat a man, his legs splayed straight out in front of him. He had thinning gray hair and a full beard. Katie couldn't tell his height for sure, but given his huge belly, she guessed that he weighed over two hundred pounds. He sat staring, expressionless, the phone receiver pressed to his ear. A torn cord dangled from the useless receiver.

"Hello, sir," Katie said softly, not wanting to startle him.

The man gave no response.

Katie continued to watch him. She noticed drying blood smeared on his hands. She guessed that he had probably punched the mirror and nicked his fingers and knuckles.

She heard Westboard rustling through some mail on the counter.

"You find a name, Matt?"

"Still looking." He held up a piece of junk mail. "Unless his name is Current Resident."

Katie smiled slightly, watching the man stare off into space. Then his head rotated slightly. His eyes fixed on her.

"Dan," was all he said.

"Sir? Your name is Dan?"

"Yeah. Dan."

"Dan, are you okay?"

"Yeah. Dan."

"Okay, Dan. What's your last name?" Katie spoke slowly and in an even voice. Though he appeared harmless, she knew that forty-eights could radically change moods at any moment.

"Danny. Danny Boy."

Katie paused. "Are you hurt, Dan?"

Dan gave her a quizzical look. He stuck his index finger deep into his mouth and pulled it out, making a popping sound. He kept the phone to his ear with the other hand.

"It's Dan Steiner," Matt told her. He showed her an envelope. "It's from Mental Health."

"Nancy is my counselor," Dan said.

"Nancy?"

"Yeah."

"Nancy what? What's her last name?"

"Sinatra. Nancy Sinatra."

Katie took a deep breath. She heard Matt checking the refrigerator and cupboards. She knew he was checking to see how much food Dan had, if any. A person could only be committed to the Mental Health Ward at Sacred Heart if they met certain criteria. Being suicidal, homicidal or unable to care for themselves were the most common reasons police officers encountered.

"What's going on tonight, Dan?" she asked. "Are you upset?"

Dan shook his head slowly.

"Why did you break up the house?"

"They called me."

"Who?"

"Nancy Sinatra at Mental Health."

"Did that make you mad?"

"I was reading."

"All right," Katie said. "I can understand that. No one likes to get interrupted when they're reading. Are you hurt?"

But Dan was staring at the wall again and did not answer.

"Plenty of canned food and goodies in here," Matt told her. "Even so, with this behavior…"

"I agree. He needs to go up to the hospital." Katie wasn't dreading the report now nearly so much as she was dreading the possibility of Dan refusing to go. If he fought, he would be a handful. Forty-eights sometimes seem almost supernaturally strong and didn't always respond to pain compliance techniques.

"I have to go now," Dan said suddenly into the phone receiver. "My friends are here."

Dan pulled the phone away from his ear and slowly lumbered to his feet.

Great, Katie thought. He stood about five-ten and his upper body was as broad as his middle. *He'll be as strong as an ox.*

Dan walked directly towards Katie, staring at a spot past her shoulder. His expression was benign. She and Westboard stepped aside cautiously and allowed him to pass.

Dan hung up the phone and turned to face them.

"My friend is sad."

"Why?" Katie asked.

"I had to hang up. He's lonely."

"I see." Katie thought for a moment. "Dan, you said I was your friend, didn't you? You told your friend on the phone that I was your friend, too, right?"

"Him, too," Dan motioned at Westboard.

"Yes. Him, too." Katie struggled not to grin. The guy was funny. "Dan, would you like to take a ride with me? Up to Sacred Heart Hospital?"

"In a police car?" Dan grinned, child-like.

"Yes. To see Nancy."

His face fell. "Nancy?"

"Yes. In my police car."

Dan shrugged. "Yeah. Of course, I'm supposed to call Fred back."

"He'll be okay."

"Yeah."

Katie found a light jacket for Dan and handed him his tennis shoes. It took him almost five minutes to put them on. He tied each bow meticulously.

"Okay." He stood up. "Ready."

Katie led him out of the house. As they were halfway down the walk, Katie remembered to ask him where his house keys were so that they could lock the house.

"They are in hyper-space," Dan said matter-of-factly.

"Great." She cast a glance backward at Westboard.

He mouthed the words, "I'll look." Katie nodded her thanks.

Once at the car, she paused again. Department policy stated that everyone an officer took into custody and transported must be handcuffed. This applied whether the custody was benevolent or an arrest situation. However, Katie knew that the rule was occasionally violated when it better suited the situation. For instance, the rape victim she transported the previous night had ridden in the front seat with her.

Still, she could, actually *should*, handcuff Dan. He might remain cooperative for the ride, but he could go ballistic in the back of her patrol car. Uncuffed, he could cause a lot of damage, maybe hurt himself, to say nothing of being difficult to control once she stopped the car. She'd heard of it happening every so often to an officer. She was pretty sure *that* was a fun one to explain to a supervisor.

Then again, Dan had blood on his hands. In this age of communicable diseases that were blood-borne, Katie didn't really like to touch someone else's blood without rubber gloves.

Katie considered briefly, then said, "Dan, you know you have to behave in my car, right? Your best behavior?"

"Yeah. Best behavior."

"I mean it, Dan. If you don't behave, my boss will get very mad at me. He will ask me why I didn't handcuff you. Do you want to be hand-cuffed?"

Katie saw horror enter Dan's eyes. She worried that she'd said too much.

"No! Handcuffs hurt! Send them to hyper-space!"

Katie waved her hand and made a whooshing sound. "There— gone. They will stay in hyperspace, as long as you behave. All right?"

"Behave. Yes. All right."

Katie opened the driver's door and popped the security button in the doorjamb to release the door to the back seat. As she stepped away from the car, she said, "Okay, Dan, get in."

Dan immediately climbed into the driver's seat.

"Dan—" Katie protested.

Dan began pushing buttons on the computer and the radio keypad. He moved quickly to the steering wheel, moving it from side to side as he adjusted the wiper blades and the heater. Since the car was turned off, none of the instruments responded. He gave a tug on the shotgun in its secure slot and moved on to the car stereo, pushing several buttons and twisting a dial.

"Busy guy," Westboard commented as he walked up. He handed Katie the house keys. "The place is locked up."

"Thanks." Katie said. She turned back to Dan. "Are you finished, Dan? Can we take a ride now?"

Dan sat still for a moment, staring through the windshield.

"Dan?"

His head rotated slowly toward her. "Of course, my favorite cat is an elephant," he said.

"Mine, too. Now please get out of my seat and get in the back."

Dan struggled out of the front seat and walked gingerly around the rear door and into the back seat. Katie shut the door.

"Sheesh. He is out there," Westboard said. "I feel like we're taking the Rainman into custody."

Katie cringed. She knew Dan probably couldn't hear them, but she didn't want to hurt his feelings or get him riled up. "At least he's not violent," she said. "Just…a little loony."

"I'll say."

"Did you see any meds in the bathroom?"

"Nope. None in the bedroom, either. But you know that typewriter in the living room?"

"Yes."

Westboard handed her a sheet of paper and said, "A book of poetry by Ralph W. Emerson was next to it."

Katie looked at the sheet of paper. A single line was typed over and over about thirty times.

The strong gods pine for my abode.

"What poem is this from?" she asked.

Westboard shrugged. "Couldn't tell ya. I didn't see it on the page the book was open to." He motioned to the sheet of paper.

"There were about fifteen or twenty of those stacked next to the typewriter, though."

"I wonder what the deal is with that?"

"Dunno. You want me to follow you up in case he gets excited?"

"No," Katie said. "I'll be fine. Thanks, Matt."

"Enjoy the ride in the police car," he said slyly and walked toward his own car.

Katie got into her driver's seat. She pulled a baby wipe from her patrol bag and wiped everywhere Dan had touched. As she cleaned the steering wheel, she looked into her rear-view mirror at Dan. The bearded man was staring off at nothing again.

"Dan? What's this from?" She held up the paper with her free hand.

Dan looked at her but didn't answer.

"What poem?"

"I don't know."

Katie held back a sigh. She balled up the baby wipe and slid it into the small plastic garbage bag. Then she started the engine. Instantly the windshield wipers began to flap violently. The stereo blasted static. She quickly hit the right buttons to stop everything, feeling like a three-year-old had been playing in her car.

She glanced back at Dan. He stared back, unaffected and not at all curious.

"So you like Emerson, then?" she asked.

"To me, he tastes like ketchup," Dan replied.

Katie put the car into gear and reset her trip odometer. "Ketchup?"

"Ketchup."

"What about T.S. Eliot?"

"Mustard."

"Of course," Katie said, smiling. She informed dispatch that she was en route to Sacred Heart with a forty-eight. On the way up, she wondered which poet tasted like mayonnaise.

0607 hours

Connor O'Sullivan sat in the lobby of the Internal Affairs office at 1098 West Mallon Avenue. Anthony Battaglia sat next to him in the corner. The dark-haired officer leaned into the wall and slept, snoring lightly.

How the hell can he sleep sitting in IA, Sully wondered. He must not think he did anything wrong. Either that, or he was consigned to his fate. Who knew?

Hart kept them both waiting. Sully figured that was how he showed his dominance. Hart was important. They were not. Therefore, they arrived early and waited for him.

At nine minutes past the hour, Lieutenant Alan Hart entered the lobby of the IA office.

Sully took one look at his thin, smug face and felt a stab of anger replace his concern. Battaglia's light snore next to him gave him confidence.

Hart cast a disapproving look at the slumbering Battaglia. Then his eyes flicked to Sully. "You're first," he said in a clipped tone.

"Good," Sully answered. "I'm ready."

Hart turned stiffly on his heel and marched back toward the interview room without a word.

Sully stood and followed.

Screw Hart, he thought, and smiled.

Battaglia's snores trailed after him.

0659 hours

Katie Macleod set her pistol on her nightstand and kicked off her shoes. The fog of sleep was already creeping in at the corner of her eyes. Other than Danny Forty-eight, the previous night had remained relatively quiet. She wondered if she were crazy or if she really had detected a slight sense of disquiet in the city last night. It had been a Wednesday evening, which was usually the busiest of the four true weekdays (she considered Friday part of the weekend—it was already in full swing by the time Graveyard shift came on duty). People slogged away for a couple of days, but then Hump Day came along. Many felt like they needed a little release, just enough to get them to the weekend. So the bars were a little busier. Domestic arguments went up, too.

Not last night, though. The streets were nearly bare all night. When she drove by the bars in her sector, she noticed some closing early for lack of customers, well before the required two o'clock. There weren't many cars out and fewer pedestrians. Overall, she had the sense of a city that was nervous.

It's probably just me.

Probably. She'd taken the rape report from Maureen Hite. She'd heard the radio news reports calling this guy the Rainy Day Rapist. She was probably just amplifying what she saw due to her own behind-the-scenes knowledge.

Right?

Or was it because *she* was nervous?

Because of what happened.

The thought came to her unbidden and unwelcome. Once it had sprung up in the early morning light, though, she took a hard look at it.

Was that the reason?

Katie unbuttoned her jeans and wriggled out of them, tossing the clumped denim into the laundry hamper in the corner of her room. She did the same with her shirt and underclothing, then pulled the long blue flannel pajama over the top of her head. As the warm material slid down her ribs and hips, a shudder went through her.

Do I even want to think about this?

Robotic, she pulled the shades closed on the bedroom window. The bedroom darkened. Natural light seeped around the corners of the window shades and splashed weakly against the wall. More light spilled in through the open bedroom door.

Katie closed the door and slid beneath the covers of her bed. The initial coolness of the sheets gave way as her body warmed the bed. She resisted shivering, afraid that if she started, she might not stop.

I thought I was over this.

She knew that was a lie the moment she thought it, though. What happened to her wasn't like the flu. She wasn't going to "get over it" and "just move on." She knew enough from the police training she'd received on the subject to know that was true.

Still, everyone deals with the trauma differently. Some were devastated. Some survive. Some leave it behind. Some face it. Some embrace it.

And some push it deep down, don't they, Katie? But it doesn't always want to stay down deep, does it? Not this, not the child on the bridge, not a dozen other things that you face but yet do not face.

She closed her eyes tightly and exhaled.

And just like she had always done when the pressure became too great, she let the images and emotions wash over her. She opened her mind and heart, spread her spiritual arms wide and accepted everything that came.

All the ugliness followed quickly.

Phil. That'd been his name. An upperclassman at Washington State University. They'd met at a party. Katie recalled the thrill of that first kiss with him. Such a naïve emotional reaction. Because next came the groping hands and the refusal to stop.

Don't be a goddamn tease.

The back bedroom sanctuary had quickly become a prison. She couldn't scream, couldn't move. He'd slapped his palm over her mouth, mashing her lips into her teeth, almost like a grotesque antithesis of that first kiss just minutes before.

Then what felt like cold steel being driven into her.

You'll do what I say, tease.

How long had that gone on? How long did it take him? She imagined it was a thousand years of staring up at the textured ceiling in the dim light of that bedroom. And when he'd finished, the dead weight of his spent body disgusted her even further. She tried to wriggle out from beneath him. He didn't resist, finally pushing himself up and buckling his pants.

You liked it. Don't forget that.

Like she could ever forget what happened. How stripped and vulnerable she felt. How much courage she had to raise just to slink out of the house and run to a pay phone. Too afraid to even call the police, she'd dialed her mother's number, praying the woman would be awake and not drunk.

She had been awake, but Katie could hear the slur in her mother's sleepy hello. It didn't seem to matter, though, because she spilled out the entire story on the phone, rushing her words, using them to fight off the tears that wanted to return.

And then her mother answered.

Well, at least you weren't a virgin.

The words struck Katie like a sheet of freezing water. The threat of tears was immediately staved off. Without a word, she hung up the phone.

After that, she never told anyone else.

Not the police. Not a single friend. Not any of her lovers. None of her brothers and sisters in the badge.

No one.

Not ever.

Her mother never mentioned the rape, either. At first, Katie thought that was because she didn't know how to deal with it or what to say. She could understand that. But when her mother expressed only confusion at why Katie would change her college major from veterinary science to criminal justice, she realized that it wasn't discomfort at all.

Her mother had simply been too drunk to even remember the conversation.

That left only two people in the world who knew the truth about what happened. She doubted that even Phil remembered it the way it really happened. His bashful glances her way over the next term told her that he was either too intoxicated to have a clear memory of the event or he wanted it to appear that way. She wondered what he told his friends about it and about her. She even wondered how he rationalized things in his own mind in order to deal with it.

Or maybe it was easy for him. Who knew?

Sometimes Katie thought the whole thing was her fault. If only she hadn't gone to the party. Or had a few drinks. Or danced with him. Or kissed him. If she'd avoided any one of those things, then the rape would never have occurred.

Other times, she wanted to scream out in frustration. She wanted to claw back at the images of him on top of her. She wanted to take back what he tore from her.

Most of the time, she wanted it to have never happened. And that was how she dealt with it every day since it happened. She simply pretended it happened to someone else. After all, no one else knew about it and Katie MacLeod planned on keeping it that way forever. Even if it meant facing down these memories every so often, when it was too difficult to keep them tamped down inside anymore.

Even if it meant passing through them again to take away their potency.

Everyone deals with trauma differently, she knew. And sometimes even the same person deals with it differently at different times.

Some people faced things head on, absorbed the pain and moved on.

Some ran away.

Katie took in a deep breath and let it out. Sweat dampened her entire body beneath the blanket, but she felt stronger.

Because even though she sometimes hid, she didn't ever run.

As if on cue, the telephone at Katie's bedside rang shrilly. She jumped at the sound, then realized she'd forgotten to turn off the ringer. She reached for the telephone, unsure until the phone was at her ear, if she would answer it or simply turn off the noise.

"Hello?"

Maybe it had been a desire for human company that drove her to answer the phone. Something to extract her from her memories. If that were true, she instantly regretted it when the voice at the other end of the connection came through.

"Kay-die?"

The slurred version of her name caused her to flash to her mother, but the voice was distinctly male.

"Is thad yew, Kay-die?"

Stef.

"It's me," she answered, her voice tight. "What do you want?"

"Oh, Kay-die," he said, his voice dissolving into several teary grunts and huffs. "Oh." He took another breath, then said, "*Hola, chica.*"

Katie felt strangely cold. The natural response from the time they dated – *hola, chico* – never even threatened to come out. It was as if the pity and the anger that she had intermittently felt for Kopriva had called a truce. With the two emotions leaving the battlefield, all that remained was a strange emptiness.

"What do you want, Stef?"

"I jes' wanna talk with you. I wanna –"

"Stef, we have nothing to talk about," she told him.

"Nu-nu-nothing?" he stammered back in a surprised tone.

"Nothing," she repeated.

"How can you say that to me?" he asked her, pain evident in his voice.

Pity may have quit the field, but at that question, her anger reentered the fray. "How could you say the things you said to me? How could you be so selfish?"

"I—I—"

"You act like everything that happened last year only happened to you." Her mind's eye flashed to a picture of Amy Dugger that she had seen in the Dugger's kitchen while she'd been assigned to wait with the family. Her jaw clenched. "Well, it didn't. Those things happened to the rest of us, too."

"You didn't kill anyone," Kopriva answered back, his slur seeming to dissipate with those particular words. "I did."

"We all have our own ghosts, Stef. But you decided not to face yours. You decided to check out instead." Katie shook her head. Now pity had heard the call of battle and reappeared on the field. "I can't have you in my life. Not if you won't face up to your demons. I can't get dragged down into that."

"Whaddayou know?" Kopriva snarled. "Little Miss Perfect Princess. You don't know shit!"

An ironic laugh forced its way out of Katie's mouth before she could stop it. "Oh, Stef. Like you know. You don't know anything about me. Not really."

"I tell you what I know. I know that you don't care about—"

"Don't call me anymore," Katie interrupted, her voice hard. "If you do, I'll get a no-contact order."

Kopriva stopped talking. Stung silence radiated through the telephone receiver toward her.

"Goodbye, Stef," she said, and hung up.

She turned off the ringer and curled up into a ball under the blankets. She let the ghosts and demons wash over her until weariness finally pulled her into a sleep so deep that even those specters could not follow.

EIGHT

Thursday, April 18th
0917 hours
Day Shift

Tower stood in the doorway of the crime analysis unit with a package of Hostess donuts in his hands. He waited until Renee looked up from her desk and spotted him there. Her expression remained momentarily angry. He raised the box of donuts and affected a contrite expression.

Renee's features softened slightly. She waved him into the office.

Tower grinned.

"Don't smile at me, John," she said. "The donuts get you in the door, but not off my shit list."

Tower's grin widened.

"I mean it, John."

"I know."

"You can't just talk to me like I'm some idiot or something."

"I know." He held out the donuts. "Peace?"

Renee stared at him, as if gauging his sincerity. After a moment, she accepted the box from him. Then she held out her empty coffee mug. The words on the side read, *Given enough coffee, I could rule the world.*

"Coffee's over there," she said.

"Yes, ma'am," Tower said lightly, snapping a salute.

Renee raised a single eyebrow. "You might want to lay off the smart alec shtick for a little while. I still haven't decided if I forgive you."

Tower held up his empty hand in an open palm, *mea culpa* gesture and moved across the room. He filled her cup with the rich brew, along with a Styrofoam cup for himself.

"You could've brought flowers," Renee said.

"Oh, yeah. *That* wouldn't start rumors."

"What'd I say about the smart alec thing?"

Tower brought her the cup of coffee he'd poured. "That was sarcasm. It's different."

"It's close enough."

Tower shrugged. "Probably. Anyway, you can't eat flowers. You can eat donuts."

Renee didn't answer. She eyed the box, then cracked the lid. "One won't hurt."

Tower suppressed a laugh. If Renee wanted to eat twenty donuts, she probably could do so without gaining an ounce. She remained slender, despite spending her days behind a desk in a small office filled with snack food. It didn't bother Tower, but he was pretty sure every woman in the department hated her for exactly that reason.

Renee bit into the donut and chewed slowly. Then she sipped her coffee. "You should've gone to the bakery," she said. "You got these at a convenience store, didn't you?"

"No," Tower lied.

Renee turned the box and read the code from the label. "The Circle K, huh?"

"How'd you know that?"

Renee smiled humorlessly. "I know everything. It's my job."

Tower shrugged. "Can't argue that. But a donut is a donut."

Renee lowered the box. Her eyebrow arched again. "Excuse me?"

"You heard me."

She raised the half-eaten donut in the air. "This is barely a donut. Real donuts are things you buy at the bakery." She raised her cup. "A real donut complements real coffee." She lowered the cup. "You know, I'm only eating this because you're trying to make up. Otherwise, I'd put them out for visitors."

"I know."

Renee took a bite and held the box out toward him.

Tower waved off her offer. "Can't feed the stereotype."

Renee swallowed. "But I can?"

"You're not the police. You only work for the police."

"The public doesn't know the difference," she said.

"True," Tower agreed. "But the public is mostly ignorant."

"I've developed a theory about that, by the way," she said, breaking off another piece of donut and tossing it in her mouth.

"About what? Why the public is ignorant?"

"Uh-uh." She chewed and swallowed and gave it another coffee chaser. "About cops and donuts. How the stereotype started."

Tower raised his eyebrows. "Really?"

She gave him a slight smile and took the last bite of her donut, making him wait. When she'd finished chewing and tossing back another shot of coffee, she went on. "It's simple, really. People forget that we haven't always been this twenty-four hours, seven days a week society. The pace of life wasn't always this fast. Take 7-11 stores for instance. Do you know where the name came from?"

Tower did, but he shook his head no. He didn't want to interrupt her.

"Those were the store's business hours. Seven in the morning until eleven at night. What was so novel about that, you ask? Well, everyone else except bars and taverns were strictly nine to five. Maybe eight to six. It was a big deal to be able to run to the store for milk at ten-thirty at night when the Safeway was closed."

She took another pull of coffee and waved her hand. "Of course, now there are tons of businesses open twenty-four hours a day. Not just convenience stores, but gas stations, restaurants and grocery stores. Everybody has twenty-four hour service."

"Not banks," Tower said.

"Not so. ATMs." She shook her head. "No, John, we've seen a very radical shift in the last half-century. The era of convenience is firmly entrenched in our social structure."

"So cops eat donuts because it's convenient?"

She took another sip and rolled her eyes at him. "Are you purposefully being obtuse?"

"Yes. But it's not much of a stretch for me."

"I don't doubt it. Do you want to hear my theory or not?"

"Yes, ma'am."

She leaned forward. "Back in the times before 7-11, when everyone closed down at a reasonable hour and went home, we still had cops out on the beat, right? Graveyard shift had to be unbearably long. By two or three in the morning, I'll bet you that the officers out there thought they were the last people alive on earth. They'd welcome human contact. They'd be looking for it. So who was open at that time of night?"

"Bars?"

"Yeah, all right, until two in the morning. *If* it were a weekend. But how long would a bartender want to stay after a long night? Not long. He'd be wanting to tally up the receipts and get home to bed. By two-thirty, even the bars were dark back then. But who comes to work about three, three-thirty in the morning?"

Tower shrugged.

She smiled. "The baker. The baker comes to work early and starts baking. He throws on a pot of coffee for himself and for his friend, the local cop. The cop swings by, has some fresh coffee, some conversation and a donut. The sugar and caffeine give him a boost through to the end of his shift. The baker doesn't have to worry about getting robbed when he opens his shop. Both parties benefit from the arrangement."

"No doubt."

Renee leaned back in her chair and crossed her arms. "And that, detective, is how I believe the cop and the donut stereotype came to be."

Tower set down his Styrofoam cup on her desk and clapped. "Brilliant. And all these years, I just thought it was because donuts tasted good."

"That's why you're a detective and not an analyst."

Tower nodded, letting a more serious look seep into his face. "You're right, actually. That's why I'd like to talk to you about those questions you wrote last time I was here."

She held up a finger. "You're forgetting something."

Tower sighed and hung his head. "The donuts aren't enough?"

"Do you have any experience with women at all, Detective Tower?"

"Apparently not."

"Apparently *so*," Renee replied. "Because you know exactly what you need to do."

Tower looked up and met her eyes. "Yes, I do." He took a deep breath and said in a sincere tone, "I'm sorry, Renee."

She paused, as if savoring his discomfort. Tower waited in silence until she finally gave him a quick nod. "Apology accepted."

"Thank you. Let's get busy, then."

Renee poised her fingers over the keyboard. "Just speak the word, master."

Tower smiled. "Actually, I was thinking more about those questions you wrote down."

Renee reached into a file on her desk and removed the slip of paper. Without a word, she handed it to Tower. He glanced down at the neat feminine script.

Why does he rape?
Who does he hate?
Is he evolving?

Tower sighed. "I know I was frustrated before, so that was why I snapped at you. But, truly, I have no clue what the answers to any of these questions are."

"It's like I said, John. You have to use your imagination. Why would a man rape?"

Tower shrugged. "Hell, I don't know."

Renee chuckled and shook her head. "Sure you do. Every man knows."

Tower cocked his head at her. "Are you saying every man is a rapist?" he asked. He'd heard about some kooky women's libber saying something like that once upon a time, but he thought it was stupid. He'd seen plenty of rapists since being assigned to the Sexual Assault Unit. Most of them were scumbag pieces of—

"No," Renee said, "of course not. But every man can imagine why a rape might occur."

"Sex?"

"Give the man a prize."

Tower shook his head. "But I thought rape was about power, not sex. That's what all the advocates say. That's what most of the training I've gone to says, too." He shrugged. "I even heard one statistic where something like forty percent of rapists can't even get an erection."

Renee nodded. "I heard that one, too."

"So?"

"So what?"

Tower cocked his head the other direction. "Are you trying to frustrate me on purpose?"

"It *is* fun," Renee said. "And so easy."

"I'm glad I amuse you."

Renee smiled. "Back to the question at hand. Power or sex? Sex or violence?"

"Easy," Tower said. "Power and violence."

"I think you're right," Renee said. "I think all the advocates and the experts and so forth are right, too. It *is* about power and it *is* about violence. But sex is the *vehicle* for all that power mongering and violence."

"So...?"

"So, in a very real way, it is also about sex. It sure as hell isn't about badminton."

Tower paused, thinking about her words. Then he said, "So he rapes for power, but it is still important to him that sex is the way he gets the power?"

"I think so. Not just with this guy, but with most of them."

Tower shrugged. "Okay, could be. How does that help us?"

Renee returned the shrug. "I don't know if it does help a whole lot. But it's a start. Move on to the next question."

Tower glanced back down at her list. "Who does he hate?" He looked up at Renee. "Do you mean groups of people? Like immigrants or women or something?"

Renee shook her head. "Not really. I mean something more specific. If he hates women in general, for example, it is usually because of a specific hate for a specific woman. Or women."

"Someone who hurt him?"

"Yes."

"Like a girlfriend."

"Or a mother."

Tower raised his eyebrows. "Oh...I see. Mommy issues." He twirled his finger at his temple and stuck out his tongue sideways.

Renee wagged her finger at him. "You shouldn't make fun, John. Our parents have a huge impact on who we become. Messed up parents usually create messed up kids."

"Maybe he was an orphan. Maybe he hates his mother for giving him up for adoption."

Renee peered closely at him.

Tower raised his palms up in a placating gesture. "Seriously."

Renee considered. "I suppose it could be. But I wouldn't think that a sense of abandonment would result in such a powerful reaction."

Tower chuckled, shaking his head slowly.

"What?" Renee asked.

"Listen to us," Tower said, "a couple of junior psychiatrists."

Renee shrugged. "You don't need a degree to figure out bad guys. This is a sick guy, John."

"Duh."

"I'd be willing to bet this all came from childhood." Renee looked down at her notepad and traced the letters absently. "I can imagine some young kid with an absent or abusive father, or a domineering mother. Or someone else and something else. It doesn't matter. What does matter is that through alternately neglecting and inflicting pain on this child, who only wanted love and protection, someone who was supposed to care for this little boy created a monster instead."

Tower looked at her askance. "You're...*sympathizing* with him?"

Renee nodded. "You bet. As a child, I sympathize with him from here to Cleveland."

"He's a violent rapist," Tower reminded her.

"Yes, he is, John. As an *adult*." Renee tapped the tip of her pen on the pad in front of her for emphasis. "As a *child*, I cry for this person."

Tower shook his head. "I don't know how."

"You remember Amy Dugger, John?"

Tower's eyes narrowed. "Of course. Why on earth would you bring up that little girl?"

"They found her dead body in a field," Renee said.

"I know. I was there."

"And forensics said she'd been sexually assaulted."

Tower clenched his jaw. "Your point?"

"My point," Renee said, "is that what that little girl went through was hellish, but it only lasted a few days. Imagine if it had gone on for years. And then imagine if she survived that beating and got away from her kidnappers. Does your heart go out to that little child, John?"

"Of course it does," Tower snapped. "It *did*. It *does*."

"I know," Renee said quietly. "But now imagine what kind of adult that kid would probably grow into. With all that pain to deal with, she'd probably want to inflict a little of it back onto the world. She might have kids of her own someday. And because of what she's learned as a child, and since they make such convenient targets, she might decide to hurt her own kids. Maybe even kill them. Now when you get called to the scene of that homicide, are you going to feel sorry for that adult? That child-murderer?"

"No," Tower whispered.

"But you felt sorry for the little girl she used to be."

Tower stood quietly, saying nothing.

"That's how I feel about this guy, John," Renee explained. "My heart bleeds for him as a child. As an adult, though, I hope he comes at you with a knife when you find him. That way you can blast the sick fuck right out of his asshole rapist shoes."

Tower nodded slowly, slightly surprised at the vehemence in Renee's words. "He is sick."

"And he's gaining momentum. He's evolving."

Tower looked down at the list in front of him. "Which brings us to number three."

"And the most important one right now," Renee added.

"Why's that?"

"Because while answers to the first two questions might help you understand the guy or have an advantage when you interview him, neither question gets you any closer to finding him. Neither does this one, but it has a direct impact on your investigation."

"How so?"

"Because if he is evolving, and I think he is, then it won't be long before merely controlling and raping his victims won't be enough."

"Meaning he'll start hurting them more?" Tower asked, but he knew that wasn't what Renee was getting at.

Renee met his gaze directly. "Or maybe he'll start to kill them."

1534 hours

At three-thirty every day, Wendy Latah left her North Central High School classroom with her students' homework tucked into her grade-book. In her history class, there was an assignment every single day except on those days right before a vacation break. Every student's grade was recorded daily. A good grade in her class required diligent, consistent study. Those students who couldn't handle that either failed or were transferred into Mr. Julian's considerably less stringent government class.

As she shuffled down the mostly empty hallway of the school, she thought about how much she loved teaching history. Her father, a history professor at Eastern Washington University, had taught her the merits of courage and resolve. He had also taught her to look at history objectively and not to judge according to the standards of *this* time, but the standards of the time in which those men and women lived. In history, he taught her, there is seldom struggle between wholly good and wholly evil. There is only the struggle of people. Maniacs like Hitler were only the exception that proved the rule.

History was nothing more than a study of people, her father had taught her. History is made every day by great leaders and small nobodies alike. Strength of character, courage, diligence and honesty, were traits *all* people could portray.

Wendy frankly wished that even a tenth of her father's wisdom had been passed onto the students today. Each day when she emerged from her classroom and walked the halls of North Central High School, she was astounded at how much things had changed since she graduated in 1967. The open disrespect, the profanity, the violence. No one could have conceived of such a thing even when she began teaching in 1972. Now she knew of two different teachers this year that had been assaulted. Another teacher had a student who brandished a knife in the classroom. And worst of all, her best friend, Anna McHugh, had been forced to call the police when she saw a gun in a student's waistband in her classroom. The subsequent arrest led to the discovery of drugs in the student's sock. He had been a sophomore, only fifteen years old.

All of this had prompted Wendy to go to The General Store, which carried firearms and sporting equipment. Her unique knowledge of history gave her the understanding that all things change. Those that become the victims of that change are those who refuse to acknowledge it. So she had reluctantly purchased a small caliber handgun which she kept in her bedroom nightstand drawer. Of course, she couldn't bring a gun to school, so she'd also bought a small canister of pepper spray which she kept in her purse on her key ring.

But the change pained her. She resented the need for her response. So she tried to keep as much continuity in her life as she could. Thus, every day at three-thirty, she left her classroom. Grade book and homework under her arm, she walked out to the parking lot. Her car was in the same parking space every day, where she had parked it when arriving at six-thirty that morning. She removed her keys and unlocked the car door. The parking lot was strangely empty, but she knew that all sports and activities had tapered off in expectation of the upcoming spring break. In fact, her students had groaned when she had assigned homework, just one school day before the break.

Discipline, she thought. They would thank her at their ten-year reunion. Or perhaps their twenty.

As she swung her car door open, she felt an arm snake around her waist and pull her forcefully backwards. She let out a small cry before a hand clamped firmly over her mouth.

"In the car, bitch," the assailant grunted at her. Her old Nova had a bench seat. She slipped to all fours, her knees thudding painfully on the bottom of the doorframe. She felt him thrust forward with his hips, forcing her onto the front seat. He climbed in after her.

Wendy fumbled with her key chain. Her breath shot forcefully in and out of her nose.

The man shoved her down onto her stomach. The smell of the cloth seat covers filled her nostrils. His hand slipped underneath her long skirt and grab at her undergarments.

My Lord! She tried to scream in terror, but the noise was muffled by the car seat. What would a high school student want with her? She was fifty-six years old. Her thin body had none of the curves she saw on the female students in the halls. Why was this happening?

His hands found the waistband and ripped her underpants away. She yelped into the seat again. She felt his fingers probe forcefully. Tears of pain sprang into her eyes and rolled down her cheeks.

Why?

Why was this happening?

He rammed his fingers into her, causing her to recoil in pain with each thrust. His hand pressed down on her shoulder blades, keeping her pinned to the seat.

Why was for history to discover, she thought weakly.

"Lying old bitch," he muttered. "Get what you got coming."

She let out a frightened moan. Her fingers scrambled for the small canister of pepper spray on her key chain.

"You could have done something." His voice had a faraway quality to it, despite being laced with anger. "You could have told somebody. Made her stop."

His fingers drove upward. Wendy yelped in pain.

He ignored her. "But no, you were too busy being the perfect little teacher."

What was he talking about?

The tip of her fingers tapped the cylinder of the pepper spray. Her hand swallowed it up and she clutched it in her fist.

"Payback is a bitch, though," he continued. "And, I'm going to fucking kill—"

She aimed blindly over her shoulder and shot.

He gave a sharp cry of surprise and pain. Immediately, she felt his hand leave her upper back. The rest of him seemed to pull away, too. Wendy rolled quickly onto her back, took a hard look into his bewildered eyes and sprayed again. This time she emptied the can into his face.

Orange foam coated the black ski mask he wore. His enraged eyes, already red and watering, glared at her from out of the mask. "You fucking bitch!" he roared at her. The force of his words sent spittle flying, the color of carrot peels.

Wendy responded by thrusting her foot at his groin. Her kick landed just below the navel and doubled him over with a grunt.

Without pause, she turned over again and crawled across the front seat. She reached for the passenger door with her left hand. She pulled on it, but it didn't open. She glanced up frantically. The peg-like latch was in the down position, still locked.

Behind her, she heard the man growling in pain and spitting out profanity.

Wendy dropped the empty canister from her right hand. She stretched her hand upward toward the door lock. The pepper spray in the air had a wet feel to it. She felt her eyes begin to burn. The tickle in her throat became a cough. Her hand closed on the door lock and lifted it.

A crushing weight dropped down on top of her. She collapsed painfully into the seat. Her forehead banged into the side of the door.

"You disgusting bitch," she heard him growl as he dragged her toward him. "I am going to lay the whammo on you!"

There was a ripping pain in her right shoulder as he flipped her onto her back. His hand grasped her by the throat. Reflexively, she clutched at it with both of her hands, but her strength was no match for his.

He squeezed.

She stared upward into his eyes. The black ski mask was coated with orange spray. Tears ran from his eyes and dripped orange onto her face.

Too old for a student, she thought. *Those eyes are far too old.*

His words rang in her ears. Not the profanities, but the almost familiar tone that he used. How he spoke as if he knew her. As if she'd betrayed him somehow.

Maybe he's a former student.

Maybe he's someone that I failed.

And that was the last thought that Wendy Latah had as she saw a clenched fist descending on her.

1609 hours

Officer Giovanni watched the ambulance pull out of the parking lot with the matronly assault victim in the back. Through the back windows, he saw Mark Ridgeway's short brown hair as he rode with her to the hospital.

I hope she makes it, he thought to himself. The woman reminded him of his sixth grade teacher, Mrs. Maloney. Of course, Mrs. Maloney had been a little heavy-set, but she'd been very kind and patient. And she always smiled at him when he did well. That had been better than a gold star any day of the week.

He turned away from the ambulance and back in the direction of the crime scene. Yellow tape cordoned off the corner of the parking lot and the 1970 Nova. The driver's door stood wide open. Offal from the medics packaging lay scattered around on the ground near the door where the medical crew had worked on her prior to loading her onto a gurney for transport.

Gio walked to the edge of the crime scene tape. Jack Stone stood glumly at the entrance with clipboard, logging who entered and left the scene.

"You're not going in, Gio," Stone told him flatly. "I've already got you logged out and I don't want to start another line."

Gio frowned at him. He wondered briefly what Stone's problem was, but then realized it was the same problem he always had—he was Jack Stone. This was just one more thing for him to bitch about.

As if to prove the point, Stone continued, "I shouldn't even be keeping this log. I'm senior to you. You should be doing this crap job. Or some rookie."

Gio made a sad face and pretended to play a violin.

"Screw you, Giovanni," Stone said and turned his back on him.

Gio stepped under the tape and into the crime scene. He ignored Stone's muted curses and walked closer to the car. Major Crimes Detective Joseph Finch was crouched on his haunches, examining the scene. His partner, Elias, spoke with another teacher, who was the woman who had found the victim.

"She was barely breathing when I got here," the woman told Elias, who busily scratched out notes while she spoke. "There was this gurgling sound when she tried to breathe." The woman brought her hand to her mouth, fighting back tears. "It was horrible."

The spicy remnants of oleoresin capsicum drifted toward Gio's nose. Always sensitive to the stuff, he covered his nose and mouth and moved away. He wondered if the guy had used the OC on her or if she'd used it defensively.

"Giovanni!" came the gruff voice of Lieutenant Crawford. "If you're not going to do anything in the crime scene, get the hell out of there."

"Sorry, El-Tee." Gio ducked under the tape and ignored Stone's self-righteous beaming.

Crawford lit up his cigar and took a deep puff. "What'd medics say?"

"She's pretty bad," Gio answered. "One guy thought she might have a subdural hematoma, whatever that is."

"Blood on the brain," Crawford explained.

"Sounds serious."

Crawford gave him a withering look. "It is. Did they say anything else?"

"No, not really. They were working pretty frantically on her before the ambulance got here. I got the impression they thought she might not make it."

Crawford glanced toward the car inside the crime scene. "That their mess?"

"On the ground, yeah."

Crawford grunted. "You start a canvass for witnesses yet?"

Gio shook his head. "Not yet."

"Do it. Call down to the General Detectives if you need more bodies."

Gio walked away, keying his mike. "Adam-254?"

"Adam-254, go ahead."

Gio recognized Trina's voice. That made him smile for a moment. When he'd gone out with her, she had liked to do this little thing with her—

"Gio!" Crawford bellowed after him.

"Adam-254, go ahead," Trina repeated.

Gio nodded to the lieutenant. As he walked toward him, he transmitted. "I need two more units here to help with the witness canvass."

"Copy."

"Yeah, El-Tee?"

"You get the names of all the medics that were inside this crime scene?"

"Jack has that."

Crawford glanced over at Stone.

Stone shrugged. "I got everybody but the guys on the paramedic unit over there." He pointed at the small paramedic truck on the other side of the crime scene. One medic was busy repacking the equipment while the other stood by, watching the cops work.

Bullshit, Gio thought. He knew Stone had those names. He just wanted to get back at him by sending him on an errand.

"Go get those names," Crawford directed him.

Gio opened his mouth to argue, then closed it. Crawford would still send him no matter what. And if he argued, all that did was provide more entertainment for Stone. Instead, he turned on his heel and trudged around the crime scene to the medics.

"How's it going?" he asked the one packing the gear. He wore no rank insignias on his uniform, so Gio figured the other guy was a boss.

"It's going," the medic answered. "Too bad about that lady, huh?"

"Yeah."

"She reminded me of my tenth grade teacher, Mrs. O'Halloran. Very nice lady."

"I know the feeling," Gio said. "Listen, can I get your names for the crime scene report?"

"Sure. I'm Terry. That's Art."

Gio took out his notebook. "Last names?"

The medic laughed. "Oh, sorry. Mine's Wylie. His is Hoagland. We're out of Station Three."

Gio jotted the information down. "Thanks. Did you work on her?"

Terry shook his head. "No, it was mostly Art, at least until the ambulance got here."

At the sound of his name, the tall, slender medic turned toward the two of them. "What's that?"

"Just talking bad about you, boss," Terry said.

"Like that's anything new."

Gio smiled lightly at the banter and turned to go.

"Officer?"

Gio stopped. "Yeah?"

Art stepped closer to him. "I'm no cop or anything, but there's something I think you should know."

"What's that?"

"Well, I noticed something strange about her clothing."

"Damaged?"

"No, not really. But when I first arrived, I noticed that her skirt was pushed up a little bit. I didn't think anything of it, but then we ended up cutting it off while we were working on her. It was one of those long thick denim skirts and it was getting in the way. Anyway, when we pulled it aside, that's when I saw that her undergarments were pulled down."

"Pulled down?" Gio repeated.

Art nodded. "Yeah. About three quarters of the way down from the hip toward the knee."

"Could that happen by accident?" Gio asked, though he figured he already knew the answer. "From her thrashing around in a fight or something?"

Art shook his head. "No, I don't think so. This was too far down for anything like that. I think they were deliberately pulled down by her attacker."

"Which means..."

"Which means this isn't just an assault," Art finished. "Yeah."

"Way to go, Columbo." Terry said. He looked up at the sky. "Is it raining?"

Gio didn't bother giving him a disapproving look. He turned and trotted back to the crime scene, ducking underneath the tape. He heard Stone's infuriated yell from the opposite side, but ignored it.

"Finch?" he asked the detective surveying the scene.

Finch looked up at him calmly. "What is it?"

"The medic over there said that when he got here, the victim's underwear was pulled down almost to her knees."

Gio expected some surprise, but got none. Instead, Finch merely pointed his pen at the ground. "That would explain the condom."

Gio followed his gesture. An unopened condom lay on the ground in the midst of all the medic's torn gauze wrappings.

"Holy shit," he muttered.

Finch turned his head and called over his shoulder. "El-Tee!"

"What?" Crawford bellowed back.

"You better call Tower."

And after that, the crime scene went quiet for a while.

1811 hours

Detective Tower stood outside of the sheet drawn between the patient's bed and the rest of the emergency room. When the doctor exited the patient area, they dispensed with any pleasantries.

"Do you believe she was sexually assaulted, doctor?"

The doctor nodded. "I would say so. There's some obvious vaginal trauma."

"Any semen?"

"None that I could see. The swabs will tell the true story, though."

Tower didn't hold out much hope for that. Not if his hunch was right. "Is she still unconscious?"

The doctor nodded. "Yes. She was struck numerous times with a blunt object in the face and head."

"Like a club?"

The doctor shrugged. "Could have been, but it looks more like a fist to me. We're going to do a CAT scan on her to see what the extent of the injuries are."

Tower shook the doctor's hand briefly and thanked him. The doctor gave him a short nod and walked away quickly to the next patient. Tower had learned long ago not to detain emergency room doctors for any longer than necessary. There was always another patient waiting.

Ridgeway appeared at his side. "She wake up?"

"No."

Ridgeway shook his head gravely and said nothing.

"Mark, do me a favor?"

"Yep."

"When the rape kit is ready, will you run that and all her clothes over to property?"

"Sure."

"Not that it'll speed things up, but mark the lab items as a rush, too."

"You got it."

Tower nodded his thanks and left the emergency room. As he walked to his car, he tossed things over in his mind. The engine rumbled to life and he headed for the station.

A flare of anger shot through his chest as he recalled Wendy Latah's swollen and bruised face. Her driver's license photo had shown an elegant older woman with delicate features. The slender woman in the hospital bed had resembled a badly pummeled boxer after a lopsided match.

Who would do such a thing?

Exactly my problem, Tower thought. *Who?*

He tried to consider alternatives to what seemed almost like a certainty to him. He forced himself to spend the time to look at it from another angle, even though, in his heart, he knew.

Maybe it was a student? He gave the thought a half-hearted analysis. Why would a student attack a teacher? Vengeance for a poor grade? Just plain cruelty?

Well, if by some strange confluence of events it actually was a student, that student's identity would come out very shortly. It was obvious that Wendy Latah had put up a good fight. The empty canister of pepper mace found in the vehicle spoke to that. Even without the canister, there was no mistaking the lung-biting odor of cayenne pepper in the air. Whoever she sprayed looked like a pumpkin-head right now. A parent was going to notice that and get to the bottom of the story, either from the kid or from the news.

If it were a student.

Tower frowned. He knew it wasn't. That condom seemed to scream the obvious at him.

This was the Rainy Day Rapist, not some vengeful student. And he had a feeling that no one was going to notice this pumpkin-head and call it in. Things were not going to be so easy. And why should it be? Nothing on this case had been yet.

He allowed himself a half-hearted hope that Diane in Forensics might be able to life a print from the unused condom. But the way his luck was rolling so far on this case, he didn't invest a lot of emotional energy into that small hope.

Tower pulled into the station and parked.

He knew he had to go see Crawford. The Rainy Day Rapist was escalating. It was time to change the way he was doing things on this case.

2008 hours

Captain Michael Reott slid open his desk drawer. Reaching inside, he brought out a cigar box. Then he flipped open the box and pulled out one of his remaining four cigars.

Lieutenant Crawford watched him from his chair on the opposite side of the desk. "You're not going to light that."

Reott looked up at him. "Hell I'm not."

Crawford allowed a slow smile to spread across his round face. "That's what I like about you, Mike. No respect for authority."

Reott bit off the butt-end of the cigar and spat it into the trash-can. Then he offered the box to Crawford.

Still smiling, Crawford took one.

"It isn't about not respecting authority," Reott said. "It's about finishing out on my own terms."

"Meaning?"

"Meaning that it doesn't hurt a single soul if I want to smoke in my own office. I've been doing it since I made captain eleven years ago."

"Well," Crawford said, "there you have it. What's a little thing like state and federal law to stand in the way of tradition?"

"Shut up," Reott said, striking his silver Zippo lighter. "And open that window."

Crawford twisted the latch and opened the window while Reott drew smoke from his cigar. The pungent smell of burning tobacco filled the room. When he'd finished, he handed the lighter across the desk to Crawford, who lit his own cigar.

The two men sat in silence for several moments, smoking and thinking.

Finally, Crawford said, "Tower wants to put together a task force."

"We should."

"Investigations or Patrol?"

"Both," Reott answered. "You run it. Tower will be lead investigator, but use patrol officers to flesh out your numbers."

Crawford nodded, recognizing the wisdom in Reott's decision. Using patrol officers kept the Patrol captain's hand in the operation. Crawford's boss, the Investigative captain, was generally considered second only to Lieutenant Hart in the dipshit category. The presence of patrol officers in the operation kept Reott involved. Between the two of them, they could fend off any goofy ideas Captain Dipshit came up with.

"We should get some information out to the public, too," Reott said.

"Not about the task force?"

"No. Not yet, anyway. Just some general personal safety information."

Crawford drew in a deep drag of the cigar. He let it out in a billowing blue cloud. "That's probably way overdue. I imagine people are getting jumpy out there."

"They are." Reott took a large puff of his own cigar. "I met with a downtown business group over lunch today. They're worried about their families and their female employees. And the Chief told me on his way out of the office that the Mayor called him twice today. Apparently, a large number of people are calling City Hall."

"It's the goddamn media," Crawford said. "They go and call this freak The Rainy Day Rapist and all of the sudden everyone is scared."

"You have a wife, right?"

Crawford paused in mid-puff. "You know I do."

"You want her going out by herself right about now?"

Another puff. Then, "No."

"There you go."

"Fine," Crawford said. "I see your point. But mine still stands. The media fans the flames."

"Maybe. But we'll get some personal safety information out there in the short term. Meanwhile, you fire up your task force. Get the Prosecutor's Office on board, too."

"You want me to let a lawyer get involved? Mike, you want us to catch this guy or just sue him?"

Reott waved his comment away. "Just get him involved. It'll mostly be for show this early on. But when we catch the guy, having a prosecutor ready to step in will streamline the process. Might not be a bad idea to have him help Tower with any search warrants, too."

Crawford sighed. "All right. You're the boss."

"Don't forget it," Reott said, but his voice was mild.

"How can I, what with you throwing your authority around all the time?"

"Captain's Prerogative," Reott said. "And here's one more thing—I'm going to use Pam Lincoln at the newspaper for the personal safety stuff. If she's game, I also want you to give her some background on the case. See if she wants to cover the task force from the inside."

Crawford gave Reott a wide-eyed stare. "Well, why don't we just send out a flyer to the guy? With the newspaper reporting every step we make—"

Reott leaned back and put his feet up on his desk with a weary sigh. "Try to keep up, huh?"

Crawford fell silent. He thought for a moment, drawing smoke and blowing it forcefully toward the open window. Then he said, "You think she'll hold the story until we catch him?"

"Of course she will. It's an exclusive."

"I don't know..." Crawford said, trailing off in a doubtful tone. "I think that might be going too far."

"She's an honest woman," Reott told him.

"She's also a reporter," Crawford replied. "A reporter with *bosses*. And from what I've seen down at the River City Herald over the past twenty-some years, they've got such a thing down there called Editor's Prerogative."

It was Reott's turn to fall silent. He smoked and thought.

Crawford waited.

Finally, Reott sighed and shrugged. "She's never screwed us over yet. I should at least keep her updated ahead of the rest of the crowd."

"Okay," Crawford said. "That's fair, I suppose. But I don't know how long she'll be able to hold out if we don't nail this guy."

"Then I guess your task force better get the job done."

Crawford gave Reott a mock salute with his cigar hand. "Yes, sir."

Graveyard Shift
2334 hours

Thomas Chisolm sat in the dim light of his living room, staring at the dark television. He'd cracked open a Kokanee shortly after an evening run and sipped it in the bathroom while showering and drying off. Once dressed in his rumpled boxers and gray Army T-shirt, he flopped on the couch, hoping that the beer and television would help him find sleep.

Instead, he'd sat staring at the dead screen, the remote untouched on the small coffee table. He stared at the shadowy figure of himself reflected back at him. Every so often, he took a pull from the bottle of beer until it was empty. Then he rose and opened another.

Back on the couch, he closed his eyes and leaned his head back. He wanted very badly to sleep, but knew it was a virtual uncertainty. Not when the ghosts wanted to visit him. Not when they wanted to cry out to him, accuse him.

He thought briefly of Sylvia, the woman whose picture remained taped to his refrigerator despite the fact she'd gotten married to someone else almost two years ago. Why couldn't he let her go?

He knew why. Because she could see him. She understood him. That is why he had loved her so much.

And that was why she had left him.

Chisolm took another long drink of Kokanee. He pushed back against the pain, muttering to himself.

"Pussy," he said. "Mooning like a fifteen year old boy in love with a cheerleader."

His words fell flat in the silence of his home, so he followed them up with some more.

"Here's to you, T.C.," he said, raising his bottle. "The one person in the whole world who truly understood you decides she doesn't like what she sees. What does that tell you?"

Not everyone can handle the ghosts, that's what it tells me.

"Bullshit," Chisolm muttered unconvincingly, but he knew it wasn't. People just wanted to live in their pretty little worlds where everything is easy. They didn't want to see the hard side of things. "They don't want to see the ugliness," he said aloud. "And when they do see it –"

He broke off, because the answer was too plain. When people saw the ugliness, they reacted by blaming the ones who were confronting it. That's what happened in Vietnam. That's what happens every day in police work. And that's what happened with Sylvia.

Chisolm drank again, then lowered the bottle to his chest.

"Fuck that," he whispered.

He pushed against the memory, opening his eyes and staring at the ceiling.

But there were other ghosts in his mind that would not be still. When he forced Sylvia away, another set of eyes came forward.

Young eyes, but hard.

Eyes that did not blink. They only stared.

Pleaded.

Accused.

"It was just another direct action," he said huskily, staring at the twisting texture of the ceiling. "Some fucking NVA colonel that military intelligence had pegged as an up-and-comer. We go in, Bobby Ramirez and I, to this little village in the middle of nowhere. Our job is to take the guy out, quick and silent."

He stopped. Sipped his beer.

"We did," he said, his breath whistling across the bottle mouth.

That's not all, though, is it?

"No," Chisolm whispered. "It isn't."

He'd ducked into a hooch inside the village to avoid a roving guard. There, he'd interrupted an NVA soldier raping a young woman.

Mai. You know her name is Mai.

"Mai," he whispered.

He'd killed the NVA soldier without a second thought. Then, in what he now remembered as a moment of incredible arrogance, he kept her calm by pointing to the subdued flag on his shoulder. He remembered how her fear seemed to diminish when he'd smiled at her, then slipped out of the hooch and back into the night.

After he'd finished the mission, they returned to that village with regular army units two days later. All of the colonel's troops were gone. As Chisolm swept through the village, he swung into the hooch to check on the young girl. Like a sick version of déjà vu, he found her struggling with an American soldier.

Chisolm took a long, deep drink from the Kokanee bottle. He lowered his eyes, returning his gaze to his shadowy reflection in the dead television screen. He recalled the brief struggle with the American troop, then the face-off that occurred when the soldier's platoon mates showed up. All three of them left after Chisolm stared down the barrel of his M-16 at them.

What was worse, though, was the young girl's –

Mai, goddamnit! Her name is Mai!

—accusing eyes when she slapped at his chest and shoulders, chattering in Vietnamese, demanding to know why he hadn't killed the American just like he'd killed the NVA.

There were nights like these that Chisolm wondered if maybe he should have.

Six months later, he came across her in a Saigon bar, all tarted up and swaying to the music. When she spotted him at a table, waiting for Bobby Ramirez to finish having his fun upstairs, she'd been all over him. Rubbing, cooing, asking him if he wanted a good time. All the while, though, her eyes radiated the same dead, accusing hatred they'd held back in that hooch in her tiny village in the middle of the jungle.

You let me down, those eyes said.

Chisolm left the bar and waited across the street. He sipped whiskey until Ramirez staggered out of the bar, looking for him. Then they walked away and never looked back.

But now I spend all my time looking back, Chisolm thought. *Just seeing all of the ghosts of those I've failed.*

He drained the beer, but made no move to get another. Instead, he stared into his own eyes in the reflection of the black TV screen. He didn't like what he saw, but he knew what he'd see if he looked away.

NINE

Friday, April 19th
Day Shift
1456 hours

Tower stood near the corner of the small conference room, sipping coffee from a Styrofoam cup. He'd watched people slowly trickle into the meeting, guessing at their identities as soon as they came through the door.

The prosecutor was easy to pick out. Patrick Hinote had the confident stride of a veteran attorney and a firm handshake. Of course, the nice suit and the briefcase provided a couple of slam-dunk clues. Tower didn't award himself any points for figuring that one out.

Next to arrive were a pair of women. The first was a slender woman with a shock of coppery hair drawn back in a ponytail. She looked about thirty to Tower. Accompanying her was a younger, heavy-set woman wearing a pair of round, thin-framed glasses. Her black hair was cut in a tight bob.

Advocates, Tower guessed.

Patrick Hinote introduced them. "Detective Tower, this is Julie Avery and Kami Preston."

Tower held out his hand. The dark haired woman reached out first. "Kami Preston," she said, her tone terse and business-like. Tower shook her hand. Her grip was firm but not overbearing.

Patrick put his briefcase on the conference table. "Kami is assistant counsel on this case."

"Nice to meet you," Tower said.

Great. Rookie lawyer.

He moved on to Julie Avery. She gave him a pleasant smile as she took his hand. He expected her grip to be much softer, but she surprised him with an even firmer grip than Kami's.

"I'm on the Prosecutor's Crisis Team," she told him.

"Oh?" Tower nodded. He'd been right about at least one of them, then. She was a rape advocate. "That's great."

Julie's smile broadened. "You don't sound too convinced, detective."

She's direct, Tower thought. He cleared his throat nervously. "No? Sorry, I'm just a little distracted by this case."

The truth was he'd worked around advocates before on other cases. For the most part, they were helpful, both to the victim and for his investigation. He'd heard horror stories about situations where an advocate interfered with an investigation or tried to play junior attorney, but he'd personally never seen it. Most of the time, they offered an ear and a resource to the victim, which made that victim a better witness in the criminal case.

Still, they weren't going to have any victims at this meeting, or as part of the task force. So why did the prosecutor bring along an advocate?

Tower sipped his coffee and retreated toward the corner of the room. The foursome stood around awkwardly for several minutes until Lieutenant Crawford and Captain Reott arrived. Renee entered the room only a few moments later. Introductions were made all around and the meeting began.

"Let me get straight to the point," Captain Reott said. "The police department is forming a small task force to deal with this so-called 'Rainy Day Rapist.' We want to get the Prosecutor's Office on board right early on to make sure that when we get the guy, he's stays got."

"I appreciate that, Captain," Patrick said. "We'll help in any way we can."

Reott nodded his understanding. "I'm sure you will. Right now, what we're thinking is this. If Tower needs any search warrants or arrest warrants, you'll assist him so that there's no chance of it getting shot down later on by some judge. Also, if there are any more assaults, I'd like you to respond to the scene to offer any advice or assistance."

"We can do that," Patrick said. "I'd like to get copies of all the incident reports to review."

"I'll ship them to you," Tower said.

"Thanks. In the meantime, could you give us a brief synopsis of where things are at?"

Tower glanced at Crawford, took a deep breath and sighed. "The truth is, we're nowhere."

"Detective, I realize you may have a difficult case, but—"

"I'm not exaggerating," Tower interrupted. "We have very little in the way of witness testimony and no physical evidence that points to a particular suspect. Even if the guy came in and confessed, I don't know if we could convict him off the evidence we've been able to collect."

"Do you have any DNA?"

Tower shook his head.

Kami Preston scrawled furiously on the yellow legal pad in front of her.

"Any injuries the attacker may have sustained in the commission of the offense?" Patrick asked.

"His last victim, a schoolteacher, blasted him with a small canister of pepper spray," Tower explained. "But within a few hours, all evidence of that was probably gone. One trip through the washing machine cleans the clothes. A few hours and lots of water takes care of the spray effects on the bad guy's eyes and face. So if he lives alone, and he probably does—"

"Why do you say that?" Julie asked him.

Tower glanced at her. "He's a rapist."

"That means he lives alone?"

"I just think it would be hard to—"

"I wonder, detective, if you are falling into the trap of stereotyping your suspect."

Kami Preston paused in her feverish writing and looked up. Tower felt her eyes and those of everyone else in the room boring into him.

"Excuse me?" He asked, stalling for time. "Stereotyping?"

"Yes," Julie answered immediately. "It's a common mistake. There are a lot of myths surrounding rape. It wouldn't be good to…"

Jesus, she's a pit bull, Tower thought. *And she's all over my ass.*

"…immediately assume that a certain myth or stereotype holds true. In fact, it may even hamper your ability to discover…"

Tower held up his hand, interrupting her. "The thing about stereotypes, Ms. Avery, is that while they might make some people of a particular political persuasion uncomfortable, they became stereotypes for a reason."

"Really?"

"Really."

"And what, pray tell, is that reason?"

"Because they are usually true."

"That's a rather ignorant view of the world, don't you think?"

"No," Tower said. "It's a rather realistic one."

"All right, that's enough," Captain Reott said. "Let's remember we're on the same team here."

"Just a friendly discussion, Captain," Tower said icily.

Reott shot Tower a warning glare before continuing. "I think what Detective Tower was getting at was that if the suspect lives alone, there won't be any witnesses to him coming home covered in pepper spray. Isn't that right, Detective?"

Kami Preston renewed her frantic note taking.

Tower shrugged. "Sure, that's part of it."

"What's the rest, then?" Julie asked.

Tower glanced at Renee, then back at the advocate. "Well, it's just a theory, but I think it's clear that this guy is pretty angry at women. Probably too angry to be in any sort of relationship right now."

"Whose theory is this?" Patrick asked. "Has the FBI profiled this guy or something?"

That's just what we need, Tower thought. *The Feebs.*

"No," he told the prosecutor. "But—"

"I have," Renee said.

All eyes turned to Renee, including Tower's. He regarded the analyst with mild surprise.

"Go on," Patrick said.

Renee cleared her throat. "I've reviewed all of the witness statements, as well as Detective Tower's investigation of the crime scene. The medical evidence, too. Based on all of that, I think we have someone with obvious anger issues toward women. I believe he is acting out his anger at one or possibly two women by attacking another, unrelated woman. It's called psychological transference."

The assembled group digested her words. Tower allowed himself a little smile. Despite the fact that he'd been a jerk to Renee, the analyst was sticking up for him. He glanced over at Julie. The copper-haired woman was nodding her head slightly in agreement.

"Indulge me for a moment," Patrick said, "but why wouldn't he just strike out at the person he's angry at?"

"Could be any number of reasons," Renee answered. "She could be unavailable, located far away. If it is a mother or grandmother he's angry at, she could even be dead. But more likely, he is too intimidated by that person to strike directly. If it is a maternal figure, she'd have had control over him for most of his adult life. That grip may still be too strong, even now. So instead, he lashes out at other women. In doing so, he symbolically lashes out at her."

"You think it's a mother figure?" Julie asked her.

Renee turned to the advocate. "I believe that is the most likely candidate, yes. Even though it *is* a bit of a stereotype."

Julie's eyes widened slightly at the comment. Then she pressed her lips together and gave Renee a small nod. *Touché*, she seemed to say.

Tower watched on, amazed.

"Of course," Renee continued, "as we see that the violence in his surrogate assaults is escalating, that gives me concern that he may be girding himself for a strike at the true object of his anger."

Patrick nodded. "Meaning he's working up the guts to go after Mommy Dearest."

"Possibly," Renee said. "Either way, there's no denying that his violence is escalating."

"It would appear so," the lawyer agreed. He turned back to Tower. "Do you agree with her assessment, detective?"

"Yes," Tower answered immediately.

"So what I'm hearing is that we have no substantive witnesses for a rapist that is leaving virtually no physical evidence of any prosecutorial value and who is becoming progressively more violent. In fact, what I'm actually hearing is that this may become a homicide case before it is over." Patrick sighed. "Wonderful. So what are we going to do?"

"That is what this task force is going to address," Captain Reott said. He pointed at Tower. "Detective Tower remains lead investigator, with you and your staff to assist him. Lieutenant Crawford will head up the task force. Lieutenant?"

Crawford began speaking without preamble. "The task force will consist of two parts." He held up one finger. "The first part will be a pair of my Major Crimes detectives who will be available for any investigative follow-up that Tower needs done."

"Such as?"

"Canvassing for witnesses, monitoring and screening the tip line, things like that. Shoe leather and grunt work. They get anything hot, they'll bring it to me and Tower."

Patrick nodded and motioned for Crawford to continue.

The lieutenant held up a second finger. "The second part will be a decoy detail. We'll run a decoy officer around the city in a variety of locations that Renee here believes would be likely targets for the rapist. The decoy will be dressed as a jogger. There'll be a two-officer cover team assigned to her at all times. Our hope is that the scumbag decides to go after our decoy. If he does, we take him down."

Patrick considered the plan. He traced a stick figure on the top of the notepaper, the only writing he'd done during the meeting so far. Next to him, Kami Preston's pen skipped across the yellow page in front of her.

"Let's say you catch the offender," he said. "From what you've already told me, you have no evidence to link him to these other attacks, correct?"

"That's right," Crawford said. "But if we bag him on an attempted rape, we might be able to get a search warrant for his car and his house. There may be evidence from the other rapes in one of those two places."

"That's a fishing expedition, Lieutenant," Patrick said. "You know that no judge will sign a search warrant for that. The warrant has to be to look for evidence related to that specific arrest."

"I'm not asking you to put in the search warrant that you're looking for evidence of the other rapes. But if you can get into the guy's house, and while searching for evidence of the most recent assault, the detective comes across evidence of the other assaults, well that's just lucky."

"That's pretextual."

"It's good police work," Crawford said.

"Maybe so," Patrick replied, "but it would be attacked in court and likely suppressed as evidence. Avoiding that sort of thing is, I believe, why my office was brought on board at this early juncture, correct?"

Crawford ignored his question. "Even if you don't get enough for a search warrant, we'll have the guy on an attempted rape. That's a solid charge."

"I agree," Patrick said. "But how will we know it is the right guy?"

"The rapes stop," Crawford told him. "Or maybe he confesses."

"Both would be nice," said Patrick.

"The most important thing is to stop this guy, one way or another," Captain Reott said. "Before another woman gets hurt."

"I agree," Julie said quietly.

"Me, too," Tower added.

There was a moment of silence in the room. Then Patrick asked in a soft voice, "What do you think the odds are of this tactic drawing out the rapist?"

"Not very good," Crawford admitted. "But a hell of a lot better than doing nothing at all."

Graveyard Shift
2108 hours

Lieutenant Robert Saylor put aside the "hot board" full of briefing memos after he read the final one aloud to the assembled graveyard patrol officers. Just in case he wasn't finished, though, Officer Katie MacLeod kept her pocket notebook in front of her.

"Last item," the lieutenant said. "As most of you already know, the Rainy Day Rapist struck again yesterday. That makes his third victim. This one was a fifty-six year old school teacher."

Angry muttering erupted and rumbled through the roll call room.

Saylor raised his hand for quiet. "In response to this, a task force is being formed to focus on this case until he's caught. Investigations is heading it up, with Detective Tower still in the lead. However, Patrol will assist. I've been asked for four volunteers. One will be a female decoy, three will rotate as part of a two-officer cover team."

Katie swallowed. A small surge of adrenaline pulsed through her limbs.

If they need a female, there aren't many to choose from. They'll probably ask me to –

Officer James Kahn raised his hand. "El-Tee, I nominate Hiero for the job of female decoy," he said.

The assembled group burst out in raucous laughter. Katie reluctantly allowed herself a small smile. Humorous moments from James Kahn were infrequent at best. Of course, it figured that he'd choose something like this to joke about. In addition to being the platoon grump, Kahn was also a dyed-in-the-wool skirt-chaser. Katie didn't know what women saw in him, other than the badge, maybe. He reminded her of an older, less handsome and much crasser version of Giovanni.

Hiero, who sometimes rode partners with Kahn, waited for the laughter to subside. Then he shook his head. "Sir, if you assign me, the first thing I'm doing is filing a sexual harassment suit against Jimmy here. It's hard enough fending off his clumsy advances all night. If I have to wear a skirt –"

Another round of laughter exploded around the room. This time, Katie didn't join in. It always amazed her how quickly gallows humor swept in to displace the anger and concern.

"All right," Saylor said, raising both hands up for quiet. "Joking aside, this is a serious assignment. Sergeants, meet me after roll call so we can get the task force personnel figured out."

Saylor turned and strode from the room.

"A little touchy, isn't he?" Kahn muttered, returning to grouch mode. Katie figured he'd spend the rest of the shift that way, maybe the rest of the week.

Sergeant Shen looked around the table. "I guess he figures that these assaults are a pretty serious issue, that's all."

"Everything we deal with is serious, Sarge," Kahn said.

"So it is," Shen agreed. "Is anyone interested in volunteering for this task force?"

No one looked at Katie, but she felt the attention of her entire platoon on her. Warmth rushed to her face. Her heart pounded in her ears.

Don't ask me to do this. Ask me anything else, but not this.

She licked her lips. Since coming on the job five years before, she'd been involved in a variety of sticky situations. An armed robber fired shots at her once in a dark construction lot. A drugged out wife-beater threatened her with a bloody knife. And, of course, she faced the unwinnable situation the previous spring on the Post Street Bridge.

She faced every one of those situations head-on. She pushed through them. She survived.

I don't want to do this.

Besides, how many rape reports had she taken? Dozens, at least. And how many rapists had she arrested? Ten or so? More?

She'd never been afraid of any of them. So why was she afraid now?

I do NOT want to do THIS!

A couple of her sector mates had turned their eyes toward her during the brief silence following Shen's question. She looked up at each of them, then at Shen. The sergeant regarded her calmly.

I don't want to do this.

I don't-

"I'll be the decoy," she told Shen. Then, clearing her throat, she repeated, "I'll do it."

Sergeant Shen nodded his thanks.

Katie MacLeod, who sometimes hid but never ran, nodded back.

2127 hours

Sergeant Miyamoto Shen closed the door to the sergeant's room behind him as he entered. Lieutenant Saylor sat reviewing and approving patrol reports. He glanced up as Shen entered and set aside the stack of papers.

"How'd it go?"

"Did anyone volunteer from the other two sectors?" Shen asked him.

Saylor shrugged. "A few cover officers."

"But no decoys?"

Saylor shook his head. "There's all of three women on graveyard right now. One of them is MacLeod, who's yours. The other two females weren't interested. One of them is going on vacation tomorrow and the other one...well, she just wasn't interested."

"MacLeod volunteered," Shen said.

"I figured she would. She's got grit."

Shen nodded thoughtfully. "She's a warrior, I agree. But everyone has limits."

Saylor looked closely at Shen. "You don't think she's up to it?"

"I'm sure she is. That's not what I mean."

"Then what?"

"It's just that she's been through a lot in the last couple of years. I don't wonder about her ability to handle any one incident, just about how she'll handle the cumulative effect of all of them."

Saylor considered, then shrugged. "That's the life of a cop."

Shen pressed his lips together in obvious disagreement. "I just don't want to lose a good troop because we push her too hard or ask too much of her."

He may be right, Saylor thought.

Nonetheless, he reached out and clapped Shen on the shoulder. "Relax, Sergeant. We ask too much of these men and women every day. At least, we ask them to face the possibility of paying too much. They can handle it. MacLeod can handle it."

"I'm sure you're right," Shen said, but his voice had a hint of a doubtful tone.

"I am," Saylor assured him. "Now, who should we assign as cover officers?"

"As soon as she volunteered, Battaglia and O'Sullivan offered to serve as cover officers."

"Are you all right with that?"

Shen nodded. "Both are good cops, if a little immature at times. And they like MacLeod. They'll take the job seriously."

"Who's your number three, then?"

"I'm going to assign Chisolm. The first night of operations for the task force is tomorrow and he'll be back from his days off. He can rotate through with Battaglia and O'Sullivan."

Saylor nodded his approval. The presence of a veteran officer like Chisolm would keep Battaglia and O'Sullivan grounded.

"Good choice," he agreed.

"Let's hope they're successful," Shen said.

God willing, Saylor added silently.

2319 hours

He felt it in his chest. It was like a burning pain at times. Other times, it felt more like a cold knife. No matter what, it welled up inside like a tsunami, forcing against his throat, his limbs, his mind.

It made him rock hard.

It made him tremble.

Hookers weren't helping anymore, he discovered. He tried to go with one earlier in the day, but had to stop. He felt the energy, the power, surging inside him. He didn't know if he could stop himself once he started. He didn't believe that River City would care much about a dead hooker, but he didn't want to waste his power on such a worthless target.

He wanted...no, he *needed* a real woman.

Someone who was closer to *her.*

He pulled in a deep breath of the cool night air. Sitting on a bench in Riverfront Park, he enjoyed the quiet of the night around him. The Looking Glass River flowed gently through the center of the park, located just on the fringe of downtown River City.

He liked it here. It was quiet, with only the light hiss of nighttime traffic in the distance. The air was cooled by the river. The coolness felt good on his face, eyes, and as he drew it into his throat. Although he'd been able to wash out all of the mace that woman had sprayed him with, a light burning remained.

His mind flashed to the front seat of the teacher's car. She reminded him so much of Mrs. Reed, or what she would probably look like know. Sure, he hadn't gotten the chance to fuck her –

Bitches ruin everything, don't they?

—but he definitely laid the whammo on her, didn't he? She got a good finger-banging first, then a good old fashioned beating. And if his eyes and throat hadn't been burning like hellfire, he would have finished the job.

He smiled.

The park was nice for other reasons. People felt safe in this park. The wide paths and frequent lighting gave them a sense of security. Unarmed patrols of rent-a-cops bicycled through periodically, heightening that perception of safety.

But it was all an illusion.

No one was safe from him.

That made him smile even wider.

He'd been watching them pass by for over an hour now. Short, tall, fat, thin, beautiful, ugly. Didn't matter. They were all bitches, every one of them.

Every *womb* of them.

He chuckled to himself, despite the burning anger in his chest. Was that really what he was doing? Showing every one of these bitches what he should have taught his mother instead? He would have, too, if she hadn't been put in the ground by cancer before he got the chance.

How many of these surrogate sluts would it take before he could believe that his mother got the message? How long before she heard the news in hell?

He drew in another deep breath of the cool night air that was stroked by the river. Maybe it didn't matter, he decided. Every time he did it, the pressure went away for a little while. Sure, it came back even stronger, but there was still some relief.

And there was something else. The first time, it was all about relief. But after that, he realized something was happening. Only a little at first, but it grew by leaps and bounds, until it was now even stronger than that pressure in his chest.

He liked it.

He liked the power. Their screams. The begging. He liked to inflict pain. To control the fate of the bitch in front of him.

It made him strong.

Important.

Hell, if he believed in God, he might even believe that he was one with God in those moments.

But since he knew there wasn't a God, what did that make him in those moments?

His cheeks ached. He realized that he'd been smiling so hugely that the muscles in his face were fatigued. With purpose, he relaxed his face into what he hoped was an open expression. He pretended to stare out at the river while watching for women walking through the park.

But inside, he answered his own question.

It makes me a god.

The frequency of foot traffic had dwindled significantly since he first sat down. He'd seen a few candidates pass by, but none were quite right. There were a variety of reasons that might be. He was smart and not about to make a mistake that would allow the clueless police department to catch him. So if there were too many people around to see, he let the ones pass who were otherwise perfect. He let the ones with too much confidence pass on by, too. He'd learned from the teacher not to underestimate anyone.

The river flowed lazily in front of him. It had the help of a small dam at the west end of the park. In the distance, though, he could hear the rush of water. Most of the park was really an island, bordered on the north by the river in its true form, crashing over rocks with a powerful current. But the south side of the park enjoyed the quiet, slow roll of the part of the river controlled by man.

Eventually, though, after the waters passed the island park, they flowed back into one crushing current, tumbling over the rocks and headed toward a waterfall just before the Post Street Bridge.

He was like the river, wasn't he? Some things nature controlled, some things he controlled. He could channel the river, his hatred. He could bottle it up and slow it down. Make it beautiful for others to see. But eventually, the fork in the river flowed together again. It always did.

He changed his thoughts, moving more toward the moment at hand. The park was good for other reasons, more practical ones. While there were several footbridges that provided access to the island, there were escape routes from every part of the park. All of the city streets that bordered the one hundred acres were arterials. They all had places to park a car. Bus stops were a dime a dozen. A man could slip out of the park and melt away into the city.

The light clacking of footsteps roused him from his philosophical contemplation. A short woman came into view on the other side of the river. Her quick steps brought her to the wide foot bridge and headed in his direction. She carried a folder of some kind under her arm. The footbridge was well lit, so he was able to see her conservative business attire easily.

Probably a secretary, he thought. *Working very late. Maybe with the boss, the slut.*

She continued north across the footbridge. He couldn't see her features exactly at this distance, but as she drew nearer, he gave a small gasp.

Jenny.

His girlfriend.

Ex-girlfriend, he reminded himself.

Dark anger rose up in his chest. Who did she think she was, anyway? Breaking up with him? Like she was something special. She was just another stupid, worthless bitch. Just like—

He glanced at her again.

It wasn't Jenny. She was built the same, had the same hair, but it wasn't her.

Still...

When she reached the end of the footbridge and turned his direction, he made his decision.

He rose from his seat and walked up the pathway eastbound, approaching the huge clock tower that reached upward into the night sky. At the clock tower, he could continue east or turn north. North led up a small rise and another path. East led to the Washington Street overpass about thirty yards farther on. Under the overpass was about fifteen yards of darkness.

He turned left and headed north, up the hill.

Trying not to appear like he was hurrying, he took long strides. His ears strained for the click-clack of her heels. He canted his head slightly and searched for her out of his peripheral vision.

She continued east.

Maybe she was headed toward the bus stop on Washington. A steep set of winding stairs led from the park path to the street above.

He had marked that earlier as an excellent escape route. Now, it might just be her destination.

When he reached to top of the short hill, he turned east himself, following another path. His heart thudded in his ears. Excitement caused his fingers to tingle.

A slutty secretary. Or maybe some hoity-toity business bitch. Either way, he was going to lay the whammo on her. He was going to lay it on her so hard that Jenny would feel it wherever she was. And his mother was going to feel it from her ringside seat in hell.

As soon as he believed he was out of her line of sight, he sprinted. There was no overpass at the top of the hill because Washington became a three-block tunnel. He hurried east. Once he'd gone far enough that he was sure he'd passed over the tunnel below, he cut south through the low, trimmed bushes. He had to get to the east side of the overpass below before she did. That would be the best place.

The bushes became larger as he continued south. The neatly trimmed standard fell by the wayside, with chaotic natural growth taking its place. He scrambled through them and around a few trees. This would be a better place, but how was he supposed to get someone into this thicket? He could see the river below, but not the overpass yet.

She couldn't have made it through yet, could she?

He looked further along the eastbound path below and saw no one.

She had to still be coming. Had to be.

He ducked beneath a tree limb and around a thick shrub. He was definitely on a downward slope now. The few trees gave way again, leaving only bushes in his way. He continued forward.

The steep set of stairs came into view, thirty or forty yards ahead, by his reckoning.

No sign of her.

He smiled. He was going to make it. He was going to peek around the corner into that dark underpass and see her shadowy form coming toward him. Her clicking heels would echo under there. He'd wait until she was three quarters of the way to him, then he'd charge her. One crack in the mouth and she'd be quiet. Then he'd push her face into the wall and nail her.

And then—

The natural growth gave way to manicured bushes again. Right at the edge of the bushes, his foot struck something heavy and he tumbled forward onto the grass with a grunt. He was able to get his hands out to break his fall. The damp grass was slippery enough to cause him to slide several feet.

"What the hell, dude?"

He looked up. A tall, thin young man sat near the edge of the bushes. The kid was a flurry of movement, which took him a moment to understand.

He was pulling on his pants.

The smaller, shadowy figure beside him drew the blanket up to cover herself.

"What's your problem, perv?" she asked in a shrill voice.

"I'm gonna to kick your ass," the young man said, kicking his feet through the bottom of his pants.

He sat still for a moment. Down below, he recognized the distant echo of clicking heels on asphalt.

The young man pulled the trousers over his hips.

"I'm just out for a jog," he told the young man, disguising his voice slightly.

"Bullshit," the kid said, scrambling to his feet.

"I was."

"Bullshit. Who jogs through the bushes with all these open paths?"

"Yeah," the girl said. "And at night? You asshole pervert."

He looked down at the overpass. The secretary or whatever she was emerged from the underpass and started up the steep stairs. To safety.

Goddamn it.

He'd missed her.

"I'm gonna kick your ass," the young man told him again.

He turned back toward the skinny little bastard, anger coursing through him. He stood up and growled, "You ruined everything."

"I'm going to ruin your face, asshole."

The young man stepped toward him confidently, his fists balled at his side.

The anger turned cold inside. He had to be smart. He didn't need any attention.

The tension in the young man's body was obvious, even in the moonlight. He bounced with every step he took forward.

He waited patiently for the punch to come.

When the young man loaded up his punch and prepared to throw it, he was ready. Hell, he could have been ready three times over, it took the kid so long.

The punch came and the kid's whole body behind it. If it landed, he'd probably be knocked out. But it wasn't going to land.

As the punch neared his head, he slipped to the side, ducking out of the way. The young man's fist whipped past his ear, but did not connect. The forward momentum carried the young man past him, causing him to slip on the grass and tumbled several yards down the hillside.

He didn't wait for the kid to recover. Like a jackrabbit, he bolted back up the hillside, cutting through the bushes and around the few trees. Behind him, he heard a shout, but he kept on. When he broke through the brush and onto the path, he turned sharply to his left. The path yawned out in front of him. He took off, running with long strides that ate up the ground.

Even with a head start, he wondered if the kid might catch him. He was tall and thin, so he was probably a good runner. Still, he had no shoes on. That'd slow him down, whether he chose to run barefoot or paused to pull on some shoes.

As he reached the bottom of the sloping hill, the path split into three directions. He glanced over his shoulder for anyone in pursuit. No one.

He cut to the right, making for the footbridge that led off the island and into the parking lot where his car was safely parked.

Even if the kid was still chasing him, he didn't know which way was the right way to turn. And he had the girl to get back to.

To finish with.

Like he should have finished that office bitch.

He pushed the thought of failure out of his mind and kept a steady run. His throat still burned with the after-effect of the mace. It seemed like his own body was mocking him. Calling out to him.

You're nothing.

You're worthless.

You're like your father.

He glanced over his shoulder again. Still no pursuit. Maybe he was away clean. He slowed to a loping jog. His breath rattled in his ears.

He *was* like his father, at least in one way.

He knew how to treat women.

His father may not have taught him anything else worth a damn, but he sure taught him that.

He taught him about the whammo.

He taught him plenty.

When he reached the edge of the bridge, he cast another backward glance. Nothing. He let himself fall back to a trot as he veered to the left. Ahead, the trail led to the parking lot where he'd left his car.

Frustration gnawed at him. The pressure in his chest made his hands tremble.

Bitches ruin everything.

He would have to hunt again another night.

TEN

Saturday, April 20th
Graveyard Shift
2126 hours

Katie MacLeod adjusted the strap of the purse on her shoulder. The bag hung awkwardly at her side, an uncomfortable add-on that she couldn't get used to. She found it both amusing and frustrating that it would matter what kind of purse she carried. But she became familiar with her purse when she was off duty in much the same way she became familiar with her police equipment on duty. Now, she was melding the two and it was all wrong. The strap on this one was too wide, but not long enough. The weight of the fake leather was off. The heavy police contents of the purse made it even worse. Unlike her own purse, which felt snug against her side when she gripped it, this one seemed to sway even when she tried pinning it with her elbow.

And besides, the purse was ugly as sin.

"This purse is so ugly," she muttered, "even my Aunt Thea would throw it out."

She wondered if Battaglia and O'Sullivan could hear her when she spoke that low while moving. When they'd tested the wire, they'd been able to hear her clearly from a block away, but that was with a clear line of sight and while she was standing still.

"It's even uglier than that," she muttered again, this time slightly quieter. "Even Batts would have the sense to throw it out."

She stopped on the wide footbridge near the carousel. Below the bridge, The Looking Glass River streamed past languidly. The water gave off dark reflections of the trees along the bank and the taller downtown buildings just a block or so away. A lamp post behind her threw a yellowish light that cast her shadow onto the water.

Katie took a deep breath and let it out slowly.

I can do this.

She knew she wasn't alone. Detective Tower was perched at the top of the clock tower, watching with a pair of binoculars. A SWAT sniper with a night vision scope stood by with him, just in case. O'Sullivan and Battaglia were at the pavilion in the middle of the park with a golf cart, ready to respond wherever she needed them. That should make her feel better, she reasoned.

The brick-like transmitter taped to the small of her back should have made her feel safer, too. Tower had a receiver. So did Sully and Batts. They could hear everything she said. Everything that happened around her.

If that weren't enough, she had a police radio in her purse.

And her gun.

So she was safe.

Then why am I so afraid?

She focused on the question for a moment. She'd been on undercover specials before. They'd done a half dozen hooker special details over her career in which she'd posed as streetwalker and snared prospective johns. Last summer, she went on loan with the dope unit for almost a month and made hand-to-hand buys. Once, there'd been a rash of purse snatchings and she'd been tasked to stroll around downtown with all the other shoppers until the maggots tried to grab her purse, a much nicer one than the ugly bag they'd issued her tonight.

The point was, she'd done these kinds of sting operations before. She'd even been wired before. So tonight shouldn't be any different.

A slurred, whispering voice from the past answered her question clearly.

Don't be a goddamn tease!

Katie took in another deep breath and let it out.

This is no different, she told herself. *No different.*

Do your job.

Katie heard the sound of approaching footsteps. She glanced up. A man jogged lightly in her direction from the north. Katie looked away.

"Someone's coming," she whispered into the microphone taped to her chest.

She kept her eyes averted, hoping to lure him in. A confident woman won't look away, but a victim would. So she stared into the water, watching him approach on the edge of her vision.

He trotted closer. Fifteen yards now.

It can't be this easy, she thought.

Her hands were ice cold and slick with sweat.

Ten yards.

"Nice night," the man said in a pleasant voice, his breath only slightly quickened from his exertion.

Katie looked up.

His eyes were on her.

She took in his face, his eyes, his frame. She figured he might be a habitual jogger and had great wind. That's why no exertion in his voice. Or he was the Rainy Day Rapist and only started jogging a block away.

He continued to meet her gaze as he came closer.

Five yards now.

Katie didn't answer him.

He smiled.

Katie popped the clasp on her ugly purse. She slid her hand inside and wrapped her fingers around the handle of her Glock. The cold, hard plastic gave her little comfort.

Three yards.

Two.

One.

And he whisked past her.

Katie watched him go. She realized that she'd been holding her breath and let it out in a whoosh.

"Goddamnit," she muttered.

The jogger glanced over his shoulder at her, then shrugged and went on.

"Who tries to pick up women while he's out jogging at night?" she said, staring after the retreating jogger in amazement. "What is he, Giovanni's brother or something?"

Katie released her grip on the Glock. She hesitated, then left the clasp unhinged as she turned to walk away from the footbridge. With an effort, she forced herself to walk without any confidence. To accomplish this, she hunched her shoulders forward and shuffled her feet. She picked a spot on the path just a couple of yards ahead of her and stared at it while she walked. Every once in a while, she glanced up nervously, then returned her gaze to the ground.

Where next?

A quick look told her she was at a fork in the path. North led through a wooded area beside the YMCA building. That path eventually flowed out of the park to a parking lot next to the River City Flour Mill, an historic building full of shops that Katie was pretty sure would never sell anything as grotesque as the purse she was hauling around Riverfront Park.

Turning east would lead her toward the clock tower and under the Washington Street Overpass. Beyond that was an area known as the Lilac Bowl, a grassy hillside bordered by bushes and some trees on the north.

Katie paused, shuffling to a stop. She wondered where an aggressive rapist might lie in wait. Where might he strike?

She glanced to the dark path through the wooded area to the north. Images of Phil and the sound of his slurred voice came unbidden into her mind. She tried to brush them aside, but his voice kept whispering in her ear—

You liked it. Don't forget that.

—accusing her. She felt pressure against her lips, reminiscent of his hand clamped across her mouth.

Katie felt her breath quicken. Sweat dampened the nape of her neck. She breathed in through her nose, but instead of the clean smell of river air and damp grass, the only scent that filled her nostrils was the ghostly aroma of Phil's rum-coated breath.

She stood at the crossroad, unmoving.

2129 hours

Tower peered through the binoculars at MacLeod.

"If she goes north, my vision will be obscured by those trees," he told Officer Paul Hiero.

"That's all right," Hiero told him, eyeing her through the rifle scope. "I should be able to pick her up with the night vision pretty well."

Tower picked up his radio and keyed the mike. "Ida-409 to Adam-122."

O'Sullivan answered immediately. *"-22, go ahead."*

"She's at the fork just north of the footbridge."

"Which footbridge? There's about seven of 'em."

Tower frowned, but Sully was right. "Near the carousel," he transmitted. "If she goes north, we'll have a limited view of her from here."

"Copy. You want us to move?"

Tower considered for a moment. Then he pressed the transmit button again. "Not yet. If we lose sight of her, I'll let you know. If that happens, you two get down to the wide bridge that leads to the Flour Mill. If she's not on the bridge, come south and find her."

Sully replied with a brief click of his mike.

Tower looked over at Hiero. Dressed in all of his SWAT regalia, complete with his baseball cap turned backward, he reminded Tower of every clichéd version of a SWAT officer that Hollywood had ever created. He considered humming the TV theme song, but instead raised his binoculars back to his eyes.

Katie still stood at the fork in the pathway.

"Come on, MacLeod," he whispered. "What are you going to do?"

2130 hours

"You think Tower's an asshole?" Battaglia asked. "Because *I* think Tower's an asshole."

Sully shrugged. "I don't know. What kind of an asshole?"

"What's that supposed to mean?"

"It means, East Coast or West Coast asshole?"

Battaglia narrowed his eyes. "Like there's a difference, other than accent."

"Oh, there's a difference," Sully said, "but I wouldn't expect you to know."

"Why? No, wait—don't tell me. It's because I'm Italian, right?"

Sully shook his head. "No, because you're a philistine."

"I'm full of what?"

"Exactly," Sully replied.

2131 hours

Katie looked down the pathway into the dark.

Everything in her police experience told her that rapists weren't boogeymen. They didn't jump out of bushes and attack strangers. In all of the rape reports she'd taken—and being a female cop, she'd been stuck with an inordinate number of them—she discovered that the suspect was almost always someone the victim knew. Maybe not someone they knew very well, but knew all the same. They came dressed as frat boys, like Phil had. It was never a stranger who leapt out of the darkness. Rapists don't do that.

This one does.

Katie turned east.

*   *   *

"She's going east," Tower transmitted.

"*Copy,*" Sully answered over the radio.

Tower peered at Katie through his binoculars. "She's doing a good job of looking scared," he said quietly. "Look at her poor posture. The way she's walking and looking down the whole time. You see that?"

"I see it," Hiero said.

"She's a natural decoy."

"Maybe she's not pretending," Hiero said.

Tower broke away from his binocs to look at the sniper. "You think she's scared?"

Hiero raised his eyebrows and turned down his mouth in a facial shrug. "I would be."

"Even with back up?"

"It *is* Sully and Battaglia," Hiero half-joked.

"Fine," Tower conceded with a small smile. "How about a sniper, then?"

This time Hiero shrugged with his shoulders. "I'm not that great a shot."

2132 hours

Katie made her way east, shuffling along with her shoulders bent and her head low. She paused at the railing near the duck feeding station. Her presence brought over a few mallards that she figured were insomniacs. In the darkness, the green feather headdress appeared black. They quacked at her, at first in appreciative tones, then in demanding ones. When she didn't break out any bread or other goodies, the quacks seemed to take on a derogatory tone. Finally, the ducks paddled away in disgust.

You are losing it, MacLeod, Katie told herself. *Attaching human traits to water fowl?*

She stared into the water for several minutes, bringing her breathing under control. Slowly but surely, she forced it to become deep and regular. She noticed she was shivering from the sweat.

It was time to move again.

Katie turned and shuffled along toward to the clock tower, her ears perked for anyone approaching her. The park seemed strangely empty for a Saturday night. Usually couples strolled along the pathways, out for romantic walks after dining downtown. Kids hung out around the carousel and tried to get away with skate-boarding where it wasn't allowed, keeping the park security guards busy. Old, lonely people walked their dogs.

But not tonight.

They're all afraid.

Katie knew it was true. Ever since the media grabbed hold of the story about the Rainy Day Rapist, people were scared to go out at night.

She didn't blame them.

Even so, a small surge of anger raked through her belly. One man was doing this. One man was preying on the fears of an entire city. One man was imposing his will. And he probably got off on it.

Katie clenched her jaw at the thought.

She paused at the base of the clock tower, once again at a crossroads. One pathway led up the hill to the north, toward the pavilion where Sully and Battaglia were staged. Continuing east led her to the Washington Street Underpass.

In the distance, the darkness of the underpass looked like an inky blot.

She headed for the darkness.

2135 hours

"You're full of crap," Battaglia said.

"Ask Gio," Sully replied. "His parents are from Brooklyn. I'll bet he knows."

"He doesn't know because you're making it up."

"No, I'm not."

"You are."

"Look," Sully said, "it's simple. Here in Washington, you use the word 'asshole' to mean, like, a jerk or something. Only more harsh, right?"

"That's what it means," Battaglia told him. "That's what the word means *everywhere*. An asshole is an asshole."

"Not back east," Sully argued, shaking his finger back and forth. "Back there, especially in New York and in Jersey, it's not such a strong word. It means something more along the lines of 'schmuck' or whatever. It's a softer word."

"Asshole is never a soft word."

Sully affected a Brooklyn accent. "What am I, an asshole ovah heah?"

"Oh, nice. Make fun of my people."

"That's how your people use the word."

Battaglia shook his head. "I think we use the word to describe the Irish."

The radio squawked, pre-empting Sully's reply. *"Adam-122?"*

"Twenty-Two," Sully said into the portable radio.

"She's headed for the Washington Street Overpass," Tower transmitted. *"I'll lose sight of her when she goes underneath."*

Sully pressed the transmit button. "We'll take the path up top and get an eye on her when she comes through the other side."

"Good. Copy that."

Sully slid the radio into his jacket pocket. "Let's go, asshole."

"East Coast or West?" Battaglia asked, firing up the golf cart.

"Both," Sully assured him.

2136 hours

Katie forced herself to maintain her hunched posture. She shuffled her feet and looked down. Somehow it was easier than before, almost as if hunching made her a smaller target and therefore safer. Tension laced her shoulders and neck as she made her way toward the darkness under the roadway.

She paused a few yards from the underpass. The blackness inside caused small waves of apprehension to ripple through her lower stomach. She recalled her irrational childhood fears—the open closet door at night, the boogeyman under the bed.

That back bedroom with Phil.

Her father always told her that her bedroom was exactly the same place with the lights off as when the lights were on. There was nothing different once the light went away.

Katie was twenty-seven years old now, and she knew what her father said wasn't really true. Things happened in the dark that never happened in the light. People hid in the dark. They did evil in the dark. There was pain in the dark.

She didn't want to go into the dark.

2137 hours

"She's stopped," Tower reported. "Why is she stopped?"

Hiero shrugged. "I don't know. You're the detective."

Tower ignored the jibe. "Maybe she sees something under the overpass?"

"Could be."

"Or some*body*. Can you see under there at all?"

Hiero trained his night scope ahead of MacLeod. "Only a few yards in. We're too close and up too high. The angle's bad."

Tower cursed. "What does she see in there?"

* * *

The area under the overpass couldn't be longer than twenty-five yards, Katie estimated. That was it. Twenty-five yards. That's maybe thirty paces.

That's all.

To her right, the slow current of The Looking Glass River drifted past. An iron fence ran along the shore to keep people from swimming in the water, which was far colder, deeper and faster than the average jerk realized.

They were usually drunk, Katie mused, her mind flitting away for a moment, almost as if it were trying to avoid what stood in front of her. And, drunk or not, most of the would-be swimmers were dissuaded by that fence.

Her focus came back when she looked beneath the underpass. The left edge of the pathway was lined with a sloping rock wall that rose up and receded away into darkness. Katie knew that transients sometimes slept up underneath the bridge in the deep recesses of the scattered rocks.

She peered into the blackness, wishing for a flashlight. There could be a half dozen transients camped back there, wrapped up in sleeping bags or laying in wait.

Or just one rapist.

She clenched her jaw.

Knock it off, Katie.

She took a deep breath. "Toughen up, buttercup," she whispered to herself.

She wanted to move forward, but her feet wouldn't budge.

There's nothing there that isn't there in the day time.

Katie blinked and stared into the darkness.

You don't have to go in there.

The words floated through her mind in an unrecognizable voice. The voice was at once soothing and taunting.

Just walk around.

Katie let the air out of her lungs. She drew in another deep breath, tasting the damp river air. What if she didn't go forward? What would be the issue? There'd be no issue, right? She was just being safe. No one would even know.

She'd know.

Katie exhaled in a long, steady breath. She slid her hand inside her purse and wrapped her fingers around the reassuring grip of her pistol.

You don't have to—

"Shut up," Katie whispered.

She stepped forward into the darkness.

2138 hours

"Not yet!" Sully yelled, just as Battaglia made a hard turn off the path and into the thinning bushes and trees.

Battaglia opened his mouth to tell Sully to shut his Irish pie-hole when he drove the golf cart into a raised tree root. The tire rode up the thick, twisted growth as readily as any man-made ramp. The cart tilted.

"Fu-uh-uh—" Battaglia began.

The golf cart toppled onto the driver's side.

Sully landed in a heap on top of Battaglia.

"She's heading in," squawked the radio.

Sully rolled off the top of Battaglia's sprawled form and scrambled to his feet. The radio lay on the wet grass nearby. He snatched it up, wiping away the dew.

"Copy," he transmitted, then turned to Battaglia. The dark-haired officer climbed to his feet, rolling his head on his shoulders, testing his neck. Sully heard popping noises.

"You okay?"

"I think so," Battaglia grunted. "Just a little whiplash."

"Then help me pick this up. She's going under the bridge."

"I heard the radio," Battaglia said. He grabbed the front corner of the golf cart. "I'm not deaf."

Sully slid the radio into his jacket pocket. "No, but you're apparently legally blind." He put his hands underneath the rear corner and squatted down. "On three?"

"Just like *Lethal Weapon*."

Sully counted three and the two officers heaved the golf cart, righting it.

"Let's go!" Sully hopped into the driver's seat.

"Hey!" Battaglia protested.

"You had your chance, Crash."

Battaglia scowled but stepped around the front of the cart and into the passenger seat. "Go!" he told Sully.

Sully punched it.

2139 hours

The soft rubber soles of her shoes thudded on the asphalt path. The dull echo bounced around the underpass, ricocheting off of the rock wall and dying on the wide expanse of river water to her right.

Katie stared straight ahead, but she scanned the area to her left with her peripheral vision. Her ears strained to pick up any stray noise, any indication of an attacker.

Her body leaned forward, wanting to move faster. Her legs wanted to sprint. She forced herself into the hunched, submissive posture she'd used before. A moment of focus allowed her to rein in her feet.

To her left, she sensed motion.

A fraction of a second later, she heard the clattering of stones, upset at the top of the wall and tumbling down.

She tore her pistol from her purse and whipped it in the direction of the noise. In an instant, she put the front sights on the blur of motion and pressed the trigger.

*   *   *

Sully slammed on the brakes. The golf cart slid on the slick, wet grass. The downward slope of the Lilac Bowl forced both officers to lean back hard to avoid tipping the cart over again. As it was, the rear end of the square vehicle spun forward as they came to a stop, leaving them stopped askew.

"You see her?" Sully asked.

Battaglia shook his head. "She must still be under the—"

KA-BLAM!

The sharp report of gunfire echoed up the hillside, followed by the sharp zing of a ricochet.

Sully punched the accelerator while Battaglia jerked his gun from its holster. They blasted down the grassy hillside, slipping and sliding crazily on the wet turf.

*   *   *

"Holy shit!"

Tower heard the gunshot simultaneously through the wire transmitter and as it echoed up to the top of the clock tower.

He clicked the mike. "Shots fired! Under the bridge! Get down there!"

There was no reply.

"Maybe she smoked the creep," Hiero said.

Tower snatched his Glock from the shoulder holster underneath his left arm. He took a step towards the long, narrow flight of stairs, then glanced back at Hiero. The SWAT sniper knelt calmly in a solid, supported stance, his eye pressed to the scope.

"Go," Hiero said. "I'll cover from here."

Tower bolted for the stairs with a curse. The route to and from the top of the clock tower was more like a leaning ladder than a staircase. Reluctantly, he slid his pistol back into his shoulder holster and snapped it in place. Before he put the radio in his jacket pocket, he pressed the transmit button again.

"Adam-122, are you there?"

No answer.

Tower paused, the only sound his own labored breathing.

He pushed the button again. "Adam-122, do you copy?"

Nothing.

Tower cursed again, slipped the radio in his jacket pocket and began climbing down the steep stairs.

2140 hours

In the darkness, under the overpass, the smell of cordite hung in the air. Katie's ears hummed from the after-effects of the gunshot. She stood stock-still, staring in the direction she'd fired.

Then she heard motion to her right.

Approaching feet.

She wheeled toward the sound, her gun at the ready.

*   *   *

Battaglia squinted, but it didn't help his vision any. All he could make out was one standing shadow. He scanned left and right for targets, but saw none.

Sully caught up to him and passed him by.

"Katie?" he called.

Battaglia moved with him, his gun in the low ready position.

*   *   *

Katie lowered her gun as soon as she recognized Sully and Batts.

"Jesus," she breathed. She'd never been happier to see the twins before.

"Where is he?" Battaglia asked, his gun sweeping the dark area atop the rock wall. "Did he get away?"

"No," Katie said, and hung her head.

"What is it?" Sully asked.

Katie put her pistol back inside the purse and secured the clasp. Hesitantly, she said, "I think I just shot a rat."

"Seriously?" Battaglia asked, flashing his light along the rock wall. "A rat?"

"I think so," Katie said, her voice wavering.

"You shot a *rat*?" Battaglia marveled.

"Shut up, Batts," Sully said. He put his hand on Katie's shoulder. "Are you okay?"

Katie swallowed and nodded. As the adrenaline and fear dripped away, she felt a sense of shame seeping in. Sully's warm hand on her shoulder did little to comfort her, even when he gave her a reassuring squeeze.

Battaglia's sweeping flashlight beam came to a stop at the base of the wall. "Found it."

Katie looked at the small brown form under the cone of light. Her feeling of shame and embarrassment stopped seeping and started gushing.

"Jesus, MacLeod," Battaglia said in amazement. "You ten-ringed the little fucker."

2141 hours

"Code 4," squawked Tower's radio just as he burst from the base of the clock tower and sprinted toward the underpass. He slowed to a mild run, and pulled up to a stop once he saw the three shadowy figures underneath the bridge.

"What happened?" he asked, his breath labored.

No one answered.

"What happened?" he repeated, this time with a little more urgency.

"Uh..." Battaglia said.

Sully stepped forward and explained.

Tower listened, his lips pressed together. His first reaction was a surge of frustration, but it was his second reaction that won the day.

He burst into laughter.

Katie, Sully and Battaglia did not join in. The three patrol officers stood watching him while he laughed for several long moments. Apparently, they'd had their chance to laugh already. He didn't care. He thought it was funny.

"Well," he said, "At least it was a bulls-eye shot. I imagine that Sergeant Morgan would be proud of you, MacLeod."

None of the officers replied.

Tower wiped his forehead again, his laughter fading into a light chuckle. Sergeant Morgan, the grizzled range master, was famous for his oft-repeated words of advice such as 'focus on the front sight' and 'you can't miss fast enough.' He warned every officer and detective that they never knew when they could end up in a gunfight. Somehow, Tower found his pearls of wisdom hilarious when applied to this particular moment.

"Glad you're amused, chucklehead," Sully finally broke in. "But now what do we do?"

Tower paused. "Do?"

The patrol officers exchanged glances.

"Asshole," muttered Battaglia.

Tower shot him a glare, but before he could answer, Katie responded.

"We have to call a sergeant. It's an A.D."

Tower frowned, his mind whirring. An accidental discharge was a serious matter. The last officer that had one was suspended for a week. Of course, it had been his second incident, but still...

"If we call a sergeant, Katie gets suspended," Battaglia said. "It's that simple."

"And if we don't," Sully said in a glum tone, "and someone finds out about this, we all get fired."

"Call a sergeant," Katie said. "I messed up. I'll deal with it."

"No way," Battaglia said. "I'm not hanging you out."

"Me, either," Sully said. "I'm just making sure we all know the risk."

"There's no risk," Katie said. "Call the sergeant."

"You'll get a day off," Battaglia said. "At least. And if Hart gets his teeth into it—"

"I'll take my chances."

"Look, there's no harm here," Battaglia argued. "No one got hurt."

"That's not the point."

"It *is* the point," Battaglia told her. "You thought you saw something, you cranked off a round. Big deal."

"I'm not saying it's a big deal," Katie said. "But I had an A.D. And we have to report it."

"Why should you get suspended a day for something this stupid? I mean, it's a dead rat. That's all."

"He's right, Katie," Sully said.

Katie shook her head at both of them. "Well, while we're at it, why don't we just throw down a little rat gun next to the corpse? Then we can claim he drew first and I had to shoot him in self-defense. How would that be?"

Tower listened to the discussion, his lips pursed. He was tempted to go with Battaglia on this one. Aside from the dead rodent, this really was a no-harm, no-foul situation. And he worried about negative press that might come out of the event, both with the department brass and the actual press.

They could probably get away with it, he knew. Toss the rat in the trash. Find the expended brass that was ejected when Katie fired the round. It'd be easy for her to switch the magazine in her gun with another of her full magazines she routinely carried on her gun belt. Even getting her a replacement round for the fired one wouldn't be difficult.

Then all four of them would have to agree not to say a word.

Five of them, he corrected. Hiero was up in the tower.

Five people would have to keep quiet about it. That meant no storytelling, no playful ribbing.

It meant withstanding any questions that might come from a sergeant.

Or from Lieutenant Hart.

If it came to Hart, that meant sitting in Internal Affairs. Being tape-recorded. Being asked very specific questions.

Lying. That's what it really meant, Tower realized. It meant lying.

Tower flashed back to his academy days, remembering the words of the training officer, Sergeant DeMarcus. He'd said a lot of things, but there were a couple of things he repeated over and over again. Chief among them was, "Integrity is the coin of our trade. Never sacrifice your integrity, because you're worthless without it."

Still, Battaglia had a point. No one had been hurt. Katie was a good troop. And he didn't want anything to affect his task force. Catching the Rainy Day Rapist was the most important thing here, not some policy violation.

Tower considered a moment longer, then made his decision. He cleared his throat. "We're not calling a sergeant."

All three patrol officers swung their heads toward him.

"Excuse me?" Katie said.

"This is my investigation," Tower said. "And this is an investigative operation, not a patrol operation."

"How do you figure that?" Sully asked. "There's five of us out here and four of us are patrol officers."

Tower shook his head. "Irrelevant. This is an investigative task force. All of you are on loan."

"Whatever," Katie said. "We're not covering this up. I'm the one who—"

"I didn't say we were covering it up," Tower interrupted. "But we're not calling a sergeant about it."

"What, then?"

Tower pointed at Sully. "Find the ejected casing."

Sully hesitated.

"Trust me," Tower said.

Sully reluctantly pulled his flashlight from his back pocket without a word. He clicked it on and began to sweep the ground with the light beam.

Tower turned to Battaglia. "Toss the rat in a garbage can. Use a pair of rubber gloves."

"What?" Battaglia protested. "Why am I on rat duty?"

"Just do it, please."

"I don't even have any gloves on me," the officer complained.

Tower reached inside his jacket pocket and removed a pair of forensic gloves. He tossed them to Battaglia. They struck him on the chest and fell to the ground at his feet.

Battaglia sighed. "Well, they're dirty now."

Tower ignored him. He turned to Katie. "Walk with me," he said.

The two walked out of the underpass, back toward the clock tower. Once they were under a streetlight, Tower stopped. He looked into Katie's eyes and said nothing. The officer returned his gaze evenly, her jaw set. But he saw something in her eyes, a flicker behind her anger that he couldn't quite identify.

After a few moments, she broke the silence. "I'm not sweeping this under the rug, Detective."

"Neither am I."

"It sure looks that way."

Tower shook his head. "Don't worry about it. I'll make a report to my Lieutenant in the morning. If I know him, he'll make a report directly to the Patrol Captain."

Katie narrowed her eyes. "What about IA?"

Tower shrugged. "That'll be the Captain's decision, won't it?"

Katie stared at him. Tower could see her mind working behind the stare. He knew she was wondering if this was tantamount to covering it up or not. He knew it wasn't. He knew that someone, either Crawford or Reott, was going to have MacLeod standing tall in the office for an ass-chewing. Whether they decided to go to IA or not was up to them. He'd satisfied his responsibility by reporting the incident.

"Are you sure?" Katie finally asked. "Is that above board?"

"Reporting an A.D. to the Captain of Patrol? Are you really asking me if that's above board or not?"

Katie considered, then shook her head. "I suppose not."

"You'll get your ass chewed," Tower told her.

"I deserve it."

"Maybe," Tower conceded.

"Definitely."

"Either way," Tower said, "I'm more concerned with this: are you okay to do this decoy job?"

Katie swallowed. Tower watched her eyes for the flicker he'd seen before.

"I'm fine," Katie told him.

"You sure?" Tower asked.

"Positive."

Tower searched her eyes. He saw nothing but resolve.

"All right," he said. He reached out and clapped her lightly on the shoulder. "Let's go try a different park, then. I want to catch this son of a bitch."

ELEVEN

Sunday, April 21st
0316 hours

The four police officers sat tiredly at the all-night diner. Katie picked at her English muffin, tearing off small pieces and nibbling them. She washed every bite down with ice water. Sully and Battaglia each nursed their own cup of coffee but Tower drank cup after cup, refilled by Lauren, a buxom and flirtatious waitress. She poured for Tower but leaned near Sully to reach across the table and fill the cup.

"She likes you," Tower commented to Sully after the waitress bounded away with an energetic bounce.

Sully grunted but Katie saw that he was hiding a small smile.

Battaglia glanced up from his cup. He followed her descending frame with his gaze, then shrugged. "She likes everybody with a badge," he said. "She gets around, from what I hear."

"You listen to Kahn too much," Sully said, a little defensively.

"As a matter of fact, that was the particular skirt chaser who gave me the scoop on this one," Battaglia said.

Typical, Katie thought. Kahn or Giovanni chases after any woman with a pulse and the guys figure them for a stud. This waitress may or may not be just as promiscuous and she's somehow a slut. *Nice double standard.*

"Kahn's an asshole," Tower muttered.

"Which kind of asshole?" Sully asked.

"Shut up with that," Battaglia told him. He turned to Tower. "He ain't an asshole. He's our platoon mate."

"Maybe so," Tower said, sipping his fresh coffee, "but he's an asshole."

"Really? And why's that?"

"He'd fuck a catcher's mitt, for starters," Tower told him. "On top of that, he treats women like shit."

Amen, Katie voiced silently.

Battaglia thought about it for a minute. Then he said, "I'll give you the catcher's mitt thing. But he's no different than Gio on day shift. Who are we to tell him not to love 'em and leave 'em?"

"We're nobody," Tower said. "I didn't say he should change. I just said he's an asshole for being that way. He's an asshole because he tells women lies to get them into bed and then he dumps them."

"How do you know?"

"I know. He did it to a friend of Stephanie's."

"Well, maybe your wife's friend was a bitch," Battaglia suggested.

"Stephanie is my girlfriend, not my wife," Tower corrected, "and her friend is a sweet kid who got caught up in the badge and promises Kahn made. Anyway, it doesn't matter. I'm just saying that your asshole platoon mate might just be saying this waitress is a slut because she wouldn't go out with him."

"Maybe he knows because he banged her," Battaglia countered.

"Then he's got no class," Tower said.

Battaglia sighed. "Well, I can't argue that one." He looked around the table at Sully and Katie. "Thanks for standing up for our platoon mate, guys."

Katie shrugged. "Face it, Batts. Kahn *is* an asshole."

Sully nodded in agreement. "She's right. I'd drive ninety miles an hour on winter roads and fight a dozen pissed off bad guys to save his neck, but that doesn't change the fact that he's an asshole." He thought about it for a moment, then added, "West Coast."

Katie looked askance at him, but he shook his head at her.

Whatever, she thought to herself. Those two had so many inside jokes between them that it was like their own little language or something.

"If that's settled, let's debrief tonight's events," Tower said, his voice dropping into a slightly more official tone. "Aside from the incident under the bridge, what's your input?"

No one answered right away. When Katie looked up, she realized everyone was looking at her. She reached for water glass and took a drink.

"Do you feel safe, MacLeod?" Tower asked her.

A surge of anger spiked in her chest at his question. "As safe as any police operation," she said coolly. "Listen, guys. I'm sorry about the bridge thing. I guess I was a little jumpy, but I'm fine now." She looked around at each of them. "Really."

Sully and Battaglia nodded. She could tell they believed her. That was expected. They'd worked with her for over a year now. They knew how she handled herself on the job.

Tower didn't respond to her statement. He merely watched her, his eyes appraising her constantly while he sipped his coffee. It made Katie nervous and angry at the same time.

"There is something I'd change, though," she said, moving the conversation away from her feelings and to something more concrete.

"What?" Tower asked.

"This," she said, setting the brick-shaped transmitter and all its wires on the table in front of him.

"You don't want to be wired?"

"Not with this. It's awkward and probably visible, even through my clothes. Plus, if our guy spots it on me, he won't take the bait."

Tower sipped his coffee, then shrugged. "Sorry, MacLeod. We're not the FBI. We don't have the latest and greatest equipment. We're River City PD, which means—"

"Which means we've got crap," Battaglia finished.

Tower didn't argue. "We've got what we got."

"Can you give it to the tech guy and see if he can rig it to look like a walkman?" Katie asked. "Then I can wear jogging clothes and it'll look like I'm listening to music."

"What about your gun and other gear?"

"I have a fanny pack that'll work."

Tower nodded. "Okay, I'll drop it off this morning and see what they can do. Anything else?"

"Yeah," Katie said. "Can I get some new back up other than these two clowns?"

Tower chuckled. "Nice."

Battaglia and Sully exchanged a glance.

Katie used the moment of silence, which she knew was the calm before the storm, to sip her water and lean back in her chair. She knew that the exaggerated Irish and Italian accents would come out next, that the insults would fly, that the waitress would be back to flirt with Sully some more and that when it was all finished, she would be ready to go home and sleep.

Things were once again as they were supposed to be.

0756 hours

Heather Torin rose from a night of broken sleep and drifted into the kitchen. She rummaged around for a coffee filter in the cupboard. Suppressing a yawn, she slipped the filter into the coffee-maker, dumped in some coffee and poured water. Then she hit the start button. The ritual had become such second nature that she sometimes barely remembered being awake for it.

She opened her front door. Outside, heavy droplets of rain cascaded downward, thumping loudly on the plastic-covered newspaper. She retrieved the paper, shook off the excess water and went back inside. The cool, wet air served to wake her up. As she unwrapped the *River City Herald* and threw away the plastic wrapping around it, the smell of brewing coffee brought her some familiar comfort.

Routine was how she'd battled her depression in the past two months. The security she had known her entire life living in a city that was once voted as an "All-American City" had been shattered on that wet day early in March. Since then, she'd kept to her routine, clinging to it with urgency. She rose from bed. She drank her coffee and read the paper. She ate breakfast. She went to work, ate lunch, came home. In the evening, she watched mindless drivel on television – situational comedies, for the most part – and kept her brain from having to revisit those frightening moments in Clemons Park.

It seemed to work.

Most of the time.

Most of the time, she was so busy focused on the task or activity at hand, her mind didn't have the opportunity to wander. That focus, coupled with her familiar routine, kept the rising panic in her chest at bay, even though she sometimes still jumped at sounds in her office. Even though she still viewed every man who walked past her with fear and suspicion. Despite all of that, she kept it under control.

Most of the time.

But not at night.

It was her dreams that had her at a disadvantage. She couldn't push them aside with routine or busying about some task. She was vulnerable to whatever dreams may come, and those that came seemed bent on some sort of emotional revenge for having been suppressed during her waking hours. In vivid detail, she heard the sound of her own pounding feet through the wooded area. She felt him knock her to the ground. She smelled the damp earth. She saw her own vision blur with tears.

Only, in her dreams, these terrible dreams, he didn't stop. He didn't run away. In her dreams, he finished his cruel assault on her. He tore at her clothing. He struck her. He screamed at her—

I'll lay the whammo on you, bitch!

—until she stopped fighting him and covered her ears. And then it became worse. Then came the sex. In her dreams, it was a cold, cutting hardness. In her dreams, she cried out, but no one came to help her.

Now, in the light of the morning, she poured a cup of coffee and tried to shake free of those dreams. She settled into the chair at her kitchen table and opened the newspaper.

The headline blared at her from above the fold.

RAPIST STALKS RIVER CITY!

Heather Torin stared down at the thick black newsprint. The corners of her vision collapsed. A rush of darkness pushed inward like a wide tunnel, then a small one. Before her vision became a pinpoint, the sensation subsided. She gulped in her breath. Hot coffee splashed onto her shaking hand and she jerked it away, dropping the cup. Brown coffee splattered across the kitchen table. The cup rolled onto the floor and shattered.

The words seemed to scream upward at her. She wanted to push the paper away. This didn't belong in her daytime life. She didn't want to see it, didn't want to know it. But here it was. It was real and it was directly before her.

Leaving the spilled coffee and the broken cup for later, she read:

RAPIST STALKS RIVER CITY *by Pam Lincoln*

A serial rapist is at work in our city, police have confirmed. There have been at least three women raped within the past two weeks and police officials believe it has been the work of the same suspect.

"There are certain similarities in these attacks that lead us to believe it is the same man," Lieutenant Crawford of the Major Crimes Unit told reporters on Saturday.

Police have refused to identify the names of the victims, but a source at the River City School District has confirmed that a North Central school teacher may have been the most recent victim. The teacher was assaulted in the school parking lot Thursday afternoon.

Lieutenant Crawford also declined to describe the "similarities" that linked these assaults. Citing a fear of copycats as well as "an investigative need to withhold certain specifics in order to successfully prosecute," he would only say that the rapist did not appear to be using any weapons in his attacks.

"This is typical," said Miranda Rice of Sexual Assault Survivors, a support group for women who have been sexually assaulted. "The police in this case are more

concerned with winning a trial two years from now than saving a woman today."

"Not true," says Julie Avery, a rape advocate who works on the Prosecutor's Office Crisis Team. "The police are working very hard to catch this man."

Avery adds, "Still, women should take extra precautions until he is caught."

Dubbed "The Rainy Day Rapist" by local media, the name is somewhat of a misnomer. Although it has been raining during some of his assaults, Lieutenant Crawford dismisses that as coincidence.

"This has nothing to do with the weather," he said.

While police officials would not confirm nor deny the identity of the most recent victim, they did identify where the assaults occurred. The most recent assault did, in fact, occur at North Central High School. Prior to that, a woman was victimized near Friendship Park on River City's northern edge. The first assault occurred near the bottom of the Post Street Hill in Clemons Park—

Heather Torin froze.

Clemons Park.

The same place he'd attacked her.

She shook her head. That couldn't be a coincidence. It had to mean something. She didn't know what, but maybe the police would.

She stared at the two words on the newspaper page for a long while, trying to summon up the courage to call. Calling would mean talking. Talking would mean thinking. It would mean bringing the dreams out into the daylight.

What would everyone say?

What would they think of her?

If she talked about it, would this fear that she seemed to be able to keep bottled up in her dreams come out into her waking hours? Would it rampage about, making her jump at every noise and cringe at every passing man?

The strong aroma of the spilt coffee washed over her as she sat and stared down at the newspaper. Her heart thudded in her ears. She felt every pulse in her fingertips. Her gaze traced through the story again.

"At least three women," she read quietly.

Three.

Four. It's been four.

Or more, she realized. It could be more. There could be other women out there just like her. How many women had this man attacked that police didn't even know about? How many more would he—

Heather Torin stopped thinking and reached for the phone.

0817 hours

Janice Koslowski stared down at the crossword in front of her in frustration. The rainy day had her in a foul mood and the puzzle in front of her wasn't helping. Usually, she was able to knock out the *Herald's* crossword within an hour, but she'd been at today's version for almost two. She found this more than a little frustrating. Worse yet, she didn't have any excuses. She couldn't blame it on too many interruptions. For one, she'd been a dispatcher for twenty-two years. Multi-tasking was second nature to her. Handling routine radio traffic while working a crossword presented no difficulty for her whatsoever.

But secondly, it hadn't even been very busy so far this morning. Sunday mornings were typically slow and the falling rain outside only served to help that phenomenon. People were either recovering from Saturday night or just holing up inside for a slow, lazy, rainy day.

So that meant she couldn't think of an excuse for not knowing a seven letter word for "Ancient Civilization" that ended in an 'E'.

"You're frowning," Carrie Anne called from her nearby supervisor's station.

"It's raining," Janice answered, setting down her pencil.

"Uh-huh," Carrie Anne answered knowingly.

Janice sighed. The two women had worked together for too long. They knew each other's tells. Janice was glad they didn't play bridge against each other – there'd be no mystery in who was holding what.

"I can't get this one particular clue," she admitted. "It's an ancient civilization that ends in the letter E."

"Ugh," Carrie Anne grunted, wrinkling her nose. "Don't ask me. Maybe if it *started* with E, I could help. Even then, Egypt is about the only one I can think of. I hate History. It's boring."

"Maybe that's why it's in a crossword puzzle," Irina commented dryly from her position on the south side channel.

"How about Greece?" Elaine guessed from the data channel station.

"Only six letters," Janice pointed out.

"Oh, right." Elaine frowned. "Carthage?"

"Eight letters."

"Darn," Elaine muttered.

"Learn to count," Irina said in a sing-song voice, her back to the other dispatchers.

Elaine met Janice's gaze and mouthed the word 'bitch.'

Janice shrugged. She tried to stay out of the occasional sniping that went on between the dispatchers. Before she had to find a way to gloss over the exchange between Elaine and Irina, her terminal dinged lightly.

She read the screen. It was a 911 transfer, marked as a cold call. The victim wanted to report an attempted rape that occurred back in March near Clemons Park. Janice checked on her list of available units, preparing to dispatch Officer Giovanni. Then something in the call struck her. She paused. Her first thought was of The Rainy Day Rapist, but this was a month old. Then she recognized the name of the park. This was where the first rape had occurred. In fact, she'd sent Gio on that call, too.

"Carrie?"

"Yeah?"

"I think you might want to page Detective Tower on this call."

Carrie tapped the keys on her keyboard, then paused while reading. After a few moments, she said, "You think it's the guy he's looking for that tried to rape her, too?"

"Clemons Park is where the first one happened. It could be a coincidence, but—"

"But he'd rather know that now than tomorrow," Carrie Anne finished. She nodded. "I'll page him. Good spot, Janice."

Janice grinned. "Thanks."

She turned back to her crossword puzzle, but couldn't concentrate. A single thought ran through her head. What if this is what broke open the case? What if this was how Tower caught the guy?

She looked up at her screen and read through the call again. She wondered for a moment what made the woman wait so long to report it, or why she decided to report it now. Either way, as far as Janice was concerned, Heather Torin was a brave soul.

Janice smiled to herself. For a rainy day, this might actually turn out to be a good one.

0946 hours

Detective John Tower sat at the small kitchen table across from Heather Torin. Julie Avery perched on the edge of her chair next to her. She held Heather's left hand in both of her own. Heather dabbed at her eyes with a tissue.

"All I can remember is his eyes," she told them both in a quiet voice. "They were so angry. So...*hateful*. And I was so scared."

Julie patted her hand. Heather smiled at her through her tears.

Tower looked on, grateful for the connection that the two women seemed to have made. Although he'd interviewed scores of rape victims, he still felt uneasy asking the hard questions while trying to provide some kind of emotional support. Julie's presence lifted one of those concerns from his shoulders and allowed him to focus on the investigative issues.

"Did he display any weapons, Miss Torin?" Tower asked.

Heather shook her head. "Just his...body."

Tower nodded. "You mentioned that he was able to tear off your shorts and underclothing."

"Yes."

"Did he take off his own clothes?"

Heather shook her head again. "No. I think he was going to, but then he just...stopped."

"Stopped?"

"Yes. He sort of shuddered and stopped."

Tower glanced over at Julie, then back at Heather. "Do you think he—"

"Yes, Detective," Heather said, nodding. "I've had a lot of time to think about this, and I think that he...finished...you know, before he meant to."

Tower nodded. A premature ejaculation. That would indicate significant sexual excitement on the suspect's part, which somewhat shot to hell Julie's theory about rape. His reaction to the information was strangely devoid of any satisfaction, however.

"Did he hit you after that?" Tower asked.

"No. I mean, he tackled me to the ground before that, but after?" Heather thought a moment, then shook her head. "No. He threatened me, though."

"How?"

"He told me not to move. He called me names."

"What did he call you?" Tower asked.

"Bitch," Heather told him. "He called me a bitch and he said that if I moved, he'd lay the whammo on me."

Tower's eyebrows shot up. "He used that word? Whammo?"

"Yes."

"You're sure about that?"

Heather swallowed, then nodded her head. "I'm sure. I hear it over and over again every night."

Tower took a deep breath and leaned back.

Son of a bitch.

It was the same guy.

Heather watched him for a moment. Then she asked, "Is that important? What he said?"

Tower nodded. "It's very important."

"So...I did the right thing? Calling, I mean."

Tower smiled warmly at her. "Yes, ma'am. You did a very brave thing today. And it was definitely the right thing to do."

Heather Torin smiled back at him through her tears. "Thank you," she whispered.

Tower reached out and touched her lightly on the shoulder. "Thank *you*."

1011 hours

The cell phone didn't have the greatest reception, but Janice could hear Tower's voice well enough to understand him.

"Your hunch was right," the detective told her. "This is definitely the same guy."

A small thrill of satisfaction ran through her. "I hope it helps you catch him."

"It might. But you catching it when you did probably got the information to me a day early, at least. I didn't have to wait for a patrol officer to take the report, turn it in and have it make its way through the system. Who knows? It might have even slipped through the cracks somehow."

"I doubt that," Janice said.

"It happens sometimes. But either way, good work."

"Thanks. I'm glad I could help."

"You did."

Janice glanced down at her incomplete crossword puzzle. "Hey, you know anything about history, John?"

"Huh?"

"I'm doing the crossword puzzle and I can't get this one clue."

Tower chuckled. "You and your crosswords."

"I hate losing," she said. "Besides, you owe me now, don't you?"

Tower laughed. "You didn't waste any time cashing in that chip, did you?"

Janice smiled, even though she knew Tower couldn't see it. "Well, let's face it. When are you ever going to have an opportunity to pay me back, anyway?"

"*Touché*," Tower said. "What's the clue?"

"It's an ancient civilization, ending in E."

"Uh...Rome?"

"No. Seven letters."

There was a long silence on the other end of the phone. Finally, Tower said, "You got me. History was never my strongest subject."

"Oh, well. Thanks for trying."

"No problem. Thanks for your help today."

"You're welcome." Janice hung up.

"Were you right?" Carrie Anne asked her.

"Tower thinks so."

"Yay!" Carrie Anne clapped lightly. "Great work!"

Elaine joined in with the clapping, but Irina studiously ignored them all.

She is kind of bitchy, Janice thought, but she smiled anyway.

1014 hours

Tower sat in his cruiser and focused on the pad of paper on his clipboard, scratching out notes of his interview with Heather Torin. Julie Avery remained inside with the victim, giving him an opportunity to record what she'd told him. As he wrote, an idea formed in his head.

The rain splattered on his windshield in a chaotic rhythm. It made him wonder about the rapist's rhythm. His attacks had seemed to have no connections thus far. Renee had tried to find a pattern, but there wasn't any. Time of day varied. There was no perceivable connection between any of the victims, nor did they seem to be any glaring similarities between the victims themselves. The only consistent thing had been his modus operandi. His method. His actions and words. And even that seemed to be changing.

Evolving.

That was the question Renee asked about him. Was he evolving? The answer, unfortunately, seemed to be a clear "yes." He seemed to be evolving into something more violent each time out. Tower shared Renee's concern that he might transition from rape to sexual homicide.

"The Rainy Day Killer," Tower muttered. "The press would have a field day with that one."

He figured his suspect probably would, too.

Tower stopped writing notes and leaned back in his seat. Maybe this was the break that Browning had promised would eventually happen. He knew this was the same guy. The M.O. was the same and the "whammo" phrase was too unique to be a coincidence. Up until now, those had been the only constants between the assaults.

Not anymore.

Now he had two assaults that occurred in the same location. The assault on Torin was somewhat bungled. Five weeks later, he hits again, this time successfully raping Patricia Reno.

In the same park.

"Why would he attack two women in the same place?" Tower asked aloud.

The rain pounded down on the hood and roof of his car. He thought about his own question for a few moments. Then he picked up his cell phone and dialed Renee's number. She picked up on the second ring.

"Renee? It's John."

"John Tower," she said. "My fourth favorite detective. What can I do for you?"

"Fourth? Who's ahead of me?"

"Browning," Renee answered matter-of-factly, "and then Finch and Elias."

"I can understand Browning," Tower conceded, "but Finch and Elias?"

"Seniority counts," Renee said. "What's up?"

Tower filled her in on his interview with Heather Torin.

"It's definitely him," she concluded. "The M.O. and the whammo key word? No question."

"So tell me if my thinking is good here," Tower said.

"Probably not, but go ahead."

Tower ignored her joke. "I asked myself why a guy like this would attack two women at the same park, five weeks apart. And I come up with two answers."

"Which are?"

"I think he attacked the second victim in the same place because the first victim never called the police. There wasn't any news coverage at all. Nothing in the paper or on TV. So he figured it was still a safe location."

"Could be."

"I figure that he picked that location because it was perfect for his plan. He'd want to use it again if it wasn't burned."

"Could be," Renee repeated. "What's the second reason?"

"Well, this new victim described him having a premature ejaculation, right? I may be wrong, but I think you could take that as an indication this was his first assault. The excitement was too much for him because he'd never done it before."

Renee paused on the other end of the line. Tower wished he could see her expression in order to gauge her reaction. Instead, he waited impatiently for her reply.

A few moments later, she said, "It makes sense, I suppose. He was clearly less violent with your victim from today than later victims. If he's building up to sexual homicide, I would suspect that each time he rapes, it becomes less and less about *sexual* domination and more and more about *violent* domination."

"That fits your theory that he's evolving," Tower said.

"Don't suck up, John."

Tower laughed. "All right, all right. But you can see where I'm going with this, can't you?"

"Not beyond the theory that this new report may have been his first, no. So enlighten me, please."

"What I'm thinking is that *if* the attack on Heather Torin was his first attack and *if* Patricia Reno was victim number two, then these attacks came early on in his development as a rapist. And even though he may be turning out to be more violent, he's also becoming more sophisticated and more daring."

"Point, please?" Renee urged.

"The point is that wouldn't a fledgling criminal start his career pretty close to where he felt safe?"

"Safe?" Renee asked.

Tower didn't answer. He waited.

After about ten seconds, Renee spoke again. "You mean his home, don't you?"

"Yep."

"You think he lives somewhere near Clemons Park?"

"I think there's a good chance of it, yeah."

Renee remained quiet. Tower listened to the static on the connection until she spoke again.

"You may be onto something, John. It makes sense."

"That's what I wanted to hear."

"Are you going to deploy the Task Force accordingly, then?"

"I think so," Tower answered. "Not at Clemons Park, though. That's too obvious. Can you do some research for me?"

"I live for research," Renee gushed in a half-sarcastic tone, but Tower could hear the tinge of excitement in her voice. He felt the same touch of excitement himself. They might be getting somewhere.

"I need a few options," he said. "Find me a few areas in the area of Clemons Park that might be good fishing holes."

"Aye, Aye," Renee replied. "Anything else?"

"No, that's it—oh, wait. Janice was asking me a question I didn't know the answer to."

"Imagine the odds of that."

"Har-de-har-har. It was for her crossword puzzle."

"What was the clue?"

"Ancient Civilization. Ends in E. Seven letters."

"Hittite," Renee answered immediately.

"How'd you know that?"

"I know everything," Renee told him. "It's my job."

She hung up.

Tower scratched out H-I-T-I-T-E on his notepad. Then he counted the letters. "There's only six," he mumbled, smiling to himself. Well, maybe Renee didn't know *everything*.

Sudden pounding at his passenger window startled him. Julie Avery stood at the passenger side of his cruiser, knocking frantically on the window. He pushed the automatic door lock. She pulled open the door hurriedly and hopped inside.

"You made me jump," he told her.

"Sorry," she said. "I just wanted out of the rain as quick as I could."

"How'd things go in there?" Tower asked.

Julie pushed the hood of her jacket back and rubbed her hands together for warmth. "Can you turn on the heater? I'm freezing."

Tower started the engine and put the heater on.

"Thanks," Julie said.

"Can you not talk about it?" Tower asked. "Some kind of client privilege or something?"

Julie shook her head. "No, she said I could share anything with law enforcement. But there's nothing more to tell. We talked about programs available to her and the importance of following through on getting help."

"You think she will?"

Julie shrugged. "Probably. She called the police after more than a month. That tells you something."

"I suppose so," Tower said.

Julie glanced over at him, blowing breath onto her hands. "You know, you did a good job in there."

"Thanks."

"I don't mean on the investigation," Julie said. "I mean, I'm sure you did fine on that, too. But I meant with Heather. You made her feel good about her decision. That's important."

"She did the right thing," Tower said.

"I know. But telling her that helps."

"Good to know," Tower said.

Julie dipped her head toward his clipboard. "What's that? Your notes?"

Tower looked down at the scrawled notes. "Yeah. Just so I don't forget anything."

She cocked her head to read the words he'd written. "I don't mean to be nosy, but what does 'Hittite' have to do with anything?"

"Huh?"

Julie pulled her hand away from her mouth and pointed at the word on his notepad. "There. Hittite. What's that mean?"

"Oh," Tower said. "Uh, nothing. It's unrelated. A history thing someone asked me about."

Julie nodded slowly. "I see. Well, just in case it's important, Hittite has three T's in it, not two."

Tower frowned.

"It's H-I-T-T-I-T-E," Julie spelled.

"I know," Tower replied, tossing the clipboard into the back seat. "I was...just writing fast."

Julie smiled and blew on her hands.

Tower dropped the car into gear and pulled away from the curb. Half a block away, he smiled, too.

TWELVE

Sunday, April 21st
Graveyard Shift
2204 hours

"Are we done yet?" yawned Anthony Battaglia, rubbing eyes with the heels of his palms.

"Don't do that," Sully said.

"Do what?"

"Yawn. Don't do it. You'll get me started."

Battaglia sighed. "This is never going to work. We're wasting our time."

The two officers sat in a gray 1978 Chevrolet Caprice, affectionately dubbed "The Gray Ghost" by the officers in the patrol division. The Ghost was the only civilian vehicle currently available to patrol for use in any undercover operations. Parked along the curb at Corbin Park, they watched Katie MacLeod walk around the park, feigning a workout in the cool, wet air.

At least it stopped raining, Sully thought.

The park ran about six blocks long and two across, making it a natural place for joggers to get in a run. Detective Tower sat alone in a small Toyota truck on the opposite corner of the park. With this configuration, MacLeod never left the sight of at least one cover team.

"Why won't it work?" Sully asked, suppressing a yawn.

He had to admit he had his own doubts, but he was curious why Batts thought so, too. He watched as MacLeod approached a modest copse of trees near the far end of the park. That was a worry spot, according to Tower, given the rapist's methods. If he was going to make a move on a woman in this park, the detective had told them that his bet was on that small treed area.

"There's only about six billion reasons," Battaglia answered.

"One for every person in the world, then."

"Huh?"

"One for every—oh, never mind," Sully shook his head. "Just give me some of those reasons, my brother."

"I will, my brother." Battaglia held up a finger. "First off, we're sitting here in the Gray Ghost. Every criminal in River City knows this is a UC vehicle. This car is so burnt, charcoal pieces fall off as we're driving down the street."

"True," Sully conceded. "But this guy probably isn't your typical doper or thief. He might not know it's an undercover ride."

Battaglia snorted. "*Everyone* knows the Gray Ghost. And even if by some strange chance this maggot didn't, how hard is it to figure out that two guys sitting in a car like this for any length of time are cops on a stakeout? Even an Irishman could figure it out."

"Oh, tha's a fine funny jest," Sully said in thick brogue. "You're a laugh fest. So what's your solution?"

"To the car problem or the two guys problem?"

"Either." Sully shrugged. "Both."

Battaglia took a deep breath and let it out. "Well, Tower's a dick, right?"

"I thought you said he was an asshole."

"Haw, haw, haw," Battaglia guffawed. "I meant detective. He's an *investigator*."

"Duh."

"So, duh, maybe he could talk to his detective buddies over in Narcotics and get us a decent ride that isn't like driving around a neon sign that says 'cop'. I mean, come on. Some of those guys are driving Mustangs and BMWs."

"Not all of them."

"Bull crap. It's like frickin' *Miami Vice* over there. Plus they've got extra cars they've seized."

"Those are the cars they use for undercover buys, right?"

Battaglia shrugged. "So?"

"So I'm sure they don't want them getting burned off in a patrol operation," Sully pointed out.

Battaglia's eyebrows flew up. "A *mere* patrol operation? Well, I suppose not, but last time I checked, this was an investigative operation, headed up by a detective and commanded by the Major Crimes Lieutenant, so–"

"Okay, okay." Sully raised his hands in surrender. "Even so, according to you, we're still going to look like two cops sitting here, no matter what we're driving."

"That's easy." He pointed toward MacLeod as she emerged from the other side of the treed area. "She's past the red zone."

Sully grunted. Maybe Battaglia was right about this being a waste of time.

"So you solve the two guys problem like this," Battaglia continued. "Get me a woman partner."

"Oh, I'm sure Rebecca would be totally cool with that happening."

Battaglia shrugged, a mischievous twinkle in his eye. "Rebecca doesn't have to know every little thing I do."

A spark of anger flared in Sully's stomach. "Now you're just being an idiot."

"What? How?"

"You'd step out on your wife? That's stupid. And with someone here at work? That's even stupider."

Battaglia raised his hands in a placating gesture. "Easy, Irish. I'm just saying that if it was a man and a woman sitting here, it might look like a date or something. That's all."

"It might look like a couple of folks committing adultery, too."

Battaglia laughed. "I suppose it might. But either way, Mr. Rapist Asshole isn't going to pay too much attention, is he?"

Sully scowled. "Not nearly as much, no."

"When did you get so Ten Commandments, anyway?"

"I'm not. Rebecca's a good woman, that's all."

"I know. I married her."

"I know. I was there." Sully pointed to his chest. "Best man, remember?"

"I do," Battaglia said, "though right now you're acting more like you were the maid of honor."

Sully fell silent. He knew Batts loved his wife, but he sometimes thought his partner took her for granted. He hadn't figured out yet if that was because Battaglia actually did take her for granted or if he himself put Rebecca on too much of a pedestal. He figured it might be some of both. In any event, Battaglia and his wife seemed oblivious to his feelings and he intended to keep them that way.

"Check this out," Battaglia said in a slightly lower voice.

He pointed, and Sully followed his gesture. A pair of men in dark clothing had appeared out of an alley and walked quickly to the edge of the park. After looking left and right, they turned and strode purposefully in MacLeod's direction.

"Did Tower say anything about this guy having a partner?" he asked Battaglia.

Battaglia shook his head. "Nope. But what would that asshole know?"

Sully didn't answer. The pair was less than two blocks away from MacLeod's location. With both sets of people walking toward each other, the distance closed rapidly.

Battaglia lifted the portable radio to his lips.

2206 hours

"Adam-122 to Ida-409, you seeing this?"

Tower pressed the mike. "Affirmative."

"You want us to move on them?"

He clicked the mike again. "Negative. Let's see if they make a move."

There was a pause, then an abrupt click in response. That was Battaglia's way of telling him that he and O'Sullivan didn't agree with his decision. Tower didn't care. Instead, he focused on Katie's exercise-walk gait as she rounded the corner of the park and turned to face the oncoming duo.

He wondered briefly if it were somehow possible that there were two rapists. He'd read cases in which rapists had partners, but they were rare. Especially when you factored in that it was a serial situation. Most partner jobs were spontaneous and had a definite alpha male forcing the issue.

Still, the purposeful stride of the two men in dark clothing concerned him. Were they planning to rob her? Or had he and Renee made a colossal error in analyzing the evidence?

He pressed the transmit button on his radio. "-409 to Adam-122."

"Twenty-two," came the clipped reply.

"See how close you can get," he instructed, "but stay darked out."

2207 hours

"Copy," Battaglia said, then tossed the radio over to Sully. He put the car in gear and gave the accelerator a light nudge, sending the Gray Ghost rolling forward.

"Flip a U-ie," Sully told him. "Come in from behind them. Otherwise, they'll spot us and know something's up."

Battaglia waited until they reached the intersection where Howard Street ran into the park. Avoiding the brake pedal, he swung the car in as tight a circle as he could, turning around and facing the other direction. Without hesitating, he accelerated to the far end of the park. He made the turn northbound without braking and without chirping the tires.

"They're about thirty yards apart," Sully estimated. He lifted his small binoculars to his face and peered through them. The motion of the car made him jiggle too much to get a clear picture through the glasses.

"You think they're going to rob her?" Battaglia asked him.

"I don't know."

Battaglia grunted in response. He turned west and pointed the Ghost directly at the pair of walking men. He accelerated as gently as possible, easing the car up to speed.

"Get right up on them before they have a chance to attack her," Sully ordered.

"Tower said to wait—"

"I don't care," Sully said. "I'm not waiting until they club her over the head or something."

Battaglia shook his head. "She sees them. She'll be fine. Let's wait until they make a move."

Sully took a deep breath and let it out. He knew Battaglia was right, but it rankled him to put MacLeod in that kind of danger. Then again, she was a cop. She had to see them approaching, as they were within twenty yards now. Besides that, she had a gun in her fanny pack.

"Okay," Sully agreed. "But get close."

"What do you think I'm doing?"

"Imitating Driving Miss Daisy."

Battaglia didn't bother to reply. He let off the gas and put the car in neutral, allowing it to roll forward at fifteen miles an hour. "It's like a Stealth Chevrolet," he whispered to Sully.

Sully smiled absently. "It'd be nice if it came equipped with missiles, because these two are going to bolt as soon as they spot us."

"One for each of us."

"And MacLeod gets dealer's choice on who she wants to chase."

"Where the hell is Tower?" Battaglia groused. "Is he some kind of chicken or something?"

Sully didn't answer. He watched as the two men closed the gap between them and MacLeod.

Ten yards.

Now five.

Three.

2208 hours

When the first man reached for her fanny pack, Katie twisted forcefully away. She turned her left side toward him and pulled her Glock.

"Police!" she shouted, pointing the muzzle into the face of the more aggressive of the two. "Don't move!"

The man's eyebrows shot up. Surprise flashed across his rugged features.

"*Chto?*" he asked in a guttural tone.

"Don't you move!" Katie repeated. "Show me your hands!"

The man's surprise melted into a cold smile. "Okay, yeah," he said, raising his hands slowly.

A blur of movement came from his right. Katie jerked her pistol in that direction, but a crushing pain exploded at her elbow. Her gun flew through the air and fell clattering onto the pavement beside her. She cried out and staggered back a step. Before she could recover, the man who'd struck her glided forward, his eyes intense. His leg flashed out, catching her in the upper thigh. A shockwave of pain blasted down to her toes and upward into her chest. Her air left her. She sank to her opposite knee, struggling to keep her hands up.

Without hesitating, both men bounded away.

*   *   *

"Jesus! I told you!" Sully yelled. "Go, go, *GO!*"

Battaglia gunned the engine and fired up the headlights at the same time. The two shadowy figures scampered off to the north. As soon as they hit the north curb, they split up and ran in opposite directions.

"I got this one!" Battaglia shouted, pointing at the one running west. He slammed on the brakes, jammed the car into park and leapt from the driver's seat in foot pursuit.

Sully scrambled out of the passenger seat and sprinted toward where MacLeod knelt, holding her leg.

"Are you okay?" he leaned down and asked her.

"Fine," she said through gritted teeth. She reached for her gun, picking it up off the asphalt. "Go."

Another set of headlights flashed on, bathing her in a yellowish glare. Sully glanced up at the lights, then straightened and raced eastbound after the second suspect.

＊　＊　＊

Tower watched the attack on Katie in horror. For a moment, he froze in place. Then a pair of headlights flooded the scene in front of him and spurred him into action. He started the Toyota's engine and hit his own headlights.

O'Sullivan was leaning over a kneeling MacLeod. He glanced up in Tower's direction, then dashed away toward the northeast.

Tower cursed at his own hesitation. He dropped the small truck into gear and tore up to MacLeod's location. As he arrived, the young officer stood up, clearly favoring one leg.

"Are you hurt?" Tower asked, slamming the truck door and walking toward her.

Katie laughed ruefully. "I think my pride just took a serious beating."

"How's your leg?"

Katie tested it gingerly, limping for several steps. She grimaced each time she put weight on her left leg.

"It'll be fine," she told him through a pained expression.

Tower brought his portable radio to his mouth. "Ida-409 to Adam-122. Update."

There was no response.

"Adam-122, an update!" Tower barked into the radio.

Katie reached out and grabbed his wrist. He met her eyes and she shook her head. "Can't you hear it?"

Tower's eyes narrowed. "Hear what?"

2209 hours

"Police!" Battaglia yelled with each exhale. "Stop!"

The man in front of him didn't slow or pause. With each stride, he seemed to pull farther away.

Battaglia renewed his effort, forcing his legs to pump harder and faster.

The suspect seemed to sense his advance and answered with a burst of his own.

You son of a bitch.

"You better quit running!" Battaglia yelled. "If I have to catch you, I'm going to kick your ass!"

Instead of slowing down, the suspect seemed to find an extra gear. He sprinted forward along the sidewalk, slowly widening the gap between them.

Battaglia pushed on, his breathing labored, his lungs burning.

* * *

Sully stretched out his stride, trying to eat up as much ground as possible with each step. The suspect in front of him was shifty, cutting through two yards and over one fence already. He ran in a zig-zag fashion, almost as if he expected Sully to start firing rounds after him.

"Police!" Sully yelled for the third time. "Stop!"

The suspect's only reaction was to hop over a four-foot chain-link fence and sprint for the alley.

Feeling much lighter in civilian clothes than his usual uniform, which came complete with duty belt and bulletproof vest, Sully vaulted over the fence easily, barely needing to use his hands on the top edge.

The suspect turned back westward once he reached the alley. Sully momentarily lost sight of him behind a garage. Without pause, he sprinted after the dark figure.

*   *   *

"Hear what?" Tower asked her again.

"You've lost your patrol ears," Katie told him. She limped over to the Gray Ghost and leaned inside the passenger seat, fishing for something. When she removed her hand, Tower immediately recognized what she held.

The portable radio.

Tower frowned. "You mean..."

Katie nodded. "Yeah. They're out there chasing bad guys in the dark without backup and without a radio."

2210 hours

"Goddamnit!" Battaglia yelled. "Where the hell did he go?"

He slowed to a walk, trying to listen for sounds of movement in the alley. The only noise that filled his ears was his own deep, ragged breaths.

The suspect had managed to get almost a block between the two of them before cutting into the alley. Battaglia walked down the dirt alley, looking left and right for hiding places, just in case the suspect had gone to ground.

But he knew that isn't what happened.

Nope, the guy didn't stop and hide. He just outran your fat, Italian ass.

Battaglia sighed. He wasn't fat. And the son of a bitch was *fast*. Carl Lewis fast. Hell, he was *The Flash* fast.

The residential alley was quiet except for the sounds of his own breathing and the thud of his boots on the hard packed dirt and gravel. He thought about stopping and calling for a K-9 to track the suspect, but he knew it was useless. He didn't have a radio to call for patrol units to set up a perimeter. Without a hard perimeter to contain the suspect, the K-9 track was useless. Even if the dog caught the scent, the suspect's head start would never be overcome. He could keep running for an hour and they'd never catch up. And as fast as this guy motored, five minutes was all he needed to be halfway to China.

Battaglia continued his lonely walk down the dark alley.

*　*　*

The suspect reached the end of the alley and turned south. As he cut to his left, he slipped on a patch of wet grass and tumbled forward onto the sidewalk. Sully heard him grunt in pain. Before the man could scramble to his feet, Sully was on top of him.

"Down on your stomach!" He ordered as he grabbed the suspect's arm at the wrist.

"Yob tvaya mat!"

Sully didn't know what that meant, but from the tone he figured it wasn't compliance. The thin man slipped and turned underneath him, trying to escape.

"Police! You're under arrest!" Sully barked at him, refusing to release his grip on the man's wrist.

The suspect answered by rolling onto his back and throwing a punch at Sully's head.

*　*　*

"Take the car," Tower instructed Katie, "and go after Battaglia. I'll try to find O'Sullivan."

Katie nodded. She slammed shut the passenger door of the Ghost and limped hurriedly around to the driver's side.

Tower returned to his truck, reversed the engine and headed off toward the northeast.

Katie's leg throbbed as she adjusted the seat to reach the pedals. She was grateful that the Ghost was an automatic. Operating a clutch right now was probably not an option.

She put the car into gear and flipped around to go after Battaglia.

* * *

The punch whizzed by Sully's face, grazing his cheek and temple.

A shot of anger exploded in his chest. First this guy attacks Katie, then he runs from them and now he was going to *punch* him?

"Enough of this shit," he growled at the suspect.

He slipped to the side, drew back his knee and drove it into the man's buttocks. The man grunted in surprised pain, but managed to throw out another punch toward Sully. This second punch was a wild one and came nowhere near hitting him.

"Stop fighting!" Sully shouted. He slid to his left and fired his opposite knee. This one thudded into the soft tissue below the rib cage.

The suspect howled in pain. He curled his body into a fetal position.

Sully transitioned quickly into an arm bar, controlling the man's elbow as well as his wrist. Using his leverage, he forced the suspect onto his stomach. Once he had that accomplished, he shuffled forward and lowered his left knee across the back of the man's neck. Now he controlled three points – the head, the elbow and the wrist.

He'd won.

Propping the elbow against his right knee, Sully fished in his belt-line for the handcuffs hanging half-in and half-out of his jeans. He was grateful to find they hadn't fallen out in the chase or during the brief struggle.

Like every other time he'd won a foot pursuit or a fight, the clicking sound the cuffs made when he ratcheted them onto the suspect's wrist was like a symphony to his ears. As the second cuff clicked into place, a pair of headlights turned the corner and illuminated the two of them.

2212 hours

Katie found Battaglia trudging up the middle of Howard Street, three blocks from the park. If the lack of a prisoner didn't tell the story of what happened, the sour expression on his face would have.

She slowed the Ghost, pulling up next to him. Without a word, Battaglia opened the door and dropped into the passenger seat in a huff. He slammed the door and stared straight ahead.

Katie didn't say a word. She drove to the next block, turned and headed back toward the park.

"God*damn*it," Battaglia muttered, staring out the window in sullen anger.

"Don't feel bad," Katie said, her leg still throbbing with each heartbeat. "At least you didn't get your ass kicked like me."

Battaglia sighed. "I guess this is the loser car, then, huh, MacLeod? All passengers must have gotten their ass kicked or been outran by a suspect?"

"I guess so." She was quiet a moment, then said, "I hope Sully and Tower have better luck catching their guy."

"Sully is the reincarnation of Bruce Jenner," Battaglia said. "He'll catch his guy. Besides, he went after the slow one."

The pair rode in silence for a block. Then Katie said, "Bruce Jenner isn't dead."

"Huh?"

"Bruce Jenner is still alive."

"So?"

"So you can't have a reincarnation of someone who is still alive. That's not how it works."

"Whatever," Battaglia said, shrugging away her comment. After a second, he shook his head to himself. "That son of a bitch was *fast*."

"Kicks like a mule, too," Katie added. She reached down and massaged her bunching quadriceps.

"You all right?"

"Hurts like hell," she said. "But what's worse, these guys weren't even who we were after. They're not rapists. Probably just a couple of crooks who saw an opportunity to rob someone."

"Assholes," muttered Battaglia.

2249 hours

Tower stood in the small observation room next to Katie. Both stared through the one-way glass at the slender man seated in the interview room. Under the light, his features were clearly Slavic.

"He looks Russian," Katie guessed.

"Safe bet," Tower said. "There's been thousands of them pouring in to River City since the fall of the Soviet Union."

"We've noticed it on patrol," Katie told him. "All across the boards, too – witnesses, victims and suspects. A noticeable increase in contacts with Russians."

"Well, this one is definitely in the 'suspect' category. The question is, of what?"

Katie shook her head. "He's not a rapist. They went for my fanny pack. It was a straight up robbery."

"Which one went for the bag?"

Katie pointed at the man in the interview room. "He did. The one that got away is the one who kicked me."

"Did he say anything that made you think he might be after more than money?"

"He didn't say anything at all," she answered. "He just reached for my fanny pack. It was a robbery, not a rape. Besides, you never said anything about The Rainy Day Rapist being a team."

Tower shrugged. "This isn't an exact science. I could be wrong."

"You know you're not."

"I could be."

Katie snorted lightly. "You're wasting your time."

"I'm paid by the hour," Tower said. He squeezed Katie on the shoulder and left the observation room. As he stepped through the doorway, he almost bumped into Lieutenant Crawford.

"Sorry," he murmured.

Crawford ran his hand through his thinning, tousled hair. "See me in my office after your interview, Tower."

"Yes, sir."

Tower took three hurried steps to the interview room door. At the door, he took a deep breath and put on his game face. Then he turned the knob and went in.

The man looked up at the sound of his entrance. His face was calm, despite the small scrape on his cheek and the smudge of dirt on his forehead. His eyes fixed Tower with a hard, appraising stare.

Tower sat down opposite him. For a long minute, the two men looked intently at each other from across the small table. Neither blinked.

"What's your name?" Tower finally asked.

The Russian did not speak. His flat expression radiated a cold hatred back at Tower.

"Do you speak English?" Tower asked.

"*Da.*"

"Then answer my question. What's your name?"

A small smile curled at the edge of his thin lips. "Do you know that I could refuse to tell you? Or give you any name I wish? You would never know difference. You not have my fingerprints."

Tower matched his smile with his own. "Let's start over. You know you don't have to talk to me, right?"

"*Da.* Of course."

"And that you can have an attorney, if you want?"

The Russian snorted. The line of his mouth went straight and hard, all hint of the smile gone.

"You don't want an attorney?" Tower asked.

"In my country," the Russian replied, "we have saying. God, he want to punish mankind, so he send lawyers."

Tower allowed himself a small grin. "I think we just found something to agree about."

The Russian did not return his smile, but instead shook his own head. "I no need lawyer. I do nothing wrong."

"Well, since you know so much," Tower said, "do you know that I can hold you until I do identify you? Even if that means sending your prints back to Moscow?"

The Russian shook his head again. "No. Is America. You will set me free."

Tower chuckled. "Hate to break this to you, pal, but that isn't how it works. Even here in the Socialist Republic of Washington, we can hold people who commit felonies until they're identified."

"What is felony?"

"A crime," Tower said. "A serious one."

"What crime? I get scared because girl point gun at me and then men chase. You should arrest her, not me."

"She's a cop."

The Russian blinked. "She is cop, this girl with gun?"

"Yep."

He shrugged. "But I no do nothing. She is one who points gun at me. Crazy, this girl."

"What's your name?" Tower asked again.

The man considered, then shrugged again. "Is fine. I no do nothing wrong, so I tell you."

"Thank you. What is it?"

The Russian drew himself up in his seat. When he spoke, his voice had a touch of pride in it. "I am Valeriy Alexandrovich Romanov."

"Your name is Valerie?"

"*Nyet.* Valeriy." He pronounced it slowly. "Vuh-LAIR-ey. You see?"

"Here in America, that's a girl's name."

Romanov shrugged. "Many things different between America and my country."

"Yeah?" Tower asked. "What do they do with rapists over there?"

"What is this word? Rapist?"

Tower raised his hand and made a circle with this thumb and forefinger. Then he lifted his middle finger and thrust it in and out of the hole he'd created.

Romanov's eyes narrowed. "You think I try make sex on this girl?"

"Didn't you?"

"*Nyet.* I no do nothing." Romanov shook his head. "I no need to do that. I get woman when I want. Many woman."

"Well, it ain't about the sex, pal," Tower told him. "It's about other things. Like being angry at women. Or being an inadequate. You know, stuff like that."

Romanov glared at him. "I no do nothing," he repeated.

"If I run your name through Interpol, what will I find?" Tower asked him.

"Go find out," Romanov told him. "I no tell you shit."

"I'll bet you've got a record over there, Valerie."

"Valeriy," Romanov corrected.

"I'll bet that record will tell me a whole lot of interesting things, Valerie," Tower continued, ignoring his correction. "I'll bet you'll have a whole slew of indicator crimes like weenie waving, minor assaults, the whole gamut."

"What are these things you say?" Romanov asked. "*Negavahru po angliscky.* I no speak English much."

"You understand me perfectly well."

"*Nyet.*"

"How many women have you attacked here in River City, Valerie?"

"I no do noth—"

"How many did you rape?"

"*Nyet.* You think I do that, then you more stupid than I first think."

Tower watched Romanov while they spoke. He knew the Russian was lying about the attempted robbery, but everything he saw told him the man was being truthful about the subject of rape.

Which I already knew, Tower thought to himself. No victim mentioned accents. None mentioned a second suspect. He was wasting his time.

"Maybe you're right," Tower told Romanov. "Maybe I am stupid. Maybe you aren't a rapist. But I saw you try to steal that fanny pack."

"*Nyet*. Is not true."

"I watched you reach right out and try to take it. So did three other cops, including the 'girl' you tried to steal it from. Now, are you going to sit there and deny that?"

Romanov gazed back at Tower, his countenance flat. "I no do nothing," he said.

Tower sighed and stood up. "Well, then I guess you'll like it here in America, Valerie. Because we throw innocent people who 'no do nothing' into jail, too."

The corner of Romanov's mouth twitched into a smile. "I very scared at U.S. jails," he said, his voice dripping with sarcasm. "So much worse than Russia."

Tower waited a moment longer, but could think of nothing to say, so he turned and left the room.

2310 hours

Katie sat in the women's locker room, her leg propped up on the long bench that ran down the center of the aisle. Her locker stood open, a calendar depicting a lighthouse displayed on the inside door.

I'd like to be there right now, she thought. Yaquina Head Lighthouse, on the coast of Oregon. Surrounded by fog. The smell of salt water in the air. A brisk wind making you glad that the door to the lighthouse was so close.

Of course, she probably couldn't climb the stairs right now with her throbbing quadriceps. She kneaded the bunched muscle and grimaced in pain. She'd trained in defensive tactics ever since the academy. That repertoire of kicks included one very similar to what the Russian suspect had used on her – a hard, low blast to the quadriceps. Although she'd taken those shots in training, it had never been full force. Usually, she knew it was coming and had time to turn her leg or retract it defensively. There'd been soreness, but never the kind of cramping, pulsating pain this kick had wrought.

A loud knock came at the locker room door. A moment later, the door nudged open a crack.

"All females decent in there?"

Katie grinned. The gravelly voice of Thomas Chisolm always made her feel better. "It's all clear," she called back.

The door swung open. Thomas Chisolm strode into the room. He spied Katie in her gym shorts and averted his eyes. "Jesus, MacLeod, you didn't tell me you were half-naked."

"Don't be such a prude. They're workout shorts."

Chisolm kept his head turned, but stole a glance at her out of the corner of his eye. "All right, then. I'm just a stranger to what goes on in the women's locker room. Never know what to expect."

"Oh, it's pretty much what all you guys imagine," Katie said. "When we're not standing around naked and rubbing lotion on ourselves, it's a big lesbian love-fest."

"Save that for Giovanni," Chisolm said. "Or Sully and Battaglia. They might just believe you." He looked around. "It *is* nice in here, though."

"You want the full tour?"

Chisolm shook his head. "Nah. I didn't come to compare digs." He reached into his back pocket and removed a small jar. "I brought you some magic juice."

Katie squinted at him. "Magic what?"

Chisolm approached and swung his leg over the bench, straddling it at her feet. "Sully said you took a hard kick to the leg?"

Katie pressed her lips together. "Yeah, so?" She wondered if the two of them were yukking it up over the girl getting her ass kicked. Well, at least she hadn't let the guy get away in a foot pursuit.

Chisolm pointed to her propped leg. "This one?"

Katie nodded.

Chisolm settled onto the bench. He twisted the top off the small container and dug his first two fingers inside. When he removed them, his fingers were coated in a thick gel.

"What is that?" she asked him.

"I told you," Chisolm said with a grin. "It's magic juice. Now, where did that bastard kick you?"

Katie shook her head. "No way, Tom. You're not putting that stuff on me. Not without telling me what it is."

"Calf or quad?"

"Quad," Katie said, "but what the hell is that?"

Chisolm fixed her with an amused look. "You don't believe in magic, MacLeod?"

"No."

"How about secret medicine?"

"No."

"Wow." Chisolm motioned toward her quadriceps. "Does it hurt?"

"Yeah," she admitted.

"Throbs? Tries to cramp up?"

"Both."

Chisolm proffered his gooey fingers to her. "That's what the magic juice is for."

Katie hesitated, then said, "All right. I trust you."

Chisolm smiled. "Good." He held his fingers out toward her hand.

Katie shook her head. "Uh, no. I don't want to touch that stuff, whatever it is. You do it."

"Fair enough," Chisolm said. He reached toward her leg. Just before touching her, he paused. "This might hurt a little."

"Hurt? But you never said—"

Chisolm smeared the thick yellow goop over the skin of her quadriceps. The cool sensation made her gasp lightly, though it wasn't entirely unpleasant. Then Chisolm dug his fingers into her muscle, rubbing in the ointment.

Katie exhaled sharply. Jolts of pain zipped from her leg outward through her entire body. All of her muscles tightened up. She gripped the sides of the bench with her fingers and let out a quiet curse.

Chisolm said nothing. His strong fingers kneaded her leg muscle, the roughness of his skin scraping and sliding across hers. The two remained silent while the veteran officer worked in the ointment. The coolness spread across her entire outer thigh. She could feel the sensation seeping into the muscle.

Katie noticed that Chisolm focused on her leg with the clinical distance of a family doctor. She wondered for a moment how many of the other men she worked with would be comfortable rubbing medication onto her leg without making it into something more. How many of them would be able to do something like that and then not run off to the rest of the platoon to spill the secret like some kind of schoolboy?

To be fair, she wondered how many men she'd feel safe enough with to let herself be touched? And were there some that she might react to with a hand on her leg? More than one kind of reaction, she decided, depending on who it was.

The last thing she noticed before Chisolm drew his hands away was that he had studiously avoided the inner thigh.

"There," he said, twisting the cap back onto the container. "Give it about ten minutes to dry before you put anything over the top of it."

Katie gazed down at her leg. The skin bore a yellow tinge. The cool sensation seemed to be shifting into something warmer in the brief seconds since Chisolm's touch.

"You want to tell me what it is now?" Katie said. "It's starting to get warm."

"Good," Chisolm said. "It should feel like a heat pad for a few hours."

"That doesn't answer my question."

Chisolm slid the canister back into his pocket. "Well, let me put it this way. Do you remember when you were a kid and had a stuffy nose? Your mom probably put some of that vapor rub stuff on your chest before you went to bed, right?"

"My dad usually did stuff like that," Katie answered, "but yeah."

"Well, this is sorta like a Ben-Gay version of that. With a little aspirin mixed in." Chisolm shrugged, then added, "And a couple of herbal remedies I read about a few years ago."

Katie looked at him in wonder. "Wow, Tom. I never figured you for a medicine man."

Chisolm grinned broadly. Katie noticed that the thin white scar that ran from his temple to the corner of his mouth faded into his laugh lines a little when smiled like that.

"Once you hit forty, MacLeod, you look for relief anywhere you can find it," he said, lifting his pant leg and wiping the excess gel on his own lower calf. "See?"

"Old age and Russians that kick like Chuck Norris," Katie said. "An odd combination for a cure, even if it is magic juice."

Chisolm faked a scowl. "Who's old? I said forty." Then he smiled and tapped Katie lightly on the shoulder with his left hand. "Rest up, MacLeod. We're back at it tomorrow."

"Thanks," Katie said, her gratitude genuine. "And I will. See you tomorrow."

Chisolm winked at her, rose and left the ladies' locker room.

2321 hours

Tower sat in Crawford's office, rubbing his sleepy eyes. The heavy breathing of the Major Crimes Lieutenant irritated him, but he tried to hide his frustration.

"You sure hit a home run with that interview, Tower," Crawford said sarcastically.

Tower shrugged. "I'm not much of a diplomat."

"Why exactly is he in custody?"

"We tried to catch a trout and landed a perch."

"What the hell does that mean?"

Tower rubbed his eyes again. "It means he didn't do the rape, so we lost nothing there. And we have witnesses on the robbery attempt, so who cares what he says?"

"Nice attitude," Crawford said. "This task force of yours is not only crapping out, but it is causing collateral damage."

"Collateral what?"

"Collateral damage," Crawford repeated. "First, you've got MacLeod cranking off rounds under the bridge at no one. Now you're arresting Boris."

"MacLeod's thing was an accident," Tower said in a low voice. "And the Russian tried to rob our decoy."

"There was nothing accidental about MacLeod firing her duty weapon without cause. It was a choice."

"It was a reaction."

"It was a reaction that makes me wonder if you picked the right patrol officers to support your operation, detective," Crawford snapped. "And when I get called down here in the middle of the night on a goddamn attempted robbery call, something is definitely wrong."

"I'm sorry," Tower said. "There's only about two hundred thousand people in this city. Half are male. That leaves me one hundred thousand suspects. If you filter out non-whites and those too young or too old, that leaves about fifty thousand potential rapists. The odds that this particular guy will bite at our decoy aren't that great."

Crawford gave him a dark look. "I'm not interested in odds, Tower. I'm interested in results. You better figure something out."

"I'm working on it," Tower said.

"If you can't handle it, I can put a homicide detective in charge," Crawford told him.

Tower gritted his teeth. "It's my case. It'll make."

Crawford sighed and leaned back in his chair. "Then what's your next move?"

"We tried south of Clemons Park and it didn't work. We'll try to the north of it next." He peered at Crawford through sleepy eyes. "What are you going to do about MacLeod's A.D.?"

"Never mind. Concentrate on catching your bad guy."

"I just don't want that hanging over her, is all," Tower said. "Distracting her."

"If she's distracted, replace her."

"I don't want to replace her. She's good."

"Good at what?" Crawford snapped. "Killing rats or getting robbed?"

"No," Tower said, his voice tightening up. "She's good at looking like a victim. She's good bait."

"Everybody has to be good at something, I guess."

Tower clenched his jaw. *Why does Crawford have to be such an insufferable prick every day of his life?*

"Meanwhile," the lieutenant said, "keep her focused or replace her. I'll tell you what we'll do about the A.D. after I meet with the Captain."

"I thought this was your operation."

"Watch it, Tower."

Tower held up his hands in a peaceful gesture. "I'm just asking."

"What you're being is a smart ass," Crawford snarled. "Besides, it *is* my operation. But MacLeod is Patrol, so I'll let the Patrol Captain decide what's to be done about her accidental discharge."

Tower nodded his understanding.

And I'm sure the two of you will make that decision over a couple of stogies in his office. You prick.

"Anything else you want to say, Tower?"

"No, sir."

Crawford nodded. "All right, then. Have there been any other developments in your case, besides the screw-ups by your task force team?"

"None," Tower told him sullenly.

"No lab results? Nothing from Crime Analysis?"

"Nope."

"Any tips?"

"Nothing credible."

Crawford swore and rubbed his eye. When he'd finished, he looked up at Tower. He seemed to appraise the detective for a few moments, then said, "Go home and get some sleep. You look like shit."

"Thanks, boss," Tower dead-panned.

"I'm serious," Crawford said. "Get some sleep."

Tower rose from his chair. "I will," he said, and left.

He planned to do exactly what Crawford ordered. He just wanted to stop by his desk and review the files once more. In case he missed something.

When he'd settled into his chair and switched on the desk lamp, he figured maybe he'd check for any Field Interview Reports from patrol, too. And he might as well check on a few tips while he was at it. Just in case.

He wouldn't be long.

Fifteen, twenty minutes. Tops.

But it was almost three in the morning when he finally switched out the light at his desk and drove home on deserted streets. As he stood undressing in the darkness of his bedroom, he could hear Stephanie's light, rhythmic breathing. He slid in next to her, kissed her bare shoulder and fell asleep in less than ten seconds.

THIRTEEN

Monday, April 22nd
Day Shift
0812 hours

Lieutenant Alan Hart proofread his first of his two reports to the Chief of Police. The complaint against O'Sullivan and Battaglia flowed nicely, laying out the facts of the complaint and his findings in a clear, succinct, but complete fashion. His eyes flicked over the familiar words, slowing down at the RECOMMENDATION section long enough to enjoy his own prose.

Clearly, both officers employ a great deal of irreverent humor in the course of their daily work. While humor is a common response to stress and can provide some relief to the tension associated with police work, it is not appropriate for officers to direct it maliciously toward the citizenry. The testimonial evidence uncovered in this case leads this investigator to the unavoidable conclusion that both officers are guilty of doing exactly that with regard to Mr. Elway, the complainant. Not only was Mr. Elway ridiculed and insulted, but this occurred while he was attempting to report a felony crime.

This investigator does recommend a finding of FOUNDED with respect to the complaint of POOR DEMEANOR and INADEQUATE

RESPONSE. This finding should be entered for both officers. This investigator recommends the following sanctions: One (1) day suspension for Officer O'Sullivan and a three (3) day suspension for Officer Battaglia. The difference in the sanction is justified due to the use of profanity by Officer Battaglia.

Nothing Follows.

Lieutenant Hart smiled. It was a well-written summary. Hopefully, the Chief would see things his way. These two clowns needed to get a firm message from management. Police work was not a big joke, no matter how much they might think so. A suspension might just get their attention. If it didn't, well then it was a nice springboard to termination if they didn't get with the program.

He closed the file and slid it into a confidential envelope. Then he reached for the Chisolm file, which he'd just completed earlier that morning. While he wished he'd been able to find a bigger hammer for this one, he figured he'd just have to settle for what the case gave him.

He flipped open the file and skimmed his report. Once again, he slowed at the RECOMMENDATION section and read carefully.

Officer Chisolm's speed may have been justified, given the nature of the call which he was assigned to assist. However, if one concedes that the response speed was appropriate, it naturally follows that the officer should have engaged his emergency equipment. The use of overhead lights is the lowest acceptable measure, though the intermittent use of a siren to clear traffic may have also been in order, depending upon traffic control devices and the number of civilian vehicles present.

This precaution may or may not have occurred to Officer Chisolm, but in either event, he did not utilize this equipment as per policy. Rather than address this fact in his interview, he chose instead to become defensive and shift blame. As the transcript indicates, Officer Chisolm focused upon the criminal record of the complainant instead of his own actions. Although he rightfully identified the nature of the complainant's offense, that fact had no bearing on the question of this investigation – did Officer Chisolm drive in an unsafe manner without using the appropriate emergency equipment as outlined in Policy 44A? The evidence clearly answers this question emphatically in the affirmative.

Given that this transgression is firmly established, what should the sanction be? Under most circumstances, with no mitigating factors, this investigator would recommend a written reprimand for the involved officer. However, Officer Chisolm has shown a history of working outside of policy, flaunting rules and displaying considerable disrespect to his superior officers. This behavior can be, and frequently is, contagious. Additionally, this investigator saw very pointedly during the interview process that Officer Chisolm did not believe he had done anything wrong. He certainly did not express any remorse or accept any level of accountability for his actions. Therefore this investigator recommends a harsh sanction—a five (5) day suspension.

Hart smiled grimly. He knew five days was excessive, but it was a calculated play on his part. Any more than five days might start to seem ridiculous and would probably be rejected outright by the Chief. But by recommending a five day suspension, he'd planted the seed that a suspension was warranted. The Chief might – probably would – reduce the sanction to one or two days, thinking he was going easy on Chisolm. And that played right into Hart's hands.

Of course, if he had his way, he'd have fired a malcontent like Chisolm a long time ago.

But he wasn't Chief.

Yet.

Hart smiled. A stint in Internal Affairs looked great on a résumé when you walked into a promotional evaluation for the rank of captain. Especially a résumé that showed that the time spent in IA was an active one.

Yes, he'd make captain next time around. And the irony that he'd make it off of holding certain officers – two clowns and a burnout – accountable was not lost upon him.

Hart slipped the Chisolm file into a confidential folder. He glanced through the small window in his office. Outside, a light misty rain was spitting water against the glass. He stood and reached for his raincoat. His smile spread across his face for a moment before he forced his expression back to neutral.

It wouldn't do to look as if he *enjoyed* delivering these files to the Chief. Even if, in fact, he *did*.

No, a future captain had to keep up appearances.

Hart opened the office door and stepped out to do his duty.

2232 hours

He sat in the small lounge, reading through the editorial page a second time. In addition to the scathing Op Ed article about the police keeping a serial rapist a secret, there were several letters to the editor. The ones that expressed outrage at the police were amusing, but there was the one that caught his interest. He read it over and over.

Dear Editor:

I hope that the River City Police Department understands what it is like to live in fear of a man like the Rainy Day Rapist. Never knowing when he might strike. Looking into every face with suspicion. Afraid to live our lives the way we want to out of a perverse terror that at any moment we might become a victim.

This doesn't just change my life every day. It destroys my ability to live.

V. Rawlings.

He smiled.

This wasn't something he intended. He'd considered that he may have to outduel the police once things started rolling. Some bitches just didn't know how to keep their mouths shut and it was inevitable that law enforcement would get involved.

But the press? This was...unanticipated. And while he hated the current incarnation of his nickname in the media, he knew it would change soon. After he laid the whammo on the next one. More of a whammo than his father ever laid on any bitch, that was certain.

This next one would be almost like the first again, he mused, lifting his drink to his lips. He sipped the cognac (a gentleman's drink, something else his father would never achieve nor understand), savoring the smooth bite of the alcohol. He'd only meant to have one, but then he got to reading the newspaper article, then the Op Ed and finally the letters to the editor. Especially the one written by V. Rawlings.

He wondered what the 'V' stood for.

Valerie? Vanessa? Veronica?

Victoria?

The last was his favorite of the lot, though he imagined that the pedestrian broad who wrote that letter was probably more of a Vicky than a Victoria.

He chuckled.

Vicky the whining bitch. That was probably it.

It didn't matter. What mattered was that she was afraid of him. He was – how had she put it? Not ruining her life, but destroying her ability to live.

That was very satisfying. Not as good as laying the whammo on those other women, but there was a certain fulfillment to knowing that he was affecting more than just one bitch at a time. They were all sisters, after all.

Just like *her*.

And now he was making them all feel it. Fear. Apprehension. An unsettling feeling in the pit of every one of their stomachs.

Well, as far as he was concerned, they could just reap it.

Fucking reap it.

And then some, because more was on the way.

He drained the last of his cognac, even though such an act was decidedly ungentlemanly. Three cognacs in, he didn't really care. Right now, he just wanted to get home and start planning for his next one.

The new *first* one.

2235 hours

Katie had refused to walk in the rain. When Tower argued with her briefly, she flat out told him that she wasn't going to catch pneumonia instead of a rapist. Tower relented and the group retreated to Mary's Café to wait out the downpour. They sat and talked idly about everything but police work – sports, movies, vacation plans, along with a little bit of department gossip. Tower noticed that MacLeod was quieter than Sully or Battaglia. She sat, fiddling absently with the fake headphone wires on the mock-up of a walkman that the tech guys had put together for her transmitter. He wondered if something might be wrong with her. Maybe she was stressing over the accidental discharge. Or some personal issue. Then he realized that Chisolm was just as quiet and that it had been Sully and Battaglia who carried most of the conversation. And the two of them could talk non-stop, especially when they were together.

When the rain let up half past ten, Tower laid down enough money on the table to cover everyone's coffee.

"Let's get to it," he told them.

Sully and Battaglia grumbled, but Chisolm nodded his thanks. Katie rose without a word. She adjusted the disguised transmitter as she stood.

"You still want to focus north of Clemons Park?" Chisolm asked.

"Yeah. Unless you've got a better idea?"

Chisolm shook his head. "No, that's as good as anywhere. It's all a shot in the dark, anyway."

"Glad you're so optimistic."

"Just realistic, Cochise."

Tower smiled at the nickname. He didn't know Chisolm very well, but he knew he only used terms like that with people he liked. Since he was pretty sure Crawford hated his guts, it was nice to have someone around who liked him.

"You and MacLeod can ride with me," he said. "We'll drop her about a block from the target area."

The group filed out of the diner.

2239 hours

His car warmed up quickly and he started north on Monroe. The arterial ran from downtown all the way north to the city limits, making it a convenient road for him. He only needed to get out of the low valley area surrounding The Looking Glass River, though. The first real hill came just a few blocks before Garland, another main arterial. He lived up above that first rise, on Atlantic just a block south of Garland.

He took a deep breath and let it out. A glimmer of irritation fluttered through him. He could feel the impact of the three cognacs he had at the lounge. While the effect wasn't unpleasant, the impairment irked him. He couldn't afford for some overly aggressive patrol officer to pull him over and arrest him for drunk driving.

He kept his car pointed carefully north and drove.

2240 hours

"This is good," Chisolm suggested.

Tower slowed but didn't stop. "You sure?"

Chisolm nodded. "We're right at the base of the hill here." He pointed. "Look, there's a minor tree line here for several blocks along Mona Street. Behind that, heavy bushes and some trees all the way up the hillside. No houses. It's a perfect location for an ambush."

Katie watched, fascinated with how quickly he evaluated the topography. A small chill went through her, though, when he mentioned the word 'ambush'.

As if sensing her unease, Chisolm shifted his gaze to her. "Don't worry. If we post up at opposite ends of this street, we should have good visibility. You'll have an eye on you the majority of the time."

"I'm not too comfortable with anything less than one hundred percent surveillance," Tower said.

"Probably not possible. But you've got the transmitter for whenever she's temporarily out of sight."

"I'll be okay," Katie said. She looked back and forth between the two men. "Really."

"All right," Tower said, giving in. He slid the receiver earphone plug into his ear. "Go ahead."

Chisolm opened the passenger door of the Toyota and slid out. Katie followed him. Once outside, she voice checked her fake walkman transmitter.

"Loud and clear," Tower reported.

Katie fired him a thumbs up.

"How's the leg?" Chisolm asked her.

Katie adjusted her fanny pack. "Still sore. But that goop really helped, whatever it was."

"I told you what it was. Magic juice."

"Right. Well, it helped. Thanks, Tom."

Chisolm grinned. "Good hunting," he told her.

Katie took a deep breath. She hunched her shoulders and looked down at the ground in front of her. Then she began to half-limp, half-shuffle toward Mona Street.

Behind her, she heard the Toyota truck door close. Tower's voice floated across the wet air to her.

"Magic juice, Tom?"

"Shut up, Tower."

Katie smiled and limped forward.

2244 hours

At the last minute, he decided to cut over to Post Street. It ran closer to Atlantic. The Garland Theater was at the corner of Monroe and Garland, anyway. This time of night, there'd be a show getting out and he didn't want to get caught up in that traffic.

He slowed for Cora Street, but refused to turn there. The very sight of the letters on the white street sign sent a surge of rage barreling through his chest and out to his fingers. He didn't want to think of the name Cora. He didn't want to hear the name. He certainly didn't want to drive down a street named for that worthless bitch of a mother.

Looking down, he saw that his knuckles were white where he gripped the steering wheel. One at a time, he let go and flexed his fingers, trying to work out the angry tension. In the process, he passed by Cora Street and continued north.

The next street was Mona Street.

He turned right.

2245 hours

A pair of headlights washed over her from behind. This time of night, there wasn't a lot of traffic on this residential side street. This was only the fourth set of headlights to spotlight her like this.

Katie didn't care for the vulnerable feeling it gave her. As each car approached, she felt at a complete disadvantage. The people in the car could see her clearly. The most she ever saw were shadowy silhouettes as the vehicle passed by.

She sighed, letting that sense of vulnerability flow through her. She hoped that it made her look even weaker to anyone that drove by.

* * *

Look at this.

From behind, he saw the slender form shuffling along, head bowed. No confidence there. And as he drew closer, he spotted the walkman clipped to her waistband. This one would be so easy...

No. It was too easy. And he hadn't planned for it. Best to stick to the plan. That was how he'd had success so far.

Still...

He cruised past her as slowly as he dared without attracting attention. He angled his head to get a good look at her while pretending to adjust his radio.

She was pretty.

And she looked scared.

He continued onward, his internal debate raging.

* * *

"How about that one?" Tower asked aloud, even though he knew MacLeod couldn't hear him. The wire was a one-way transmitter.

Even so, she spoke aloud as if anticipating his question. "Nothing there. Silver four door Tempo or Topaz. Guy didn't even look at me. He was fiddling with his radio."

Tower cursed. He broadcasted the information to Sully and Battaglia, who answered him with a dismissive click of the mike.

He sighed. It was going to be a long and fruitless night, he could tell.

✸   ✸   ✸

He turned onto Post and drove north for a block, his mind racing. The arguments played themselves out in his head, one concern at a time.

There were plenty of trees all along that street. Only a couple of houses over the entire three blocks and all of them were dark.

But she might continue on across Post. Or she might even turn up the steep hill, especially if she's out for exercise.

She might. But she might turn around and head back along Mona Street. If she did, the site was too perfect to pass up.

There's too many people.

No. It was almost eleven at night. It's cold, dark and the tail end of a rainy day. There's hardly anyone else out.

No. It's not smart. You've got to plan.

He set his jaw. Planning was important, but sometimes opportunities occurred that weren't part of the plan. A smart man took advantage of these opportunities.

That's the cognac talking.

No, he decided. It wasn't.

It wasn't the cognac at all. It was the new him. And that unlucky bitch just made his new self one lucky man.

He turned onto Glass Street and pulled his car to the curb just around the corner. A half block up the street was one lonely, dark house. Below him lay a tumble of bushes and a few scattered trees before the small thicket of trees that lined Mona Street.

At first, he reached for the glove compartment for his ski mask. Then he stopped. He wouldn't need that precaution any more, would he? He looked down at his hands, flexing them wide open and back into fists. No, he wasn't going to have to worry about this one telling tales on him. Not once he laid these hands on her.

He exited the car. The fresh air filled his lungs. He smiled because even the world smelled new to him.

2249 hours

"My fingers are getting cold," Katie murmured, knowing Tower could hear her on the other end of the transmitter. She imagined him sitting in the truck with Chisolm, the white plug stuck in his ear.

Warm and cozy in that truck, she corrected herself. While she was out here like a worm dangling on a hook, hoping that a shark came along to take a bite.

And on top of that, she had cold fingers.

"I'm going to have to start jogging to keep warm," she said in to the transmitter.

Of course, that was hardly true. The street took a decidedly uphill swing as she approached Post. The effort she expended climbing up the rise kept her core warm enough. It was just her fingers that didn't benefit from the exertion.

Katie raised her hands to her mouth and blew on them. When she reached Post, she paused and looked around. It took her several moments to spot Tower's Toyota truck. He'd picked a good spot, nestled between two other parked cars on the side of the street. From there, she figured they had a good view of her for most of her route along Mona Street. The only blind spot might be the area she'd just trekked up, but Sully and Batts would be able to see her from their end.

"One more pass," she said quietly. "Then we're going for some more coffee."

Tower flashed his headlights, indicating he'd heard her transmission.

Katie turned and started back west on Mona Street.

2250 hours

Walking through the bushes soaked his clothing with a freezing wetness, causing him to shiver. He ignored the sensation and pressed on. The cognac kept him warm inside. He'd be taking a hot shower soon enough, anyway.

He spotted her coming back westbound from crest of the rise to Post Street. A thrill shot through his limbs, causing a sudden erection.

He'd been right.

He crept past a leafy bush and stepped behind a wide pine tree near the base of the small rise.

He crouched and watched her shuffle toward him.

He waited.

2251 hours

Katie breathed onto her frigid fingers again. She decided that she didn't want coffee, after all. On a night like tonight, some hot cocoa was in order. She'd forgo any marshmallows or whipped cream in the interests of not appearing too girlish in the presence of her platoon mates, but secretly she was glad that she could do girl things like that on occasion.

Right now, she marveled at the absolute reverse chivalry at work in this operation. All four men were sitting in dry, warm cars while the sole woman on the team was trudging back and forth on wet pavement in the cold.

Well, Katie thought, *we wanted equality. If this is how it feels, then I guess this is how it feels.*

As she shuffled down the rise, she leaned back slightly to slow her descent. Her bruised quadriceps protested with small yelps of soreness.

There's another point for equality, she thought. That Russian hadn't even hesitated before blasting her in the leg. Even the criminals had left chivalry by the wayside in favor of equality.

Katie caught her toe in a crack in the asphalt, causing her to stumble. She windmilled her arms and regained her balance before she fell to the ground. She winced as the sudden movement put all of her weight momentarily on her injured leg.

She stopped and took a moment to catch her breath. Flexing and stretching her left leg, she thought about asking Chisolm for another dose of his magic juice.

* * *

Why was she stopping?

He watched her intently from twenty yards away. His body pressed against the tree in front of him. The odor of wet bark filled his nostrils, but he was already imagining the smell of her fear.

She'd stumbled and almost fell. Now she stood in the street, working her left leg as if testing the muscle. He admired her athletic form, resenting it at the same time. She probably thought she was something special, this one. She definitely needed to be knocked down a notch or two.

Still, what about the leg? Did she pull something when she tripped? It didn't look like that bad of a stumble, but you never knew.

A weak leg meant a weak runner.

This was going to be easier than he thought.

* * *

"That didn't sound good," Tower said.

"What did it sound like?"

"Like she fell down or something," Tower said. He raised the field glasses to his eyes and scanned the dark street in front of him. "I can't see her, either."

"Those aren't worth much of a damn at night," Chisolm told him.

"I don't care if all I see is a shadow, as long as I know it's her." Tower lowered the glasses and shook his head. "I'm not seeing anything."

"Check with the others."

Tower raised the radio to his mouth. "Ida-409 to Adam-122."

"Go ahead."

"Do you have a visual on MacLeod?"

"Affirm. She's near the base of the rise that leads up to Post."

Tower copied, looked over at Chisolm and shrugged. "Sorry. Paranoid, I guess."

Chisolm grinned. "Don't be. A healthy dose of paranoia is the reason I'm sitting here and not in some military cemetery."

2252 hours

He hesitated.

While she'd been stretching, her athleticism first irritated him. Then it set him thinking. Athletic people tended to be more confident than their sedentary counterparts. And she looked like she was in too good of shape to employ walking as a means of fitness.

When she finished stretching and resumed walking, he smiled to himself. Her shoulders slumped. He eyes fell. Even her walk was an insecure shuffle.

Maybe she hurt her knee. Maybe this was how she was rehabbing it. That would explain why the small trip worried her so much.

That made sense. And just because she was in good shape didn't mean she wasn't weak. The way she moved, it was obvious that something had happened to her in her past. Maybe she'd been some sort of victim before. If that were so, he was certain that she'd be more scared in the next five minutes than any other time in her pitiful, waste of a life. At least she'd have the opportunity to take part in his new beginning. At least she'd accomplish something in the brief moments left to her in this world.

He took in a deep breath. Things were falling into place nicely.

*   *   *

Katie focused on the small pools of water collected in puddles along the roadway as she shuffled slowly along. She drew her cold fingers into her middle and allowed herself to think about how good that hot cocoa was going to taste in about twenty minutes.

She wondered who would pony up and pay for the cocoa. She figured it would be a dead heat between Tower and Chisolm. Battaglia was too self-centered and Sully would be too conscious of the fact that they were both single. He wouldn't want to send mixed messages. It was an unfortunate by-product of all the sexual harassment training that officers went through. A cup of coffee sometimes just can't be a cup of coffee.

Katie figured Tower would still buy the cocoa because it was his operation and Chisolm would do it because...well, because he was Tom Chisolm. He just did things like that.

Her mind drifted to the events in the park two nights ago. She still hadn't heard from any of the brass what was going to happen with her accidental discharge under the overpass. Tower told her before shift that he'd reported the incident to Lieutenant Crawford, who was going to discuss it with Captain Reott, the Patrol Captain. After that, who knew what—

The movement surprised her. The flash of shadow made her gasp. Before she could react, an arm had already snaked around her throat and pulled her tight against the body that appeared behind her.

She struggled, trying to reach for her fanny pack, but the attacker's other arm wrapped around her chest and squeezed.

Her breath left her.

He grabbed onto her right wrist and drew him to her.

She felt his hardness grinding into her buttocks through his clothing and hers.

Katie froze.

* * *

"What the–?" Sully raised his binoculars.

Battaglia stirred next to him. "What?"

The scene through his binoculars was dark and difficult to make out. He saw a flash of shadow near the sidewalk, but it seemed to disappear into the trees.

He lowered the binoculars. "I can't see her. Check with Tower."

* * *

"Adam-122 to Ida-409."

Tower raised the portable radio and answered, "Go ahead."

"We've lost our visual on her. Do you have an eye?"

Tower shot an alarmed look at Chisolm. Then he answered, "No. She hasn't come back into view yet once she headed down the rise."

"Copy. We should roll in and check it out."

Tower considered for a moment. If they rolled in and all was fine, they risked blowing the cover of the operation. But that didn't matter if MacLeod were in danger. And besides, if all was well, who was really going to see that the operation was burned?

He pressed the transmit button. "Let's go."

* * *

"Don't you move, bitch," he grunted into her ear.

Katie's knees went weak. Terror enveloped her as if she'd plunged into a freezing lake. Unable to think or move, she felt herself drift toward the bottom.

It was him.

The Rainy Day Rapist.

But to her ears, he spoke with Phil's voice.

Her heels drug across the sidewalk and into the brush.

* * *

The words broadcasted over the transmitter were scratchy and distant, but they still managed to send a shock wave through Tower.

"Don't you move, bitch."

"Oh, God," he breathed.

"Go!" Chisolm hollered at him, ripping his pistol from its holster. "Go, go, *go!*"

Tower started the truck, racing the engine. He slammed it into gear and punched the accelerator.

* * *

Ten more yards.

Ten more and then he was going to make this bitch pay. Tear her clothes away. Fuck her like she's never been fucked before. Lay the whammo on her.

All the way.

His breath came quickly as he dragged her into the foliage.

2253 hours

His grip around her body was stifling. She could barely breathe. She stared out into the darkness, but it was the shadows of the past that washed over her.

Her own pleas.

Don't do this.

His forceful replies.

You'll do whatever the fuck I tell you to do, bitch.

And afterward, the condemnation.

You liked it. Don't forget that.

A wet, leafy bush raked across her face, spilling cold water onto her cheek and down her neck. His ragged, excited breathing rang in her ears. His hardness bumped and grinded against her backside as he pulled her deeper into the brush.

Katie tried to cry out, but nothing happened. She felt strangely paralyzed, her limbs and mouth refusing to obey the weak commands that came from her mind.

Am I going to die?

*   *   *

He stopped near a pine tree. It was far enough away from the street to be out of sight through the other bushes and trees. And this one seemed too scared to scream for help. Just in case, he released her wrist and grabbed a handful of hair. With a jerk, he pulled her head back.

"I'm going lay the whammo on you, bitch," he whispered directly into her ear. "If you make a sound, I *will* kill you. You understand?"

The woman didn't respond.

He yanked hard on her hair, pulling her head further back.

"Fucking answer me!"

*   *   *

Katie felt no pain, only pressure. When he jerked her hair, it forced her head back. She stared up at the dark expanse of the sky. There were no stars visible through the cloud cover.

"Fucking answer me!" he growled in her ear.

Still unable to speak, she bobbed her head slightly in understanding. But in that moment, she felt a tickle of warmth in the pit of her stomach.

Fear melted away.

Who the hell do you think you are, you piece of shit?

The tickle became a flare and the flare turned into a blaze. Voices from the past echoed through the wet brush that surrounded her.

Don't be a goddamn tease.
You liked it. Don't forget that.
At least you weren't a virgin.

Hot rage engulfed her.

*   *   *

He felt her try to nod her head in submission. That was all he needed from her before taking care of business.

With a hard shove, he threw her face-first into the ground. He heard her grunt as she landed. Even that modest amount of pain made him feel good. Of course, it was nothing compared with what was to come.

He dropped on top of her, straddling her just below her buttocks. Leaning forward, he pressed his left hand onto her upper back, pinning her to the earth. With his free hand, he reached for her waistband.

She squirmed beneath him. Without hesitation, he threw a hard punch into her kidneys. She let out a yelp as the blow landed.

He grabbed her waistband at the small of her back and tore it downward.

She twisted underneath him, scrambling onto her side.

"Stop moving, bitch!" he said through gritted teeth.

"Fuck you," she growled back.

The words surprised him. So did the tone. There was fire in those two words. He felt it radiating upward toward him.

A white fury swept over him.

How *dare* she?

He slid upward, straddling her waist. Ignoring her struggling, he cocked his fist and began raining punches down on her head and face.

"You want the whammo, bitch, you got it."

*   *   *

The first blow stunned her. She didn't see it coming, but only felt the raw force collide with her forehead. She battled with a dark fog that seemed to be settling in across her vision.

"You want the whammo, bitch, you got it," she heard him say.

Reflexively, she raised her own hands to fend off his punches. The next one landed on her forearm, followed by a shot that she caught on the wrist. That punch drove the heel of her own palm into her mouth.

Katie twisted and moved, trying to avoid each punch as they came out of the darkness.

*　*　*

Most of his punches weren't landing solidly, but he didn't care. The sheer exhilaration of raining his hatred down on this worthless bitch filled every part of his being. If it took another dozen blasts for him to catch her with one that put her out, so be it.

It felt good.

No.

It felt *great*.

Perfect.

Fulfilling.

He raised his fist for another punch.

That was when he heard the unmistakable sound of tires screeching to a halt, followed by slamming doors. Yells came next, several voices at once.

"Straight through there!"

"Katie!"

"Police!"

Police? How the hell did they get here so quick?

Flashlights darted through the darkness. The beams bounced and bobbed in his direction.

He turned to look down at the nearly defenseless form beneath him.

She twisted and rose toward him. Then he saw stars.

*　*　*

The punches stopped suddenly. In that brief moment, she heard tires on asphalt. Doors slammed. Familiar voices called out to her.

She moved without thinking, twisting underneath him. She torqued her body, forcing herself upward from lying on her side. As she reached a sitting position, she drove her elbow toward his head, following through like a baseball player swinging a bat.

Her elbow connected with something hard. Pain jolted through her arm, causing her to cry out again. Her arm fell to her side, sagging and useless.

* * *

The blow caught him behind the ear, stunning him.

Stars dancing in darkness paraded across his vision. He shook his head and the stars faded away quickly.

And his fury returned.

He realized she was sitting up, her face even with his chest. She was too close to hit with any force. He knew he had to run in the next few seconds or he'd be caught. But he wasn't going to let this bitch get away with hitting him.

He reached behind her again, grabbing a fistful of hair. With a powerful yank, he pulled her away from his chest, creating enough distance between them for him to blast her with his right fist.

He put everything he had into that one punch. He knew he was only going to get one, so it had to count. When it landed against her face, the force of the blow reverberated up and down his arm.

She went limp.

That felt wonderful. Better than sex.

Reluctantly, he released her head, letting her flop to the wet ground. Then he clambered to his feet and sprinted away. Behind him, the sound of men scrambling through the bushes and calling out –

"Katie!"

—filled the air.

He ran, joy and anger still coursing through his blood.

* * *

Tower was the one who found her. She lay stunned on the wet grass.

"MacLeod?" He knelt down next to her. "Give me some light!" he yelled out to whoever was nearby. Almost instantly, he and Katie were awash in a powerful flashlight beam.

"Is she all right?" Sully asked him.

Tower didn't answer. Her face was bruised and bloody, but the fact that her eyes were closed and her mouth slack concerned him even more.

"MacLeod?" he asked her again, giving her a gentle shake. When she didn't respond, he glanced toward the bright light. "Call for medics," he ordered.

* * *

Chisolm crashed through the wet bushes and past the dark trees. He tried to light up his path as much as possible, while still shining his light up ahead for a sign of the suspect. While he ran, he reached for his radio.

"Adam-112, foot pursuit!" he shouted into the portable radio.

"Adam-112, go ahead."

"In pursuit of a rape suspect," Chisolm bellowed into the mike. "We're Mona and Post, northbound through the wooded area."

"Copy."

Chisolm gulped in a breath as he side-stepped a large root and hustled around a tree. He paused and swept his light beam ahead of him again.

Nothing.

Think, Tom. He can't be that fast.

Chisolm glanced around. Maybe he was, but maybe not. He might have gone to ground, trying to hide in the bushes to avoid them. Either way, they needed to secure the area.

"I need a perimeter," he told Dispatch. "Get me units up the hill on Garland at Post and at Monroe." He figured that if he hadn't gone to ground yet, that perimeter might hem in the suspect.

Battaglia appeared at his side, breathing heavily. "You see anything?"

Chisolm shook his head.

"You hear anything?" Battaglia asked.

"Not with you talking," Chisolm said. He raised the radio to his mouth. "And start a K-9," he added.

He stood in the small wooded area and waited for the K-9. The sound of speeding police cars rushing past on Post and the reflection of the flashing red and blue lights as they zipped up the hill gave him some hope. If this guy had decided to hide, the dog would find him. If he'd continued to run, Chisolm's only hope was that he wasn't a fast runner. Hopefully, the perimeter would be in place quickly enough.

Constant chatter issued from his portable radio as the dispatcher and officers coordinated the perimeter positions. Chisolm knew it was necessary, but he was impatient to get on the air to inquire about Katie's condition.

A few minutes later, he heard the heavy steps of Shane Gomez, the K-9 handler. His partner, a jet black German Shepherd named Čert, ran toward Chisolm in desperate lunges. Every surge forward pulled Gomez along as he held onto the dog lead. Chisolm braced himself in case the dog mistook him for the suspect, but the muscular canine brushed past him without acknowledgement.

Gomez reined in his partner. "Čert!" he yelled, pronouncing it 'Chairt.' The dog whined back at him, then yelped his dissent. Gomez gave the lead a short, firm pull. "Sadni!" he ordered.

Čert reluctantly sat, but not before issuing two more angry barks at his handler.

Gomez grinned excitedly at Chisolm. His hair was just as black as his dog's and his large, muscular frame made Chisolm think of him as a human version of the K-9 he was partnered with.

"He's got a good scent," Gomez said. "Anything I need to know?"

Chisolm shook his head. "No known weapons. Last seen northbound."

Gomez gave him a short nod. "Okay. Cover me. And stay close."

"You bet."

Gomez turned his attention back to Čert. "Let's go, boy. Fuss him up. Get that bad guy!"

Čert yelped and lunged forward. Gomez and Chisolm scrambled after him, with Battaglia struggling to keep up.

"Still northbound through the woods," Chisolm reported to Dispatch. "Nearing Glass."

"Copy."

Chisolm kept pace with Gomez and Čert. The black dog was almost invisible in front of him. The only signs of his presence were the sound of his paws scrambling over the dirt and leaves and the deep huffs of his breath. Occasionally, he let out a yearning whine. Chisolm assumed that was to let his handler know he was still hot on the trail. Of course, with the demon dog, it could simply be a desire to catch up to his prey and get his crushing jaws wrapped around it.

The thought didn't disturb Chisolm at all. In fact, he hoped Čert went straight for the groin.

Battaglia had fallen back too far to be an effective cover officer. Chisolm kept his eyes trained to the left, right and behind of the K-9 handler. During a track, Gomez focused on his dog, reading the reactions to determine what the dog was sensing. That left him vulnerable. Chisolm's duty was to protect the handler. He kept his flashlight ready, but avoided using it. He didn't want to back-light Gomez, thereby making him an easy target.

"*Baker-126*," Chisolm's radio crackled. He recognized James Kahn's gravelly voice. "*I've got a vehicle that just crossed Post at Glass. Eastbound. You want me to break perimeter and stop it?*"

Gomez reined up with Čert. He turned to Chisolm. "It's your call," he said, barely breathing heavy. "But I've got a strong scent here."

Chisolm considered. If Tower was right and the guy lived in the area, the odds were that he'd try to run home. If that were the case, the dog would track directly to his front door. And if the perimeter managed to hem in the suspect, breaking that perimeter now would risk giving him an opening to escape through.

He raised the radio to his mouth. "Negative," he said. "Hold perimeter."

Gomez gave him a nod in agreement.

"*Copy*," Kahn replied. "*But if you've got any mobile units, have them check east of Post. There's not a lot of vehicle traffic out tonight.*"

"*Baker-127*," came Officer Hiero's voice. "*I got that, from Ruby and Sharp.*"

"That'll work," Chisolm said, slipping his radio back into the holder on his belt.

Čert whined impatiently.

"Let's go," Gomez said. "Get him, boy!"

2301 hours

"I don't need to go in an ambulance," Katie argued, her words slightly groggy.

Tower shook his head. "It's the medics' call, MacLeod."

"Then I'll refuse and they can A-M-A it."

"You can't invoke Against Medical Advice when you're on duty," Tower lied. "Just take the ride."

Katie's jaw set, followed by a wince. Tears formed in her eyes, though Tower couldn't tell if they were the result of pain, anger or perhaps embarrassment. Maybe some of all of them, he decided, and reached out to touch her hand.

"It'll be all right," he said in low voice that he hoped no one else besides the medics could hear.

Katie didn't answer, but after a moment she nodded in acquiescence.

Without hesitation, the medics raised the gurney and slid her into the ambulance. One medic crawled in after her while the second slammed the door behind them. The second medic turned to head toward the driver's door.

Tower grabbed his sleeve. "Which hospital?"

"Sacred Heart," the man answered.

Tower glanced down at his nametag. It read *A. Hoagland.*

"Is she going to be all right, Hoagland?" Tower asked.

Hoagland gave him a neutral look. "She took some heavy blows to the head. I think she has a concussion at the very least. They'll do some tests on her up at the hospital to see if she sustained any injuries more serious than that."

"But she'll be okay?"

Hoagland bit his lip. "It's hard to say with head injuries, but she's coherent now, so that's a good sign."

Tower clenched his jaw. "That doesn't sound too promising."

Hoagland reached down and removed Tower's grasp from his sleeve. "Head injuries are tricky, but she looks good right now." He put his hand on Tower's shoulder. "She looks like a fighter to me. I think she'll be all right."

Tower nodded.

"I've got to get her transported," Hoagland said. Without waiting for a reply, he turned and hurried to the driver's door. Within another moment, the ambulance's engine fired to life and it lumbered forward. Tower watched the flashing lights atop the large, white box approached Post, slow, then turned right and disappear down the hill.

2303 hours

Chisolm followed Gomez and Čert out of the bushes and onto the sidewalk. His uniform was soaking wet, but he ignored the chill. Čert charged eastward along the sidewalk. Gomez loped along behind him while Chisolm sprinted to keep up.

About twenty yards from the intersection, Čert stopped. He dropped his nose lower toward the ground, sniffing urgently. Chisolm stopped and drew in deep breaths while he waited. The street was clear of foot traffic. There were no cars. He glanced over his shoulder. There was a single house up the street without any exterior lighting. Other than that, all was clear.

The dog seemed to be wandering in a large circle, searching for scent. He whined again, but even Chisolm could hear that the sound was now frustration, not eagerness. A sinking feeling settled in his stomach.

Gomez didn't give up. He worked Čert up and down the sidewalk on both sides of the street for several minutes, trying to pick up the scent. They always returned to the same point on the sidewalk, where the dog finally sat down and let out an angry, mournful howl.

"Shit," Chisolm finally muttered.

Gomez sighed and ran his hand through his hair. "He must have jumped in a car, Tom. That's the only thing I can figure happened."

"Shit," Chisolm repeated. He realized that meant the car that Kahn had seen was probably the suspect. He raised the radio to his lips. "Secure the perimeter," he said.

"*Copy,*" the dispatcher replied. "*Secure the perimeter.*"

The two men stood on the wet sidewalk, brooding. Čert whined, his tone suggesting that he commiserated.

We almost had him. The thought throbbed in Chisolm's skull. *We almost had him and it's my fault he got away.*

Gomez knelt next to Čert and rubbed the dog's head. "You did a good job, boy," he whispered. "It's not your fault."

"Shit," Chisolm said a third time. He couldn't think of anything else to say.

2304 hours

At first, he'd fought the terrain, blasting through the bushes and bouncing off the trees. The water from the bushes he forced his way through soaked his clothes to the skin. That coldness jarred him enough. He put aside the absolute ecstasy that hummed through his body and tamped down the rage that was seething and bubbling beneath it. Instead, he focused on his escape.

Instead of blindly running, he dodged and slipped around trees and bushes. That sped up his progress considerably. When the hillside steepened, he leaned forward for balance, even using his hands to pull himself along.

He kept his ears piqued for the sound of pursuit, but for some reason it fell off almost right away. Had he outrun them? Outrun the *police*? That surprised him, but it made him smile in spite of the cold and the darkness around him.

He hurried forward.

He burst out the bushes and onto the street near his car. Without hesitation, he sprinted to the car, got in and started the engine. Then he sat for a moment, thinking.

Which way to go?

The police weren't stupid. They had radios. There would soon be cop cars all over the neighborhood. What would they be looking for? Probably a man on foot. But they had seen his car when he drove by. Would they remember it and make the connection? Did they write down his license plate? Take his picture?

He decided in an instant, flipping a quick U-turn on the small street.

It was too narrow for a complete turn, so he bounced up onto the sidewalk with his front tire. Once he was pointed back east, he drove forward. He paused briefly at the stop sign, then crossed Post and continued east at the speed limit.

He frowned as he drove. If they had his license plate, they'd soon have his address. Going home could mean walking into a trap.

This wasn't something he'd planned for. He never imagined his own home as a danger. Home was his sanctuary. He'd have to trust it was still safe.

Drive home. Throw his clothes in the washer. Shower. Think of an alibi.

If the cops came, he'd bluff. That was the only play he had right now. Later, maybe he could come up with a different plan for another time, but for now, he'd bluff.

His frown turned into a scowl. Did they have his picture?

Did that bitch get a look at his face?

He shook his head. It was too dark. She didn't see him.

He reached Atlantic Avenue and turned left. Two blocks later, he turned off his headlights and cruised quietly up the street. His block was still. Most of the lights inside the small ranchers and brick single story houses were turned out for the night. It was too cold for anyone to be sitting out on the front porch. No one would notice his stealthy approach.

He pulled into his driveway and shut off the engine. Before exiting the car, he took several deep breaths. Then he went inside.

2310 hours

Officer Paul Hiero turned onto Atlantic just as the order to secure the perimeter came over his radio. He frowned, knowing that meant the K-9 track had failed. Which meant the suspect had escaped.

He cruised slowly northbound along the residential street. Most of the lights inside the houses were turned off. Outdoor lights burned over the front doors of almost every porch. The occasional flicker of a television behind curtains told him that some people were still awake, but the majority of people in the neighborhood had already called it a night. That didn't surprise him. The neighborhood consisted largely of retired folks and working class families. The retired folks went to bed early because they were old. The working families had either school or a job to get to in the morning.

Hiero sighed. This was a waste of time. There was no way a scumbag rapist would live in a neighborhood like this.

Nonetheless, he drifted along the street, watching for any pedestrians or anything suspicious. There was nothing, just as he expected.

When he reached Garland, he stopped for the stop sign. He lifted the radio mike and spoke into it. "Baker-127, clear of the call."

"Copy, Baker-127."

He turned right and headed back east to Baker Sector.

FOURTEEN

Tuesday, April 23rd
Day Shift
0611 hours

Tower stood in his kitchen, staring at the small cactus in a coffee cup that was on the windowsill. That cactus was his sole contribution to the flora and fauna life in his home. All the rest came with Stephanie as she slowly moved in. As he sipped the strong coffee from his own cup, he ran the events of the previous night through his head.

He tried to work up some anger toward Kahn for not breaking perimeter to go after the car. Or at Chisolm for directing him not to. But in the end, he knew it had been the right decision. Besides, he'd been too worried about MacLeod's injuries to even be aware of the track. It wasn't until she'd been shuttled off to the hospital that he turned his attention to the activities around him.

He took a long sip of the brew in his cup. The bold blend overwhelmed his mouth with taste. As he swallowed and enjoyed the after-scent of the coffee, he decided that even if there had been mistakes made by the officers, it had been his task force. He should have foreseen the mistakes or prevented them. Or had a better plan.

The cactus on the windowsill looked dry. He supposed that was the cactus's nature, but that didn't stop him from reaching out and dribbling coffee over the top of the spiky bulb. The steaming hot liquid washed down the green cactus and darkened the dry earth beneath it.

A shuffling sound arose behind him.

"John, what're you doing?"

"Watering the plants," Tower said evenly.

Stephanie brushed past him toward the cupboard containing the coffee cups, leaving a trail of bed-warmth from her body in her wash. She poured herself a cup and sidled up next to Tower.

"You didn't get in 'til late last night," she said.

Tower grunted and took another sip.

"You should have woken me," Stephanie said, giving him a gentle nudge with her hip.

Tower sighed. "I was exhausted."

"What happened? Did you catch the guy?"

"Nope." Tower reached out and dribbled some more coffee onto the cactus.

Stephanie watched him. Then she said, "You know, some people believe that plants can feel pain. You could be burning the hell out of that poor cactus."

"Those people are idiots," Tower remarked. He gave the cactus one last splash of coffee. "Besides, cactuses are tough."

"Cacti," Stephanie corrected.

Tower sighed again, a tickle of irritation going through him. "Thanks. Are you getting into crosswords or something?"

"What?"

"Never mind." Tower drank the last of his coffee. He thought about pouring himself another cup but hesitated. He should get to work. Of course, he knew what was waiting for him there.

Questions.

And Lieutenant Crawford.

He poured another cup.

"I saw your sister yesterday," Stephanie said. "Little Ben sure is cute."

Tower smiled in spite of himself. His nephew was a cute kid, and he was proud of the boy. He didn't know if he'd ever have kids of his own, but somehow being an uncle to Ben made that concern less worrisome.

"Thought that'd make you smile," Stephanie said. Then she assumed a mock pout. "Although, it'd been nice if the prospect of waking me up for sex had done the same thing."

Tower leaned over and kissed her temple. "I really was exhausted, babe. And I had a bad night."

Stephanie leaned in and nestled into his chest. "Well, I'll tell you what. When you have bad nights like that and you're tired, wake me up anyway. I'll make your night better. And I'll even do most of the work."

Tower kissed the top of her head. "Okay. You got it." He kissed her head again, pausing to smell her hair. "Thanks," he whispered.

In that moment, it didn't matter to him that Crawford was probably already waiting to chew his ass at the office. Or that the Rainy Day Rapist was getting the better of him. For those few seconds, it didn't even matter that Katie MacLeod was up at the hospital. All that mattered was the scent of her hair and the closeness of her body.

"Thanks," he whispered again.

0630 hours

He sat at his kitchen table, staring down at his uneaten breakfast. The reality of his near capture the previous night settled in after he'd slept for a few hours. He'd been foolish to attempt something with no plan. And to risk doing it without his ski mask was doubly foolish. What if she'd seen his face?

The entire scenario played itself out behind his eyes. Spotting her while driving by. The rush to grab her. The quick response of the police. Her rebellious words—

Fuck you!

—once he had her in the wooded area rang in his ears. So did the beautiful sound of his fist slapping into her face. The memory of the sweet limpness of her body afterward still made his fingers and palms tingle hours later.

But he forced his mind to ignore that for a moment. He worked on the events some more, thinking things through. He supposed it was possible, though not probable, that there had been police officers that close simply by chance, but he doubted it. And one of them had called out a name.

"Katie," he breathed.

If they knew her name, then they knew who she was. So that meant she was with the police. Or she *was* police. Probably a decoy.

Yes, he decided. That was it. He'd fallen for a decoy.

The idea made him grind his teeth. Still, even with all their planning, his unplanned actions had won out. He'd escaped, leaving behind a limp body. Not a dead body, granted. But a limp one was pretty good for the time he'd had to work with.

So now their little ploy had failed. He knew their game. He could stop what he was doing. Maybe even move to a different city and start over.

The thought caused his jaw to clench even tighter. He didn't want to be dictated to by the police. He'd never considered them as rivals before because he'd been so focused on his work, but now he knew that was exactly what they were. Rivals. Enemies. And there was no way he was going to allow them to beat him. Especially not some bitch cop who thought she could trick him.

No. He'd stay. He'd just have to be more careful.

The first thing he needed to do was get them to stop with the decoys. After that, he needed to finish the job with this Katie the Cop bitch. The prospect of that made his whole body tingle.

Still, first things first. How to get rid of the decoys?

He stared down at his uneaten blob of scrambled eggs. Next to the plate was the *River City Herald*, still folded and unread. His mind drifted to the letter V. had written—

Was it really Victoria, he wondered. He thought so.

—the day before. He recalled how good the letter made him feel when he realized that at any given time, Victoria or some other bitch like her was walking around afraid of him.

He reached out and touched the newspaper. A thought struck him. He considered it for a few moments, liking the idea better and better the more he thought about it. Finally, he smiled.

It would work, he decided. He lifted his fork and scooped up his lukewarm eggs into his mouth, gobbling down his breakfast.

Then he rose from the table, found a coat and left the house in order to find a payphone.

0707 hours

Katie MacLeod stared up at the ceiling. The faraway beep of medical monitors seemed to echo down the quiet hallway. She imagined a four-foot bunny rabbit stepping lightly along on the red balls that each beeping sound created.

Beep.

Out her door.

Beep.

Down the hallway.

Beep.

Past the nurse's station.

She blinked. She took a deep breath. The sound of the air sucking into her lungs sounded like a hurricane.

A small voice in the back of her mind screamed out, "You're loopy, MacLeod. You're doped up!" but she brushed the voice away with a giant light blue feather. The effort made her exhale, then swallow. That seemed to take five minutes. And it created another hurricane, followed by a waterfall.

A stocky nurse bustled into the room. "How are we this morning?" she asked in a blasting, cheery voice that seemed harsh against all of the softness in Katie's world.

"Gooooood," Katie managed to reply. She'd wanted to tell this loud, happy woman all of the secrets of the world that she'd discovered, but she didn't know how to put those colors and sounds into words.

The nurse glanced at her chart. "Mmm-hmmm. I'll bet. Well, just so you're aware, the doctor has ordered us to taper off your magic juice by noon."

Magic juice? Katie flashed to the women's locker room at the police station. Chisolm's rough hands digging into the little jar. The heat on her leg.

Was Chisolm a doctor? Was he *her* doctor?

Of course he was. That made sense. Chisolm took care of things.

Chisolm was always there.

Chisolm was a four foot bunny who could dance on red balls down *any* hallway.

"The doctor will be in himself once your test results are in," the nurse said. "Until then, you just rest, okay? We'll check in with you every so often, all right?"

She wanted to tell her that Chisolm could just make more magic juice if she needed it. He had plenty of beeps. And besides that, she had just figured out where God really came from. She couldn't wait to explain it to Chaplain Marshall, who would be disappointed that Captain Jean-Luc Picard wasn't somehow involved.

"Goooooood," Katie said.

0714 hours

Pam Lincoln rubbed her tired eyes. Being the crime beat reporter meant a lot of late nights. Most police action that was newsworthy took place in the evening hours, so she was up monitoring her scanner. She kept her pager and cell phone at her bedside even after she turned in, just in case she got a call. Not only did she have a few officers who were willing to tip her to the events that might make the cops look good, there were a couple of disgruntled ones who let her in on the more scandalous occurrences as well. Plus she had half a dozen stalwart citizens from both sides of the pro-police/anti-police fence who also monitored the scanner frequencies. Not much occurred without her getting at least a whisper of it.

Despite the need for late nights, her editor required her to be at her desk every day at seven sharp. He didn't seem to care that her work carried her until at least midnight every night or that she was frequently woken up in the middle of the night to cover something big. He was an old school journalist who idolized two things: Walter Cronkite and a seven A.M. start time.

Pam sipped her triple-shot vanilla latté through two skinny straws. She thanked the coffee gods for caffeine and the fact that there was a drive-through latté stand approximately every fifty yards in River City. Seattle may have been the birthplace of the 1990s coffee craze, but River City certainly embraced the notion.

As she got her oral caffeine infusion, she reviewed her notes. There wasn't much from the previous night.

There'd been a violent domestic dispute in Browne's Addition, but she'd already written up the brief paragraph on that story. Except for the names and the address, it could fit any dozen other domestic violence assaults she'd reported in the past three years.

On the north side, officers were briefly in foot pursuit of a rape suspect, but that petered out before she'd been able to get to her car. The only real interesting aspect of that call was that an ambulance had responded. She wondered if the Rainy Day Rapist had struck again, but she doubted it. Captain Reott had assured her that she'd get a call any hour if there were any developments on that case.

That left a vehicle pursuit which occurred out in the County. The suspect had been a four-wheel drive truck that simply went off road and lost the Deputy Sheriff, who couldn't follow in his Chevy Caprice. That might make for a mildly humorous piece, but Pam didn't think it was worth embarrassing the Deputy. It never was, in her mind. Unlike some of her colleagues, she knew that cops were people, too, just like everyone else – not simply convenient targets.

So all in all, she had a puny paragraph about a DV to hand into Mr. Seven O'Clock.

Her phone rang. She glanced down at the caller ID, but didn't recognize the number. She lifted the receiver.

"Pam Lincoln, River City Herald."

There was a pause. She could hear the flow of traffic in the background and guessed immediately that her caller was on a payphone.

She squinted. Now, why would someone call her on a payphone? Leaning forward, flipping open her notepad and fished around in her drawer for a pen.

"Hello?" she repeated, her interest piqued. She found her pen. Quickly, she held it poised above the steno pad.

"You wrote the piece about the Rainy Day Rapist," a male voice said. Something sounded wrong in the tone and inflection, but for a moment, she couldn't pinpoint what it was.

"Yes," she answered, "I did."

The voice fell silent again. A car horn honked in the background.

"Can I help you with something?" she asked in her most open voice.

He chuckled. "Yes. Yes, I think you can." He paused a moment. She figured out what was wrong with the voice. He was trying to disguise it somehow. She started to make a note of that on her steno pad.

That's when he dropped his bombshell.

0741 hours

The Chief of the River City Police Department sat at his desk, his hands folded on his lap. Across from him sat Captain Michael Reott of the Patrol Division and the head of Major Crimes, Lieutenant Crawford.

"I'm not sure these answers are satisfactory," he told the both of them. "In fact, I have to tell you that, in my opinion, they're not."

Crawford squirmed in his seat, his lip curled up as if he were about to deliver a retort. The Chief looked at him placidly, waiting to see if he said anything, but ultimately the Lieutenant remained silent.

The Chief turned to Reott. "You're the ranking officer here. Explain to me why this occurred."

Reott didn't blink. "Sir, at each stage of this operation, Lieutenant Crawford assessed the situation. He took into consideration the officers who were involved, what actually occurred and what was at stake. In each case, he determined that the best course of action was to press on and continue with—"

"Do you agree?" The Chief asked him. Crawford wasn't Reott's immediate subordinate, but he was pretty sure he knew how the Captain would answer.

"Absolutely," Reott told him without hesitation. "He made the best decision at the time with the information available to him at the time."

The Chief wasn't surprised. Still, he asked, "When exactly were you made aware of these decisions?"

"As soon as it was practical," Reott answered.

"*Specifically*," The Chief said, "when?"

"No later than the following morning. Earlier, in some cases."

The Chief nodded. Reott had always been a stand-up leader when it came to his troops, so his response was exactly what The Chief had expected. He admired the Captain's loyalty. Still, he was disappointed at the turn of events.

"Just so I'm clear," he said, "let's recap how this task force has progressed."

Crawford clenched his jaw and exhaled heavily, but Reott's expression remained impassive.

The Chief continued. "The team was out for three total nights. The first night, no rapist. But MacLeod has an accidental discharge under the Washington Street Underpass. And yet she goes back out again the next night anyway. The second night, no rapist again. And MacLeod is assaulted in an attempted robbery. Even after that, she goes out again a third night. This time, we actually get *the* rapist. But the cover team blows it and MacLeod ends up in the hospital while the rapist gets away." The Chief rested his elbows on his desk and steepled his fingers in front of him. "Does that about sum things up?"

"No," Crawford began, but Reott cut him off.

"Yes, sir," the Patrol Captain said in an even voice. "That is what occurred."

Crawford looked away and sighed heavily, but said nothing.

The Chief gave him an appraising look. "You know, Mike, I'm not a detective anymore. But I was at one time, years and years ago. Back in those days, we learned all about behavioral cues. And I have to tell you, as rusty as I am, it still looks like the Lieutenant here has something to say."

He smiled humorlessly at Crawford. In his peripheral vision, he saw Reott turn to the Major Crimes Lieutenant as well.

Crawford stewed for a moment, as if engaged in an internal debate. He glanced at Reott, then leaned forward. "It's not as clear cut as all that, Chief."

The Chief held up both his palms. "Educate me, then."

Crawford wiped the sweat from his lip and cleared his throat. "Well, I'll deal with things in the same order you did, I suppose. For starters, not getting a bite from the rapist that first night was expected. It'd be like winning the lottery to catch the guy the first time out."

The Chief made what he hoped was an expression of mild agreement.

"The A.D.," Crawford continued, "was just nerves. MacLeod was in a dark place and there was movement. She shot a rat."

"And what if it had been a bum?" The Chief asked.

"A transient," Reott corrected.

"When I talk to the camera, they're transients," The Chief said, unfazed. "In this office, they're bums." He turned to Crawford. "Answer the question, Lieutenant."

"If it were a bum," Crawford said, "MacLeod would have killed him."

The Chief nodded.

"And," Crawford added, "if my aunt had balls, she'd be my uncle."

The Chief raised his eyebrows, but said nothing. His silence seemed to embolden Crawford, who pressed forward.

"I told the Captain about the accidental discharge. He was considering a summary judgment in the matter rather than sending it to Internal Affairs."

"Which means?" The Chief asked, his voice sounding a little tight to him.

"Which means a formal letter of reprimand."

"How does that impact her?"

Reott answered before Crawford could speak. "According to Lieutenant Saylor, she's just been given a position as a Field Training Officer. A formal reprimand would revoke her FTO status for six months."

The Chief pursed his lips. That actually seemed a little harsh to him, but he left it alone for the time being.

Crawford pressed on. "The second night was just bad luck. There's no way the team could have predicted a robbery attempt. The coverage on it was good. One of the suspects was captured, interrogated and charged."

The Chief nodded, saying nothing.

"The third night," Crawford continued, "was a stroke of good luck."

"*Good* luck?" The Chief asked.

"Yes," said Crawford. "Good luck. A victim came forward who hadn't yet spoken to police. Her attack came in the exact same place as the victim we thought was number one. Tower and Renee in Crime Analysis both theorized that the suspect lived near that location. That was why they were at Corbin Park on night two and Mona Street on night three."

"Tell me where the luck comes in," The Chief asked.

"We found him," Crawford answered. "Just three nights into the operation, we found the son of a bitch."

"How do you know it was him?"

Crawford grunted. A smug look overcame him. "MacLeod was wired. Tower reviewed the tape. The guy used some unique phrases. It was him. No doubt."

The Chief gave Crawford a long glance. He wondered for a moment if he should lay into him for his demeanor, but he figured Reott would take care of that later. Instead, he conceded the point. "Okay, so we got lucky. We failed to capitalize on that luck."

Crawford nodded in agreement. "You're right, sir. But the officers on the scene made the best call they could under the circumstances. They didn't have the benefit of twenty/twenty hindsight."

"Maybe so," said The Chief, a whisper of frustration creeping into his chest. "But the end result is that I have an officer up at the hospital and a rapist still on the loose."

"I'm aware of that, sir."

"I'm glad you're so aware, Lieutenant." The Chief was unable to keep the sarcasm out of his voice. "Now, tell me what you plan to do about it."

He saw Crawford's eyes flash in anger, but the Detective Lieutenant held his tongue. "We stay the course," was all he said.

The Chief raised his eyebrows. "Stay the course? You don't think your operation is burned?"

Crawford shook his head. "Damaged, yes. But burned? No. We just need a different decoy and we can keep moving forward. A guy like this won't stop. We'll catch him. We just have to stay the course."

The Chief looked over at Reott. "Mike, do you agree with this?"

Reott looked uncomfortable. After a moment, he opened his mouth to speak. Before he could say anything, The Chief's telephone rang.

He glanced down. The ringing line was his private number. Not many people had that, so he figured he should answer it.

"Excuse me," he said to Reott and Crawford, then lifted the receiver. "Hello?"

"Hello, Chief. This is Pam Lincoln."

The Chief didn't miss a beat. "Hello, Pam. What can I do for you?"

"I just wanted to make you aware of something before I took it to my editors," Pam said.

The Chief narrowed his eyes. That didn't sound good. "I appreciate that," he said. "Go ahead."

"I got a call from a man about twenty minutes ago who claimed to be the Rainy Day Rapist," Pam told him.

The Chief paused. "Really?" he asked.

"Really."

He looked at the two men across from him. "Pam, let me put you on speaker phone," he said. "I'm in a meeting right now with Captain Reott and Lieutenant Crawford."

"I'm not surprised," Pam said. "Go ahead and put me on the speaker phone."

The Chief pushed the speaker button and rested the receiver back on the cradle. "Can you repeat what you just told me, please?"

"Certainly. I received a call about twenty minutes ago from a man who claimed to be the Rainy Day Rapist."

The Chief watched as the eyebrows of both men flew upward.

Crawford withdrew a notepad from inside his ancient sport coat. "Do you know what number?" he asked.

"Yes, I do." Pam recited the number slowly while Crawford scrawled it onto the notepad. "But I think it was a pay phone," she added.

"What did he say?" The Chief asked her.

"He said that the police tried to catch him with a decoy," Pam said. "He also said that he badly assaulted the decoy before escaping from the area. Is that true?"

No one answered her. The three men stared at each other during the long silence.

"I thought I was going to be kept up on this operation." Pam Lincoln's voice from the telephone speaker broke the silence. "I'm already aware of a foot pursuit and a K-9 track for a rapist up at Mona and Post last night. I also know that there was an ambulance dispatched to that same location."

There was another silence.

Again, it was the reporter's voice that broke the silence. "Are you still there, Chief?"

The Chief cleared his throat. "I am. Pam, thank you for calling me about this. We were just discussing the matter in this meeting. I'm sure the lieutenant would have updated you."

"Okay," Pam said, her voice neutral.

"Are you anticipating running this story?"

"I have to, Chief. If I don't pass this onto my editor, I'm fired. It's that simple."

"I understand," The Chief said. "If that's the case, then please give Lieutenant Crawford a call at his office in five minutes. Do you have that number?"

"I do. What can I expect from him?"

"Everything," The Chief told her.

"Nothing held back?"

"Not unless there are clear security concerns," said The Chief.

"Or specific medical privacy issues," Reott added quickly.

"Of course," The Chief said.

"I understand," Pam said. "I'll call in five minutes."

"Thank you," said The Chief. He pressed the button to disconnect the call. Then he looked up at both men. "Well, I guess that settles whether the task force is burned or not."

Crawford's face bore a sour look. "I'll let Tower know it's over."

The Chief nodded. "Good. And do right by Pam Lincoln. She didn't have to call us. She could have gone straight to her editor. We might still be able to minimize looking like the Keystone Kops on this one."

"I will," Crawford said. He stood and left without another word. As he swung the door open, Lieutenant Alan Hart stood outside, his fist poised to knock. Crawford gave him a distasteful look and brushed past him without a word.

The Chief hid his own feelings toward the Internal Affairs Lieutenant. "Come in," he told him, gesturing to the chair just vacated by Crawford.

Hart strode in, his back ramrod straight. He stood next to the chair, then paused and looked at The Chief.

"Please," The Chief said. "Have a seat."

Hart nodded briskly. He sat down, his posture remaining erect.

Before Hart could speak, Captain Reott stood. "Unless you need me, Chief, I have some things to attend to."

The Chief nodded.

Reott glanced at Hart, his disgust plain. Then he left the room, pulling the door shut behind him.

The Chief turned his gaze upon Hart. "What can I do for you, Alan?"

"A couple of things, sir. First, I wanted to discuss your findings that you issued on my investigations of both Officers O'Sullivan and Battaglia, as well as Officer Chisolm."

"Refresh my memory," The Chief said. "The one with O'Sullivan and Battaglia was...?"

"A demeanor issue, sir. And an inadequate response. It was in regard to a stolen vehicle. Mr. Tad Elway was the complainant."

"Ah, yes. I remember now. I think I decided on a letter of reprimand on that one?"

"Yes, sir." Hart bobbed his head. "I just wanted to express that, with all due respect, I thought that was a little bit lenient."

"Noted, Lieutenant," The Chief said, his voice dropping into a growl. "Anything else?"

Hart seemed to catch the audible clue. "Uh, no, sir. I'm sure you made the right decision. Anyway, I was more concerned with the Chisolm matter."

"The driving issue?"

"Yes, sir."

"The one with the child molester complainant?"

"Well..uh, yes sir."

"I dismissed it," The Chief said.

"I know," Lieutenant Hart said, then hastily added, "Sir."

"Then what?"

"Well," Hart said, "in light of last night's events, I believe another investigation is in order. Clearly, Chisolm made some errors during last night's operation."

"Hard to say," The Chief said, "since we weren't there."

Lieutenant Hart pressed his lips together, clearly in disagreement.

The Chief leaned back in his chair. "Tell me something, Alan. What's your beef with Thomas Chisolm?"

Hart's cheeks turned red. He swallowed hard and clenched his jaw. Finally, he answered, "He doesn't think the rules apply to him, sir."

"Why do you suppose that is?"

"Because," Hart answered, "Thomas Chisolm thinks that it is his personal responsibility to save the world. If rules get in the way of that, he just disregards them."

The Chief considered Hart's words. After a few moments, he had to concede that despite being a pompous, self-serving boob, the man was correct on this count. Chisolm *did* think it was his job to save the world. Still, as Chief, he'd rather have one Thomas Chisolm than fifty Alan Harts. Then again, he realized that he could probably only afford to have one Thomas Chisolm around.

"My decision stands, Lieutenant," The Chief finally said. "But I appreciate your input."

Hart's face took on a pinched look. His cheeks remained flushed, but he stood erect, nodded, said "Thank you, sir," and turned to leave.

"Lieutenant?" The Chief said to him before he reached the door.

"Yes, sir?"

The Chief eyed the ambitious lieutenant. Then he gave him a short nod. "After this Rainy Day Rapist thing is put to bed, I'll reconsider your request to look into the operation. But not until."

Lieutenant Hart seemed to be suppressing a smile as he said, "Thank you, sir," and strode from the office.

The Chief leaned back in his leather chair. Like it or not, his job was a political one. He needed someone like Hart to watch the troops. Not that most of his officers weren't stand up cops, but having Hart lurking in the wings had much the same effect that a locked door did on an honest man. He viewed it as an insurance policy of sorts.

But all the same, it irked him to see how much Hart seemed to revel in potential mistakes by officers. It appeared as if the arrogant, self-righteous bastard felt like every one of those mistakes was his chance to show everyone how much smarter he was than everyone else.

Which, in the Chief's opinion, he wasn't. He was a useful tool. Maybe even a round peg in a round hole, but one that he viewed as a necessary evil. And there was no way Lieutenant Alan Hart was going to make Captain, at least not while he sat in the Big Chair at the Big Desk.

The Chief of the River City Police Department let out a long sigh. It was on days like this that he wished he drank before five o'clock.

1432 hours

Katie's head throbbed while she listened to the doctor's explanation.

"You definitely suffered a concussion," he told her, "but based on the results from the tests we ran last night, there was no significant brain trauma beyond that. So, with the exception of the bruises, swelling and small cuts on your face, you came through this assault rather well."

Then why do I feel like shit? Katie wondered.

"There's really no reason to keep you here in the hospital any longer," the doctor continued. "I've already signed your discharge papers. The nurse will be along in a few minutes with your release instructions and a prescription for the pain you might encounter over the next few days."

"What's the prescription for?"

The doctor smiled. "Ibuprofen," he answered. "What were you hoping for?"

"Magic juice," Katie replied.

The doctor smiled at her. Katie tried to smile back, but the soreness on her cheek and the cut inside her mouth caused her to wince instead.

"I think you'll find the ibuprofen will keep the pain under control." Then he added, "Without the disorienting side effects."

Katie nodded. Parts of the last twenty-four hours held a dream-like quality. Mostly, she remembered floating peacefully. The rest had already slipped away, just like dreams tend to do the morning after.

"If you feel spacey or have any other symptoms of disorientation, give your regular doctor a call. Same thing if you're overly nauseous. That's a sign that you haven't come through the concussion yet." The doctor glanced down at her chart. "Other than that, you're good to go. Do you have any questions?"

"Just one. How long before I can go back to work?"

"That's up to you, I suppose," he said. "But I'd give it a couple of days, at least. After that, if you're symptom free and feel up to it, there's no medical reason not to."

"Thanks, doctor."

The doctor gave her a warm smile, replaced her chart and left the room. A few minutes later, the nurse arrived as promised. She went over the release paperwork in painstaking detail, causing Katie's headache to get worse. Finally, after it seemed like she'd scratched out her initials enough times to buy a house or settle a peace treaty, the nurse told her they were finished.

"Do you want some help getting dressed?"

Katie shook her head no. "I'll do it myself."

"All right. Just buzz when you're ready to go. We'll need to escort you out to the police car."

"Police car?"

The nurse gave her a confused look. "You're the cop, right?"

"Yes, but—"

"Once the doctor discharged you, we called the police. It was in the instructions on your chart. They've sent a car to transport you home."

"Oh." Katie supposed it made sense. She had no other way home, anyway.

"Well, I'll leave you to it," the nurse said, and left.

Katie swung her feet off the bed and stood. The tile was cool, even through her hospital issue socks. She shuffled over to the mirror. Once there, she took a hesitant look at herself.

A large bruise was painted across the left side of her face, coating the entire cheek and under her eye. Even a day later, the noticeable swelling gave her the look of a boxer after a twelve-round slugfest. Another smaller bruise appeared like a shadow on her forehead, along with a narrow, red splash on her chin.

"Ugh," she said back to the reflection.

She moved to the closet. The soreness and bruising throughout her limbs and torso punctuated each movement. When she reached for the closet door, it exposed her forearm, which was dotted with large splotches of dark bruising. And to top it all off, her leg was still tender from where the Russian kicked her.

"I should have been a firefighter," she said, reciting a common police officer lament.

Inside the closet, the only clothing she saw was a neatly folded pair of dark green surgical scrubs and a pair of slippers. None of her own clothing was present.

Katie frowned. The expression made her wince, though not as badly as her earlier attempt at a smile. Where were her clothes?

A moment later, she realized that they had probably been seized as evidence. Someone, probably Tower, had taken possession of the clothes, bagged them, labeled them and logged them onto evidence at the Property Room.

For some reason, the thought bothered her. Maybe it was the idea of someone handling her undergarments. It gave her a feeling of vulnerability, almost as if her privacy had been violated.

Or it could be that victims had their clothing booked on as evidence. Not cops. And she was a cop, not a victim.

Katie shrugged away the thought. Instead, she focused on changing into the scrubs. The process was more painstaking than she expected, as every muscle she used to strip off the gown and slip on the clean hospital gear seemed to scream at her in protest.

Eventually, she managed to finish the job. She shuffled back to the bedside and pushed the call button for the nurse. A few moments later, the nurse appeared with a wheelchair. Before Katie could object, she raised up one of her hands.

"It's hospital policy," she said, "so don't even think to argue."

"Who's arguing?" Katie answered.

"Most cops do," the nurse told her, "so I figured I'd make things clear right up front." She swung out the foot posts and gestured for Katie to sit down.

Katie lowered herself into the wheelchair. Part of her felt humiliated at using it, but another part of her was grateful for the ride. She settled in without a word.

The nurse put a small blanket on her lap. "We don't have any jackets," she explained. "It's rainy out."

"Figures," Katie mumbled, pulling the blanket toward her middle.

The nurse wheeled her out of the room. Thomas Chisolm stood in the hallway, wearing jeans and a windbreaker. Katie raised her eyebrows in surprise. "Tom?"

Chisolm shrugged. "I asked Dispatch to let me know when you were getting discharged. I figured you'd need a lift home."

Katie didn't know what to say. Eventually, she settled with a mumbled, "Thanks."

"No problem," Chisolm said. He motioned to the wheelchair. "May I?"

"No," the nurse said. "I have to wheel her to the door. Hospital policy."

"Okay." Chisolm fell into stride beside them as the nurse walked quickly to the elevator. They waited in silence for the elevator to arrive, then jockeyed their way inside.

"Where are you parked?" the nurse asked.

"Outside the E.R.," Chisolm told her.

Her disapproval was plain on her face as she punched the appropriate floor. "That's reserved for on-duty personnel."

"I'm never off duty," Chisolm told her lightly. He caught Katie's eye and gave her a wink.

The nurse didn't reply. Once they exited the elevator, she rolled Katie toward the Emergency Room entrance at something that seemed just shy of the speed of sound. Katie realized after a few moments that she was actually gripping the armrests of the wheelchair tightly.

"Hi, cop," came a deep voice to her right.

Katie turned to see a heavy-set bearded man sitting in one of the alcoves. His placid features were immediately familiar to her. After a second, she recognized him. It was Dan, the Forty-eight who liked Emerson. Or thought he tasted like some kind of condiment. She wondered if he was still in the hospital from the call she had with him last week or if this was a completely new trip.

Before she could answer, Dan's flat expression turned to a scowl of concern. "Oh," he said. "Cop got hurt."

In the next instant, the Dale Earnhardt of the nursing profession had her out of Dan's sight.

Katie sighed to herself.

Cop got hurt? Yeah, you could say that.

Just as quickly, the threesome reached the entrance. "Okay," said the nurse. "Here we are."

Katie stood slowly. Chisolm reached out to help her, but she shook him off with a quick head motion. Once she was on her feet, she opened the blanket and wrapped it around her shoulders like a cloak.

"Okay, I'm ready," she said.

She and Chisolm walked out the sliding glass doors of the E.R. toward the nearby row of cars. Chisolm pointed at the blue Ford truck in the second slot underneath the awning. "That's me."

Katie nodded and shuffled toward the truck. She was glad that she didn't have to walk in the rain. It was a cold, spitting mist that she imagined would sink the chill straight to the bone. At the passenger side, Chisolm unlocked the door and opened it for her. This time, she let him help her ease up into the passenger seat. Then he closed the door and went around to the driver's side.

As the two of them snapped their seatbelts into place, Chisolm broke the silence. "What was up with Nurse Ratched in there?"

Katie grinned, then winced. "Don't make me laugh, Tom. It hurts to smile."

"Sorry." He started the truck and put it in gear. "So where am I headed?"

Katie recited her address, knowing that Chisolm would have no difficulty finding it. That was the way it was with cops in general, her included. They didn't want directions, just an address. Every one of them knew River City inside and out anyway.

"Sergeant Shen said to give him a call sometime in the next couple of nights to let him know how long you'll be out," Chisolm told her, pulling out onto Eighth Avenue.

"Okay."

Chisolm drove in silence for several minutes. The stop and go motion of the truck made Katie feel tired again. She started thinking about her bed and how good it was going to feel to slip between the covers and sleep for another year or so.

As they pulled onto the Monroe Street Bridge, Chisolm cleared his throat. "Uh, Katie?"

"Yeah?" She stared off to the right toward the falls near the Post Street Bridge. Images of her experience there the previous year flashed through her mind's eye. It was almost as if she could see herself on the bridge, her pistol pointed at the insane man who stood dangling his own infant son over the edge of the railing. She looked away.

"I'm...sorry," Chisolm said.

"Huh?"

"I said I'm sorry. I let you down."

Katie turned his direction. The muscles in his jaw were bunched. He stared straight ahead at the road in front of them.

"Tom, you didn't —"

"Yes, I did," Chisolm interrupted, his voice intense. "I was supposed be your cover and I let you down."

Katie didn't want to argue. She just didn't have the energy. Instead, she adjusted the blanket around her shoulders. "It's okay," she said.

"No, it's not," Chisolm said. "I should have been there."

Katie thought about telling him that he was always there when it counted, but she sensed that he wasn't going to hear her words. So she simply sighed and murmured, "You were there. And I'm fine. I'm just tired and I want to go home."

Chisolm didn't reply. He just kept driving.

FIFTEEN

Wednesday, April 24th
Day Shift
1109 hours

After calling sick into work, something he had done only twice since taking the job, he gathered up a notebook and a pen. Then he headed to the library.

The newspaper article had been perfect. Not only did the reporter detail the task force's unsuccessful attempts to trap him and thereby neuter the cops, but there'd been an additional benefit. The bitch he nearly killed was identified in the article as Officer Katie MacLeod (said to be "resting comfortably" at the hospital, he noted with disappointment). That revelation made him so happy that he almost considered a second phone call just to thank the reporter for supplying the information. But that was a risk he wasn't willing to take. It wasn't worth it.

There were other risks, though – ones he *was* willing to take. But that would take some careful planning.

At the library, he headed to the newspaper archives in the basement. He had some research to do.

2218 hours

Officer Matt Westboard cruised down Madison Street toward downtown. He was returning from Sacred Heart Hospital, where he'd dropped off another Forty-eight. Unlike the one he'd helped Katie with the previous week, this person's mental problem was more dangerous. She'd been threatening to kill herself with pills.

Once she voiced that threat to Westboard, he had little choice but to transport her to the Mental Health ward for an evaluation.

Gratefully, such calls generated only a brief report. He was already down a burglary report in addition to this mental health hold and his shift was barely more than an hour old. He wondered if it were going to be that sort of night – the kind where he got buried under an avalanche of paper.

Westboard passed Second Avenue and continued north. He was getting into an area of downtown that bustled with drugs and other criminal activity, most of it culminating on a stretch of First Avenue known as The Block. Every time he drove through this section of downtown on his way back north, he seemed to get sidetracked with something. It never failed. As if to offer proof in the matter, he spotted a woman mid-way up the street. She leaned into a car window at the curbside, cocking her hip provocatively to the side. Her huge mane of blond hair bounced as she bobbed her head in agreement with whatever the driver was saying.

Westboard recognized her as a prostitute immediately. He slowed down and watched.

With an almost prey-sense, she looked up and saw his patrol car. She glanced back at the driver and said something. The driver looked over at Westboard's approaching vehicle. Without hesitation, he pulled from the curb and drove away. The woman did the same thing, walking quickly in the opposite direction.

Westboard debated briefly as to whether to stop the hooker or the john. Truth be told, his sympathies lay more with the prostitute, but he knew that it was better to attack supply than demand.

He pulled alongside her, angling his car toward the curb and coming to a stop just ahead of her path. Then he activated his overhead flashers.

The woman didn't try to run. She threw up her hands in mild frustration, then crossed them and waited.

Westboard advised radio of his location, then exited the patrol car. "How's it going?" he asked pleasantly.

"Fine until you showed up," the hooker shot back.

Westboard nodded knowingly as he approached. "Isn't that how it always is? The cops show up and spoil the fun."

She narrowed her eyes at him, unsure how to take him. "Usually," she answered.

Westboard stopped next to her. She looked around twenty-five years old to him. At this range, he could see the acne scars that she was trying to hide with heavy makeup. The woman was thin with very little curve in the hip. Westboard made her for a heroin user. She wasn't twitchy enough for a crack whore.

"Do you have any I.D.?" he asked.

She sighed, then reached into her small purse and withdrew a driver's license.

Westboard thanked her, looking down at the card. Her name was Toni Redding and she was younger than he'd thought by about five years. The photograph on the driver's license was only about two years old, but the woman who smiled out of it might as well have been an entirely different person than the one standing before him. The young woman in the photograph had a full face and a vibrant smile. Her eyes shined with life and hope. When he glanced up at today's Toni, her eyes were flat and dead. Only her hair, long, blond and flowing, seemed to come from her previous life.

She seemed to read that he was comparing the picture with her current state. "That was a while ago," she explained.

Westboard nodded. He removed his portable radio, switched over to the data channel and gave the operator Toni's name and birthdate. "What'd that guy want?" he asked.

Toni eyed him carefully. Then she said, "Directions to the freeway."

Westboard smiled. "Well, he left heading the wrong way."

Toni shrugged. "So I'm bad with directions. Is that against the law?"

"Not the last time I checked. If that's what you were doing."

"It was."

Westboard nodded again. "Okay. You live here in town, Toni?"

"What do you care where I live?"

"Just passing the time while I wait for your name to come back."

She gave him another suspicious look, then shrugged. "I've got a place in Browne's Addition."

"Not far, then."

"No. It's like ten blocks."

Westboard immediately thought that if Sully or Battaglia were here, one of them would pop off with something about how convenient that made it for her to walk to work. The quip was humorous, but he figured it would be unnecessarily cruel to cut on Toni. He'd already interrupted her trick. No need to ridicule her, too.

"How long have you lived there?" he asked instead.

"A few months. Why? You a real estate agent?"

Westboard raised his hands in mock surrender. "Easy," he said. "I'm just talking with you."

"I don't like talking to cops."

"Most people don't. But it hurts less as you go along."

She gave him a curious look, but he noticed that her jaw wasn't set as rigidly as when he'd first approached her.

"*Baker-124?*" his radio crackled.

"Go ahead," he told the dispatcher.

"*Redding is clear with prostitution entries and a suspended driver's license.*"

"Copy, thanks." Westboard handed the driver's license back to Toni. "Here you go. I'm supposed to seize that when it's suspended, but you go ahead and keep it."

Confused gratitude crept into Toni's eyes. Westboard didn't tell her that his ulterior motive was making sure she had good picture identification for the next cop that stopped her.

"Thanks," she said.

"No big deal," he told her. "Listen, you don't have any warrants and I'm not going to arrest you for soliciting tonight. But you need to scat out of the area for the rest of the night. If I see you down here later on tonight, I'll have to take you in."

Toni scowled, though not as harshly as before. "The charge wouldn't stick, you know."

"I do," he said, "but you'd still spend the night in jail instead of in your apartment."

She sighed in resignation. "Okay. You win. I'm out of here."

"Be careful," Westboard said.

She turned to go, then paused. She cast a sideways glance at Westboard over her shoulder. "Hey, is that cop all right? The woman cop that got beat up a few nights ago?"

"Yeah," Westboard said. "She's fine. Why?"

Toni shrugged. "I just wondered." She turned to leave, then paused again. "I hope you guys catch that asshole."

"We will."

"Because he's an asshole."

"I agree."

"There's lots of men who are assholes, if you really stop to think about it," Toni said.

"True enough," Westboard agreed. "You come across a fair number that type?"

She gave him a measured look before asking, "Do you really care?"

"Of course."

Toni turned back to face him. "I run into them every night. Some nights are worse than others."

"Maybe you should get away from this life," Westboard said quietly.

Toni looked away, absently rubbing her hands up and down her arms. "Maybe I will. Or maybe you should mind your own business."

Westboard shrugged in mild agreement. An awkward silence fell between them for several seconds. Westboard expected her to turn and leave, either in an indignant huff or the practiced casualness that he'd come to associate with prostitutes. When she remained standing near him, looking everywhere but his direction, he finally broke the silence, asking her, "Toni, is there something you want to tell me?"

She met his gaze, then lowered her eyes to the ground. "I don't know. Maybe."

Westboard realized what she was working herself up to. He made it easy for her. "Have you been assaulted?"

She nodded. A tear formed in the corner of her left eye.

"Sexually?" Westboard asked.

She wiped angrily at the tear, nodding again. "Yeah. A few times. But there was this one guy who almost choked me to death about a week ago. He was a bigger asshole than the others."

Westboard reached out and put his hand on her shoulder. "What happened?" he asked her in a soft voice.

"He picked me up. We did our deal, you know? But then in the middle of it all, he started choking me. I almost passed out. Then he threw me out of the car onto the ground." More tears spilled down her cheeks. "I thought he was going to kill me."

Westboard nodded his head in understanding. He gave her shoulder a squeeze. "Did he say anything?"

"Yeah," she said, sniffling. "He said he only let me live because I was beautiful." She laughed nervously through her tears. "Like I'm supposed to forgive him because he threw out a lame compliment or something? What an asshole."

Westboard removed his notebook from his breast pocket. "I'd like to do a report on this, Toni. If that's okay with you."

"Sure," she said, taking a tissue from her purse and wiping her nose. "Like it'll ever go anywhere. Most cops just think getting raped goes with the territory."

"It doesn't," Westboard said. "I don't."

She stared at him in appreciation, but suspicion still rimmed her eyes. "Yeah, all right. Let's make a report."

"Is there anything else you can remember about this guy?" Westboard asked.

"Yeah," she said. "He said something strange to me while he was choking me. Something about how he was going to put the whammy on me or something like that."

Westboard felt a surge of adrenaline in his chest. "He said that to you? Whammy?"

Toni nodded.

"You think you'd recognize this guy if you saw him again?"

"Absolutely." She nodded emphatically. "He was an asshole. I never forget those guys, because I won't get into a car with them ever again."

Westboard raised his radio to his lips. "Baker-124."

"*Baker-124, go ahead.*"

"Page Detective Tower to my location."

"*Copy.*"

Toni watched him carefully. "Is that important?" she asked him. "What I said?"

He nodded. "Oh, yeah. Very important."

Thursday, April 25th
Day Shift
1044 hours

Katie tapped lightly on Lieutenant Saylor's door.

"Come," she heard him say.

She opened the door and leaned in. Saylor sat at his desk, reviewing a thick stack of paperwork. He looked up as she entered.

"Ah, MacLeod," he said, setting down his pen and turning to face her. "Come on in. Have a seat."

Katie sat down gingerly in the chair at the side of the lieutenant's desk.

Saylor watched her carefully. "How're you feeling?"

"Sore," she admitted. "But nothing's broken."

"Good." He paused a moment, then asked. "How are you feeling about what happened?"

Katie shrugged. "I'm fine."

"It was a bit of mess out there that night, from what I can gather," Saylor said. "Do you think you might want to talk to someone about it?"

Katie looked up at him, annoyed. "You mean a shrink?"

Saylor didn't waver. "Or a counselor. Or a Peer Assistance Team member. Anybody you want. If you want."

Katie shook her head. "I'm fine. Things go wrong sometimes. Shit happens." After a moment, she added, "sir."

Saylor raised his hand to his chin and scratched it absently, watching Katie silently. Then he said, "All right. That's your call. Moving along, then – when do you think you'll be back to duty?"

"Tomorrow," Katie said. "I probably could tonight, but I think I could use another day of rest."

"I'm sure that's true. Is that the timetable the doctor recommended?"

She nodded.

"All right," Saylor said. "It's settled, then. One last thing, though. Do you feel up to giving a statement to Tower tomorrow morning? He's been asking about you."

"Sure."

Saylor gave her a warm smile and held out his hand. "I'll be glad to have you back, MacLeod."

Katie took his hand. "Thanks, Lieutenant."

1144 hours

He sat in his car, eating an apple from his sack lunch. The tart taste barely registered as he studied his notes.

It was amazing to him how much you could learn about a person just by going to the library. And not a famous person, either. Just a regular, every day public servant.

He now knew that Officer Katie MacLeod was twenty-six years old. That piece of knowledge took a little bit of quick math after he came across the newspaper article from 1991. The story detailed the swearing in of several brand new River City officers, including one Kathleen Maria MacLeod. Both she and another of the recruits, Stefan Kopriva, barely made the twenty-one year old age cut off in order to get hired and were the youngest in their class. Somehow this passed for news in River City, but he didn't dwell on the poor journalism. Instead, he reveled in that little piece of knowledge about the bitch.

There was another article from 1994 when the so-called Scarface Robber was captured, but it contained more information about other officers than her. But nonetheless, the search yielded a photograph of her accompanying a wounded officer into the rear of an ambulance. The anguish on her face was plain. He wondered if she had feelings for the downed cop. Probably not, he decided. She was probably just another overly emotional female, unable to control herself under stress.

He also found a fluff piece in the city government newsletter proclaiming Katie as Employee of the Month for December 1994. The nomination letter detailed her "tireless hard work on patrol" and "pleasant demeanor with citizens," none of which really helped him much.

The most interesting news story came from the previous year. Some crazy man dropped his own baby off of the Post Street Bridge in broad daylight. And who do you suppose was there when it happened? The intrepid Officer MacLeod, bitch that she was. Apparently, she was unable to talk the man out of his horrific action. The article was mildly critical of her, though in all fairness, he couldn't see a whole lot a person could do in that situation. Despite that fact, he took some pleasure imagining the pain that encounter must have caused her.

That was nothing, bitch. You just wait until I lay the whammo on you.

That was it for archived news stories, but not for his research. He found out that the library saved all the old telephone books. He dutifully checked each one, beginning with the current year. He didn't find anything until he got back to 1991 and then he struck pay dirt. The entry read "K. MacLeod" and was followed by a telephone number.

He considered that maybe she had changed the number after becoming a cop. But he figured it was more likely that she just got it unlisted, figuring that once the current year was up, the new phone book wouldn't have a listing for her anymore. Which was quite true. And who had the time or inclination to go to the library and search through a half dozen old phone books?

So now he knew how old she was and her phone number. Thanks to Pam Lincoln's article after he called her, he knew she was assigned to the graveyard shift. A little research into the configuration of the River City Police Department gave him the hours for that shift. Those officers started work at nine P.M. and worked until seven the following morning.

Lucky him, he didn't have to be to work until eight.

He rolled down the window and tossed the remains of his apple out onto the grass. A squirrel immediately darted from a nearby tree to inspect the treasure. He wiped his hands on a napkin while the rodent snatched up the apple core and scurried back to his tree.

"Good luck getting up the trunk of that tree, Mr. Squirrel," he muttered. Then he removed his sandwich from the sack and unwrapped it. As he bit into the white bread, he imagined what kind of home Katie MacLeod lived in. Was it an apartment? Or a house? Did she live alone? Or was she shacking up like the whore she probably was?

He wondered if her home were neat or messy. What her underwear looked like.

What it smelled like.

He already knew what *she* smelt like.

He already knew that she was afraid of him. And that little spark of rebellion she displayed? Well, he had certainly beaten that out of her. When they met again, he was sure that she'd cower in his presence. And then he'd take her.

And this time, he'd finish the job.

At the foot of the pine tree, the squirrel finally gave up trying to climb and set about eating the apple core right there at the tree base. He munched his own sandwich as he watched, his mouth turned up in a smile.

Soon.

SIXTEEN

Friday, April 26th
Day Shift
0912 hours

Tower sat at his desk, tapping his pen. His Rainy Day Rapist file lay in front of him, spread out across the desk like a bad dream. He picked up Westboard's report about the prostitute Toni Redding along with his own supplemental and re-read both. The details were clear. She had to have been assaulted by the Rainy Day Rapist. That phrase about "the whammo" was just too unique to turn up being used by someone else in the same city during the same time-period committing the same crime. Even though she initially told Westboard he'd said something slightly different, when he'd asked her if it could have been 'whammo' instead of 'whammy,' her eyes lit up and she'd nodded with certainty.

Plus, the time frame was right in the middle of the explosion of rapes he'd done. It occurred just a day after Patricia Reno.

It had to be him.

He put down Westboard's report, trading it for MacLeod's account of the attack on her during the decoy operation. He already knew all of the details, but he read through them again, paging on to his own account, Chisolm's, Battaglia's, Sully's and finally Shane Gomez's brief report on the failed K-9 track.

Nothing new jumped out at him.

And that frustrated the shit out of him.

He rose and walked to the bullpen's nearby coffee pot, pouring himself a cup. He stood and sipped the brew, staring at the same comics clipped from the paper that had been hanging there for over a year. He read them anyway, trying anything to jar his mind.

There had to be something he wasn't thinking of. Something he was missing.

"Taste-testing the coffee, John?" Georgina asked him from her desk.

Tower turned to the Sexual Assault Unit's secretary. He knew the pleasant woman was a horrible gossip, but he'd always found her presence comforting. Georgina reminded him of that large-bosomed aunt who wore lots of jewelry, especially bracelets. When things were difficult, she would be the one to give you a hug and tell you everything would be all right. And it would be all right, except that she would tell the whole family anything you confided in her.

"Just stretching the brain," he told her, taking another sip.

"Always good to stretch before exercise," she said. "I wouldn't want you to strain a brain muscle."

"I'm not so sure I have any to strain," Tower groused. "At least not on this case."

"Problems?" Georgina asked, her tone a practiced casual.

Tower smiled. It would be so easy to unload on her sympathetic ear. He would feel better. Maybe even find an answer in the purging. But he'd barely be back at his desk before everyone on the department would know he couldn't solve this case.

"Just like every case," he told her. "Little hiccups here and there. You have to work through them, you know?"

Georgina nodded, trying to hide her disappointment. Then she asked, "I heard on the news that—"

Tower's pager beeped loudly, interrupting her. He gave her a sheepish grin, inwardly grateful for the easy extrication from what might have turned into a Georgina interrogation. He glanced down at the LED display.

"You want to use my phone?" Georgina asked.

Tower squinted at the number. It was Browning's desk phone.

"No, thanks," he told Georgina absently, and strode from the reception area.

I thought Browning was still on vacation.

After a short walk, he turned into the Major Crimes unit. Glenda, the Major Crimes Unit Secretary, wore a pair of headphones and was typing at something that approached light speed. Nonetheless, she spotted him and gave him a perfunctory nod as he passed.

Seated at Browning's desk with one leg drawn up under the other, he found Katie MacLeod. She wore a pair of jeans and a simple white shirt with pink trim. Her light windbreaker was folded over the arm of the chair. Despite the yellow remnants of bruises on her face, Tower was struck by how feminine she looked.

"Are you feeling all right?"

Katie dropped her head backward and groaned at the ceiling. "Everyone keeps asking me that."

Tower didn't reply.

Katie rolled her head to the side to meet his gaze. "Yes, I am fine. I just look like Boom-Boom Bassen after losing a fight."

"Boom-Boom who?"

She waved his question away. "Inside joke, I guess. He's a boxer from River City. Or he was, a couple of years ago. Anyway, I booted in a door one time while a couple inside was watching him fight on TV. I thought it was a domestic."

"Ah." Tower nodded. "I see. So...did you forget where I work or what?"

"No, I remember. I just didn't want to deal with your secretary."

"Georgina? Why?"

"She's a nosy gossip, that's why."

Tower cocked his head at her. "How would you know *that*?"

"Are you saying it isn't true?"

"No. But how do you know?"

Katie shrugged. "Last year, when Stef...when Kopriva was working light duty in your office, I'd come by to see him sometimes. She was always watching us. I asked him about it and he told me about her."

Tower nodded knowingly. The rest of that conversation would probably be too painful for either of them to discuss, so he pushed on. "Are you ready for the sketch artist?"

"I don't know," Katie said. "I didn't really see the guy. It was so dark and he came at me from behind."

"Would you be willing to try?"

"I just wouldn't know where to start."

Tower considered, then said, "Well, here's the thing. I've got another witness working with the sketch artist right now. Could you look at that drawing and tell me what you think?"

Katie shrugged. "Sure. I just don't know how much help I can be."

Tower reached out and touched her hand. It was surprisingly warm. "Anything helps, MacLeod."

He turned to go.

"Tower?"

He stopped and turned back around. "Yeah?"

She stared at him, her features hard. "I'll tell you this. If I ever hear his voice again, I'll know."

He nodded his understanding. They both knew that a voice identification was next to useless in court, but at this point he'd take an I.D. based on smell.

"I'll be back in a bit," he told her.

He made his way to the interview rooms. Inside of number three, he saw Toni Redding seated with the sketch artist, an aged art instructor from the local community college. The artist sat comfortably in her chair, attending to the sketch with short pencil strokes. Her bright, intelligent eyes darted across the drawing pad as she made adjustments. Redding, on the other hand, slouched in her chair, one leg crossed over the other. Her crossed leg bounced in a constant jittery motion that might look to the uninitiated like a sign of impatience. But Tower knew better. Toni was tweaking.

"How are we coming along?" he asked.

The artist opened her mouth, but Toni beat her to the punch. "It's taking *forever*, that's how."

"Almost done," the artist said quietly, lifting her sketch slightly in Tower's direction.

He gave her a grateful smile, then turned to Toni. "Almost done," he repeated.

Toni snorted derisively. "That's what she said half an hour ago."

Tower glanced down at the nearly complete portrait. "It won't be long now. Can I get you something to drink?"

"Coke," Toni snapped sharply. "Two of them."

Tower pressed his lips together, but didn't reply. "How about you?" he asked the artist.

"No, thanks," she said, returning to her drawing pad.

Tower headed for the refrigerator between the Sex Crimes Unit and Major Crimes. Inside, he discovered there wasn't any Coke, so he grabbed two Pepsis instead. Then he fished a dollar out of his pocket and dropped it into the coffee can inside the fridge.

Back in the interview room, Toni curled her lip at the sign of the Pepsi cans.

"I said Coke."

Tower set the cans on the table. "There is no Coke. We're out."

Toni cursed. "Pepsi isn't as sweet as Coke."

"They're cold," Tower told her. "And they're free."

Toni sighed, but took both cans. She slipped one into her purse. Then she opened the other can and took a long drink. When she'd finished, she smothered a burp with the back of her hand. "See?" she complained. "Not as sweet."

Before Tower could reply, the artist announced that she was done. She handed the pencil sketch to Tower, who examined it first. The man's appearance was nondescript. The thought that immediately leapt to his mind was 'white bread.'

Hopefully, Tower turned the sketch around for Toni to see.

The prostitute wrinkled her nose and shrugged. "It's close, I suppose."

"Close?"

Toni took another long drink of her Pepsi. "Yeah. I mean, I guess it is."

Tower looked back and forth between the two women. "You helped her with this, right?" he asked Toni.

"Yeah."

"So, you told her how he looks."

She shrugged and sipped again. "Sure."

Tower looked back at the artist. The woman's warm features didn't completely hide her discomfort. "She wasn't terribly... descriptive," she told Tower.

"Bitch, I told you exactly how he looked," Toni snapped at her.

Tower raised his hand up and held his palm in front of Toni. "Easy."

"Well," Toni protested, "she ought to draw it how I say it. That's what she's getting paid for."

"I'm a volunteer," the artist said quietly.

Toni snorted. "Figures."

Tower pushed the drawing toward her face. "How is it not right, Toni?"

"It just isn't."

"How?" Tower asked again, raising his voice slightly.

"I don't know," Toni answered, matching his intensity. "It...just...*isn't*."

Tower resisted the urge to sigh. "But it's close?"

She shrugged. "Close enough. I mean, it could be him."

Tower looked down at the drawing again. If it were an art piece, he imagined the title would be 'Ordinary, Average, White Guy.' Then he turned his attention back to the artist. "Thank you," he told her. "I can walk you out, if you want."

The artist nodded gratefully and stood up.

"Wait here," Tower said to Toni.

"Why?"

"Because I said so."

"But I've got an appointment," she complained.

"I'll write you a note," Tower said. As he exited the room, he closed it behind him and turned the lock. He glanced around and spotted Detective Finch pouring himself some coffee across the room.

"Finch? Can you watch this Wit for a minute?"

Finch cast him a languid look, then nodded.

"Thanks." Tower led the artist down the hallway and toward the public entrance to the police department. Along the way, he thanked her again. "I really appreciate you coming in to do this," he said.

"I don't mind," she said. "I like to volunteer. But the victims are usually...nicer."

"Yes, they are," he agreed.

After he showed her out, he took the drawing back to Major Crimes. Katie MacLeod stood by the coffee pot, examining the comics that Major Crimes found hilarious enough to post on the wall above the coffee maker.

"Take a look at this, MacLeod," he said, holding it out.

Katie hesitated. "You sure you want me to look?"

"Why not?"

"Well, I just don't want to screw things up for a photo lineup later. If I see this drawing now, then –"

"It doesn't matter," Tower said, even though he knew it did. She'd never be able to identify him in a lineup if this drawing looked anything like the rapist. A good defense attorney would get that identification suppressed. But right now, all he wanted to know was if this drawing was worth a damn.

Katie gave him a doubtful look, but took the drawing from his hands. She turned it over and stared at it for several long moments. Finally, she shrugged and looked up at Tower. "I don't know. This could be anyone. It looks like Mr. WASP."

"I know," Tower said. Then he urged, "But try."

Katie returned her gaze to the sketch. "Like I said, I couldn't see much. The shape of the head looks right, I suppose. I got a glimpse of his silhouette. But other than that?" She shook her head. "Sorry."

Tower took the picture. "It's okay. Thanks for looking."

"You know, there's probably a thousand guys in River City who look like that," Katie observed.

"At least," Tower agreed.

Katie nodded. After a moment, she stood to go. "Okay, well, good luck."

"Are you working tonight?"

"Yes."

"First night back?"

"Yes. Why?"

Tower reached out and touched her on the shoulder. "Be careful, MacLeod. That's all."

He turned away before she could answer, heading back to the interview room. He caught Finch's eye as he neared the door and nodded his thanks. The other detective returned his nod without a word and strolled away.

Inside, he found Toni picking at a small scab on her inner elbow. She looked up when he entered.

"What the hell?" she asked. "Why'd I have to stay?"

Tower withdrew his business card and held it out for her. She stared at it without reaching to take it for several seconds. Then she asked, "What's that?"

"What's it look like? It's my card."

"I don't want it."

"Take it. And if you see this guy in the drawing again, you call me with everything you know. If he stops somewhere, you call 911 and tell them I told you to call. Understand?"

She continued to stare at the proffered card, shaking her head. "You know what happens to snitches out on the street?" she asked him.

Tower resisted frowning. In his experience, almost everyone on the street was a snitch. They all just had different breaking points. Instead of telling her that, he said, "You've got nothing to worry about. Even in prison, no one likes a rapist, Toni. Take the card."

She glanced from his face to the card and back again.

"Take it," he instructed her again.

She sighed, reached out and snatched the card from his hand. As she tucked it into her purse, she suddenly paused. Then she looked up at him, her face brightening. "Hey, do you think there might be a reward for that? Like, some cash or something?"

Tower smiled indulgently. "I'm sure there will be."

2112 hours

Katie sat at the roll call table, focusing on Sergeant Shen as he listed several drug houses in the sector that needed attention. She felt the eyes of her platoon mates drifting to her still-bruised face. The attention made her feel warm and uncomfortable.

When he'd finished with his list, Shen looked up at the assembled group. If he sensed the discomfort among the group, he chose to ignore it. "Last thing. Sully and Battaglia, you two are doubled up tonight."

"Big surprise," muttered Kahn.

"MacLeod, you team up with Westboard," Shen added.

There was a moment of silence at the table. Even though she rode partners with Westboard once in a while, it was always at her or Westboard's request. Shen had never assigned them together.

Katie's discomfort at being the center of attention was overshadowed by a hot, dull anger that settled into her gut. Did Shen think she wasn't ready to work yet? Or was he putting her with a partner just because she was female?

Before anyone could respond to the car assignments, Shen said, "All right, let's hit the street." Then he rose and left the table without another word.

After a short pause, the platoon members stood up and made their way out of the roll call room in ones and pairs. Katie rose along with them, not wanting to give any appearance of surprise at Shen's decision. She thought about going into the sergeant's office and asking him about it, but decided not to. The truth was, a partner didn't sound too bad. Just for one night.

Down in the basement, Sully and Battaglia were in rare form. While waiting for the cars to come in from Swing Shift, they fired ethnic barbs back and forth.

"What do you call an Italian with his hands in his pockets?" Sully asked.

"What?" Battaglia asked with a scowl.

"A mute," Sully answered, laughing.

Westboard and Katie chuckled along.

"Yeah?" Battaglia said. "Well, you know that God invented whiskey strictly so that the Irish wouldn't rule the world."

Sully snorted. "Like the Italians ever ruled anything."

Battaglia snorted back. "Ever hear of Rome, Paddy?"

"Yeah, in a book about ancient history."

"At least we had an empire."

Sully affected his best Irish brogue. "And a grand empire 'twas, lad."

"You know what you call an Irishman underneath a wheelbarrow, Sully? Huh? A mechanic, that's what."

"Yeah? Well, you know what's black and blue and floating in the Irish Sea?" Sully grinned. "A guy who told one too many Irish jokes."

Battaglia grinned back and fired him a middle finger. "Like I'm afraid of you ovah heah," he said in Brooklyn-ese. "You get outta line, I'll just call Vinnie the Moose and –"

"Would you shut the fuck up?" Kahn snapped from nearby.

Everyone fell silent. The barrel-chested veteran stood holding his patrol bag, scowling at Battaglia.

"Huh?" Battaglia asked, obviously surprised.

"You heard me. I said you should shut the fuck up." Kahn's low, gravelly voice rumbled and echoed throughout the sally port. "Really, give it a try. I'm sick of your Robert DeNiro, Godfather bullshit. So you've got an Italian last name and dark hair. So what?"

"Jimmy –"

"Don't 'Jimmy' me, you goofball prick. Drop the act. This is River City. It isn't Brooklyn."

Battaglia stared at Kahn in shocked surprise. Sully chuckled uneasily. Kahn turned on him next.

"This isn't Boston, either. You're about as Irish as my goddamn boots. And I'm sick of listening to you two ass monkeys jibber-jabber like this isn't serious work we do here. It isn't a fucking joke. If the two of you realized that, if you didn't treat this job like one long goddamn stand up routine, then maybe MacLeod wouldn't be standing here looking like Rocky Balboa warmed over."

Kahn gave each of them a hard stare. Then he muttered, "assholes," and strode off to the far end of the sally port to wait for the first car to roll in. He didn't look back.

"What was that all about?" Battaglia whispered.

Sully didn't reply. He glanced sheepishly at Katie, then down at the ground.

"Jesus," Battaglia continued. "If the guy isn't chasing tail, he's a giant grouch. What's his problem, anyway?" He looked from Sully to Westboard to Katie.

No one answered.

SEVENTEEN

Saturday, April 27th
0726 hours

He spotted her as soon as she walked through the glass doors of the police department. With so little traffic on the street this early on a Saturday morning, he opted to park a half-block away to surveil the exit. He worried that he might not recognize her at that distance, but as soon as she pushed open the door, he knew.

There was still a vestige of a limp in her stride. And maybe just a trace of the shuffle he'd seen when she was playing the role of prey. As she turned and walked in the opposite direction, he stared after her. He watched her ponytail bob and bounce with each step. He thought about making it into a handle.

His eyes drifted down her body. He admired the tight curve of her hip, the upward turn of her ass. Dark, angry lust seethed in his loins.

He gripped the steering wheel and watched her.

Almost a block away, she stopped next to a Jeep, opened the door and slid into the driver's seat.

He smiled. Now he knew what she drove.

A puff of clear exhaust spurted out of the tailpipe of the Jeep. He sat and watched while Katie the Bitch Cop warmed up the engine. His palms were cool and sweaty. He wiped them on his slacks. He waited.

After a few minutes, her Jeep's brake lights flashed, then the vehicle nudged forward into the street. He watched her go, then started his own car and eased onto the street. The sparse traffic forced him to follow her at a distance of several blocks as she headed up Monroe. He watched carefully, prepared for any turn signal from the Jeep.

The Jeep continued due north, not turning, not slowing. He hung back, hoping she wasn't suspicious of him. Hoping she wasn't vigilant at this time in the morning, after working all night.

Was she going home? He was counting on it, but you never knew with cops. Or whores. Maybe she was going to a bar. Or over to some guy's house.

Maybe there was a man waiting at home for her.

He curled his lip. If that were the case, he would take care of that problem, too.

Finally, when she hit Rowan, almost five miles from the police station, she turned right.

He waited until she was out of sight, then sped up to almost fifty miles an hour to close the distance between them. At Rowan, he braked and turned. As soon as he turned onto Rowan, he saw her Jeep a block and a half to the east.

He followed.

At Calispel, she slowed and turned to the left. He slowed as well, watching her. She stopped in front of a small brick house three houses north of the intersection. He stopped, too, pulling up against the curb on Rowan. He was in the bicycle lane, but with so little traffic, he didn't worry.

She stepped out of her Jeep and headed up the walkway to the small brick house. He stared after her until after she'd unlocked the door and gone inside.

It was a small house, but not too small for two people. She could be shacking up. He had to be careful and remain aware of that possibility. But there were no other cars parked right in front of the house, only hers. The houses on each side of hers had driveways. One led to a carport, the other to a garage. Poor Katie the Bitch Cop had to park on the street.

Unless there was a garage in back.

He put the car in gear and cruised forward, past the intersection. Mid-block, he spotted the alley that ran north/south behind the house. The alley was evenly paved with asphalt, not very common in River City. Most of the alleys he'd seen were still made up of hard-packed dirt or gravel and were bumpy as hell. As he turned into the alley, he enjoyed the smooth progression northward. He counted houses, slowing as he reached the third one.

A small chain link fence. That was all. No garage. No second car.

Probably no man in the house.

He glanced down at the towel on the seat beside him. Wrapped inside of it was a knife that would put Rambo to shame. More than anything, he wanted to put on the brakes. He wanted to stop in the alley, take that knife and jump the fence. Go inside. Find that fucking cunt. Grab onto that handle of hair and give her the banging of her life. Then slit her throat. Watch her life flow out onto the floor.

His hands trembled. His hardness strained against his slacks. He realized he was smiling.

No.

He couldn't take any chances. He had to plan it out better. Look what happened the last time he went on impulse. They almost caught him in their little trap.

No, this time he'd watch. He'd plan.

This one was worth waiting for.

He rolled northbound through the alley. His hands continued to quiver, even as he turned out of the alley and back onto the street.

She's going to get what she's got coming, he told himself. *What they all have coming.*

Soon.

Not soon enough by half, but soon.

As he drifted back toward Division Street, he tried to sort out the beginnings of a plan, but the details eluded him. All he could see was that bouncing pony tail. All he could hear was her defiant voice. All he could feel was the satisfying smack of his knuckles against her cheek. All he could smell was her fear.

He rolled his head around, stretching the tight muscles in his neck. His breath came in and out in small quivering gasps. His erection ached.

He had to do *something*. This was too much.

At the first convenience store he saw, he pulled into the parking lot.

0805 hours

Katie peeled off the last of her clothing. She rubbed her sleepy eyes, causing a twinge of pain in her bruised face. Ignoring that, she found her flannel pajamas and slipped them over her head.

Bed was going to feel good. Her entire shift had been one stupid call after another. Westboard was overly protective, asking her about a dozen times how she was doing. On a fight call outside an apartment complex, Kahn had all but ignored everyone, his eyes still full of cold fire. His words seemed to have spurred Sully and Battaglia into a guilt-ridden state, which she was fairly certain they compounded while talking about it as they drove around during the shift. As a result, both of them apologized to her several times whenever their paths crossed on calls. When it came time for a lunch break, Katie talked Westboard into going somewhere with just the two of them so she could avoid more apologies.

She looked forward to forgetting about all of that in the coma-esque sleep of a graveyard officer. Putter the cat was fed and watered. Her alarm was set. She made sure the shades were pulled and secured in the bedroom. All that remained was to slide between the blankets and–

The telephone rang.

Katie sighed, annoyed. Then a tickle of anger sparked in her chest.

It had to be Stef.

She thought about letting it go to the machine. Then she thought about changing her phone number so he couldn't call her anymore. The prospect of his actions forcing her to give up the same number she'd had since first coming to River City pissed her off, so on the fourth ring, she snatched the receiver.

"Hello?" she asked, not trying very hard to keep the irritation out of her voice.

The sound of traffic in the background immediately confirmed her suspicions. It was Kopriva, calling on a payphone. She wondered if he'd been up drinking all night. The thought of listening to his self-pitying slur made her clench her jaw.

He didn't say anything right away.

"Hello?" she repeated.

Still no reply.

"Listen," Katie said, letting all of her anger flood through her voice, "this is bullshit, Stef. I told you not to call me anymore."

A car horn honked in the background, followed by the sound of an engine racing by.

"I wasn't kidding about the no-contact order, Stef. I can get one on Monday."

No answer.

Katie sighed. "Just leave me alone, all right?" She waited another moment for a reply, then started to hang up.

"Katie?" came a voice from the phone receiver.

She brought the phone back to her ear. "Stef?"

There was a low chuckle. "No. Not...*Stef*," he said in a hissing stage whisper.

She recognized the voice. Fear lanced through her stomach. For a moment, she thought it might be Phil, coming back from college to haunt her –

You liked it. Don't forget that.

—or to try to do that to her again. But after that frantic moment, her mind cleared. She knew who it was.

"Are you there, Katie?" he whispered into the phone.

She swallowed hard before she spoke. When the words came out, she tried to put an edge to them. He couldn't know that she was afraid.

"I'm here. What do you want?"

He laughed then. The sound grated against her nerves. She closed her eyes and bit her lip.

"I want *you*, bitch."

Think, Katie! Do something!

"When I find you, Katie, I am going to lay the whammo on you."

Say something!

"You're going to get it *good*."

She cast her eyes around the room, her mind racing.

"And you'll like it, too. Count on that, bitch."

You liked it. Don't forget that.

His echoing words cut through her fear and found her anger. Who the hell did he think he was? She clenched her jaw, then spoke in a tight voice. "I don't think you have the balls," she told him.

There was a pause.

Good. I surprised him.

She forged ahead. "In fact, I think you're a giant chicken shit. You only go after weak women because you're weak yourself. You don't have the guts to come after a strong woman like me because you know I'll kick your ass. You know—"

"BITCH, I WILL FUCK YOU UNTIL YOU CRY!" he screamed at her.

"I don't believe you," Katie goaded him. A flare of satisfaction went off in her chest, settling down her body in a warm glow. The tables were turned and she liked it. "I think you're all talk."

"I WILL CUT YOUR FUCKING TITS OFF!"

"You're a coward," she told him, ignoring the graphic visual.

There was another pause. She heard his heavy breathing in the receiver. The sound of traffic in the background was again audible.

How do you like that? she thought. *Not used to a woman who fights back?* A grim battle smile spread across her face.

"You're nothing but a coward," she repeated. "And I know it."

"Really?" he whispered into her ear, his voice full of barely controlled rage. "Well, I know something, too."

"Yeah? What's that?"

"I know where you live, bitch."

Then he hung up.

Katie's smile melted away.

1039 hours

Captain Reott leaned back in his leather chair, giving Detective Tower a hard look. "This really hasn't gone as you planned, has it, Detective?"

Seated next to Lieutenant Crawford, Tower shifted in his chair and looked away, his jaw clenched. "There's been some setbacks," he admitted.

"Setbacks?" Reott repeated, surprise and sarcasm plain in his tone. "In order to have setbacks, don't you have to have some progress to be set back from? Where's the progress on this case? All I've seen is more women being raped and botched operations."

Crawford cleared his throat. "All due respect, Captain, Detective Tower is my responsibility. I'll do the ass-chewing, if you don't mind."

"I *do* mind," Reott said. "Because now one of my patrol officers is the target of this whack job pervert."

"What would you have done differently, sir?" Tower asked quietly through his clenched teeth.

"Lots. For starters, how about catching the guy?" Reott snapped.

A silence settled into the room. Reott gave Tower a hard look. The detective was unshaven and wearing a pair of jeans and a wrinkled shirt along with a Seattle Mariners windbreaker. His eyes held a desperate, haunted look that worried Reott. He made a mental note to bring it up with Crawford after Tower left. This case had almost certainly become too much for one detective to handle, though he knew that was Crawford's call.

Finally, Reott rubbed his own eyes and sighed. "All right," he said. "I guess there's no profit in casting blame here. Everyone's doing the best they can with what they've been given. The question now is, how do we move forward?"

"As far as the rapes go," Tower said, "I'll keep working the case. Something will break."

Reott glanced at Crawford, but didn't reply.

"I interviewed MacLeod for about an hour this morning, after the phone call," Tower continued. "She recognized the voice, so it was definitely the same guy."

"Any chance of a telephone trace of some sort?" Reott asked.

Tower shrugged. "Maybe. The phone company supposedly keeps a seventy-two hour record of all local calls made on a rolling basis. We might be able to find out where the call came from."

"That's good."

Tower frowned. "Maybe."

"Why wouldn't it be?"

"Several reasons. For one, their techs aren't available on the weekend, so Monday is the soonest we'll be able to get at the information. Plus, they won't let us have the information without a subpoena."

"So get a subpoena from the prosecutor. Patrick what's-his-name."

"It's Patrick Hinote," Tower said. "That's no problem, just a matter of doing it. The thing is, it probably won't help us at all."

"Why not?"

"He called from a pay phone. So the odds of getting prints off that are virtually nil, especially by the time we get the information."

Reott scowled. It would be the same thing with finding any witnesses who might remember some guy who was there making a phone call two days prior. "So it's a dead end."

"The phone call is," Tower said, "but I think we have a different opportunity here."

"What's that?"

"We can stake out MacLeod's house, for one. See if we can catch the guy prowling around."

"That sounds smart. What else?"

"We stake out MacLeod."

Reott paused. "You mean use her as bait?"

Tower shrugged. "Call it what you want. He's obviously keyed in on MacLeod. We can use that to draw him out."

"No." Reott shook his head firmly. "She's been through enough with this task force. I'm not going to ask her to do that."

"Captain—"

"I said no," Reott interrupted. "This isn't some cop movie, Tower. MacLeod is not the answer."

"Why don't you at least ask her?"

"Because it isn't her choice," Reott said. "It's mine. And I'm not going to do it."

"Why not?"

Reott leaned forward and fixed Tower with a cold stare. "I don't have to explain myself to you, detective. I don't work for you."

Another silence settled into the room. Outside Reott's open window, the distant sound of tires hissing on wet pavement meshed with high-pitched birdsong.

After almost a minute, Tower broke the silence, "Captain—"

"You're dismissed, detective."

Tower gaped at him, surprised. Then he rose and stalked out of the room.

Reott watched him go. Once the door snapped shut behind him, he turned his attention to Crawford.

The Major Crimes Lieutenant looked back at him, his face saggy and his expression unreadable. "That was a little harsh, Mike," he said.

Reott didn't answer. He pulled open his drawer and withdrew a pair of cigars, offering one to Crawford. Crawford paused, then accepted it. Reott fired his up, then handed the Zippo lighter to Crawford.

Once both men had a cherry coal at the end of the cigar, the mood in the room seemed to loosen. The smoke somehow alleviated the tension in the air.

"It probably was a little harsh," Reott agreed. "But I stand by my decision."

"Which I agree with, for the record. MacLeod's been through too much already. Using her as bait would be a mistake."

"Tower doesn't think so."

Crawford drew in smoke, then blew it at the ceiling. "It's Tower's job to catch this guy. He's failing. He wants to try anything that might work."

"You think he's too close to this case?"

"Absolutely. And I wouldn't have it any other way."

Reott peered across the desk at Crawford through the blue smoke trails between them. "That's a dangerous game to play."

"We live in a dangerous world," Crawford replied easily. "Look, Tower pisses me off. That's no secret. He's a smartass who thinks he knows better than everyone else. But he's goddamn dedicated. And some days, he's a good detective." He took another deep puff on the cigar, seeming to savor the sensation. "He cares, Mike. He *cares*. And if it means catching a very bad man, then I'm going to ride that horse until it drops."

Reott turned the cigar in his fingers. "I don't know how comfortable I am with that philosophy. A guy like Tower could burn out."

"Maybe," Crawford conceded. "In fact, at some point, he probably will. He's wired too emotionally for this job." Crawford leaned forward slightly, his shoulders hunching. "But come on, Mike. You're a leader. You know you have to push your people sometimes."

"Maybe, but not like this. What you're talking about is a level usually reserved for soldiers at war."

Crawford smiled grimly. "We *are* at war. And it's a war we're losing a little more every year."

"Jesus," Reott said, shaking his head. "That's pretty dark. Who shit in your Cheerios this morning?"

"Today? The Rainy Day Rapist," Crawford said. "But he's just another in a long line of reality checks."

Reott sighed. "So where do we go from here?"

"We need a full court press," Crawford said. "I'll throw another of my Major Crimes teams into the mix and get them out there shaking bushes. You tell your patrol troops to stop and FI any single white male who looks remotely suspicious. That'll hopefully generate some leads for Tower to follow up."

Reott agreed. "Call the media, too. Get that sketch out to the public."

Crawford laughed derisively. "The Mr. Every Other White Guy drawing? We'll have sightings at every bowling alley, grocery aisle and video store."

"All the more for Tower to follow up on, then," Reott said with a tight grin. "Now what about the threat to my officer?"

"Tower's right on that count. We need to put men on MacLeod's house. The guy might be foolish enough to come poking around." Crawford considered. "And she needs protection, too."

"A bodyguard, you mean?"

Crawford shrugged. "Put her with a partner while she's on patrol. When she's not working, we set her up at a motel. Put another cop with her in the adjoining room."

"For how long?"

"I don't know," Crawford said. "You're the Captain. You tell me."

Reott smoked for a few moments, thinking. He was out of good ideas. He didn't know how long. He didn't even know if it would work or not. Finally, he nodded to Crawford. "Do it," he said, putting as much confidence into his voice as he could muster. "All of it."

2024 hours

Katie stared back at Tower, her gaze shifting between the detective and Lieutenant Saylor. "You're kidding me," she said.

Saylor shook his head. "This comes straight from the Captain of Patrol."

Katie turned her attention to Tower. "Was this your idea?"

Tower stared back at her. "Not this part of it."

Katie sighed in frustration. "I can take care of myself," she told Saylor. "I don't need a partner all the time, El-Tee. And I don't need a bodyguard. That's ridiculous."

"You've received a death threat," Saylor said.

"I get death threats once a shift," Katie replied, bristling. "Sir."

"This is different," Tower said quietly. "This guy has shown that he isn't simply talking. He acts."

She swallowed, knowing that he was right about that. Still, she wondered if this had more to do with catching a rapist or with the fact that she was a woman. If she were a man, would the bodyguard be on the table? Or would the lieutenant slap the man on the shoulder with a macho exhortation to "be careful" and call it enough?

You'll never know for sure, Katie. Just do your job.

Katie met the Lieutenant's eyes. "Fine. I'll do it."

Tension noticeably eased in the room.

"But I want to choose who my bodyguard will be," she added.

Saylor and Sergeant Shen exchanged a glance. Then the lieutenant asked, "Okay, fair enough. Who do you want?"

Katie didn't hesitate. "Tom Chisolm."

2217 hours

Tower sat on the small patio, wrapped in a blanket. A beer nestled between his legs, his right hand wrapped loosely around the neck. The ornamental blanket belonged on the small couch inside the house and barely covered his shoulders and chest. It merely provided him some temporary protection against the light mist of rain in the air.

It isn't even really falling, he thought to himself. It was almost more like a fog than rainfall. Just a light, stinging mist that bit into his cheeks and ears and coated his slacks. He felt the heaviness of the droplets as they gathered in his hair. Each time he raised the bottle of beer to his lips, the cold slap of the water smacked his hand.

I should be drinking a hot buttered rum instead.

Tower smiled grimly. *Or maybe some hot buttered hemlock.*

The enormity of the past week settled in on his shoulders with considerable weight. Captain Reott's condemnation of his lack of progress rang in his ears, louder still because Tower knew the Patrol Captain was right. What breakthroughs had he engineered in this case? The only one that could even be called progress was the victim Heather Torin coming forward and that wasn't his doing.

No, it was safe to say that he'd been about as useful as a handbrake on a canoe.

What's worse, he didn't see things improving. He still had little useful physical evidence to convict the Rainy Day Rapist, even if he waltzed into police headquarters and surrendered. In his phone conversation with the prosecutor, Patrick Hinote had expressed concern that he'd be able to overcome *corpus delecti* issues even if the suspect confessed. All in all, it was a giant bag of crap.

Tower lifted the beer bottle to his mouth and took a deep draught. The foam at the end of his drink and the weight of the bottle told him he was empty. Now he had to decide whether to go inside for another one or simply sit in the rain. Since he was four deep into the six pack of Kokanee he'd brought home after work, this initially presented a difficult logic problem. After a moment, though, the only thought that resonated with him was that beer was good and he needed more. Besides, he had to take a leak.

The rain continued to fall on him while he mustered the energy to get up and go inside. He knew Stephanie would have a word or two with him for using the ornamental blanket in such an unorthodox fashion, but at this point, he didn't care.

Tower let out a long sigh. Crawford had used the words 'full court press,' but he knew what that translated to. His case was being taken away from him. Finch and Elias were on loan from Robbery/Homicide, but it wouldn't be long before the status of lead detective would drift to one of them. Probably Finch, who was the more taciturn of the two. Tower imagined that the next crime scene would be the last where he was considered the lead, and even that one would probably be a 'collaborative' scene in order to begin the transition.

"Fuck it," he whispered. "I don't care who gets credit. I just want to catch this son of a bitch."

He wished that were one hundred percent true, but even four beers deep, he knew it wasn't entirely so. So he sat a little bit longer, paying penance with a full bladder in the cold, stinging misty rain, clutching an empty beer bottle, and thinking ill thoughts.

Sunday, April 28th
0848 hours

Katie tossed her small suitcase into the overstuffed chair. "I guess they spare no expense," she groused. "This place is barely one step above a Motel 6."

"Hey," Chisolm chided her, "I love Motel 6."

"That figures."

Chisolm shrugged. "They leave the light on."

Katie rolled her eyes and flopped backward onto the queen-sized bed. "This is so stupid. If they are staking out my house, why can't I just stay there?"

Chisolm reached for the door that separated Katie's room from his. "I guess they just want to be as safe as possible," he said diplomatically.

Katie snorted. "We both know that they're only doing this because I'm a girl."

Chisolm shrugged, swinging open the door from Katie's side. "You're probably right."

Katie paused. Chisolm's directness and honesty surprised her, as was always the case. After a moment, she followed up her thought. "Well, if that's true, then it's bullshit for them to do it."

"Bullshit for who to do it?"

"I don't know. The brass. Whoever decided."

"You think it was Saylor?"

Katie thought briefly, then shook her head. "No. He said it came straight from the Patrol Captain. And Tower said that this whole bodyguard routine wasn't part of his suggestion."

"I wouldn't think so."

Katie squinted at him. "What's *that* mean?"

"It means," Chisolm answered, turning to meet her gaze, "that if I was Tower, I'd want you at home for bait. That is, if all I cared about was catching the Rainy Day Rapist."

She considered his words. "You think that's all he cares about?"

"I think that's what he cares about *most*," Chisolm said. "Why else would he have kept you on after the accidental discharge in Riverfront Park and then the assault at Corbin Park?"

"Maybe because he knew I could handle it."

Chisolm shrugged. "Could be, but I doubt it. I've seen Tower's kind before. He's not totally hung up on himself like Kahn or Stone, but he's still pretty self-centered. I don't think he gave a whole lot of thought to how this was affecting you until after the Rainy Day Rapist grabbed onto you that night over on Mona Street."

Katie looked up at the ceiling, thinking about what Chisolm had said. She didn't want to believe it. She wanted to believe that Tower had believed in her as a cop. But she found it difficult to simply discount Chisolm's view of things.

"So you're saying Tower's some kind of an asshole?" she asked.

"No," Chisolm responded. He checked the bathroom, even going so far as to pull the shower curtain aside. "I'm saying that he's focused on himself and his case. That's his role. The captain's role is something different. He has to take more of a global view."

Katie sat up and stared at him. "Officer Chisolm," she said, affecting shock and surprise. "Did you just defend the brass?"

Chisolm chuckled. "Hey, I believe in leadership. If it's competent, that is. Saylor's a good leader."

Katie made a face, agreeing. "True. Not like Hart."

Chisolm snorted. "Why do you think they shipped that idiot over to Internal Affairs? Hell, that move alone should tell you that the Chief has a pretty good idea what the score is. He's a good leader, too. And so is Captain Reott."

Katie shrugged. She had no opinion one way or the other. Generally, she was so removed from the leadership as a line officer working graveyard that she just hoped they would leave her alone to do her job. The only time she saw or heard from them was when someone screwed up, anyway.

"What do you mean by 'global view'?" she asked.

Chisolm walked to the window and pushed aside the heavy curtain. Katie looked past him into the parking lot. He'd insisted on a second floor room, explaining that it kept the window from being as vulnerable. He gave her a similar explanation when it came to parking his car in the basement sally port and having them leave after work from that location, citing a change in pattern. "I mean, he had to balance the need to catch this prick with your personal safety. He decided that your house was enough bait and that he didn't want to risk using you."

"Right," Katie said, "and would he have made that same decision if it was a male officer?"

"I don't know," Chisolm answered, snapping the curtains shut. "I guess it might depend on the officer."

"Meaning?"

"Meaning that most officers, he'd probably do the same thing. Can you imagine the negative press if something were to happen to you, MacLeod? If they decided to use you as a worm on a hook and you got gobbled up? Even if we caught the fish, the fallout would be enough to bring down this Chief and probably the Captain, too."

"Are you saying this was self-preservation on their part?"

Chisolm sighed. "Hell, every decision has elements of self-preservation. Have you ever arrested a guy for domestic violence on thin probable cause simply because you're covered if you arrest him and you're liable if you don't?"

Katie looked away. "Sure. I suppose. PC is PC, right?"

Chisolm smiled. "Depends on if it is probable cause or *probably* cause."

Katie chuckled. "Okay, I see your point. But honestly, do you think they'd have gone the whole nine yards with a bodyguard and everything if *you* were the target?"

Chisolm's smile faded into a grimace. "Probably not."

"Because you're a man," Katie said.

"No," Chisolm answered. "Because I would have politely told the Captain to go run a leg up his ass."

Katie laughed out loud. "Oh, I'd pay to see that."

Chisolm shrugged. "When you've been here for fifteen or more years, you might know a thing or two about people that gives you a little leverage, MacLeod."

"Like what?"

"Can't tell you," Chisolm said, "otherwise it wouldn't be worth anything."

"So this has nothing to do with me being a woman?"

"I'm sure it does," Chisolm admitted, "but it is what it is."

"Oh," Katie said. "A philosopher and a medicine man. Impressive."

"Probably why you picked me as your bunk mate," Chisolm said. He pointed at the door. "I'll be right through there. When I get into my room, I'll open it from my side. We leave the doors between our rooms open. If you need some privacy, swing the door nearly shut but don't latch it."

"Yes, sir," Katie said, saluting.

Chisolm ignored her and continued. "If there's a knock on your door, you don't answer it. You come across into my room and we'll decide how to deal with it from there. Same thing with the phone. Don't answer it. Okay?"

"Okay," Katie said, firing another salute at him.

Chisolm gave her a gentle smile, then good-naturedly returned her salute. "Hey," he said. "I'm working for you here." He pointed to the door between their rooms. "I'll be right in there," he added, then turned to go.

"Tom?" Katie asked.

Chisolm turned. "Yeah?"

"Thanks," she said, her tone warm and full of gratitude. "I mean it."

"I know," Chisolm replied. "I know."

0916 hours

He cruised along Rowan, his eyes darting down every alley and into every car. He knew he had to be aware. Now that he'd tipped his hands, he figured the cops would be all over the bitch's house. Still, he had to know. He had to *see*.

Besides, even if they saw him, even if they stopped him, what would they have? He'd used a condom every time, leaving behind no evidence for them. Most of the stupid bitches hadn't fought back at all, and those that had raised some defense hadn't caused him any serious injury. If they were vigilant and somehow spotted him, it wouldn't matter. They had nothing to tie him to the rapes.

He even had his alibi worked out. His outgoing mail lay on the seat beside him. Just over on Division was a post office. If they stopped him, he'd just say he was looking for the back entrance to the post office in order to avoid traffic. They'd see the stamped, unsent letters on his passenger seat and that would convince them.

Cops, he had decided, were not that bright. They only caught on to the most obvious of facts.

When he turned onto Calispel, the first thing he noticed was that the Jeep was missing. He wondered if it were still at the police station or if she'd driven elsewhere. Perhaps tomorrow, he'd have to stake out the station and see.

The second thing he noticed was the gray four-door Caprice parked a half block from the bitch's brick house. Two clearly male figures sat inside.

Cops.

Jesus, he thought. *Could they be more obvious?*

He fixed his gaze straight ahead, then made a point to feign that he was fiddling with the radio as he rolled up the street at just under the speed limit. He used his peripheral vision to check the two of them out as he passed the gray car. They appeared to be deeply involved in a conversation.

Probably sports, he guessed. Cops were all the same. In all likelihood, arguing about the prospects of the Seattle Seahawks or the Seattle Mariners. Or, if they had a more local focus, the minor league hockey team, the River City Flyers. Some sort of knuckle-dragging sports endeavor that people with low IQs seemed to enjoy.

As he neared the end of the block, he signaled and turned right. A quick glance in his rear view mirror told him that the gray car was not following him. That meant they hadn't even noticed him.

Good. That would make things easier.

Mid-block, he paused and peered down the alley. He saw no cars. No coverage. Could it be that they were only watching the front of the house?

He smiled. Things just went from easier to perfect.

The waiting would be the hardest part, he realized. He'd have to rein in those powerful emotions. He couldn't afford to let them spill out anywhere. Not on those useless prostitutes. Not on any other deserving women. No, he had to save his energy for the one that got away.

He had to be smart.

He had to be careful.

He had to plan.

Most of all, he had to be patient. And he knew he could. He'd already proven it.

Part III

October 1977
Seattle, Washington

Every sweet has its sour; every evil its good.
Ralph Waldo Emerson

EIGHTEEN

October 1977

Anticipation. As a child, anticipation ruled his life early on. There was no double-edged aspect to that particular brand of anticipation, either – not for a seven year old, at least. The joy of anticipating an event like Christmas (or in this case, his father returning home after a long deployment) occupied his mind and kept his thoughts alive all hours of the day. Nothing could dampen his enthusiasm. Not the long wait, which was usually where that other edge cut the other direction. No, waiting was just fine with him. In fact, the longer he had to look forward to something, the better the experience.

His mother seated sullenly in her chair didn't leach away his happiness, either. He didn't entirely understand why she wasn't as excited as he was, but figuring that mystery out wasn't a requirement for him to be excited for the big event.

He had a few strange memories from the last time, but they weren't scary so much as puzzling, so he simply brushed them aside. Those shadowy recollections from when he was only five didn't matter, anyway.

What mattered was that his daddy was coming home.

That was all he cared about.

It didn't matter that his daddy hadn't remembered his birthday back in August when he turned seven. He was an important man on a big ship. He was really, really busy. He had to watch over all the other sailors. And he had to fight the enemy. He couldn't be asked to do all of that and still remember a birthday, could he?

Then again, a birthday was a super big deal. It was as big as Christmas *and* Halloween. Sure, he cried when his dad didn't call or send a present. Then his mother gave him a sharp one across the cheek and told him to 'button it up.' She told him he was old enough to figure out what his old man was all about. She said that he could expect more of the same disappointment from him, if he ever came around.

He quit crying then, because he knew she'd lay another slap on him if he didn't. He said, "Yes, Mother," because she liked to be agreed with and she liked to be called Mother (never 'mommy,' she hated that word, said it was a peasant's word), then waited for her to present her gift to him. His heart sank as soon as she produced the wrapped present. He could tell by the shape that it was clothing. He didn't want clothes. He wanted Lego's or Army men or maybe some cars, but not clothes. Clothes were awful. In fact, as far as a birthday gift went, clothes completely blew chunks.

His mother's mouth hardened into a tight line. He knew what that meant, so he manufactured a smile. He pretended he was opening up a G.I. Joe complete set of action figures and tore off the wrapping paper with gusto. The plaid pants with reinforced knees and the matching turtleneck stared up at him in silent mockery.

Under his mother's hateful stare, he managed a smile. He said, "Thank you, Mother." Then he rose and tried to give her a hug. After all, even if her gift was the most stupidest gift ever, at least she got something for him. At least she said 'happy birthday' to him when she woke him up that morning. She even hinted that she might make some cupcakes, though he knew there wasn't any cupcake mix in the cupboard and she wasn't likely to go to the store because it wasn't Wednesday and besides that, her 'goddamn check' hadn't come in the mail yet (he always knew when that check had arrived, because for a day or so, the hard line of her mouth relaxed just a little bit and she seemed a little more at ease).

She allowed him a brief, cursory hug, then pushed him away. "Put your new clothes away," she said, then motioned at the wrapping paper on the floor. "And clean up this mess."

So he did, and that was it for his birthday. No cupcakes, either – he was right on that count – but she did make chili for him that night, which was his favorite. They sat in silence at the rickety kitchen table while he ate his chili and she drank her special stuff from a water glass. He wasn't allowed to drink her special stuff, which was fine with him. He smelled it once and it hurt his nose. Besides, whenever she drank it (which was every day), it made her breath stink. Worse than that, it made her be mean to him.

None of that mattered now. Right now, he sat at the rain splattered window of their apartment and stared out at the gray street, waiting. His daddy was coming home. Everything was going to be better.

Maybe his daddy would bring his birthday present with him. Maybe he didn't forget, but just couldn't send it home. It wasn't like there was a mailman who went out into the middle of the ocean to pick up mail, right? So they probably had to wait until the ship came into the dock before they could send mail. His daddy's ship was out in the ocean for a long time, so that explained it.

A present between his birthday and Christmas. The prospect of a gift during that long present drought amped up his level of excitement even more. That would make up for a lot. It would make up for his daddy being gone, for the smacks and whacks he took from his mother, for all the troubles at school. A present in between his birthday and Christmas might just solve everything in the whole world, at least for a little while.

He figured his daddy could solve the rest. He could tell his mother not to drink any of her special stuff and then she wouldn't be so mean to him. Maybe she'd even stop slapping him. And since his daddy was a boy, too, maybe he could help him with some things.

School, for instance. That was his biggest problem besides his mother. Maybe his daddy could help him with school. Maybe he could tell his mother that he didn't have to go to school anymore. He hated going now, but his mother made him go there anyway. He was in second grade and it was terrible. He'd liked Kindergarten. They got to play and take naps and eat snacks. The teachers never got mad when he had an accident or did something wrong. Miss Reed had been his favorite. She was really, really tall and pretty and had long, long hair and she smiled at him and called him 'Jeffrey' instead of 'Jeffie.' She always liked his art projects that he made, too. He tried to give them to her, but she made him take them home to his mother.

"I'm sure your mommy will want to put them on the refrigerator or something," she'd said, and because she was so beautiful, Jeffrey wanted to believe her. So he took the colorings and the finger-paintings and the macaroni projects home. He showed them to his mother (never 'mommy'), who gave them a critical glance and tossed them on the table.

"Miss Reed said you should put them on the fridge," he told his mother.

"Miss Reed does not run this house," his mother snapped back. She took another drink from her water glass full of her special stuff. "Go do your chores and I'll think about it."

He did as he was told, but the colorings and finger-paintings and macaroni projects only sat on the table, never on the fridge. Sometimes, they sat for a day or two, sometimes for weeks. Her water glass full of special stuff made little ring marks on some of them. He imagined those to be like the little happy faces Miss Reed drew on papers when he wrote his numbers and letters really good.

Eventually, though, all of those papers all ended up in the kitchen garbage, covered in coffee grounds and empty bottles of her special stuff.

Once, he drew a picture of his family. The three figures took up the entire piece of construction paper. He made sure his mother and daddy were standing next to each other, holding hands. He gave his mother a giant smile, but then he drew the eyebrows wrong. They slanted inward toward the center, giving her an angry look. He tried to fix it, but everything he did just made things worse—

"All you ever do is make things worse!"

—so that his mother looked like she was enraged. There was nothing he could do, so he moved on to his daddy. He made sure to draw his Navy uniform as best that he could. He used the one picture he had as a guide, even making certain that he put the right number of stripes on his sleeve. Three below, then one on top with an eagle. After that, he carefully colored it in, taking his time and staying mostly inside the lines he'd drawn. When he'd finished, he thought it was perfect. In fact, it was probably the best drawing he'd ever made. Miss Reed agreed with him, putting her gentle, warm hand on his shoulder when she told him so.

"It's a beautiful family drawing, Jeffrey," she said, her voice soft and comforting.

He tried to give it to her, but she declined as always. "It belongs on your refrigerator, for your family to see."

She was right, of course. Miss Reed was always right. She knew everything, he figured, or just about everything. So he took it home. Instead of presenting it to his mother so that she could toss it on the table on top of his other work, he found a piece of tape and put the drawing on the refrigerator himself. He stood in the kitchen and looked at it. After a few seconds, he realized that he'd started to cry and he didn't know why. The picture made him happy when he looked at it, but it made him sad, too. That was confusing. He wasn't sure what to think about it, but he didn't know who to ask. His mother would probably slap him and tell him to 'button it up' or 'zip it.'

He left the picture up. Maybe it would make his mother happy. Maybe she would agree with Miss Reed that it belonged up there.

By dinnertime, his mother discovered it. She ripped it from the refrigerator and shoved it into his face. She screeched about how he'd drawn her, asking him if he thought she was really that evil. She asked him if he wanted her to die and called him an ungrateful bastard. He thought the 'pain you've caused me' speech was coming, but then she veered into a series of insults against his daddy. She called him names he'd never heard and didn't understand, but he could tell all of them were bad.

He stood in the kitchen, shocked at her rage. Inside, all the happiness that had come from drawing the picture seeped away and that part of him filled with more of the same sadness.

Near the end of her tirade, she tore the drawing into strips. She forced him to put the paper into his mouth and chew it up. He cried and begged her, but she slapped him hard and pressed forward. He chewed on the paper, his mouth quickly drying. He feared that she would make him swallow it. He knew that he'd choke to death on the huge wad in his mouth. Instead, she directed him to spit it into the garbage, take another strip and chew some more. They stood in the kitchen for fifteen long minutes while he chewed up and spat his entire drawing into the garbage can.

"That's your goddamn family," she snarled at him, pointing at the clumps of chewed up paper.

He didn't understand exactly, but somehow he knew she was right.

When Kindergarten ended, he remembered how sad he was. He cried and clung to Miss Reed's leg on the final day. He wanted to ask her to be his mommy instead of his mother, but even back then he knew that wasn't the way the world worked, so he didn't bother to ask. He just cried and hung on until she gently pried his fingers away.

"You'll have lots of fun in first grade, Jeffrey," she told him, giving his shoulder a squeeze. "You're a nice boy and everyone will love you, just like we all did here in this class."

He believed her, and that represented the first real betrayal besides his mother that he could remember in his life.

The lie hadn't been immediately apparent. First grade had been all right at first, even though the elementary school was much bigger than where he'd gone to kindergarten. He got lost on the first day, but a nice woman almost as pretty as Miss Reed found him wandering and took him to his class.

He soon discovered that there were no naps or any snacks. There was recess, which somewhat made up for it, but not completely. And the boys and girls in his class seemed to like him. Some of them, at least. But then he discovered that there were second-graders, third-graders and fourth-graders at the school, too. Some of them liked to pick on the younger kids.

The fourth-graders were the worst. They pushed him down. They took his milk money away. When it was his turn to play four-square, they made him go to the back of the line. Sometimes, they pretended to be nice and let him play dodge ball, then all of them hurled the red rubber balls at him at the same time. Once, the force of Hugh Jessup's throw knocked his head backward and into the wall. He fell to the ground, dazed. Black walls rushed in from the edges of his vision, collapsing toward his center. He may have passed out – he couldn't remember. He remembered that no one noticed, though. The fourth-graders who'd thrown the balls (except for Hugh Jessup – he was a third grader who was big and so they let him play, too) scattered. The foursquare games, basketball, tetherball and tag all continued around him while he sat against the red brick wall, blinking. His head throbbed and when he reached back, he felt something warm and sticky. He looked down at his fingers and saw blood. The sight scared him at first, but what he worried about even more was everyone knowing. Everyone laughing. So he wiped the blood behind the knee of his Toughskin jeans and sat still, collecting his senses.

When the bell rang, he went inside and told no one. He sat in class and pretended everything was fine. Then, just five minutes into class, Laurie Phillips, who sat right behind him, yelled out, "Ewwww, gross!" and pointed at the back of his head. Everyone turned to stare at him. The kids behind him followed Laurie's finger and made disgusted sounds themselves. Kids to the side leaned backward and tried to get a look at it.

All of this attracted the attention of Mrs. Piper, his new teacher. She stalked to his seat, turned his head and gasped. Then she yelled at him and sent him to the school nurse. He felt every eye in the room upon him as he rose from his seat and slunk out of the classroom.

The nurse cleaned him up, dabbing gently at the back of his head with a washcloth. She told him it was only a small cut and wouldn't need any stitches. Heads bleed, she said. She was nice, he decided. Maybe there were only so many nice people in the world. Maybe that was it. Then she called his mother and he decided that nice people didn't know everything. When she asked him how it happened, he briefly considered telling her. He knew instinctively, though, that the worst thing in the schoolyard world was a tattletale. He knew she couldn't save him from the fourth-graders and if they knew he'd tattled, then things would get worse. So he told her he tripped. He wasn't sure if she believed him, but she didn't ask any more questions.

When his mother saw it, she flew into a rage. At first, he thought she was angry at him, the way she snatched his hand and dragged him out of the apartment. But as she stalked down the street, jerking him along behind her, he realized they were going back to the school.

Once there, she found her way through the mostly empty building to the office. The principal was still at his desk doing paperwork. His mother barged into the principal's office, screaming and pointing at the cut on the back of his head. She hollered about things he didn't understand like "improper supervision" and "negligence." She threatened to "sue the whole goddamn city."

Jeffrey watched her in amazement as she railed against the principal, who sat stiffly in his chair, absorbing the verbal barrage. He realized that, despite the fact that he didn't understand half of what she was saying and that she used some bad words and that he could smell the strong wash of special stuff coming off of her while she yelled, she was sticking up for him.

She was defending him.

And it felt good.

The principal waited until her ranting tapered off, then apologized. He said that the school's insurance would pay for any medical costs. He said he would have a meeting with all the teachers about playground safety. He offered to give them a ride home.

His mother stared back at the principal, showing no reaction to any of his entreaties. Finally, she raised her finger in the air and waggled it at him.

"My son gets hurt again, mister, and I will *own* this school!" Then she took him by the hand and strode out of the office without a backward glance.

On the way home, he positively floated along the sidewalk, his feet barely touching the ground. His mother grumbled about the conversation she'd just had with the principal, her head lowered toward the ground. When they got home, she poured a second glass of the special stuff, even though she still had one that was half-full next to her chair in the living room. After a long drink, she sat down at the kitchen table and wept.

Jeffrey hadn't seen her cry for as long as he could remember. He stood off at first, unsure what to do. Eventually, though, he was drawn to comfort her. He reached out with his small hand and touched her shoulder.

She looked up, saw him and opened her arms.

Gratefully, he fell into them. She pulled him tight to her bosom, sobbing.

"It's just you and me, Jeffie," she said between sobs. "You and me against the world."

He stayed against her chest, hugging her for as long as she allowed it. Then, like a light switch had been flicked, she stood abruptly, shrugged him off and went to the bathroom. He sat down in her seat, feeling the warmth from her body fade. When she returned, her mouth was a hard line again.

"Don't make me come bail you out of trouble like that again," she told him, waggling her finger at him in the same way she'd done in the principal's office. "Stop making problems for me. Don't I have it hard enough already?"

"Yes, Mother," he said. He felt tears welling up, but fought them down. His mother's tender moments were few and far between and she didn't put up with any bawl babies outside of those special times.

Strangely, the worst thing about first grade was that they all called him Jeffie again. No one called him Jeffrey, not even Mrs. Piper. She didn't pay particular attention to him, either. She was stingy with the smiley faces and gold stars, too, though she was pretty free with the red ones. He didn't like the red ones so much, but a star was a star. Still, he didn't offer any of his drawings to her and she didn't tell him that they were worthy of the refrigerator at his home.

He made it through the school year somehow. He dealt with the nicknames of Jeffie Booger Eater (because he'd picked his nose one time and someone saw him, then told everyone that he'd picked his nose and eaten it, which was a lie but everyone believed it anyway so the name stuck) and Jeffie the Queer (which he didn't understand except that it came from the fourth graders and was really bad). He just kept thinking about summertime and his birthday and how someday his daddy was coming home to fix things.

At the end of the year, he didn't hug Mrs. Piper and he didn't cry. Summer came and it was better than school, even though his mother drank her special stuff most of the day every day. Sometimes she went to the park, though, and let him play on the bars there. Those days were the best, even though it was usually overcast and cool.

His birthday came (including his single gift of clothes from his mother) and before he knew it, it was time for school again.

Second grade was much worse than first grade.

Everyone remembered him, for starters. The same old names from first grade popped up again. New ones sprang into being. He learned that 'queer' meant a boy who likes boys instead of girls, but it still didn't make much sense to him. At school, he was starting to dislike boys *and* girls, so he didn't know if that made him queer or not queer, but it didn't matter because they stilled called him that name.

On the third day of school, disaster struck at recess. He'd somehow managed to secure one of the swings and even though he knew he had to pee, he didn't want to give it up. If the fourth-graders realized he'd made it to first in line and was swinging and having fun, someone would do something about it. Maybe even Hugh Jessup, who was a fourth grader now and bigger than any other boy in school. So he held it and he swung and swung, pumping his legs and soaring into the air and back down again. He kept swinging and soaring as the pressure in his bladder grew. Finally, he couldn't stand it anymore. He decided he needed to stop and go to the toilet.

He tried to slow down, but that takes forever on a swing. The urgency from his bladder told him he didn't have that kind of time. He drug his feet lightly on the dirt patch below the swing, resulting in only a marginal braking. So he tried planting his feet more firmly instead. That resulted in his shoes catching the soft dirt, digging in and yanking him from the swing. He went tumbling from the swing, rolling into a heap on the grass several yards in front of the swing set. The force of his landing jolted him enough that he let loose of his bladder, accidentally wetting his pants.

A crowd surrounded him. At first, there was mild concern that he was hurt. That seemed to quickly fade into curiosity about any injuries he might have incurred. Then someone spotted the giant wet spot on his crotch, pointed and screamed it out for the whole world to know.

After that, all the other kids called him Jeffie Pee-Pee Pants.

His second grade teacher, Miss Guidry, didn't notice a thing for the last two hours of school, but that didn't surprise him. She was older than dust. She probably couldn't even smell any more.

He didn't tell his mother about the incident, but she figured it out easily enough when he came home reeking of urine. She shrieked at him that he was a disgusting, dirty little boy, that he was just like his father and that he made her sick. She smacked him in the head several times, then hauled him to the bathroom by his hair. In the bathroom, she pushed him roughly into the bathtub and turned on the shower. He yelped at the cold water, but she gave him another smack, so he kept his mouth clamped shut. She never adjusted the water temperature, letting the ice cold water rain down on him as he sat huddled in the bottom of the tub, shivering. After what seemed like hours, she switched off the water and asked him if he learned his lesson.

"Yes, Mother," he answered, because he knew it was the right thing to say. He didn't know what the lesson was supposed to be, other than don't pee your pants at school, but it was too late for that lesson to do him any good.

Still, maybe his daddy knew the answers to that, too. Maybe he could help him. Tell him how to deal with the third and fourth-graders (and, truth be told, most of the second-graders, too and a few of the first-graders) that made school so miserable. His daddy could teach him how to fight. He was in the Navy and that was like the Army and everyone knew that soldiers knew how to fight. Heck, that was their *job*.

His daddy was coming home.

He'd know how to handle the pee problem. He'd teach him to fight those bigger kids. Or maybe he'd smack them around himself. Maybe he'd show up in his uniform and grab Hugh Jessup by the collar and give him a bare butt spanking for everyone to see. And then he'd tell them all that Jeffrey was the best kid in the school and they better believe it or he'd be back.

So he sat by that rain-splattered window every day, looking out at the gray Seattle street, knowing that at any moment, his daddy would appear. He waited for the sailor uniform to appear in the parking lot. He watched for him to stride up the steps to the second level where they lived, carrying a wrapped present in his arms (or maybe a bike! That would be so cool!). He'd jump into his daddy's arms. His daddy would smell like Old Spice, just like in the commercial on T.V. He'd hug him and his daddy would hug him back and say how much he missed his little boy.

Everything would be better.

That was all that mattered.

So he watched and he waited.

November 1977

One week before Thanksgiving, his patience was rewarded and his faith destroyed, all in the same day.

He sat by the window in late afternoon, more out of hopeful habit than anticipation by that point. He read his favorite book, Dr. Seuss's *Green Eggs & Ham*, over and over again. Something about the way that the little guy was able to finally convince the grouch to change his mind about those yucky looking green eggs and green ham appealed to him.

Finishing it for the second time that afternoon, he glanced out the window. The full rain clouds above Seattle seemed to be almost trembling with the weight of all that water. It reminded him of how it felt to wake up in the middle of the night just a second or two before he had to pee. It was always a battle to push away all the sleep and scramble out of bed toward the bathroom in time to make it.

He was about to lower his eyes back to the book for a third go-round when he saw the jaunty stride of a sailor coming through the parking lot. His pea coat and sea bag slung over his shoulder were unmistakable signs of a Navy man.

Jeffrey dropped the book and pressed against the glass, staring.

Was it his daddy?

He wanted to scream out to his mother, to God, to the world, but all he could manage was a low whimper. Then a chilling thought struck him. What if it wasn't his daddy? What if it was someone else's relative? It was a large complex with lots of neighbors. Maybe—

He reluctantly tore his eyes away from the figure and fixed his gaze on the only picture of his daddy in the entire home. He didn't know how old the picture was, but it showed a rough and tumble sailor outfitted in his uniform, smoking a cigarette and eyeing the camera lens with an expression that Jeffrey couldn't entirely read.

After studying that face for a moment, he snapped his head back to the front. The sailor was closer now. In fact, he was coming directly toward the apartment.

This apartment.

Jeffrey whimpered again. It might be. It might be.

Once the sailor reached the stairs, he took them with a steady confidence, swinging around the corner on the first landing. As he turned toward the apartment window, he looked up and caught Jeffrey's eye.

It was. It *was*.

He was older than the picture, but when he met Jeffrey's eye, it was with the same expression. He paused a moment, looking at the boy almost as if he'd forgotten about him. Then a rakish grin spread over his face and he tipped him a wink.

Jeffrey smiled and waved frantically. His daddy was home and he winked at him and he was going to make everything better and tell his mother to be nice and stop the kids at school –

"What are you in here whining about?" his mother snapped from behind him. "I'm trying to take my nap and all I can hear is you making noi—"

Jeffrey turned from the window to face her. "Daddy's home!" he squealed.

Her face registered surprise for a moment, then her features sank into their customary hardness as she watched the figure pass in front of the window and try the door knob. It was locked.

"Aren't you happy, Mother?" Jeffrey asked her.

"Thrilled," she answered in a flat voice.

Jeffrey didn't think she sounded too happy, but he was too excited to worry about it. When his daddy discovered the door was locked, he began pounding on it with his palm. Jeffrey sprinted for the door. His little hands fumbled with the lock on the doorknob, then he slid the chain aside and flung open the door.

"Daddy!" he squeaked.

His daddy's eyes narrowed at the sound. "Is this my son or my daughter?" he joked gruffly.

Jeffrey's jaw dropped. He felt as if someone had just kicked him in the stomach.

His daddy laughed uproariously and pointed. "Oh, that's classic. You should see your face, kiddo." He laughed, looking up at Jeffrey's mother. "Really, Cora, you should get a look at this kid's face when I said that. You'd think I took away his teddy bear or something."

"Come in," was all his mother said. "You're letting in the cold."

"S'pose I am," he agreed, and stepped forward. He brushed past Jeffrey as he entered. The smell of cigarettes and sweat wafted over the boy, but instead of being repelled by the odor, he soaked it in. That's how dads are supposed to smell, he figured.

"Close the door, Jeffie," his mother said.

He obeyed, turning the knob lock and setting the chain. He turned around to see his mother and daddy eyeing each other in the living room. Jeffrey could feel the electric tension between them, even though he didn't understand exactly what it was or why it was there. This was a mommy and a daddy. Aren't they supposed love each other and hug and kiss and stuff?

"Glad to see me?" his daddy said.

"It's been a long time," she answered.

"Navy's a tough life," he told her. "You knew that when you signed on."

She narrowed her eyes slightly and flicked her gaze toward Jeffrey. "Like I had a choice."

He dropped his sea bag on the floor next to her chair. "You always got a choice, Cora. Hell, I could've chosen not to come home when they gave me leave."

"Why didn't you?"

He raised his eyebrows. "Because this is my family. Now, how about a drink and a little boom-boom for the sailor long-time gone?"

She pressed her lips together, glancing over Jeffrey. He followed her gaze, then nodded knowingly. "Oh, yeah. Well, then how about the drink now and the boom-boom later?"

"It's in the kitchen," his mother said.

His daddy cocked his head at her. "Then go and get it," he said in a low voice.

She paused, glancing back and forth between him and Jeffrey. Then she sighed, turned and left the room.

Jeffrey watched the exchange, astounded. His daddy turned toward him, saw his expression and tipped him another wink. "Sometimes ya gotta put a woman in her place, boy," he said with a grin. "Deep down inside, that's what really want, anyway."

His daddy removed his Navy Pea Coat and tossed it onto the small couch. Then he sat down in the chair and eyed Jeffrey for a few long moments. The sounds of clinking glasses drifted in from the kitchen. Jeffrey squirmed under his gaze.

"How old are you now, boy?" he asked.

"Seven," Jeffrey told him.

"Seven, *sir*," his daddy corrected him, shaking his head. "Didn't your mother teach you any respect?"

"No," Jeffrey answered without thinking. When his daddy's eyes narrowed at him, he added, "sir."

His daddy laughed darkly. "Well, at least you're honest, kiddo. But you look about as fucked up as a soup sandwich, you know that?"

Jeffrey blanched at the profanity. His mind worked frantically to understand what a soup sandwich was. He felt his lip quivering and put his hand over it.

His mother came back into the room with a single water glass. She held it out to his daddy. The man ignored her for a moment, studying Jeffrey closely. Then he turned to his mother. "Jesus, Cora. The kid's a mess. What've you been doing with him?"

"I've been doing the best I'm able to do, Stan," she replied evenly. "Here's your drink."

"The best you can?" He shook his head and took the drink from her hand. "That's a pretty piss-poor excuse, you ask me."

His mother said nothing.

His daddy took a large drink from the glass. After he swallowed, his face contracted in a grimace. "Vodka? Good Christ, that's a whore's drink. Don't you have any whiskey in the house?"

"I drink vodka," she answered quietly.

"Like I said, a whore's drink." He took another sip. "Damn. It doesn't get any better as you go, either." He lifted his chin in her direction. "Go to the liquor store and get a bottle of whiskey. Get the good stuff. Jack Daniels."

"I don't have any money," she whispered.

His daddy catapulted from the chair and struck her with the back of his hand. She yelped and fell back onto the couch atop his coat. "Don't start out by giving me lip, bitch," he growled at her. "Just because I've been gone a while doesn't mean I'm not still the man around here."

Jeffrey stared on in shock while his mother pulled herself up into a sitting position, holding her cheek.

"I'm...sorry," she said quietly, avoiding her husband's gaze.

"Goddamn right you are." He sat back down in the chair and took another pull from the water glass. Then he asked, "Why don't you have any money? My checks should be coming regular."

"It gets used up," she said.

"On what?" He jerked a thumb toward Jeffrey. "Ballet lessons for him?"

"Food," she whispered. "Rent."

His daddy laughed. "Food and rent? Yeah, maybe, but you manage to have some vodka in the house, too, don't you, Cora?"

She didn't answer.

He pulled roll of bills from his pocket and peeled off several, tossing them at her. "Now go get some whiskey. And make it quick."

She slowly gathered up the money, folded it and slid it into her dress pocket. Then she rose and walked to the door. "Come on, Jeffie," she said as she slipped on her jacket.

"No, he stays here," his daddy said. "Christ knows he needs to spend some time with a man. Looks to me like you've turned the kid into some kind of queer or something."

At the word 'queer', the kick to the stomach sensation repeated itself, only much harder this time. Jeffrey heard himself whimper, unable to hold the sound inside.

"See?" his daddy said over the rim of his water glass. "He needs some toughening up."

Jeffrey felt the tears rise up in his eyes. At the same time, his cheeks grew hot. His stomach roiled.

This wasn't supposed to be how it went. His daddy was supposed love him and hug him and fix everything. He wasn't supposed to be mean. He wasn't supposed to laugh at him and call him the same names the kids at school did.

"Ah, Jesus, now he's going to cry." His daddy shook his head. "This just proves my point. What are you, three?" He waved his drink at Jeffrey. "You got a room of your own?" he asked.

Jeffrey nodded dumbly, tears rolling down his fiery cheeks.

"Then go there. Get out of my sight until you decide to be a man and not some kind of little crybaby."

Jeffrey fled to his room. He leapt onto his bed, buried his face into the lumpy, thin pillow and cried. Vaguely, in the distance, he heard the door open and close and then it was silent except for his tears. His sobs racked his chest, tearing at his little lungs. He was aware of a giant pain in his chest, but it wasn't until his tears slowed down a little that he realized what it was. He'd heard of it, but never experienced it until now. His heart was breaking.

A while later, his mother returned, but she didn't come to him. More than anything, that was what he wanted right then. He wanted her to come to his door, sit on his bed and gather him up in her arms. He wanted to press his face between her breasts and finish his crying there instead of the poor excuse of a pillow on his bed. She would stroke his hair and comfort him and tell him how it was just the two of them against the world and how she would make his daddy go back to the ship or make him stop being mean and she would stop being mean and then everything would be all right.

Instead, he was left alone to cry into his flat pillow.

Eventually, his sobs ran out. He lay on the bed, curled up into a fetal ball. His cheeks remained hot, but the salty tears were drying. As they dried, he felt a tightness on the skin of his cheeks. Every once in a while, he gave a little hitch.

In the small apartment, he could hear their voices carry.

"This is the first leave you've had in two years?" his mother asked, her voice stronger than before but still a pale imitation of what he was used to.

"First one that was long enough to come home," his daddy answered.

"Your ship was in port just this Spring."

"So?"

"Why didn't you come then? If your family is so important?"

"You want another goddamn smack?" he snapped at her.

"No," she said. "I just want to know—"

"I was in the fucking brig, all right?"

It was silent for a few moments, then she asked, "That's why one less stripe? You were demoted?"

"I lost two stripes," he said, a tinge of pride in his voice. "I've earned one back since."

"That explains why the check got smaller."

"Are you starving?" he barked at her.

"No."

"No, I didn't think so. You've got enough for this shithole apartment and for food and your precious vodka, so I'd say I'm providing pretty goddamn well."

It was silent again for a little while, then he could hear them talking in lowered voices. After that, there was the rustle and clinking of items being moved. He could hear the chair slide on the kitchen floor. His mother yelped. It was quiet some more. Then came some more noises he didn't understand, sounds that he was pretty sure his mother and his daddy were making with their voices, but they weren't words. He thought about going into the kitchen to see if they were all right, but he stayed put. He didn't know who he wanted to see less at that moment, so he decided he didn't want to see either one of them.

After what seemed like a long time, the noises stopped, then changed to hushed voices again. He heard his daddy laugh derisively. "It might give him an idea what it means to be a man, that's what," he said.

The apartment grew dark as his parents talked and drank in the kitchen. He could hear their voices and sometimes the actual words, as well as the clink of glasses. Sometimes the tones were quiet, almost gentle. Other times, his father's voice boomed with laughter. Still other exchanges had the sharp edge of anger to them.

Hours later, his door swung open. He hoped it was his mother, there to comfort him, but expected it was more likely his father, there to tell him that lying on his bed like that was queer and that he was a crybaby.

"Jeffie?" his mother's voice had a softness to it, and for a moment he thought his hopes might be realized. Then she spoke again and he realized that gentleness was simply the way her voice turned when she drank a lot of her special stuff. "Wash your face and come and eat."

He roused himself from bed. In the bathroom, he splashed his face with water. Then he made his way to the kitchen.

His daddy sat with his elbows on the table, his arms crossed, holding his drink. An edgy smile hovered on his face. Jeffrey looked into his red, watery eyes for some sign of the daddy he'd been waiting for almost forever.

"Well, Jeffie," he said, his voice softened in the same way his mother's was. "Done with your little crying fit?"

Jeffrey swallowed and nodded. "Yes, sir."

His daddy's eyebrows shot up. "Hey, he's a quick learner." He glanced over at the stove where Jeffrey's mother stirred dinner. "At least there's that, Cora. I can teach this boy to be a man someday."

His mother didn't answer. She served dinner in silence, the hard line of her mouth returning. She slopped some beans in front of his daddy, then Jeffrey and finally herself. The three of them ate quietly. Once they'd finished, she cleared the plates from the table.

Jeffrey's daddy poured another drink and sipped it. He eyed the boy over the top of his glass. "So you want to learn to be a real man, kid?"

Jeffrey felt a surge of joy in his chest. "Yes, sir!"

His daddy chuckled. "All right. Good. We'll start with lesson one right now. Stop acting like a goddamn sissy. That means no whining. No crying. And stop looking like you're afraid of everything and everybody. You have to show the world you're tough, kid. Sometimes you have to prove it, too. But if you look like a little sissy, then you're going to get screwed with all the time by everybody."

Jeffrey swallowed, but nodded that he understood.

"And no more of this 'Jeffie' shit. Understand? The next kid that calls you Jeffie, you punch the little bastard right in the nose. Got it?"

"Yes, sir."

"Good." His daddy took a long drink, then sighed afterward. "Things are going to change around here, yessir."

Jeffrey grinned. Maybe his wish was going to come true after all.

At the sink, his mother washed dishes in silence.

That night, Jeffrey sat up late at the kitchen table while his father drank and told stories. He told Jeffrey and his mother about the ship he was on, which he said was the best damn ship in the Navy, and that was mostly because of him, since the entire ship was filled with idiot officers. He described the ports he'd been to in faraway lands. Jeffrey listened, wide-eyed. His mother joined them, sipping her special stuff without a word, looking down at the kitchen table. She didn't react to any of the stories, but Jeffrey figured that maybe she'd heard them before. She did shift in her seat slightly when his daddy described some of the women in the different ports he'd visited, but didn't say a word.

Jeffrey learned about port and starboard that night. He learned that a man stands up for himself. That was how he got respect. Respect meant that no one touched you or called you names.

Jeffrey thought respect sounded like the greatest thing ever invented. He started to tell his daddy about the things some of the kids at school did and said to him, but stopped when he saw the disapproval in his daddy's eyes.

"You can't let them get away with that," his daddy told him. "They'll turn you into a total wimp."

So he stopped before he got to the Pee-Pee Pants story or the dodge ball story. Instead, he promised his daddy he'd "take care of business" at school the next day.

His daddy reached out clumsily and clapped him on the shoulder. "Thas' a good boy," he said.

His mother rose from the table. "Time for bed, Jeffie."

"Jeff!" his daddy bellowed. "No more of this Jeffie shit!"

His mother didn't reply. She gave Jeffrey a withering look and pointed toward the bathroom. He slipped out of his chair, headed for the bathroom and got ready for bed.

"After I tuck him in, I'm laying down, too," he heard his mother say.

"Fine. I'll be in for a repeat performance after I finish this drink."

"I'm a little tired," she said.

"You better get un-tired," he told her.

Jeffrey put his toothbrush away and went into his bedroom. He crawled into bed, pulling the covers over him. He wasn't sure what his mother meant by tucking him in. He couldn't remember the last time she'd put him to bed. Usually she just let him give her a quick hug while she sat in her chair, watching her programs with a water glass in hand. But he was surprised when she showed up at his bedside, sitting down next to his small form.

She leaned down, her breath strong with her special stuff. Even though she hadn't tucked him in for what seemed like years, he still expected a kiss on the forehead and a whispered 'good night.' Instead, she grabbed a handful of his hair at the base of his neck and pulled it taut.

"Remember," she whispered in his ear, "he'll be gone soon. Don't you go getting any big ideas."

She gave his hair a painful tug for good measure, then released him. A moment later, she'd stood and left the room, leaving his head spinning with questions.

What did she mean?

How long would he be here? Would he have enough time to teach Jeffrey what he needed to know?

Exhausted and confused, he dropped off to sleep.

The next morning, he woke up on his own. Both his mother and his daddy slept through him making himself breakfast. He buttered his toast next to a nearly empty bottle of brown special stuff (the label said 'whiskey', so he figured that was what his mother had retrieved from the store for his daddy last night) and a pair of water glasses. Both still had some special stuff in them. He sniffed his daddy's glass and jerked his head back in surprise at how strong the smell was. He wondered how his daddy was able to put that stuff in his mouth, much less swallow it. Then he realized that it was because his daddy was tough.

He wanted to be tough, too.

He wanted his daddy to be proud of him.

He wanted his daddy to stay forever.

He reached out and picked up the glass. With a shaking hand, he brought it to his lips. Before he could drink any, the strong odor assaulted his nostrils again and he had to put the glass back on the table.

I guess I'm not tough enough yet.

Besides, he figured that his daddy might be mad if he drank any of his special stuff without asking. So that was a good reason to leave it alone, too.

He finished buttering his toast. After he ate, he crept into the living room and turned on the television. He kept the volume as low as it would go and still allow him to hear anything. Quietly, he changed the channel knob from station to station. There were only four channels to choose from. One of them had a preacher. Another one looked like a news guy. The Sesame Street channel had more news guys on it, but the final channel featured a Bugs Bunny cartoon. He smiled and sat just a few inches away from the T.V., laughing at the antics of the 'wascally wabbit.' Just to be careful, he covered his laughter with his hand.

Cartoons eventually gave way to football games, so he turned off the T.V. and tried to read his Dr. Seuss book again. It was difficult to concentrate with his ears piqued for any movement from his parent's room.

He was starting to get hungry for lunch when his mother stumbled out of the bedroom in her robe. She breezed past the living room and straight to the kitchen, where he heard her brewing coffee. Then, magically, he heard sounds of sizzling food. The aroma of bacon wafted out into the living room.

His mother was cooking breakfast. She never cooked breakfast.

He walked to the kitchen and poked his head around the corner of the doorway. He spotted his mother standing at the stove, turning strips of bacon, then cracking several eggs into a frying pan.

From behind him, the heavy thud of feet stomped out of the bedroom and into the bathroom. From behind the closed door,

Jeffrey could hear his father making retching sounds. His own stomach clenched at the sound. He covered his ears. After a few moments, the sound ended. The toilet flushed, followed by running water. Then his daddy stumbled from the bathroom and toward the kitchen. He brushed by Jeffrey without a word, sliding up behind his mother. Amazingly, he swatted her on the bottom, causing her to jump. A slice of bacon flew through the air and landed on the counter.

"Goddamnit, Stan!" she snapped. "I'm cooking your breakfast."

"The kid can have that piece," he said, motioning to the errant slice of bacon. He stood directly behind her, pressing up against her back. His arms snaked around to the front of her. Jeffrey couldn't see what he was doing, but his mother twisted and dodged in place while he groped at her. "And I'll have this one."

"I'm trying to cook," she said in an irritated tone. "Jesus, I took care of you last night."

His daddy's hand flew up and grabbed his mother's hair. He pulled hard with a backward jerk. "And what if I want it again right now?" he asked her in a low, mean voice. He jerked on her hair again. "What do you say to that, huh?"

"You're hurting me," she said.

"You even haven't seen the beginning of hurt," he told her. "You want to see hurt? I will lay the whammo on you, Cora. You won't walk right for a week. And you definitely won't be able to smart back to me with that pretty little mouth."

"The eggs are going to burn," she whimpered.

He laughed then and let her go with a slight shove. She immediately went back to stirring the scrambled eggs, then retrieved the wayward slice of bacon.

His daddy glanced over and spotted Jeffrey in the doorway. He lowered himself into the chair at the kitchen table. "I see we have a little sneaky spy in the house," he said.

Jeffrey didn't know what to say, so he replied, "Yes, sir."

His daddy laughed again. "Oh, he's learning." He reached out and swatted Jeffrey's mother on the bottom again. "You hear that, Cora? He's learning. Better than you, he's learning."

His mother didn't reply. She served them wordlessly, just as she had the night before. His daddy didn't thank her, but he tore into the food, eating quickly. Jeffrey watched him, amazed. Then he picked up his fork and tried to do the same.

Once his daddy finished eating, he lifted the water glass from last night and peered at the brown liquid. "Hair o' the dog that bit ya," he said, almost more to himself than anyone else. Then he drained the glass in one swift swallow. He grimaced, let out a small belch and sighed afterward. "Good ol' Jack," he said.

Jeffrey tried to eat his breakfast as hurriedly as possible. His daddy didn't notice. Instead, he stood with the bottle of special stuff and wandered into the living room.

When Jeffrey finished, he found his way into the living room, where his daddy sat watching a football game and sipping his drink. Jeffrey found a place to sit unobtrusively and watched the game with his daddy. Neither of them said a word, but for Jeffrey, that two hours would become quite likely his greatest childhood memory.

When the game ended, his daddy glanced over at him, seeming to just then notice he was there. He took a drink from his glass and sniffed in disgust. "Seems like it was a bad idea for Seattle to get a football team, huh?"

Jeffrey had heard of the Seahawks. Some of the boys at school wore jerseys to school with the stylized blue and green logo of the fictional bird. He himself didn't care much about football, but if his daddy liked it, maybe he would, too. In fact, maybe football would be his favorite sport from now on.

"You retarded or something, kid?" his daddy said. "I asked you a question."

"Yes, sir," Jeffrey blurted automatically.

His daddy scowled. "Yes, you are retarded?"

"I mean, no, sir," Jeffrey sputtered.

"No? You mean you like the Seahawks? They're almost as bad as Tampa Bay." He waved his hand at Jeffrey. "Now go to your room. You're bothering me."

Jeffrey spent the rest of the day in his room, listening to every whisper of movement and voice out in the living room and the kitchen. He crept out once to use the bathroom, peeing carefully onto the inside edge of the toilet bowl in order to keep as quiet as possible. He didn't flush.

There wasn't much talking between his mother and his daddy during the day, but occasionally he heard an exchange, though he couldn't make out the words most of the time. Once, the words were sharper and he heard some sort of tussling. This was followed a smacking sound, which made him jump. There was a pause, then more tussling, but it was quieter and more rhythmic.

Around dinnertime, his mother brought him in a peanut butter sandwich. She had changed into her robe. He noticed a deep redness below her left eye.

He thought about asking her what happened, but instinctively, he knew. She must have made a wrong look at his daddy and so he laid the whammo on her.

He stared up at her, torn. He felt a perverse thrill knowing that she wasn't in charge. Maybe she could still be mean to him, but she wasn't the boss anymore. At the same time, an overwhelming desire came over him to hug her and make her feel better.

Before he could act on either emotion, she thrust the plate toward him. "Eat your dinner," she told him numbly, "and put yourself to bed."

She left without another word.

He chewed the peanut butter slowly, his stomach growling while he ate. He didn't know what to think or what to feel. He was glad his daddy was home. But it wasn't working the way he'd hoped.

What could he do?

Jeffrey chewed on his sandwich, thinking.

The next morning, he went to school with purpose. At the morning recess, he waited in line to play tetherball. Most of line was made up of girls, which he thought was just fine. In fact, it was probably almost perfect. His daddy would want him to put one of them in her place.

Laura Kennedy was the one who tried to take cuts when it was his turn. She was a girl who always wore overalls to school because she said her daddy was a farmer. Once, she'd told Jeffrey that being a farmer was much better than being in the Navy, so he thought it was fitting that she be the one to step in front of him now.

"It's my turn," he told Laura resolutely.

"No, it's not," she said. "It's mine."

"I'm next," Jeffrey insisted.

"Shut up, Jeffie," Laura said. "Why don't you go pee your pants?"

Jeffrey felt a warm satisfaction coil up inside his stomach. He balled up his fist and punched Laura in the cheek as hard as he could.

His knuckles grazed her cheekbone and scraped across her ear. Laura's eyes flew open in surprise, then narrowed in anger. She punched Jeffrey in the stomach. The air whooshed out of his lungs. He sank to his knees, then curled into a ball on the ground.

Laura wasn't finished, though. She dropped on top of him, rolling him onto his back. Her knees pinned his arms to the blacktop while she punched him in the face. The first punch landed on his mouth, driving his lip into a tooth, cutting it. The second punch blasted into his eye, sending racing white dots shooting through his head. The third and final blow crunched his nose, sending comets chasing after those white dots. The warm flow of blood gushed from his nostrils, covering his upper lip.

The teacher on playground duty interceded at that point, hauling both of them to the principal's office, where Jeffrey had to undergo the humiliation of admitting that he threw the first punch in the fight. This shame was coupled with having been beaten up by a girl, even if it was a girl who wore overalls and whose dad was a farmer.

The principal gave Jeffrey a look that was difficult to decipher as the boy sat on the chair in front of his desk with a tissue pressed against one nostril. Jeffrey wanted to believe that he felt bad for Jeffrey's bloody nose or maybe that he was proud that he'd tried to put a girl in her place, but somehow he didn't think so. Then he gave both children notes to take home for their parents to sign. "Bring those back tomorrow," he told them. "And you two leave each other alone the rest of the day."

Jeffrey endured the snickers and stares for the remainder of the school day. At the final bell, he scrambled to get away from the school as fast as he could. He managed to avoid all but a couple of catcalls from other kids. Once on the street headed home, however, he slowed to a crawl. He wondered if his mother would get angry again and march down to the school. Would she find a way to 'own the school,' like she told the principal last time? He remembered how good it felt for that short time while she was sticking up for him. He momentarily quickened his pace, until he remembered her admonition afterward.

And what would his daddy say? He'd been in a fight. Didn't that make him tough? Deep inside, Jeffrey knew it didn't. He'd been in a fight with a girl. And he lost. A real man laid the whammo on girls. Laura laid the whammo on him instead.

Jeffrey hung his head and shuffled home.

When he arrived, he found his mother sitting in her chair with her glass of special stuff, watching one of her programs. She turned her gaze toward him as soon as he walked in the door. The black eye, bloody lip and swollen nose registered slowly with her. She pressed her lips together and scowled.

"What happened?"

Wordlessly, he handed her the note from the principal. She snatched it from his hand and read it, her lips moving while her eyes scanned the slip of paper. When she'd finished, she balled up the note and set it on the rickety end table next to her.

"You're supposed to sign it," Jeffrey told her quietly.

His mother turned toward him again. Her right hand lashed out, slapping him hard across the face. The force of the blow was magnified by his earlier injuries and he yelped in painful surprise. His hand flew up to his cheek. Tears stung his eyes.

"He's gone again," his mother said quietly. A cruel smile curled up at the corners of her mouth. "It's just you and me against the world again, Jeffie."

A strange combination of relief, anger and fear washed over him at those words. The tears in his eyes bubbled over and coursed down his cheeks.

His daddy was gone.

An ache appeared in his chest, almost like a jagged blade was tearing through it. He let out a small sob.

His mother reached out to him. Gratefully, he fell into her embrace, resting his face between her breasts. The sobs rose up in his chest and came out in huge, racking moans. His mother ran her fingers through his hair. For a moment, even though he hurt, he also felt safe. He also felt good. Maybe the two of them could stand against the world. Maybe she could make everything—

Her fingers twisted and tightened in his hair. She jerked his head backward to stare up at her. Malice radiated from her red, watery eyes. Her foul breath washed down onto his face. The sour stench cut through his overworked sinuses, despite the earlier bleeding and his crying now.

"He's gone," she repeated, "but you're just like him. You ruin everything, too."

Jeffrey felt something deep inside him wilt. The intensity of his sobs waned. The color in the room faded.

"You ruin everything," his mother said, and Jeffrey believed her.

October 1980

All he ever wanted anymore was snow. That was the only real wish he had left that he held out as a possibility. There had been a time when he wished for other things, but now that he was ten, he knew better. He knew better than to wish for the things that his mother or father (not his 'daddy' anymore. 'Daddy' was a baby word) would have to be responsible for making happen. Instead, he wished for things that came from outside his own house. The weather seemed to be the easiest thing to count on, and in Seattle, snow seemed like something special enough to hope for.

His father made it home once or twice a year. Jeffrey both dreaded the time and looked forward to it. He held out an insane hope that the next time would be better. His father and his mother would decide to make it so they were all a real family. His mother would stop being mean all the time. His father would want to stay. He'd tell Jeffrey how big he'd grown to be and how much he was proud of him.

But these foolish hopes didn't come true. Every time his father visited, in fact, they seemed to slip farther away. His father usually arrived in a foul mood, sometimes already drunk. Sometimes Jeffrey noticed he had one less stripe on his uniform. Other times, he'd have it back. He noticed the lines on his father's face and how he always looked tired. He seemed meaner, but not as strong.

At first, that diminishing strength only fed Jeffrey's hope. He reasoned that if his father wasn't as strong, then he wouldn't be so mean to his mother. Then things would get better. His mother, however, seemed to have other plans. In the face of his father's weakening, she grew more bold. He heard them arguing more frequently, with her voice gaining resolve. His father had to lay the whammo on her more often. Sometimes she ran into the bedroom and locked the door. Then his father would either break down the door or he would sleep on the couch. If he slept on the couch, Jeffrey made sure to leave him alone because he was always in a worse mood than usual. He didn't hesitate to give Jeffrey the back of his hand for any perceived mistake or irritation.

Once, he spilled his cereal bowl. Milk and corn flakes splashed across the kitchen table and onto the floor. His father was sitting at the table, drinking coffee and reading the newspaper. He leapt up in his chair, wiping milk off his shirt and pants.

That resulted in a spanking with his father's belt. The folded strap lashed his backside, raising red welts on his buttocks and the backs of his legs. He tried not to cry because crying only resulted in being told he was a 'sissy' or even a 'little queer,' both of which burned in his chest just like when the kids at school said it.

His mother stood in the kitchen doorway and watched the spanking. He looked up at her and pleaded silently for her to intervene. He knew she could probably make him stop, even if it meant that he decided to lay the whammo on her instead. She could make him stop. He knew it. So he pleaded with his eyes, begging her.

But she only watched the beating, her expression flat and unreadable.

The strappings only came when his father was furious or when he had a little time to think about things. Like the time he brought home his report card on the same Friday his father showed up. The littering of 'Unsatisfactory' ratings led to another session with the belt, with his father counting the strokes. He received one for every 'Unsatisfactory' on his report card.

More often, though, his father's hard palm lashed out and cuffed him in the back of the head. Sometimes he got the back of the hand across the mouth, if that were more convenient. He tried to learn what to say and do in order to avoid it, but he was unable to crack the code. He got in trouble for asking questions, but he got in trouble for being too quiet. He got in trouble for staying in his room and for 'hanging all over' his father. He was punished for not looking at his father when he was being spoken to, but other times he got the back of the hand for the expression on his face.

And yet, still he tried to impress his father. He asked his mother to let him play fifth grade football. She refused. When his father came home a few months later, he ridiculed Jeffrey for not being on the football team.

"Maybe you could be a cheerleader," he suggested, shaking his head. "Jesus, what a mess you are, boy."

Whenever his father came home, he made a point to show him he wasn't a sissy. He wasn't a little queer. He was tough. If that meant finding a way to get into a fight (never a difficult thing to do when all the other kids seemed to pick on him more every year), so be it. He'd come home with a black eye or bloody lip and a note, wearing those injuries like a badge of honor. But his father always took them to mean that Jeffrey had lost the fight (which was true, but how did he always know?) and ridiculed him all the more.

When his father was away, his mother ruled with an iron fist. Her hand was quick to slap his cheek for any reason. Sometimes there didn't seem to be a reason, but he learned not to ask her why, because that resulted in a follow-up smack.

Jeffrey stopped wishing that it would ever truly be she and him against the world. He knew that she wasn't going to love him enough for that to happen. Every so often, though, she gave him a renewed false hope. This seemed to happen in the evening and only when she'd been drinking her vodka (he didn't call it 'special stuff' anymore. That was a baby word, too) for the majority of the day. He always knew when it was coming. First, she stopped watching television. Then she brought out old pictures and thumbed through them. Next, she grew weepy. She'd mutter things he couldn't hear clearly nor understand. Then she'd call him to her, draw him to her chest and stroke his hair.

"You and me against the world," she'd whisper over and over again.

Sometimes, she'd fall asleep in the chair. When that happened, he always cleaned up the pictures. He didn't bother to look at them. Most were of people he didn't know. A few showed his mother and father much younger and smiling. He put them back in the shoebox his mother kept them stored in and covered her with a blanket. He always hoped in vain that she'd wake up and hug him in the morning like she did on those nights. Maybe she'd even make him breakfast and repeat that it was the two of them against the world. But she never did. Instead, she awoke in a foul mood, demanding silence all day because she had a 'splitting headache.'

Other times, her mood would turn before she even fell asleep. She'd push him away, toppling him to the floor. Then she'd throw down the box of pictures and hurl invectives at him. He was worthless. He was an anchor pulling her to the bottom of Puget Sound. He was everything that had ever gone wrong in her life.

Once he told her he was sorry for being all of those things. She responded with a vicious slap. "Don't patronize me, you little bastard!" she screeched.

His head humming from the blow, he blinked back and didn't reply.

"And don't you sit there and give me your father's look, either!"

He struggled to put a neutral expression on his face. And after that, he didn't say anything when her mood turned. He sat and endured it until she shouted herself out, turned and staggered away. Then he'd slip off to his bedroom and go to sleep.

There were times, though, that her weepy affection and reminisces led her to take him to bed with her. In those instances, she took him by the hand and led him into her room. Together, they curled up under the blankets. She held him close, her chin resting atop his head. The warmth of their bodies surrounded Jeffrey like heated cotton. He closed his eyes and let himself drift, always hopeful that this is how it would be forever. While she slept, her arm rested gently across him. Her breath plumed lightly in his hair. Even the rattle of a snore deep in her throat was somehow comforting.

He soon learned that even on those rare occasions, nothing good can last. When she woke first, she expelled him from her bed, calling names ranging from 'little baby' (which he understood but didn't agree with) to 'dirty little boy' (which he didn't understand but knew he didn't like to hear). In either event, she'd send him to his own bed with an ear ringing from a slap and the blankets of his bed cold. So after that, if he was lucky enough for her to want to snuggle with him, he tried hard to wake up first. Sometimes that didn't work, either, because if she remembered the night before, he'd still get the slap in the morning. But the nice thing about vodka, Jeffrey discovered, was that sometimes it made his mother forget the previous night. Maybe that's why it was a whore's drink, he figured. That's what his father said about vodka. Jeffrey thought that maybe a whore was someone who forgot things in the morning. Or maybe it was just another word for a mean mother. He wasn't sure exactly, though he had figured out that only a woman could be called a whore.

At school, he found an oasis of safety – the library. In the library, everyone had to be quiet. They couldn't call him Jeffie Pee-Pee Pants or queer-bait or any of the other dozen names that kids kept coming up with. No one was able to take his place in line or steal his milk money. There was always a librarian on duty who made sure of these things, though Jeffrey figured out that it wasn't him she was worried about so much as the sanctity of library silence. He didn't care, though. He was able to find a book, hide away in one of the study carrels in the corner and read.

The books took him to worlds far away from Seattle. He read about pirates and wizards and monsters. He read about sports heroes and war heroes and super heroes.

For his birthday that year, he convinced his mother to get him a library card at the public library. Unlike the school library, which only housed children's books, the public library had a wide array of books about anything he could imagine. She balked at first, but he said he wanted it more than any presents (she would have only bought him some clothes, anyway, he figured), so she relented. Besides, he explained to her, it was free. There was a library branch just six blocks from their apartment. This quickly became his sanctuary. He spent hours among the shelves. When he wasn't there, he holed up in his room, reading the books he checked out.

His mother only occasionally objected to his absences, but since he'd turned ten he started making his own meals and taking care of himself in every way, which left her more time to drink her whore's drink and watch her programs. About the only thing they did together on a regular basis was sit in the Laundromat once each week and watch the three loads of laundry as they were first washed, then dried. Every other interaction seemed to be in passing, sometimes punctuated with a sharp word or a stinging slap. He learned to absorb those without crying. Crying in front of his mother was almost as bad as crying in front of his father and there were far more opportunities for it.

So they settled into a routine of sorts, Jeffrey and his mother. She seemed to accept his bookishness because it freed her of dealing with him. He accepted that the cost of being her son remained the frequent slurred, angry words and hard smacks, but that they never lasted forever and he was eventually allowed to escape into a book.

Then his father came home and disrupted the truce. For those few days, Jeffrey tried to hide his reading habit while at the same time needing the escape all the more. The arguments between his parents grew fiercer and more frequent. The bruises and swollen lips appeared on his mother's face more often. At the same time, it seemed like his father only ever slept on the couch. Sometimes he went out, staying away until late in the night. Every time he left, Jeffrey hoped he was going back to the best damn ship in the Navy (even if it was full of idiot officers) instead of coming home in the middle of the night, slamming doors and singing incoherently.

Once, he ordered Jeffrey out of bed in the middle of the night and into the living room. He stood at attention, blinking stupidly through his sleepy eyes, while his father criticized him and gave him advice on how to stop being such a sissy queer boy. He punctuated his points with heavy slaps to Jeffrey's shoulders, along with admonitions to 'stand up straight like a man.'

Jeffrey stood as tall and rigid as he could at three o'clock in the morning. He pretended he was an Army soldier and stared straight ahead, refusing to cry. He knew his father hated the Army even more than he hated and loved the Navy, so pretending to be a soldier gave him a strange sense of satisfaction and strength. It must have shown on his face because his father lit into him for having a "smart ass look on that mug of yours." He followed that up with a series of hard slaps to Jeffrey's head.

"You think you're something? Huh?"

Slap.

"You aren't shit, you little shit."

Slap.

"You little whore's son. You'll never be shit."

Slap.

"Don't you fucking look at me like that."

Tears sprang to Jeffrey's eyes. He willed them not to fall.

The appearance of tears seemed to satisfy his father. He stopped slapping and laughed uproariously. "Oh, there it is. The little queer crybaby I know." He waved him away with a flick of his hand. "Get out of my sight."

Jeffrey retreated gratefully to his bedroom, but it was a long time before the burning in his belly allowed him to sleep.

On another occasion, he heard two voices come into the apartment late at night. One was unmistakably his father's deep rumbling, but he didn't recognize the other voice. It was definitely a woman's voice, though. There were some whispers and laughter and the clink of glasses, followed by some other noises that he couldn't exactly place. He heard the woman's voice cry out as if she were in some kind of pain. That's when he figured out that his father was putting her in her place. He was laying the whammo on her, just like he did to his mother.

After a while, the noises leveled off and he drifted back to sleep.

In the morning, he waited for the argument to begin, but it never came. Eventually, his hunger drove him out of his room. In the kitchen, his father drank coffee and read the newspaper. His mother sat in her chair and watched television. No one said anything.

Jeffrey made himself some toast. For now, he decided not to say anything, either. Instead, he ate his toast, then slipped into the living room. He stood next to the window and watched the sky for snow.

August 1982

His father missed his twelfth birthday, which was no surprise.

Slightly more surprising was that so did his mother, even though she was there. She tried to make up for her forgetfulness several days later. She took him to McDonald's for a cheeseburger and then to the movies. Together, they sat in the darkened theater and watched *E.T., the Extraterrestrial.* She even bought him popcorn and a soda.

More importantly, she wasn't being mean to him.

That part lasted the entire movie and until they made it out to the parking lot. In the car on the way back to the apartment, though, she noticed that he'd wiped his buttery fingers on his jeans. Her hand whipped out and caught him alongside his head, accompanied by harsh words about how he "never took care of his things" and how he "ruined everything he touched."

He clenched his jaw and said, "Yes, Mother."

At home, he tried to slip away to his room and lose himself in a book. But she caught him first. Reaching out with her thumb and forefinger, she gripped the tender skin under his chin and pinched. This was even worse than the slaps. If he tightened the muscles that ran under there, her finger pinch turned into a finger-nail gouge, followed up with a slap to the head.

"Don't think you can just run and hide," she carped at him. "That's all you ever do, is read your stupid books. You don't know how hard it is to be a single mother and to try to keep this house in order."

"Yes, Mother."

"Oh, get out of my sight," she told him. "You disgust me."

He fled to his room. The book he was reading now concerned a boy who was thirteen and going through changes. The boy discovered things about girls that Jeffrey was just starting to be interested in. Beyond that, things were happening to that boy that were also happening to Jeffrey. The one that worried him the most until he read about it in this book was that sometimes he woke up in the night and realized he'd wet the bed. At first, he was horrified because of the difficulty he used to have with wetting the bed and wetting his pants. But this was different than pee. Instead, there was less of it and it was sticky. The boy in the book called them "wet dreams" and he always had them when he thought about his best friend's sister. Jeffrey couldn't always remember what he'd been dreaming about, but the times that he did remember were confusing to him. Sometimes, he knew he'd been dreaming about the sounds that the strange woman made in the living room when his father was laying the whammo on her. Other times, he knew he'd been dreaming about his mother, though he couldn't remember what happened in the dream.

Eventually, he learned that he didn't have to be asleep or dreaming to make those things happen. He could think about things, touch himself and after a while, there was a wonderful feeling, followed by that same wet, sticky stuff. He marveled at what a wonderful secret he'd discovered. He wondered if anyone else knew about it, but he instinctively knew to keep it private.

All of the changes in his body that made him think that maybe when his father came home again, he'd talk to him differently when he saw that he was becoming a man. He'd grow big and strong. Maybe he'd join the Army and even though that would make his father angry, he'd get over it when he saw how tough Jeffrey was. He'd show him. He'd lay the whammo on lots of different girls. He didn't know how many it would take before his father would love him, but he knew that if he did it enough, eventually he would.

February 1985

High school was a nightmare on all fronts. He'd hoped he'd grow out of his troubles, but they only evolved along with him, taking on different slants and hues but finding him all the same.

His retreat into the library was a permanent one. He graduated from hiding in the stacks of books, to working as a library aide and an audio-visual aide. Returning books to the shelves and setting up film projectors occupied his time. More importantly, it kept him flying underneath the radar of some of the school's biggest bullies. He still took his share of casual barbs, as well as enduring the occasional act of intimidation. But he'd discovered a truth at home that carried over to his school experience.

He could handle it.

It would pass.

When they called him a name, he didn't react. He just waited until they got bored and moved on. Whenever some jock or headbanger knocked his books from his hands, he merely knelt down and picked them back up. Did he get angry on the inside?

Oh, yes. He fucking *seethed*. But he learned to hide it. He learned to put it away for another day. A day would come when he'd get his revenge. He realized now that it might not be until he came back to the twenty-year reunion as a wealthy success that could buy and sell every one of the loser assholes who thought they were so much better than him, but his time would come. He'd roll into town in an expensive car with a big-tittied blonde trophy wife on his arm. Everyone would try to remember what he'd been like in high school, but all they'd be able to think about would be the nice car and nice rack in front of them.

All the girls in school would be jealous, too. They'd be sorry they didn't get their hooks into him when they had the chance. Every one of them, especially the ones he thought about when he touched himself, would wish they wouldn't have been such stuck up bitches.

Still, he knew that was years away. That didn't make it easy to bear things, but it made it possible. He read books about anything and everything, learning everything he could while working in the library and hating every minute of high school.

Home was worse. His mother seemed to grow harsher each passing year. She had him doing all of the housework, even including her laundry. Her thin fingers still found their way under his chin for that demeaning pinch. "You can't do anything right, can you?" was her favorite refrain.

She'd taken to walking into his bedroom without knocking. He didn't know why she did that, other than the fact that she seemed to delight in watching him scramble to cover his erection and hide the fact that he'd been dreaming of girls at school and revenge. She'd order him out of bed to complete some mundane task like taking out the kitchen garbage, then stand there and watch him squirm while he made excuses to delay things long enough for his erection to subside.

Other times, out of the blue, she seemed to refer to his activities when she told him he was "still a dirty little boy." He pretended not to understand as embarrassment and shame swallowed him whole.

His father's visits grew more infrequent and more intense. His parents would usually drink together, which devolved into a fight without fail. Either they'd end up in the bedroom or his father would storm out. Sometimes he just didn't come back. Those were Jeffrey's favorite times. But often, he did return and never alone. He brought women home with him, turning the living room into a sexual playground. Jeffrey was at once attracted and repelled when this happened. He lay in bed and listened to the voices and the sounds of sex in the living room. Excited, he found himself masturbating furiously to the noises, then lying in bed afterward, full of shame.

The next morning, no one left their bedroom until his father roused the woman and sent her on her way, although Jeffrey sometimes sneaked out to get a look at his father's conquests. He felt a strange sense of pride while hating him for it at the same time.

Other times, his father felt the need to assert his alpha wolf status. Despite Jeffrey's efforts to avoid him and not to offer any affront, it required very little drinking before his father took offense at some slight, real or imagined. Then he was called into the living room, where he stood at attention to be berated and slapped. This worked into his father theorizing that Jeffrey thought he was "tougher than the old man." He'd challenge Jeffrey to "take his best shot," demanding it until he reached the conclusion that Jeffrey was "too much of a queer little pussy" to do so. "Get out of my sight," he'd bellow at Jeffrey. "You make me sick."

Rarely, though, and for some reason he had never been able to pinpoint, the three of them were able to co-exist in an easy, quiet truce. Jeffrey read his books in his room while his parents drank slowly and watched television. On these days, he was able to escape the house and go to the library.

Sometimes, he'd take his books and go to the mall where he'd watch the same bitchy girls from school ignore him there, too. But he'd pretend to read his book and stare that their bodies. He'd imagine tearing the clothing off of them. He saw their surprise at how tough he was, what a man he was. As that realization seeped into their eyes, he knew that his father was right about what every woman wanted deep down inside. So he imagined laying the whammo on them. If they didn't cry out with enough passion, he'd punctuate matters with a good slap upside the head.

He stored those thoughts and the sights of the girls at the mall for when he returned home at night. Lying in bed alone, he'd recall them over and over again. He obsessed and studied and dreamt and watched and masturbated.

His day would come.

He knew it would.

June 12, 1987

High school ended on a Thursday. He left just like it was any other day. Only the librarian, Mrs. Bryant, wished him a happy summer. He thanked her, wishing he could spend it with her at the library, but knowing he'd be spending as much time as possible at the public library or at the mall, looking at girls. Still, the librarian's farewell reminded him oddly of his kindergarten teacher, Miss Reed.

He wondered about Miss Reed as he walked toward home. Did she still teach? Was she even *Miss* Reed anymore, or did she marry some guy and change her name? He imagined she probably had. Looking back, he decided she was fine looking. Someone would have come along and snagged her.

Strangely, the thought made him feel betrayed. She'd been so nice to him, but he imagined that she had probably been faking it all along. Women were generally traitors, at least as much as he could tell based on the one he lived with. He wondered if Miss Reed made fun of him to the other teachers after he left for the day. He saw her getting together in the teacher's lounge and telling all the other teachers shitty things about him. Anger brewed in the pit of his stomach as he made his way toward the apartment.

He switched the scenario. Saw himself finding her at her house. Fantasized about what he would do to her.

He smiled, holding his folder and library book in front of his jeans as he walked.

At his apartment, he let himself in. His mother was taking one of her naps, so he kept as quiet as he could. In his bedroom, he put aside the book and the folder. He opened his button, unzipped his pants and slid them down his hips. Leaning back and touching himself, he imagined again what his visit to Miss Reed's house would be like.

I'd lay the whammo on that bitch.

He closed his eyes and saw it all over again, like a movie playing in his head. Coming inside the house. Maybe a hard slap across the face to get things started. Tearing away her clothing. Bending her over the couch. No, over the coffee table. Ripping her shirt off of her back as he pumped into her. Listening to her scream–

The door to his room flung open. His mother stood in the doorway, glaring at him.

Jeffrey scrambled to his feet, turning his back to her. "Jesus, Mother! Don't you knock?"

"I don't have to knock in my own house, you dirty little boy!" She cackled at him. "I knew it. I knew you were in here being nasty."

"I wasn't doing anything." He looked over his shoulder at her as he zipped his pants and snapped the button. "I was just going to change my school clothes, that's all."

She stepped into the room, shaking her head. "Liar," she whispered.

"It's the truth. I–"

"No," she whispered. "It's a *lie.*"

There was something strange in her voice that made him stop. Her words were slurred more heavily than was usual for this early in the afternoon, but he knew she sometimes started early. The difference in her voice went beyond that, however. It was oddly soft and gentle, something he could remember from years ago and only intermittently at that.

"Sit down," she said, motioning to the bed.

Hesitantly, he sat on the edge of his mattress. She lowered herself clumsily, sitting beside him. The essence of her sweat and the alcohol permeated the small bedroom. Her eyes were red and watery, their customary hardness filled with an empty sorrow that wasn't familiar to him.

"Do you think I don't know what you do in here at night?" she asked him.

"I don't do anything. I only—"

She raised her hand. He flinched involuntarily, expecting her to pinch beneath his chin. Instead, she rested her index finger on his lips, shushing him. "It's all right," she whispered. "Every boy does it. Every single little boy ends up becoming a nasty young man and then a piece of shit just like your father."

His thoughts raced. He had wondered if other boys did it, but based on the conversations he overheard, everyone denied it. He thought something was wrong with him, not just for doing it but for how often.

"You can't help it," she said in the same soft voice. "You're just like him."

She let her finger fall away from his lips.

"You even look like him. Hell, you could be brothers, you look so much alike."

He didn't know whether to be happy or not about that. Was it a good thing or a bad thing to look like your father?

His mother straightened the battered robe that covered her legs. Then she cast him a sidelong glance. "What do you think about when you do it, Jeffie?"

His heart raced. If she knew he touched himself, was it possible that she knew what he fantasized about? Could she know how he wanted to lay the whammo on the girls at school? Did she have some sort of motherly knowledge about these things? He tried to tell himself this wasn't possible, but then why was she asking him this?

"Do you think about the little pretties at your school?" she continued. "Those girls with their fluffy hair and their tight jeans?"

Jeffrey swallowed. He didn't know how to answer, but she was staring at him, so he gave her a small nod.

"Of course you do," she said, her voice silky smooth. "What boy wouldn't?" She leaned closer. "But tell me something else, Jeffie. Have you ever done more than just *think* about any of them?"

His heart pounded frantically.

She knew.

She knew.

She knew, she knew, sheknewsheknew*sheknew!*

He moved his head left and right with a frenzied shake.

She raised her eyebrow. "No? Never slipped off into a quiet place with one of those large breasted sluts?"

"No," he whispered, though he'd imagined it many times. Did she know that, too?

She smiled as if she knew everything. "Is my little boy still a virgin, then?"

He hesitated, but the admission seemed better than the alternative, so he nodded again.

"I figured as much," she whispered. She took a deep breath and let it out. The powerful odor of vodka washed past him. She glanced down at the thin wedding band on her finger. "You know what today is?" she asked him.

"Last day of school?"

She gave a small laugh. "I suppose so. But do you know what else it is? I'll give you a hint. It's a big day."

He thought about it for a few seconds, but eventually shook his head. "I...I don't know."

"I wouldn't expect you to," she said, twisting the ring. "No one in this family seems to remember."

He waited, expecting that she would tell him what day it was and why no one seemed to remember. Instead, she turned suddenly and was upon him. The force of her motion pushed him backward onto bed. Her legs straddled him. Her face pressed against his, her mouth searching for his. He parted his lips, letting out a surprised sound. Her kisses smothered his small cry. Her tongue snaked out and raked across his teeth.

No!

His stomach clenched. A hotness brewed there that filled with all the hate and love and desire and pain and confusion that he had ever felt. The tumultuous emotions broiled and twisted while her hands tore at his clothing. He lay frozen on his back. He could taste the harshness of her vodka now in the back of his own throat.

His legs trembled. He realized that his erection was straining at his zipper.

Her mouth broke away from his. He gasped for air. Her lips found his earlobe, drawing it into her mouth while her hot breath plumed into his ear.

He raised his arms up in the air, his palms open, his fingers twitching.

What do I do? How do I stop this?

She tore his jeans from his legs, sending them flying across the room. The denim struck the far wall and dropped to the floor like a dead body.

He pushed at her chest while trying to slide backwards, away from her. Her robe fell open. He stared at her hanging breasts, the large red nipples erect. She looked down at him with a mixed expression he'd never seen on her face before, but he recognized them both. Her eyes were filled with a venomous combination of lust and pure hatred.

"No," he gasped at her.

She grasped him by the wrists and pulled his open palms until they were against her chest. The warm flesh of her breasts filled his palms. He pulled weakly against her, shaking his head. His stomach clenched and roiled. She pressed his hands hard against her chest.

He felt light-headed.

"Mother, please—"

She shushed him, rocking her hips against his hardness. "Call me Cora."

"Mother—"

"Cora!" she snapped, grinding herself downward onto him. His hardness slipped inside her. Overpowering warm wetness radiated outward from down there. "Say it!"

He surrendered. "Cora, please."

She kept moving. "Please what?" she purred down at him.

All his strength faded from him. The absolute wrongness of the world at that moment came crushing downward upon his chest. He struggled to breath.

How could this be happening?

"That's right," she said. "Shut up and enjoy it."

That feeling, that wonderful feeling that he'd always associated with his fantasies coming true, swept over him. He arched his back and grunted in surprise, in horror, in ecstasy. The force of the explosion rocked through his legs and up to his chest. His grunt became a primal cry.

As soon as the fluttering convulsions faded, his churning stomach overtook him. He rolled to the left and heaved. The warm vomit spewed out onto his bed and the wall. His stomach clenched again, pulling his legs in toward his center. He was dimly aware of her slipping off of him, but his head was spinning. He clutched at his stomach and retched a third time.

Vaguely, as if it were happening to someone else a hundred million miles away, he felt her hands raining down on him, pounding with the fury of a harpy. The blows didn't bring any pain with them, nor did the familiar words she hurled at him. She'd called him all of these things before. She'd hit him before. But she'd never—

His stomach clenched, but there was nothing left to come up. All he could manage was a watery gagging.

The next thing he could remember, she was gone. He remained on the bed, gagging and shivering, curled up into a small ball. The sounds of the apartment surrounded him. Familiar sounds. The creak of the ceiling when someone walked across the floor upstairs. The opening and closing of cupboards in the kitchen. His own labored, rattled breathing. The clink of a vodka bottle on the lip of a water glass. The drone of the television.

After what seemed like hours, he rose on weak legs and made his way to the bathroom. He stepped into the shower and turned it on as hot as it could possibly go. The water splashed down onto him, washing away the sick remains of his lunch and his own semen from his body. He used soap to lather up the wash cloth and scrubbed his skin until it felt raw. Then he stood under the shower head while the hot liquid poured onto his head and coursed down his body.

When he finally shut off the water and pushed aside the curtain, he half-expected to see her standing there in the bathroom, holding a towel for him. He was alone, though, and reached for the towel himself.

What do I do next?

As he dried off, he searched for an answer. He thought at first that maybe this would never happen again, but he realized that this was just the little boy inside of him hoping against hope. Little Jeffie, wishing his mommy and daddy would be perfect.

He knew better.

No, this was just the newest evolution of how things were to be. She had to know about his fantasies. She had to know that he dreamed of the power and control over all of the girls that ignored him at school. And she wanted to take that fantasy away from him before he could make it really happen.

She would come to him whenever she wanted. She would control it. She would take it from him. She'd take his fantasy, piece by piece.

She was still too strong.

He finished drying off and went to his room. He dressed quickly, then emptied out a small sea bag that his father had left behind one of the times he'd left in the middle of the night. He pushed some jeans and some shirts into the sea bag, along with a few paperback books he'd borrowed from the library.

As quiet as he could, he slipped out of his room and into his mother's bedroom. In the top drawer of the dresser, he found a wooden box full of jewelry. Underneath that were a number of folded bills. He took both, slipping the cash into his pocket and bringing the jewelry box back to his room, where he put it into the sea bag.

His coat hung in the hall closet. He carried the bag with him, moving woodenly, without emotion. It was as if when he spewed out the contents of his stomach in the bedroom, all of his emotion had left him, too.

She didn't look up as he walked to the door. He thought about not turning around, but something made him pause. He looked over his shoulder at her. She met his eyes. He saw no remorse in them at all.

"You're leaving, then?" she asked, her slurred tone matter-of-fact.

He nodded.

"Well, good," she said. With that, she turned her attention back to the television.

He waited. A hundred things that he might say raced through his brain, but in the end, one question won out.

"Cora?" he said. Since she wanted to be called by her name so goddamn bad, then he'd do it now.

She turned her gaze back to him. "What?"

He licked his lips, then asked, "Why don't you love me?"

She smiled, a cruel grin that licked at her cheeks. "Because you are the reason my entire life has been wasted, that's why."

He expected those words to rock him in the gut like mule kick, but strangely, he felt nothing. He simply turned away from her and left the apartment.

His first steps down the street were light and euphoric. He couldn't think of why he hadn't done this years ago. Take some of her precious money and just go. He felt free. He felt like a new person.

His footsteps carried him to a bus stop. He got on without thinking. He sat and stared out the window at the wet, gray Seattle streets. His sense of freedom was short-lived. Already he felt a brewing, seething rage building in the pit of his stomach. He knew he could never be free of it. He knew he would have to come back and find her. Someday, when he was stronger. He'd come knocking on her door. She'd answer it, probably with a glass full of vodka, that whore's drink, in her hand. He'd push his way in. He'd give her the back of her hand. Then he'd lay the whammo on her, better than his father ever did. He'd control it. He'd show her what power was.

He would.

Someday, he would.

The city bus stopped near the Greyhound terminal. He exited and walked across the street. Once inside the terminal, he stood in front of the list of destinations. He didn't have much money. He couldn't go far. But he had to go far enough. Where was that? Tacoma? Vancouver?

His eyes flitted down the list until his gaze came to rest on River City. That was clear across the state, on the other side of the Cascades. Far enough, but close enough.

He smiled.

Besides, it snowed in River City.

Part IV

May 1996
RIVER CITY, WASHINGTON

Failure, then, failure! so the world stamps us at every turn. We strew it with our blunders, our misdeeds, our lost opportunities, with all the memorials of our inadequacy...
William James (1842–1910)

NINETEEN

Detective John Tower tapped his pen against his knee. A half-cup of coffee, long cold, stood next to his open case file, but instead of looking at the contents of the file, Tower stared at the picture of Stephanie on the corner of his desk.

He wondered how he'd like it if it had been his girlfriend that had been attacked by the Rainy Day Rapist, only to have the case assigned to a complete moron like himself.

No, he corrected himself. Better yet, what if she were the next victim in line, relying on him to catch the guy before he was able to assault her?

Tower sighed. He dropped the pen on top of the case file and rubbed his eyes.

You can't afford self-pity right now, John. Get your ass to work.

He opened his eyes again and paged through the case file. Nothing new jumped out at him on this, easily his hundredth time through the file contents.

Strike one.

None of the calls into the police tip line had resulted in anything of value, even though he'd run down anything remotely promising. They all just led down blind alleys, unfortunately. Most of the tips were the result of the Mr. Every Other White Guy composite that Lieutenant Crawford had released to the media. He'd spent countless hours contacting men who tipsters had been certain were "that guy on the news," only to know within moments that it wasn't the Rainy Day Rapist. Still, he had to interview each of them, get their alibi and then confirm it. That took time, but yielded no results.

Strike two.

On the scientific side of the house, there was nothing in the way of useful forensics that might help to identify the suspect.

Strike three.

There'd been no rapes or attempted rapes since the threats made against MacLeod a week and a half ago. While he was glad that was the case, there was a single positive to another criminal event – the potential for evidence.

Tower shook his head at his own morbidity. What kind of a sick bastard wished for a rape to happen just so he might have a shot at some additional evidence? It was stupid, anyway. This guy had been careful. There were no witnesses except the victims themselves and they didn't see much that helped identify the bad guy.

On top of that, there hadn't been a whisper of activity at MacLeod's house during the surveillance by officers there. No appearances by the rapist there or anywhere while she was on patrol. Chisolm reported no suspicious activity at the hotel they were staying at, either. That led to amateur hour, with Lieutenant Crawford trying to convince him that the Rainy Day Rapist had hopped a train out of River City. He wanted to shut down the operation.

So what did that make it? Strike four? Five?

Tower decided to dump the baseball analogy. Instead, he imagined this to be a back-alley scrap. One with no rules other than the most basic rules of conflict – never give up and the last man standing wins.

He wasn't going to quit. He was going to find the son of a bitch.

He reached for the small stack of tips and leafed through them. All were vague and unlikely candidates. He decided to pass them back to Crawford. The lieutenant would give them to Finch and Elias to run down, which was fine by Tower. Let those glory boy homicide dicks do a little work for someone else for a change, instead of the other way around.

Tower half-chuckled, half-snorted at his own thoughts.

Jeez, am I really turning into that big of an asshole?

Rather than study that question any further, he reached for the list of license plates that the surveillance officers had jotted down. At his request, they'd noted any cars that pulled onto Calispel during surveillance, as well as cars parked a block in either direction. It was a long shot, but at this point, he didn't have much else.

Systematically, he began running the license plate numbers through the Department of Licensing computer. That gave him the registered owner. If it were a male, he'd run that male through the criminal database. He'd also run a history on the address and get any other male names from that, which he'd also run through the criminal database. Anyone with a criminal record would be a nice start, but he figured he should look hard at anyone whose car didn't belong in the neighborhood by virtue of living there. Maybe the Rainy Day Rapist had driven by to case MacLeod's house.

As he worked, he thought about the women who'd been victimized in this case. While his analytical mind worked on the license plate data, he let the unconscious part of his mind drift over the names.

Heather Torin.

Patricia Reno.

Maureen Hite.

Wendy Latah.

How were they different?

How were they the same?

How did he pick them? Was it coincidence or design?

Tower kept tapping information into the computer, reviewing the returns. Both sides of his brain whirred with activity, but the only thing that he knew for sure was that the Rainy Day Rapist was getting progressively more violent. Tower was pretty certain that if he didn't find the suspect before he struck again, the news media was going to have to change his name to the Rainy Day Killer.

Graveyard Shift
2129 hours

"So?" Matt Westboard asked Katie as soon as they were clear of the basement of the police station.

"So what?" she replied from the passenger seat, but she knew what he was asking.

"How are you holding up?" Westboard asked.

Katie gave a long, irritated sigh. "Please, Matt. Not you, too, okay?"

"What's that supposed to mean?"

Katie watched the scenery of River City's West Central neighborhood flit by. The smaller single-family homes were some of the older houses in the city. It was easy for Katie to tell which were owned and which were rentals, as the well-tended lawns and neatly painted homes alternated with the overgrown yards and houses with chipped, peeling walls. She greatly preferred working up in Hillyard instead, even though the scene there was much the same, just with homes from the 1950s instead of the 1920s. But since Westboard was driving, his choice as to where they'd patrol was pretty much the default. Maybe she'd suggest they give Hillyard a try later in the shift.

"How's Putter doing?" she asked, changing the subject.

Westboard smiled knowingly. "Your cat's doing fine. He likes to sleep on the recliner in my living room."

"And you let him?"

Westboard snorted. "He's a cat. Like I can tell him what to do."

"I don't let him sleep on the furniture," Katie objected lightly.

"Yeah, well, he's a guest, so he gets special privileges at my house."

Katie shrugged. "Your call. I hate to see how spoiled your kids will be one day, though."

Westboard didn't answer. After a few moments of silence, he repeated his earlier question. "What'd you mean before?"

Katie turned her head, facing the other officer. There was no sense of guile about him. She felt momentarily guilty for including him with most of the others. While they didn't hang out away from work, Westboard had proven to be a good friend on duty. He probably didn't deserve any attitude.

"I'm sorry, Matt," she said. "It's just been a frustrating week."

"Not enjoying your vacation with Chisolm?"

She shrugged. "That part isn't so bad. Tom's a nice guy. He gives me my space when I need it, but he'll hang out with me if I'm in the mood. We've watched Jeopardy just about every night. He's pretty good at it."

"That comes with getting old," Westboard joked. "Pretty soon, Alzheimer's will kick in and that streak will end."

"Maybe. But he's been cool through all of this. I mean, I'm sure there's someplace he'd rather be."

Westboard grinned and said nothing.

Katie noticed the grin. "What?"

Westboard shrugged and shook his head. "Nothing."

She figured it out then. "My God, Matt. You're as bad as the others."

"I didn't say anything," he protested.

"You didn't have to."

"I *didn't*," he repeated.

"You didn't have to," she repeated back. "You guys are all alike. So does everyone else think the same thing?" She imagined it were so, but had held out a futile hope that maybe, just maybe some of her co-workers would give her the benefit of the doubt. Or Chisolm, for that matter.

Westboard glanced over at her. "Oh, you mean does everyone think you and Chisolm are fooling around?"

"Yeah, that's what I mean. Duh."

"I don't know. Probably a few. That's not what I meant, though."

"Yes, it is."

"No, it's not. Honest."

Katie frowned at him. "Really?"

He gave her an emphatic nod. "Really."

"What did you mean, then?"

Westboard turned on Nettleton Street, slowing to a crawl. He scanned the sidewalks as he drove. "All I meant was that I don't think there's anywhere else Chisolm would rather be than protecting you. That's it."

Katie narrowed her eyes, thinking. "That's almost the same thing."

"Not even close."

"Saying that Tom and I are shacking up at the hotel and saying that there's no place he'd rather be than shacking up is pretty much the same thing, Matt."

"That would be," Westboard agreed. "But that's not what I said."

"It's exactly what you said."

"Okay, then it's not what I was referring to."

"Then what?"

Westboard stopped for the stop sign at Boone. He turned to look at Katie before answering. "I'm just saying that the kind of guy Chisolm is, being on a protection detail for a platoon mate is probably his idea of heaven."

"I doubt it."

"Come on, Katie. That's exactly what drives the guy. You ever hear him talk about anything away from work?"

"No, but neither do you."

Westboard shook his head. "Sure, I'm private, but at least you know when I've gone to Mexico on vacation or seen a baseball game. I told you when I bought a new truck. Chisolm ever talk about something like that? Does he ever talk about *anything*?"

Katie considered. She had to concede that Westboard had a valid argument. Even in the ten days they'd spent in adjacent rooms at the hotel, Chisolm had shared little in the way of personal information. "You could have a point," she admitted.

"I know," he said, crossing Boone and cruising slowly. "And that point is what I meant."

"Sorry, then."

"Apology accepted. Now, answer the rest of the question."

"I forgot the question." She pointed at a house on the corner of Nettleton and Sinto. Two different insulation brand names were plastered across the unfinished outside of the structure. "That place has been waiting for siding for two years now."

Westboard grunted that he knew, then gave her an impatient wave of his hand.

Katie sighed. "All right. It's just that this last week has sucked. I'm holed up at the hotel on my off time. Then I have to ride with someone every day at work."

"How has it been partnering up?"

Katie shrugged and glanced out the window. She saw a long-haired man in jeans and some kind of heavy metal T-shirt raking his small lawn under the harsh yellow porch light. He noticed the police car cruising by, stopped and stared. Katie raised her hand in a small wave. The man didn't wave back, but continued to stare defiantly at them as the car rolled past.

"Nice to have your support," Katie muttered to the closed window.

"What?"

"Nothing," Katie said, turning away from the window. "Riding partners has been...interesting."

"Interesting how?"

"Well, for starters, Battaglia hit on me all night long."

Westboard's eyebrows shot up. "No way."

She nodded slowly. "Yep. That was ten hours of the married man waltz."

"Ouch. I wouldn't have figured that about him. Sully, too, then?"

"No. Actually, Sully went too far the other way, making sure that I didn't take anything he said as a come on."

Westboard's face bore a surprised expression. "I wouldn't have figured that, either."

Katie laughed lightly. "It was kind of cute, but kind of annoying, too. And then when we ended up riding together two days in a row, it was even worse the second day."

"Who would've known the twins were actually so different?"

Katie waved his comment away. "Ah, they were both pining away for the other by midnight, anyway." She faked a deep voiced, Italian accent. "I wonder what Sully's doing on that call. Let's go see if he needs any help."

Westboard laughed at her impression.

Katie shifted into a light, Irish lilt. "Let's check up on Batts, lass. Just in case he needs some assistance."

"That's pretty good," laughed Westboard. "I think you have them nailed."

She shook her head in mock disgust. "It's like they were going through withdrawals or something."

"So how about Kahn?"

Katie wrinkled her nose. "Ugh. Too much aftershave and too much bragging. All night long."

"Figured that one. And Chisolm?"

"Chisolm was...Chisolm."

"And now," Westboard pronounced in a grand tone and a stately wave, "you have *moi*."

Katie laughed at his pomp. "It's not the company that sucks," she said, although that wasn't entirely true. Kahn's braggadocio and not so subtle hints disgusted her as much as Battaglia's flirting surprised her. But she was a big girl. She could deal with those things. "The part that bothers me is that I'm being treated like some kind of china doll. Like I have to be protected or I'll break."

Westboard shrugged. "Pretty big stuff that happened to you. And those threats..."

"Fine," Katie conceded. "But I still don't think they'd have gone to this extreme if I was a man."

Westboard's only reply was to continue rolling slowly forward through West Central. Finally, he asked her, "Does it matter?"

A warm spike of anger flared in Katie's gut. "Of course it matters!"

"Why?"

"Would you like it if they treated you different"?

"No," Westboard whispered. "I wouldn't."

"Neither do I," Katie answered.

Afterward, they drove in silence for a long while, thinking.

Thursday, May 8th
Day Shift
1018 hours

Captain Michael Reott opened the office window. He reached out through the slanted opening and caught some of the cascading rain on his hands. Then he wiped the cool water on his face and the back of his neck.

"You should leave that open," Lieutenant Crawford told him.

"Why's that?"

"Get some fresh air in here," Crawford said. "This office reeks of cigars. If the Chief ever comes in here —"

"The Chief of Police doesn't care if I smoke a cigar in my office. I'd be more worried if some smoking Nazi from City Hall came knocking."

Crawford shrugged and stirred his coffee. "Leave it open, anyway, Mike. The cool air is nice."

Reott agreed and left the window open. He sat down at his desk, reached into the drawer and removed a package of Rolaids. "Now I know why they pay us more than the line troops," he said, holding up the antacids. "I bet I spend a thousand bucks a year on these little bastards."

He removed two and popped them into his mouth.

Crawford chuckled. "That's not why they pay us more, and you know it."

"No, I suppose not," Reott said, crushing the chalky tablets with his molars. "I guess they pay us because we're the ones who have to make the tough decisions."

"That's some of it."

"Some? What's the rest, then?"

Crawford raised his eyebrows. "They didn't teach you this at the FBI National Academy?"

Reott waved his comment away. "You want to tell me, then tell me. But don't break my balls."

"Fine. They *do* pay us more to make the tough decisions. But the thing is, most every one of those decisions will probably piss someone off, right?"

Reott half nodded, half shrugged in agreement.

"Of course it will," Crawford continued. "It'll piss off the citizens, or it'll piss off the patrol cops. Or the detectives. It might even go the other direction and piss off your boss or God forbid, the Mayor. Point is, if it doesn't piss somebody off, then it probably wasn't such a tough decision."

"Agreed. So what?"

"So," Crawford continued, "if a good leader makes tough decisions and if making those tough decisions pisses people off, then pretty soon you'll have pissed off enough people that pretty much no one will like you anymore."

"You're saying that we get a little more pay in case people start disliking us?"

"No," Crawford corrected. "I'm saying that they inevitably will. And dislike is a weak word."

"Oh?"

"The more accurate word is hate. They'll end up hating you for it. As a leader, you'll eventually become something of an outcast. When that social ostracizing happens, there's only one thing left to do."

"What's that?"

"Drink."

Reott blinked. "Drink?"

Crawford nodded. "Yep. What else are you going to do? Stop making those decisions? Start making decisions based on how popular it'll make you?" He shook his head. "No. All you can do is say fuck it, and have a drink."

Reott sighed. "You're on quite a downer jag these days."

"That's life. You ought to be used to it, *Captain*."

"I'm still trying to get my mind wrapped around your point," Reott said, frowning. "The added pay is because I might become an alcoholic?"

"How'd you get to be a captain with that little brain?" Crawford asked, a roguish grin forming under his moustache.

"I took a Civil Service exam."

"Ah, that explains a lot."

"You made lieutenant the same way," Reott reminded him.

"True, but at least I've figured out why it came with a pay raise."

"So you can drink more?"

"No." Crawford shook his head. "So that when you're sitting alone at your house with no friends anywhere to be seen, crying in your cups, at least you can commiserate with a little bit finer brand of booze."

Reott let out a long, knowing chuckle. "Oh, that's rich."

"It's true."

"I know," Reott said, still laughing.

Crawford smiled and drank his coffee.

Reott allowed himself a few more quiet chuckles, thinking of the two bottles of seventeen year old Glengoyne single malt Scotch whisky at home in his cupboard. He'd dropped over a hundred bucks for the two of them right before Christmas last year, so maybe Crawford had a point.

His laughter tapered off. He resumed chewing his Rolaids and swallowed. When he'd finished, he leaned back in his chair. "So where are we on this rapist?"

"We're nowhere," Crawford replied.

"Aren't you just a little ray of sunshine?"

Crawford shrugged. "It is what it is. Tower hasn't come up with anything. The victims didn't see anything. The forensics is a bust."

"What about the composite sketch?"

"Tons of responses, just like I expected."

"And?"

"And Tower ran them all down. Most of them, anyway. I've got Finch and Elias running down some of the others, along with the other dicks in Sexual Assault."

"But no luck," Reott concluded.

"No luck," Crawford said.

"Which leaves us with what?"

"It leaves us with nothing," Crawford said, the frustration in his voice apparent.

"We can't keep MacLeod in limbo like this forever," Reott said. "How long has it been?"

"Only a week and a half."

"I'll bet 'only' isn't a word MacLeod would use to describe it."

Crawford shrugged. "You want my take on this?"

"I didn't ask you in here for your theories on police pay scales."

Crawford ignored the jest. "I think he's moved on."

"You mean left River City?"

"Yes. I think that when things got too hot, he packed up and moved on."

Reott looked at Crawford, appraising the Investigative Lieutenant's words. Finally, he said, "The investigation part of this is your call. I don't know if I agree with your theory, but it's your call to make."

"I know."

"But I'm curious why you think this guy's gone."

"He was on a rampage, Mike. He couldn't control himself. Then he almost gets caught. Now there hasn't been a stranger rape for two weeks."

"That's not very long."

"He raped two of them one day apart," Crawford pointed out, shaking his head. "No, this guy is compulsive. He couldn't stop himself if he tried."

"What does Tower think?"

"All he cares about is catching the guy. He's not going to admit the possibility that this suspect is out of his reach."

"Did you talk to the Prosecutor?"

"Yes. Patrick Hinote said he doesn't have an opinion on the matter. He's more concerned that if we do find the guy, he gets a call right away. Unless the evidence in this case opens up, a conviction is going to be tough."

"How about his team?" Reott asked. "They seemed pretty hard core during that meeting we had."

"I don't know. That's Hinote's problem and he said he'd handle it."

Reott sighed. "Sounds like just about everyone is ready to give up. I don't like that idea."

"It's not giving up, Mike."

"What would you call it?"

"Re-allocating our assets," Crawford replied immediately.

"Does that include the MacLeod detail?"

"They're your people, but I'd say yes."

Reott pursed his lips in thought. "What if this guy is just waiting for us to do exactly that? What if he's been watching for that this entire time?"

Crawford met Reott's eyes with his own steady gaze. "Well, if that's the case, then it will still be true no matter when we pull the plug on this detail, won't it?"

Reott thought about it for several long moments. He rose from his chair and walked back to the window. Reaching through the opening, he let the thick spring raindrops pepper his palms. Then he wiped the cool water on his face and neck again. "Is this one of those tough decisions we were talking about earlier?" he asked, more to himself than anyone else.

Crawford answered anyway.

"Only if you make the wrong one," the lieutenant said.

1804 hours

Tower glanced at the clock on the wall. It was after six already, which put him an hour past quitting time.

He didn't care.

Lieutenant Crawford informed him earlier that afternoon that both the surveillance and the protection details were being pulled. He took the news in stride, knowing that there wasn't anything he could do about it. Moreover, he struggled to find fault with the decision. That didn't stop him from being pissed off about it.

Listlessly, he flipped through the three most recent tips. He found nothing interesting, so he reached for another license plate and tapped the information into the computer. As he waited for the return, his telephone rang.

He snatched the receiver off the hook, hoping it was something helpful. "Tower," he barked.

"John? It's Stephanie."

Disappointment settled into Tower's chest. Was he ever going to catch a break?

"Oh. Hey."

"Don't sound so enthused," she chided gently.

"Just busy, babe. What's up?"

"Nothing. I was just wondering when you'd be home. I was thinking of cooking some steaks."

Tower felt a pang of guilt. "I, uh, I don't know exactly," he said.

Stephanie was quiet on the other end of the line. Then she said, "John, just come home. We'll have some steak and some wine and then I'll take you to bed."

"That sounds good," Tower admitted. In fact, it sounded *very* good.

"Great," she said. "Then I'll see you soon?"

Tower looked at her picture on his desk, then at the open case file. The stack of license plates next to the case file were his best lead right now, probably his only lead. He should probably finish them before calling it a night. But that would take hours.

"Steph, I don't know. I've got these license plates to check through –"

"They'll still be there in the morning, right?"

Tower sighed. "Give me a couple of hours and I'll be home."

Stephanie was silent a moment, then sighed herself. "Okay, John. Your couple of hours usually turns into all night, but okay."

"I'm sorry."

"So am I," she said, and hung up.

He stared at the receiver for a few moments afterward, shaking his head to himself. What was he doing? He was going to screw things up with this woman if he didn't pull things together pretty fast. Most women would have probably already called no joy and split.

Tower hung up the telephone and turned to back to his stack of license plates. The computer let out a soft ding. He took a look at the vehicle registration return.

Goodkind, Jeffrey A.

Tower suppressed a sigh. That certainly didn't sound like a serial rapist to him, but he'd dig into Mr. Goodkind a little bit just the same, exactly like he had all the others.

Time for another trip down another blind alley.

"Working late, John?"

Tower turned toward the voice behind him. Ray Browning stood near his desk, a light jacket slung over his shoulder.

"Just trying to find the piece that breaks things open," Tower said.

Browning nodded knowingly. He settled into the chair at the empty desk opposite Tower. "You want a little help?"

Tower shook his head. "Thanks, Ray, but no. Take off. You've got a family to get home to."

"Don't you have a Stephanie?"

"She's a big girl," Tower said. "She understands."

Browning nodded again. He adjusted the small wire frames on his nose and observed in a quiet voice, "Be careful you don't take advantage of that, you know?"

Tower cocked an eyebrow at him. "So what, you're a relationship counselor now?"

"No," Browning said. "Just someone who has gone before telling a fellow traveler about the dangers of the road ahead."

"That sounds more like Buddha than a counselor," Tower remarked dryly.

Browning let out a small chuckle. "Well, if it helps, I don't care if it makes me sound like Bobcat Goldwhaite."

"Point taken, Ray. Thanks."

"You're welcome. And the offer's open, if you want the help."

Tower shook his head again. "No, it's all right. There's nothing but grunt work here anyway."

"I've done plenty of that."

"*Boring* grunt work," Tower corrected, then added, "that doesn't net anything."

"Done that, too."

Tower smiled grimly. "I'll bet you have. But really, I'm just going to run a few more of these registered owners and then I'll head home."

Browning nodded, but Tower could tell the older detective knew he was lying. He must have understood Tower's angst, though, because he had the decency not to call him on the lie. Instead, he rose to leave.

"You should go home, too," he told Tower. "Those plates will still be there in the morning."

"That's what Stephanie said."

"She's right. Besides," Browning added, "if you leave them for tomorrow, you'll be fresher when you look at them. Detail work like that, you don't want to miss anything."

Tower nodded, but made no move to leave.

Browning gave him a warm smile. He slipped his arms into his jacket. As he adjusted it around his shoulders, he said, "You know, John, when you find this guy, he's not going to live up to your expectations."

"I don't have any expectations. I just want to stop him."

Browning's smile widened. "Don't kid a kidder," he said. "This guy has brutally raped at least four women. He assaulted a police officer. He's gotten more violent every time out. Has the teacher come out of her coma yet?"

"No," Tower whispered. "She's still unresponsive."

Browning raised his eyebrows and nodded. "And he'll be even worse the next time."

"Probably."

"So when you find him, you'll expect him to be some evil, maniacal genius. You already half-imagine him to be a man capable of sprouting horns on his head and spitting fire from a forked, demonic tongue."

"That's a bit much, don't you think?"

"Barely," Browning said. He reached up and stroked his graying goatee. "But the point is that no matter how much you've built him up, you are going to be disappointed in the end. That's because what you'll discover is that he is a sad, sick, flawed, insecure, inadequate creature who figured out how to do one thing well in life. When you take that away from him, all the rest of the bravado falls. All that's left is the weakness."

Tower stared at Browning. A sarcastic reply of "profound" died on his lips. Instead, he swallowed and thought about Browning's words. Then he asked, "Is that how it is with you? With the murderers you investigate?"

Browning nodded slowly. "Every single one of them."

Tower glanced back down at his open case file, then at his picture of Stephanie. When he looked back up at Browning, the older detective was still staring at him. His warm brown eyes radiated empathy.

"He's just a man, John," he said. Then he reached out and squeezed Tower on the shoulder. "Just a sick, sad man."

Tower nodded his thanks.

Browning turned and made his way out of the Sexual Assault Unit.

Tower thought about it a moment longer. Then he decided that Detective Ray Browning was pretty much the best cop he knew, so he should listen to the man. He pushed the **PRINT** button on the computer, getting a copy of Mr. Jeffrey A. Goodkind's registration information so that he could start with that particular blind alley again in the morning. Then he reached for the phone.

Stephanie answered on the second ring.

"Babe?" Tower asked.

"Yeah?"

"Put on the steaks," he said, "and pour the wine."

2048 hours
Graveyard Shift

Katie MacLeod laced up her patrol boots, cinching down the knot. She reached for her duty belt, strapping it around her waist. She slipped the thin leather belt keepers under her regular belt and around her duty belt to secure the two together. After a quick glance in the mirror to make sure she was presentable, she grabbed her patrol bag and left the locker room.

In the hallway that led down to the sally port in the basement, she dropped her bag. She'd pick it up after roll call on the way downstairs. She made her way toward the briefing room, but was intercepted by Lieutenant Saylor.

"MacLeod?" he said. "I need to see you for a second."

Katie gave him a professional nod, but inside she suppressed a sigh.

What is it now? I'm going into the Witness Protection Program?

The two stepped into the conference room next to the sergeant's office. Even after being on the job for five years, going into the so-called "spanking room" with a sergeant or lieutenant gave her a sense of unease in the pit of her stomach.

Saylor closed the door. He turned to face her. Up close, Katie could see the hard lines of his face. He always reminded her of a paradoxical cross between a kindly grandfather and a Marine drill instructor.

"It's been a bit of a rough ride this last couple of weeks, hasn't it?" he asked her.

"It's been fine, sir," Katie answered. Unconsciously, she found herself standing as straight as she could.

Saylor smiled slightly. "My experience has been that room service is only good for about a day or so. Usually less than that."

Katie flashed to the tasteless sandwiches and soggy fries that she'd been subsisting on at the hotel. He'd hit the nail on the head. "It hasn't been gourmet," she admitted.

"Well, I've got some good news," Saylor told her. "It's over."

"Over?"

Saylor nodded. "That's the word from above."

"Did they catch the guy?"

"No."

Katie narrowed her eyes in thought. She wondered why this change of heart had occurred. "So I can check out of the hotel and go home?"

"Yes."

"And I don't have to ride with anyone tonight?"

Saylor shrugged. "I suppose that's between you and Sergeant Shen. But there's no directive from the Captain that says you have to."

Katie stood in the small conference room, a mixture of emotions rushing through her. There was an overwhelming sense of relief and exhilaration at the situation ending and at returning to something akin to normal. At the same time, she experienced some hesitation and gnawing concern. "I wonder why now?" she asked aloud, more rhetorically than not.

Saylor answered anyway. "I think they figured he'd moved on."

"You mean left River City?"

"Maybe. Or just emotionally. There's been no sign of him these last two weeks, right?"

Katie shook her head. "Not that I'm aware of."

"Then that'd be my guess."

Katie wondered briefly why the Captain wouldn't have explained things to Saylor in greater detail, but she long ago gave up trying to figure out how the Byzantine world of the brass functioned. Instead, she wondered if 'they' meant Detective Tower or if it meant the Captain and Lieutenant Crawford. Whoever it was, she wondered if 'they' were right.

"Are you all right, MacLeod?" Saylor asked.

Katie broke away from her contemplation. She nodded. "I'm fine, sir. Just happy to be back to normal."

TWENTY

Friday May 9th
0721 hours
Day Shift

Where the hell are you, you fucking bitch?

He watched the police station from up the street. It'd been easy to find a slightly different location to park every day. At first he'd sat patiently, sipping his tea and pretending to read the newspaper while he watched the parking lot where the officers parked. He'd spotted the bitch cop's Jeep on the first day, but it hadn't moved since. He'd even checked on the weekend, but the Jeep sat there the entire time.

Sitting off her house was out of the question. Not after he'd spotted the two idiot cops up there that day. He'd driven by twice since, taking care not to turn onto her side street. Both times, he was able to pick out a surveillance vehicle. The one time he was certain the house was no longer being watched, a thrill shot through his body like raw adrenaline. He'd parked a block away and crept down the dark alley behind her house. Carefully, he entered her back yard. There was no activity inside the house. The same lights were on as before. He peered through the sectioned glass window of her back door, but saw nothing. And her Jeep wasn't out front, either.

He wanted to smash the small glass panes of her door. He wanted to go inside and find her. If she wasn't there, he wanted to wait for her. He ached for it, like a tooth throbbing in his head. But he forced himself not to. He had to wait. He had to be patient.

Headlights appeared up the street, then winked out. A gray Chevy Caprice rolled to a stop a few houses away. Two shadowy figures sat in the front seat.

He quickly lowered himself into a crouch. He waited for a moment to see if they'd spotted him, but neither door opened. Once he was sure, he crept back to the alley and headed back to his car.

Now, sitting in his car in the early morning hours, he ground his teeth together in frustration. He was tired of waiting on this fucking bitch. Obviously, they'd been hiding her from him, which enraged him all the more. If she didn't show in the next couple of days, he was done waiting. He'd find some other worthless snatch, lay the whammo on her and carve her up like a Christmas goose. That was more than his worthless father ever did, so the son of a bitch would have to be proud, wherever he was. He'd have to know who the better man was.

More than that, if he nailed someone else, they might just take their eyes off of their precious little girl cop.

Then he'd take care of her.

He smiled.

"There it is, Katie," he whispered in the stillness of his car. "If you don't show by the end of the weekend, next week is going to be very newsworthy."

He imagined the news lady, that plastic-faced talking head Shawna Matheson, reporting his deeds to the Joe and Mary Six-Pack crowd that made up the majority of River City. He could see her affected look of contrived gravitas. He could hear the emphasis she'd place on key words in her video report to make her audience listen more closely. It would be so slick, so Hollywood, and yet he knew he'd love it.

Maybe after Katie, he should go after that Matheson bitch. That'd make headlines.

That'd make him quite the man.

He'd be the Rainy Day Killer.

Or maybe the River City Killer. That'd be even better. Maybe after he took care of that Matheson snit, he'd give that reporter lady another call. Maybe he'd tell her how he wanted to be referred to. And she'd make sure it happened, or else she'd find out what the whammo was all about.

He realized he was gripping the steering wheel in two fists and forced himself to relax. It was nice to dream, but the difference between him now and him when he was younger was that now he made his dreams become reality. He wasn't fantasizing about the whammo anymore. He was living it.

The door to the police station opened. Several male officers filed out, along with a female. He peered closely, but it wasn't the one he was looking for. It was some blonde. He settled back in his seat. The floodgates were opening now. The graveyard officers would be flowing out for the next ten or fifteen minutes. Katie hadn't been part of that exodus, though. He wasn't sure if that meant she wasn't working at all, or maybe she was on a different shift. Still, she wasn't using her Jeep or staying at her house. They had to be protecting her, no question.

He ground his teeth, rubbed his palms on his slacks and waited.

Five minutes later, his faith was rewarded.

Katie MacLeod exited the glass doors of the police station. The sight of her caused him to take in a sharp breath. Excitement buzzed through his limbs. He leaned forward, almost expecting it to be some other woman that just looked like her.

No. It was her.

He stared at her as she made her way directly toward the Jeep. Her stride had a confident bounce to it that made his stomach burn. Gone was the slouch. Gone was the meek shuffle. She strode along like everything in world was right. Like she was in control of everything around her. Like she was the queen of the whole goddamn world.

"Oh, I'm going to fix that," he whispered to himself. "I am going to fix that to*day*."

0746 hours

Tower sipped a fresh cup of coffee and rubbed his eyes. He felt tired, but refreshed at the same time. On the one hand, he knew he'd had far too much wine last night. And probably too much

Stephanie, too, if there was such a thing. He was sleepy and hung over, but in the midst of that, he felt a level of relaxation that he hadn't experienced since all of this rapist business started.

When he came into the office this morning, he didn't dive straight into the pile waiting for him. Instead, he'd poured a cup of coffee and wandered around the General Detectives bullpen, shooting the bull with the detectives there. It felt good to argue about something as meaningless as whether the Seattle Mariners were going to have a good season or not.

He avoided Major Crimes, even though he felt like he owed Browning a thank you. There'd be time for that later. He didn't want to risk running into Lieutenant Crawford and having his good morning spoiled.

Now, seated at his desk, took another sip of the coffee and reached for his pile of registrations. The top one was the printout from the previous night. He scanned it.

"Jeffrey Goodkind," he whispered. "Time to eliminate another lucky soul from suspicion."

He noted the address on the registration. It was nowhere near MacLeod's house, where the vehicle had been spotted. In fact, the address on the registration put him down near Corbin Park.

Tower read the address again.

It was *very* near. Ten blocks away, in fact.

He swallowed, feeling his pulse quicken.

Careful, he cautioned himself. *It's probably just a coincidence.*

A coincidence. That was probably it. How many registrations had he checked? Eventually, one of them was going to be registered to an address near Corbin Park, right? River City wasn't Los Angeles. It was bound to happen.

Tower checked his license plate list. Next to Goodkind's plate, either O'Sullivan or Battaglia had jotted down the location where the vehicle had been parked and the time. They'd spotted the car a block away very near the beginning of their shift.

Tower figured they probably did a loop around the neighborhood before setting up shop at a good surveillance spot. So what was Jeffrey Goodkind's car doing parked a block away from MacLeod's house when he lived half a city away?

There could be any number of explanations, Tower knew. Maybe he had a friend or a girlfriend up there, for example.

On another note, it was possible he didn't even live near Corbin Park anymore. Registrations were good for a year. He could have moved. All of this could be a giant coincidence.

Tower pressed his lips together. None of those answers felt quite right.

He opened up his criminal database and fed in Goodkind's name and date of birth. Because the computer system was in-house rather than connected to Olympia like his Department of Licensing computer, the results came back almost immediately.

Jeffrey Goodkind had only two entries. The first read:

VEHCOLLSN / 07-13-1995 / ROLE: WIT

Okay, so Goodkind had been a witness in a vehicle collision the previous July. Tower selected that entry. The details flashed on his screen. Goodkind had been directly behind the number one car when it failed to stop for a red light and crashed into another car. Tower opened up Goodkind's biographical information. It also showed the address near Corbin Park.

The second entry was more confusing, and one he hadn't seen before.

JUVDEFRD / 3-14-1988 / ROLE: DEF

The 'JUV' meant 'juvenile' and the role was definitely 'defendant.' But what did the rest mean?

He selected the entry. The computer paused, then a response flashed on his screen.

RESTRICTED.

What the hell did that mean?

Tower leaned back, taking another sip of his coffee. He was starting to get a tingling in his fingertips. After another moment of thought, he hit the **PRINT** button, gathered up his paperwork and headed down the hall to Crime Analysis.

0749 hours

Where the hell was she going?

Instead of heading north as he expected, the Jeep turned south toward downtown. That confused him. When she entered I-90 eastbound, that made him wonder further. As they cruised eastward at 65 miles per hour, he started to believe maybe he'd figured it out.

She had a boyfriend.

That was it.

The little slut had a boyfriend and she was heading out to his house instead of home to hers.

He glanced at his watch. He was late getting to work now, but he didn't care. His boss was clueless. Any excuse would do. So he'd follow her out to her boyfriend's house, then go to work.

At Argonne, the Jeep slid to the right and took the exit. He followed her at a safe distance. Once off the freeway, she crossed the one way street southbound and hooked a left onto the northbound street. Ignoring the traffic behind him, he waited a few extra moments before making the turn himself. With her finally back in his sights, he didn't want to risk being seen.

Just a couple of blocks to the north, she signaled and turned into the parking lot of a Comfort Inn. He slowed, his eyes narrowing in confusion. What was she doing here? Some kind of rendezvous?

She pulled into a stall and parked. He drove past the hotel, then turned and circled around. Driving quickly around the back of the building, he pulled to a stop on the far side of the parking lot she'd just entered. He put the car into park and stared at her Jeep.

That little tramp.

Whore.

Bitch.

Slut.

She was meeting someone at the motel. Probably a married guy, he figured. But why not just take him up to her house? She lived alone. Or was it someone the neighbors knew?

He bit his lip, thinking. If they were in there having sex, they were extremely vulnerable right now. If he could find a key to the door, he could –

No!

It was too dangerous. He had to wait.

Another vehicle pulled into the lot, an old blue truck. The driver parked it next to Katie's Jeep, then got out. The man looked older than her from this distance, but that seemed to fit his theory about an affair. He made his way up to the second floor, where he rapped on a door. A woman answered.

Katie.

She smiled and let him inside.

His hands trembled. Oh, it was going to feel *good* when he finally laid the whammo on this bitch.

Sitting in his car, he debated his next move. He could go to work and wait for another day. Or he could wait here until they were finished and follow her home.

If she went home.

He sat in his front seat, clenching and unclenching his fists. He knew he couldn't leave. Not now. He couldn't wait anymore.

It had to be today.

0801 hours

"It's a sealed file," Renee told Tower.

"Sealed why?"

Renee shrugged. "Probably because he was a juvenile at the time. Whatever he did was dealt with by the courts, but then they sealed his records."

"I didn't think that extended to law enforcement," Tower said. "I mean, I knew it wasn't available to the public, but I thought we could at least view it."

"You can," Renee said, "Most of the time."

"So why is this sealed?"

Renee took in a deep breath and looked at Tower. When she didn't release the air, Tower gave her a questioning stare. Then his stomach sank.

"No. Don't tell me."

Renee let out her breath in a whoosh. "'Fraid so. The only time I've ever seen this is when the subject was a victim or a suspect in a sex crime."

"And this entry shows him as a defendant," Tower finished.

"Yes, it does."

"So he had some sort of issue back in 1988. The question is, what?"

"More importantly," Renee added, "Why hasn't he had anything between then and now?"

Tower cursed lightly. "Could a guy do that?"

"Do what?"

"Be messed up enough as a kid to get involved in some kind of sex crime and then stay clean for eight years as an adult?"

"Of course," Renee said. "The human animal is capable of incredible things. It's not terribly *likely* that he would, but it's possible."

"If that's the case, why start raping now? Built up pressure?"

"Yes," Renee agreed, "but there'd probably need to be a trigger, too. Something to set him off."

Tower took a deep breath of his own and let it out slowly, thinking. "Okay, here's what we need to do. I need to see what's in this file, for starters. I probably need a warrant for that, or at least a subpoena."

"That prosecutor, Patrick Hinote? He could help you with that," Renee offered.

"Good idea," Tower said. "I'll give him a call. Meanwhile, I need you to do as much research as you can on this Jeffrey Goodkind."

"What do you want me to focus on?"

Tower raised his fingers and counted. "Where he works, for starters. And then look for anything that fits your theory about a trigger point. Something that might have set him off."

"You got it," Renee said, her fingers already flying over the keyboard.

Tower reached for the telephone.

0825 hours

He was about ready to give up when she appeared at the doorway of the hotel room, carrying a suitcase. She stepped lightly down the stairs to her Jeep. He watched as she stowed her suitcases in the rear of the vehicle.

He frowned, deep in thought.

Here was another wrinkle. Was she taking a trip? That didn't make sense. The bags were already at the hotel room.

It dawned on him suddenly. He slapped the steering wheel twice, first in frustration for being so dense and then a second time with exuberance for figuring it out.

This is where she'd hidden from him. She'd packed up a bag and checked into a hotel room in order to avoid him. That had been her grand plan all along. The boyfriend was just an added bonus.

She went back upstairs. After a while, she appeared again. This time, she held two much smaller bags. He was fairly certain they were full of girl stuff – toiletries, makeup, curling irons and so forth. She was definitely packing up to leave.

A thought struck him and he smiled.

Maybe she was heading home.

0841 hours

"You've got to be kidding me!" Tower shouted into the phone.

"I'm sorry," the tech support agent told him. "I can't do it."

"But I've got a fucking subpoena!" Tower raged.

The phone fell silent. Then the man said, "Sir, I understand that. I'm not *refusing* to open the file. I'm telling you that I am not *able* to open the file. I can't do it."

"Why?"

"It's password protected."

"So who has the password?"

"For Juvenile Superior Court, the gatekeeper is in Olympia."

"Gatekeeper?" Tower snorted. "What the hell is that?"

The tech support agent's voice didn't waver or become defensive. "That is the term for the individual charged with the electronic security and integrity of those files. Our county Superior Court transfers the information to Olympia for central housing."

Tower shook his head. A dull pain was beginning to throb behind his left eye. "Do you have the number for this gatekeeper guy?"

The tech agent rattled it off from memory. Tower wrote it down and hung up without another word. Then he picked up the phone again and dialed. After five rings, an electronic voice answered. With growing impatience, he listened to the phone tree options, finally selecting what he hoped was the right one.

After two more rings, the line picked up. "This is Jonah Brandenburg," a voice stated, "head of File Integrity for Juvenile Defendants and Victims for the State of Washington. I'm currently on vacation and will return on May twelfth. If you're requesting information on a sealed file, please forward a request along with a subpoena to my office. I'm currently experiencing a backlog of two weeks in my response time, so thank you for your patience. If you'd like to leave a message, you may do so at the beep."

Tower hung up, cursing.

"Dead end?" Renee asked.

"Goddamn government bureaucracy," he groused. "You get anywhere?"

"Getting there," she answered.

0902 hours

At first, she'd headed back north. He'd been thrilled at that. Anticipation hummed through him so powerfully that he almost let out a preternatural whine. He breathed in deeply and exhaled long and slow to get control of the urge. His grip on the steering wheel tensed and loosened while he drove.

Halfway to her house, when she pulled into a diner, he groaned out loud.

He parked across the street and watched her go inside. A few minutes later, the older man in the blue truck arrived and went inside to meet her. They sat across from each other in a booth near the window, giving him a front seat view to their little breakfast meeting.

"I guess it's true," he muttered through clenched teeth. "Sex really does make you hungry."

He laughed nervously at his own joke, but his mind was whirring. Why didn't they just order room service? Or was this part of the façade? That if someone sees them having breakfast together in public, that explains why they were together today?

It didn't make a lot of sense to him, but at this point he didn't care. He just wished the bitch waitress would arrive with pancakes or whatever the hell they were ordering so that Katie should shove some food down her gullet and get her ass home.

He had plans for her.

0921 hours

"All right," she said. "I've got about all I think I'm going to get for a while."

Tower grabbed his cup of coffee and sidled up next to her desk. "Run it for me."

Renee picked up her notepad. "The collision report from 1995 didn't list a work location, but there was a telephone number. I did a reverse on the number. Turns out he works for Men Only, a men's suit store on Wellesley Street."

"I know that store," Tower said.

Renee cast him an appraising look. "Not from shopping there."

Tower ignored the jibe. "I drive by it sometimes. What else did you find out?"

Renee glanced back down at her notepad. "Okay, no time for jokes, apparently," she muttered, searching for her place with the tip of her pen. "I also discovered something interesting when I checked the power records for his residence. Up until April, the account was in the name of a Jennifer Gallagher. Then, in late April, the account was switched to Jeffrey Goodkind."

"What do you make of that?"

"Well," Renee said, "you could surmise several things. The first is that she moved out in April and he moved in. But –"

"But we already know that's been his address since at least 1995," Tower finished.

"Right. So another possibility is that they lived together, but changed the account over for personal financial reasons."

Tower's eyebrows scrunched. "So this guy has a girlfriend? Hard to believe."

"I think 'had' is a better word to use."

"Why?"

"I checked with the power company and the phone company for a Jennifer Gallagher. Both sources showed her with a new account as of early April."

Tower pursed his lips. "So they broke up?"

Renee nodded. "Yes, I'd say so. And did you notice the timeframe?"

"Yeah, right around the time of the Patricia Reno assault."

"A relationship ending *could* act as a trigger," Renee said.

"You don't sound so sure."

"I'm not," she answered. "A breakup is no small thing, but it just didn't seem like enough of a cataclysmic event to send a man over the edge all by itself. Not a man who has been simmering but remaining under control for eight years."

"It seems like a perfectly logical trigger to me."

"Well, either way, that's why I looked at Jeffrey Goodkind a little more closely. I called Men Only and posed as a wife wanting to bring my husband in. I told them Jeffrey had helped us out last time and asked if we could have him again. The manager said that would be no problem."

"So he still works there," Tower observed. "No job loss for a trigger."

"No. And again, depending on how important his job is or isn't, getting fired or laid off might be a big deal or might mean absolutely nothing." Renee put a check mark next to that item on her notepad. "But I had to eliminate it."

Tower nodded. "That's just good investigative technique. Process of elimination."

"Problem is, I was running out of things to eliminate."

"I run into that sometimes, too," Tower said ruefully.

"Then," Renee said, "I asked myself what the biggest stress-related event in a person's life might be. And then it all made sense."

Tower twirled his finger in a hurry-up gesture.

"Death," Renee pronounced.

"Huh?"

"Someone dying is the greatest stressor for most people," she explained. "So I checked the *River City Herald* obituaries for anything related to Goodkind."

Tower raised his eyebrows hopefully, but Renee shook her head.

"Nothing there. But when I didn't find anything, I tried a Lexis-Nexis search on the last name. There were a lot of hits, but I started with Pacific Northwest cities like Portland and Seattle."

"That's a lot of work," Tower said. "How'd you manage that so fast?"

Renee tapped her computer. "Once I had the articles, all I had to do was tell the computer to search for a mention of Jeffrey Goodkind in any of them."

Tower thought about it for a moment, then nodded his understanding. "Because he'd be listed as a surviving family member in an obituary, right?"

"There's hope for you yet, John," Renee said with a wink. "That's exactly right."

"So, what did you find?"

"In the *Seattle Post-Intelligencer*, I found an obit for Cora Goodkind who is survived by her only son, Jeffrey Goodkind."

"Amazing," Tower said. "Before computers, that would have taken days."

Renee shrugged. "Maybe. Before computers, the networks were people-based. If I didn't have this here," she tapped her monitor again, "then I'd have to know a guy at the Seattle PI. I'd make a phone call and he'd get back to me."

"Still, it wouldn't be as fast."

"Probably not. It is pretty amazing." She leaned back in her chair and looked at Tower. "But what's more interesting is the date on that obituary."

"Let me guess," Tower said. "She died around the beginning of March this year."

"February 27th," Renee reported. "Which, coincidentally, was around a week before –"

"Before Heather Torin was attacked," Tower finished.

"Exactly," Renee said. "And the death of a mother, particularly one that he likely had issues with would definitely qualify as a trigger."

"So the death of his mother sets him off," Tower said, theorizing. "Then he manages to control it again, holding it together for at least another month. But maybe he's acting hinky or something, because the girlfriend dumps him. And that pushes him over the edge."

"With the pressure of the mother's death behind it, I think that'd do it."

Tower reached out and rested his hand on Renee's shoulder. He gave her a squeeze. "Renee, you are magnificent."

"I know," she said.

Tower turned to leave.

"Where are you going?" she asked.

"Men Only," Tower said. "Sealed file or not, I want to have a chat with Mr. Jeffrey Goodkind."

0956 hours

Katie pulled up in front of her house and parked her Jeep. She cast a look at the dark red brick of the little home, enjoying the comforting sensation that the familiar sight gave her.

"Be it ever so humble," she whispered sleepily. Emotion welled up in her chest. Small prickles of tears stung her eyes. Surprised at her own emotion, she turned off the ignition and wiped away the beginnings of tears.

I'm just tired. Tired and glad to be home.

She exited the Jeep, and walked around to the rear. Exhausted from working all night and now with a belly full of breakfast, the task of hauling in her luggage seemed herculean in nature. She considered leaving it for later, but opened the back hatch of the Jeep, anyway. She gathered up all of the luggage, setting it on the damp asphalt of the street while she closed and locked the hatch. Then she trapped one of the smaller bags beneath her armpit, took a bag in each hand and made her way to the front door.

Katie remembered what Chisolm told her at the hotel and again at breakfast.

"Maybe this guy's gone and maybe he isn't," the veteran officer said. "But you need to keep your guard up."

Katie didn't want to admit to anyone that while she resented the protective measures while they had been in place, she suddenly felt a sense of vulnerability now that they were removed. That fact, in turn, made her a little bit angry at herself. How did it make sense for her to complain about something on the one hand, but then be glad for it at the same time? And then be mad about both?

Don't try to understand everything, Katie.

Chisolm didn't seem to have any difficulty understanding the paradox. He gave her a reassuring pat on the hand at the breakfast table. "You'll be fine," he told her. "You're a warrior."

That was another instance in which she'd felt emotion welling up inside her, unexpected, uncontrolled. Having the consummate warrior tell her that he looked at her as a peer gave Katie a greater sense of satisfaction and accomplishment than anything her bosses could have bestowed upon her. Respect was hard enough to get from fellow cops. Throw in being female and it got to be about three times as hard. But she had Thomas Chisolm's respect, and you didn't get any higher than that.

"Thanks," was all she'd been able to manage at the diner table, but she supposed that there really wasn't anything more that needed saying.

At her front door, she set down the bag in her right hand and unlocked the door. As she swung open the front door, the familiar smell of her home washed over her.

Katie smiled and stepped inside. She needed a shower and then a good day's sleep, but she was home.

0957 hours

He watched her step through the front door of her house. Excitement buzzed through his limbs like an electric current.

"Wait," he whispered, shifting his aching erection to one side.

She worked all night. She just had sex, then ate breakfast. It only made sense that she'd be going to bed. So he'd wait a few minutes. Let her settle in. Doze off. He'd catch her still half-asleep, so that she would wonder if the cold of his knife against her throat and him thrusting inside her was real or only just a nightmare.

And then she'd find out.

"Wait," he whispered again. "Just a little while."

1008 hours

Tower flashed his badge at the store manager. "I'm looking for Jeffrey Goodkind," he said.

The manager, a tall, effete man that reminded Tower more of a mortician than a suit salesman, leaned forward to inspect Tower's badge and identification. Satisfied, he replied, "I'm sorry, sir, Mr. Goodkind is not at work today."

"When does he work again?"

"He was scheduled to work today, but he has not yet arrived."

Tower's eyes narrowed. "Did he call in sick?"

"No."

"He just didn't show?"

The manager nodded. "Yes."

"Is that normal for him? To just not show up?"

"No," the manager conceded, then shrugged, "although, he has been acting strangely of late."

Tower raised his fingers to his face and rubbed his chin. After a moment, he realized that he was mimicking one of Browning's habits. Dropping his fingers, he asked, "Strange in what way?"

The manager shrugged. "He has just seemed a bit pre-occupied. Not as attentive to his work."

"Do you know what's been going on in his life?"

The manager's eyebrows shot up in horror. "Oh, no. Jeffrey is quite private and I would never think to pry."

Tower suppressed a sigh. Then he asked, "Does he have a locker or a work station?"

"Not really. He has his own drawer at the salesmen's desk, though."

"I'd like to see that, please."

The manager hesitated. "Do you have a search warrant?"

"Do I need one?" Tower shot back.

The manager pressed his lips together, considering. Then he said, "No, I suppose not. Right this way."

He turned and walked toward the rear of the store. Tower followed. As they passed the last rack of suits, a series of photographs lined the hallway that led to the back room where the manager was headed. Large block letters proudly pronounced, "OUR SALES TEAM IS HERE TO SERVE YOU!"

Tower slowed, his eyes passing over each photograph. When he reached the one labeled "Jeffrey Goodkind, since 1993," he stopped.

A photograph of Mr. Every Other White Guy stared out at him from inside the frame, a practiced smile on his lips.

And at that moment, Tower knew for sure.

1011 hours

The pressure was too great. He couldn't wait any more.

Staring at that hateful little brick house, his hands trembled. The pungent smell of his own sweat filled the cab of his car. He shifted in his seat, trying to get comfortable, trying to force himself to wait a few more minutes.

He glanced down at the passenger seat. The silver blade of the Buck knife radiated a cold light back at him.

The time for waiting is over.

Pick up the knife.

Go inside. Lay the whammo on that arrogant bitch. Slice her. Gut her.

Kill Katie. Kill that cunt.

Kill Cora.

He gave a short shake of his head, trying to clear his mind. He had to be careful. He couldn't let his rage get in the way. He couldn't let his mother turn his victory into another defeat by taking away what he most wanted.

Fear.

Control.

Pain.

Vengeance.

Somewhere deep inside the icy core of his soul, he felt a small flickering warmth spring to life. Katie was the only one who had thwarted him since he had become a real man. She was the only one who had defied him. Since that night on Mona Street, he'd heard his father's mocking laughter in every voice. Worse yet, he'd seen his mother's hard features in every line of Katie's face. Just like his mother had done when she attacked him and tore away at his sexual power, Katie's defiance and her escape robbed him of his manhood. It stripped him of what he'd become.

She had to pay.

His mouth curled into a cold smile. He'd send Katie to hell, where she belonged. Right next to his mother.

"I'm coming," he whispered, and got out of the car.

1017 hours

"Adam-254, Adam-251?"

Gio reached for the microphone. "Fifty-four, go ahead."

"Assist the detective. Contact Ida-409 at the west end of Corbin Park."

Gio clicked the mike, signaling he copied the call. A second click followed, presumably from Ridgeway. Gio was close to the park and drove there in a matter of a couple of minutes. As he turned off Post and into the wide lanes at the west end of the park, he was surprised to see Ridgeway already there. He pulled his car alongside.

"You got here quick," he said.

Ridgeway grunted back.

"Ida-409?" he asked Ridgeway. "That's Tower, right?"

Ridgeway nodded, but didn't say a word.

Gio suppressed a sigh. Instead he said, "You take an oath of silence or something?"

"No," Ridgeway answered, "but sometimes I wish you would."

"What's up, Grumpy Gus?"

Ridgeway's bleary-eyed stare answered Gio's question.

"Nothing's up," the veteran officer said through gritted teeth. "I'm just tired."

Gio nodded an apology. Ridgeway accepted it wordlessly and leaned his head back against the headrest.

It was at times like this Gio missed their fallen comrade, Karl Winter the most. Winter knew how to listen, especially to Ridgeway.

The best he could do was sit next to him and know when to remain silent.

1020 hours

He strode down the alley like he owned it.

He *did* own it.

He was in control.

At her small back gate, he unlatched the clasp and slipped into the yard as quietly as he could. He clutched the Buck knife in his right hand, the blade hidden by the cuff of his white shirt. The weight of the cool metal reassured him.

Confident, he walked to her back door. At the door, he peered through the small glass panes into the house.

No activity.

He strained his ears, listening for movement.

The patter of water and the rumbling whine of plumbing filtered toward him. He glanced at the marbled, frosted window a few yards to his right. Condensation formed on the outside of the window and the glass had a hazy film of steam covering it.

She was in the shower.

Perfect.

Without hesitation, he drove the metal butt end of the knife into the small glass pane in the lower left corner of the back door. He was rewarded with shattering shards of glass. Flipping the knife around, he used the blade to clear out the four-by-four-inch mini-pane of any remaining glass. Then he reached through and fumbled for the lock inside.

First the knob.

He found the small button in the center of the doorknob. Pinching it between his thumb and forefinger, he twisted it until it stopped.

Then the deadbolt.

The larger locking mechanism was easier to find and to flip to the opposite side. A solid click sent a thrill of success through him.

He opened the door and stepped through.

Inside, the heavy sound of falling water from the bathroom filled the quiet of the house. He forced himself to creep cautiously toward the sound. His eyes flitted around his surroundings as he moved.

He wondered if she brought her gun home.

If so, where did she keep it?

A quick look told him the kitchen counter was clear.

Probably the bedroom, then.

He knew he should go there first and collect it, but he was drawn to siren's song of the falling water in the bathroom. It sounded so...vulnerable. He imagined her naked body under the shower head, water cascading down upon her. Rivulets of white, foamy soap sliding down her breasts, across her stomach. He could almost see the dark patch between her legs standing out against the lather soap and her pink skin.

I'm going to tear you to shreds, bitch.

I'm going to lay the whammo on you like you've never known. And then –

The water came to a sudden stop. The sound of a shower curtain being drawn aside was muffled by the door between them.

A moment of panic struck him, but he pushed it down. Quickly, he adapted his plans. It would have to be an ambush when she stepped out of the bathroom, then.

He moved silently to the side of the bathroom door.

He gripped his knife and waited.

1022 hours

Tower pulled up next to Gio's car. The two officers looked over at him. Gio's pleasant features were expectant. Ridgeway's were sullen.

"Where are we going?" Gio asked.

Tower recited Jeffrey Goodkind's address. "It's about ten blocks away," he added. "Just up the hill."

"What's there?" Gio asked.

Tower smiled. "It *might* be the Rainy Day Rapist."

He enjoyed the surprise that registered on the faces of both officers, followed by anticipation.

"If," Tower said, "you're interested."

"Hell, yeah," Gio said.

Ridgeway gave Tower a resolute nod.

"All right, then," Tower said. "Let's go."

1023 hours

Katie scrubbed her hair with a towel, drying off. The weariness from the long night had seeped into her bones. Her muscles felt heavy and weak. The warm breakfast and now the hot shower had only made her exhaustion complete. Thoughts of flopping her head onto the pillow in her own bed and slipping into a deep sleep filled her mind.

It felt good to be home again. To dry off with her own towel. To see her own robe hanging from the back of her own bathroom door. She imagined that she'd sleep better tonight than she had for weeks.

Katie wrapped the towel up on her head. She reached for a second blue fluffy towel, drying off her body with long strokes. Slight stubble on her legs reminded her that she hadn't shaved them while showering.

Oh well. It's not like I'm going on a date.

Finished, she re-hung the towel on the rack. Then she put on her battered terry cloth robe and opened the door.

1024 hours

When the door opened, a rush of smells blasted outward, riding on the steam. Soap. Linen.

Her.

He trembled.

His fist tightened around the handle of his knife.

*   *   *

As soon as she stepped through the door, she felt an eerie malevolence in the room that made her skin prickle. Before she could calculate a response or process the sensation, a figure appeared in front of her. A bare hand shot toward her throat.

Instinctively, Katie knocked the grasping claw aside in a sweeping block with her left forearm. The collision of her fleshy muscle and his bony hand reverberated through her arm and up to her shoulder.

"Bitch!" he snarled.

Katie's eyes were drawn to his face. An enraged variation on the police sketch glared back at her.

A moment later, another attack flashed out at her. She brought her opposite forearm across to block this second attack. Something bit painfully into her arm.

He pulled his hand back. "You like that, bitch?"

Katie gaped down at her right arm. The white terrycloth sleeve was stained bright red.

The knife came slashing back at her in something akin to a sword stroke. She held up her hands defensively. The cool blade sliced through the flesh of several fingers, leaving an icy trail behind.

Katie let out a cry. A moment later, warmth flooded through her fingers. Pain throbbed in her hand with each heartbeat.

He drew back the knife to slash again, but paused a moment. He shifted the handle in his hand until the blade was pointed downward so that he could stab instead of slash. Katie stared at the silver blade tinged with her own blood. Fear raced through her body.

"I'm going to lay the whammo on you," he whispered hoarsely, his tone almost reverent.

Katie met his gaze. A sheen of lust and anger coated his eyes, radiating outward. She read her own death in the black pinpricks of his pupils.

He stabbed downward with the knife.

Katie brought her foot up sharply, driving it into his groin with every ounce of strength she could muster. Her instep landed with a solid thunk. The force of the blow rang up her leg as far as her hip.

As soon as the kick landed, his downward stab faltered and fell to his side. A low groan escaped his lips. He reached for his groin and sank to his knees.

Katie sidestepped the kneeling assailant and sprinted for her bedroom. At her bedside table, she grasped the portable telephone. The receiver slipped out of her bloody hand, falling to the floor. She knelt and picked it up. With trembling, blood-soaked fingers, she punched in the numbers $9 - 1 - 1$.

Her heart racing, she pressed the receiver to her ear.

One ring. Then two.

She watched the bedroom door, her entire body trembling with adrenaline.

Three rings.

"Nine one one, state your emergency."

He burst into the room with a roar. His face was contorted in rage.

"YOU BITCH!"

He held the knife out in front of his body in his right hand.

"I need police here *now*!" Katie screamed into the telephone.

"What is the problem?" the calm voice on the other end of the line asked.

He lunged forward, his eyes narrowed, his jaw set.

Katie tossed the telephone aside. She dove onto her bed, tucking and rolling across the mattress. As she left the far side of the bed, she fell to the floor on her knees. Scrambling to her feet, she raced toward her dresser. Her service pistol rested there.

His eyes followed her motion towards the gun, and he moved to cut her off.

*   *   *

The 9-1-1 transfer popped up on Janice Koslowski's screen. As always, the urgency of the call was indicated by the red font and the blinking letters. With a few quick keystrokes, she opened the call. Calmly, she read the text.

```
Female voice states she "needs police
here  now."  Male  voice  in  background
calling  her  "a  bitch."  Phone  dropped.
Open line, sounds of struggle.
```

Janice looked at the address. It was immediately familiar, but it took her a moment to remember why she knew it. Then she gasped. Without pause, she depressed her microphone lever and spoke.

*   *   *

"Any available units," the car radio crackled. *"Code Ninety-Nine at 5610 North Calispel. Officer MacLeod's residence. All available units, respond."*

Gio slammed on his brakes and cranked the wheel, whipping his patrol car around. Then he buried the accelerator. The police cruiser leapt forward, the engine opening up with a throaty roar as he headed north.

*   *   *

Get the gun!

Katie reached the dresser first. She grasped the pistol by the grips and popped the snap with her thumb. With her bloody left hand, she clutched at the holster and pulled.

The holster slipped from her hand.

He reached her, his free hand lashing out at her. The blow caught her square in the nose, driving her back into the wall. Stunned, she flailed at the holster. Her wet fingers were beginning to go numb. She found one of the belt loops and pinched. With her right hand, she jerked the gun from the holster.

Another crushing punch thundered into her face, this one flush in the eye. Stars ricocheted through her vision. A forceful slap knocked the gun from her hand and sent it clattering away.

He took a fistful of her hair and yanked, pulling her forward to the ground. Her vision cleared just as he jammed her face into the wooden floor of her bedroom. She felt his knee between her shoulder blades. The weight of his body pressed down on her, pinning her to the ground.

"Not so tough without a gun, are you?" he taunted her. "Without that, you're just another worthless bitch."

Katie struggled to breath. She flailed with her arms, trying to find purchase on something, trying to dislodge him from his position of control.

He chuckled darkly. "You can try as much as you want. It won't matter. I'm stronger than you. Much stronger." His voice took on a faraway note. "Finally, I'm much stronger than you."

Think, Katie! Don't let him beat you! Think!

"Cops," Katie wheezed," are...coming..."

She felt his motion shift and heard his voice nearer to her ear. "Maybe so. Maybe they'll even catch me this time. But not before I lay the whammo on you." He pressed the cold blade against her cheek. "So it really doesn't matter, does it?"

Katie stopped struggling. She let out a whimper of fear.

"That's more like it," he said. "Now, don't move."

The weight slid off her shoulders, but the blade remained resting against her face. He tore aside her robe, baring her skin. He paused for a moment. Katie felt his knife hand tremble. A cold, sick feeling broke out through her entire body. She pushed it away. Instead, she focused her anger.

Then she heard the clattering noise of his belt unbuckling.

Now! It has to be now!

Katie waited.

The unmistakable sound of a zipper descending seemed to fill the room.

You can't let this happen. Not again.

Next came the rustle of his jeans as he pushed them over his hips.

Now!

Katie waited.

When she felt the rigid warmth of his erection brush against her bare buttocks, she twisted away from the knife. Whirling and sitting up, she swung her left hand blindly, fingers extended. The knife edge of her hand caught him in the temple.

He grunted in surprise.

Katie didn't stop. She reached out with both hands and gouged her fingertips into his eyes.

A primal scream erupted from his mouth. He lashed out madly with the knife, clipping her in the shoulder with the point of the blade.

Katie yelped and let go. She scrambled backward across the wooden floor until her back slammed into the wall.

"You fucking cunt!" he yelled. His empty hand rubbed at his eyes while he held the knife out in front of him, slashing defensively from side to side. "You blinded me!"

Katie heard her own breath racing in and out of her lungs. She watched him in horror as he rose to his feet.

Where were the police?

Crouching in the corner, with the bed to her left and the wall to her right, she felt like a trapped animal. She told herself that she should get up, scramble over the bed and run out of the house. Before she could react, she heard a siren in the distance. Momentary relief washed over her.

He removed his hand from his face. Blinking, he looked around the room. For a moment, she wondered if he'd be able to see her. Then he cocked his head slightly and his gaze locked onto her.

"I hear them coming," he rasped. "And I can still see you."

Katie tensed herself to leap to her feet.

"You're fucking dead, bitch," he growled, and stepped forward.

At that moment, Katie spotted the dark black metal of her gun resting on the floor, slightly underneath the bed. She lunged for it, clutching it in her bloody hands.

His heavy thudding footsteps seemed to shake the world as he drew nearer.

Range-master Sergeant Morgan's booming voice overshadowed even that sound as she remembered his frequent advice for taking down an enemy combatant.

Fire into the pelvic girdle.

She tightened her grip on the gun.

Break the body's support.

Katie swung the gun toward his advancing figure.

If a man can't walk, he can't fight.

Without aiming, she pointed the pistol toward his waist and slapped the trigger.

The gun barked in her hands, the muzzle flashing.

He didn't stop.

She fired again. And again. The gun bucked in her hands as she brought the sights back to bear on his pelvic girdle. She blasted a fourth time, then a fifth.

He paused, then stumbled brokenly backward. With a loud crash, he collapsed to the ground only a few feet from her. His arms and chest shuddered.

Katie indexed, placing her trigger finger along the side of the pistol. She stared at the quivering heap of evil on her bedroom floor through the sights of her gun. Rage suffused her. Her own hand trembled with fury.

He tried to rape me.

He tried to kill me.

In my own home.

He should die.

With some effort, she steadied her hand. The unmistakable yelp and wail of police sirens rose in volume as they grew closer. The acrid smell of cordite and the coppery odor of blood filled her nostrils. Katie drew a bead on the back of her attacker's head, her trained eye focusing on the front sight. She moved her finger from the indexed position onto the trigger.

He should die.

A gurgling breath leaked out of his mouth.

Katie pressed the trigger slightly, swallowing in anticipation. She could do it. She knew she could. All it would take is for her to apply few pounds of pressure on the trigger and a 186-grain bullet would blast into the back of his head.

Blood coursed down her fingers and dripped from her extended hands onto the floor. The dollops that landed on the wooden floor seemed louder than her own breathing, louder than the approaching sirens.

All she had to do was squeeze. Kill him. Kill the memory of Phil. Just another pound or two of pressure and the gun would explode with the same fury and pain she'd carried with her all these past years. The blast would fill the room. The gun would leap backward in her hands. The bullet would sizzle through the air, impact his head and end his miserable life. No one would know any better.

She would feel good about it.

She would be free.

She could do it.

Another wheezing breath came out of him.

He should die.

Katie MacLeod lowered her gun.

1026 hours

Gio screeched to a halt in front of Katie's house. He leapt out of the patrol car, leaving the engine running and the door standing open. He sprinted up her walkway, his long legs eating up the ground quickly. At the same time, he drew his sidearm on the run. At her door, he stopped and checked the knob.

Locked.

Gio drove his shoulder into the door.

It didn't budge.

He cursed loudly, stepped back and delivered a powerful, thrusting kick directly next to the doorknob. With a crash, the doorjamb shattered. The door swung open and Gio dashed inside, his gun extended in front of him.

"MacLeod?" he shouted. He scanned the living room and kitchen for any movement. The bathroom door stood open, the remnants of steam still visible on the mirror. Another siren drew closer, followed by another set of tires screeching to a stop.

He could detect the unmistakable scent of fired gunpowder hovering in the air. And something else, too, but it was a moment before he recognized the odor.

Blood.

"MacLeod?" he shouted again. "Where are you?"

The only room that remained was the bedroom. He shuffled toward it, his gun trained on the doorway.

"I'm in here," Katie called out weakly. Then, a moment later, she added, "Code Four."

Gio lowered his gun but didn't holster. He strode quickly into the room. Katie sat with her back to the wall on the far side of the bed. She'd drawn her knees up to her chest and wrapped herself in her bloodstained terry cloth robe. Her wrist rested on a raised knee. A still-smoking automatic dangled from her hand.

"Are you all right?" Gio asked.

Katie didn't answer. Instead, she stared at the ground in front of her. Gio followed her gaze, moving around the foot of the bed.

In front of her lay a man, collapsed in a twisted heap, a bloody knife still clutched in his hand.

Gio covered the man with his own gun and brushed the knife away with his foot. The blade skittered and spun across the wooden floor. Then he reached for his radio.

"Adam-254, situation is Code Four here," he transmitted. "I need medics to this location." He hesitated, then added, "Two ambulances."

"Copy."

"And start a supervisor," he said. "This is an officer-involved shooting."

Behind him, Gio heard the stomping of heavy feet. Before him, he heard the rasping, gurgling breath of the downed suspect. He ignored both sounds. Instead, he stepped over the bent form and knelt in front of Katie. His uniform blocked her view of the attacker. Gio looked into Katie's eyes. He waited until their focus shifted and met his own.

"You did it," he told her softly. "You're okay."

Part V

I sit and savor that I'm alive
Abandon the world to die and thrive
Moment by black moment passes me by
Beneath a weeping sky.
Rebecca Battaglia

TWENTY-ONE

Detective John Tower stood on the fringe of the crime scene. He watched as Detectives Finch and Elias from Major Crimes worked the scene. The pair was an efficient tandem and he knew he shouldn't resent them for being inside the yellow tape, examining evidence and espousing theories. It was their job. Moreover, this was an officer-involved shooting, so it fell under the purview of Major Crimes. It wasn't their fault he was on the sidelines, so he shouldn't be pissed at them for it.

But he was.

He stood at the front of his car, sipping terrible convenience store coffee from a Styrofoam cup. The acid in the foul brew made his stomach gurgle in protest, but he ignored it. Instead, he watched the hustle and bustle of the crime scene. Watched Elias direct Diane from Forensics and other support personnel this way and that. Watched Finch's careful contemplation. He watched it all happen outside the residence and then he watched it all drift gradually inside as a careful, measured, recorded process.

A few minutes later, Ray Browning arrived. The compact, cocoa-skinned detective gave Tower a soft, sympathetic smile before ducking under the yellow crime scene tape.

Tower didn't smile back.

He knew he shouldn't resent Ray, either. But he did.

Lieutenant Crawford stood inside the crime scene perimeter, overseeing the activity but giving very little direction. Everyone knew their job, so little was necessary. He glanced over at Tower.

Even at the distance of forty yards or so, Tower could read the disgust plainly on the lieutenant's face.

Everyone knows their job, all right.

Tower held Crawford's gaze, refusing to look away.

And my job is to stand here and watch. To have it rubbed in my face.

Crawford stared back until one of the crime scene photographers approached a few moments later and asked him a question. He broke away and spoke with her. After that, he studiously ignored Tower.

"I had him," Tower whispered. "I *fucking* had him, and I blew it."

A dark green Lincoln pulled to a stop across the street. The Prosecuting Attorney, Patrick Hinote, exited along with Julie Avery. Both approached Tower. Hinote offered his hand. Tower shook it without much conviction.

Avery greeted him with a nod.

"Not how we'd have planned it, huh?" Hinote remarked, motioning toward the house.

Tower shook his head.

"What do you know?" the Prosecutor asked.

Tower took a sip of the brackish coffee. He eyed the lawyer for a moment, then said, "He attacked one of our officers. She shot him. They're both up at the hospital."

Hinote nodded, his expression calm and open. When Tower didn't continue, he asked, "I'm sure there's more to it than that, right?"

Tower motioned toward Crawford. "You can get it from him."

Hinote gave Tower a confused look, but said nothing. Without another word, he turned and headed toward the lieutenant.

Tower watched him go. Then he peeled off the plastic lid on his cup and dumped the remainder of his coffee onto the black asphalt of the street. Turning, he headed toward the car.

"Wait." Julie Avery's voice stopped him as he opened the driver's door.

He glanced over his shoulder at her. "What?"

Avery cleared her throat. "You said the officer was up at the hospital?"

"Yeah."

"Is he all right?"

"She," Tower corrected. "And I don't know."

"She? Who was it?"

"Katie MacLeod."

Avery's eyes widened slightly. "She was the decoy, right?"

Tower nodded.

"And he attacked her?"

"That's what I said."

Avery walked around the nose of his car and to the passenger side. She tried the door handle, but it was locked. "Open it," she instructed Tower.

"Why?"

"Because I need a ride to the hospital, that's why."

Tower regarded her for a moment, then nodded. He flipped the door lock switch. Avery opened the passenger door and got into the car without a word. Tower did the same. He started the car and drove away from the crime scene.

1442 hours

Beeps.

He heard beeps.

Not pleasant ones, either. No, these were insistent, shrill, accusatory beeps. He listened to the machine that made them, knowing in his rational mind that there was no emotion behind the monotonous sounds. But his rage wouldn't listen.

He heard his mother.

You are the reason my entire life has been wasted.

His father.

You little whore's son. You'll never be shit.

Maybe they were both right.

Beep... Beep... Beep.

He pushed the medication button in time with the beeps.

He wanted to go away.

He stared at the machine. He thought of how close he'd come to...to *becoming* something. Would his father have ever been proud? Would he admit who the better man was? Oh, he wouldn't show it, but if he found out his little Jeffie was the Rainy Day Killer, there'd have been a spark of pride that would've inevitably fired off in the old man's chest.

If the old man was still alive, that is.

A weak smile touched his lips.

Of course, if he was in hell, looking up, he'd have been proud, too.

But now what was he? A failure. Just like his mother said, like his father said. Even the kids in school, all those years ago, had been right. He was a broken failure, destined for prison. Still only the Rainy Day Rapist, a ridiculous name.

Motion flashed in the doorway. The dark blue of a police uniform swaggered toward him. The creak of leather seemed to dance with the beeping of his machine, with his mother's cruel tones, his father's harsh voice.

A leathery face appeared next to his. A closely cropped mustache seemed to be almost burned into the man's upper lip. The sour stench of coffee and cigarettes rolled off his tongue as he growled out his words.

"What the fuck are you smiling about, you piece of shit?"

Jeffrey forced his smile wider, a ball of spite beginning to grow in his belly.

The old cop smiled back, but his eyes were as cold as death. Jeffrey could see that even though the man was undoubtedly assigned to guard him, he'd much preferred to have throttled him. The hard eyes said it all.

"The doctor says one of MacLeod's bullets hit your spine," the cop whispered gruffly. "He says you might be a cripple."

A cripple? Somehow, the karma didn't surprise him. Why not? Everything else bad has happened to him. Why not that, too?

"I hope not," the cop said to him. "You know why?"

Some confusion overcame him. The beeps were getting fuzzier. Colors seemed to blur. He turned his heavy eyes to the cop's nametag.

M. Ridgeway, it read.

He looked back at M. Ridgeway's face. He blinked a long blink.

"Wuh-eye?" he slurred.

"Because," Ridgeway told him, "You're going to prison for a long time. And I want you to be able to feel what rape is like while you're there."

He blinked at Ridgeway, still confused for a moment. Then it dawned on him through the fog of the medication.

Of course.

He was a cop. So he hated him.

He understood.

But it wasn't his fault.

No. None of it was.

It was *hers.*

Katie's.

Bitches ruin everything, he thought. Then a soft, blessed darkness took him.

1502 hours

Katie's head rested on the hospital pillow. She wanted to reach back and fold it over for a little more support, but couldn't work up the motivation to do so. Everything hurt. Her left forearm throbbed dully. Her left hand seemed to have more of a stinging pain. Her shoulder shared the general, aching soreness which had settled over her entire body.

She imagined the real pain lay lurking below the light pain medication they'd given her. She'd refused anything stronger. She had vague recollections about bouncing red balls and the secrets of the universe from her previous trip, and no desire to experience those bizarre images again.

The doctor entered, trailed by a pair of interns. He glanced wordlessly at her chart for a moment, the spoke without looking up.

"How are we feeling?" he asked in a preoccupied, distant tone.

"Like hell," Katie answered truthfully.

"Mmmmmhhhhhhmmmm," the doctor replied, his eyes skipping over the chart. "Well, all in all, things look well." He handed the chart off to one of the interns, looking at Katie for the first time. He didn't smile. "There's really no reason to keep you any longer than overnight. Your cuts were deep, but clean. Luckily, no nerves were severed. The cuts stitched well, and scarring should be minimal. A couple of weeks of rest at home and you should be mostly recovered."

"Why am I staying overnight if I'm all stitched up?" Katie asked.

"Holcomb?" the doctor asked.

One of the interns, a rail thin kid with small spectacles stepped forward. As he spoke, his Adam's apple bounced up and down his throat. "Uh, your medical history shows a recent concussion. You were struck in the head during this assault, so there is an increased potential for another concussion."

"Excellent, Holcomb," the doctor said. He gestured to the second intern, a beefier man with soft eyes. "Bullock?"

Bullock glanced at the doctor, then at Katie. After a moment, he said, "He's right about the concussion. And your body's been through a lot today." He gave Katie a warm smile and touched her foot gently. "Anyway, keeping you overnight is just a precaution."

Katie nodded her understanding.

"Is there anything else you need?" the doctor asked her.

"No—uh, wait. Yeah. Can someone fold my pillow in half so that it's a little thicker?"

"I'll send in the nurse," the doctor said. Without further hesitation, he turned and strode out of the room, Holcomb in tow.

Bullock paused, then stepped up to the side of her bed. "Lean forward," he instructed.

With an effort, Katie did so. He folded over her pillow and replaced it. She sank backward onto it.

"Better?" he asked.

"A little."

"They're not much of a cushion, are they?" Bullock smiled.

"No."

"I'll ask the nurse to bring in another one," he told her.

"Thanks."

"Hope you feel better," he said with another smile, then turned and left.

Katie watched him go. As he exited the room, another head leaned in around the closing door. She recognized Tower immediately. He raised his eyebrows at her questioningly.

"Okay to come in?" he asked.

"Sure."

Tower swung the door open a little more and walked in. A redheaded woman in jeans and a green blouse trailed behind him. Tower saw Katie notice her and made an introduction.

"This is Julie Avery," he explained. "She works with the Prosecutor's Office as a victim advocate."

Katie gave her a guarded nod. Julie replied with a warm smile.

Tower stopped at the side of her bed. He seemed to be taking in all of the bandages and Katie's bruised and battered face.

"I look a mess, don't I?" Katie asked.

"No," Tower lied. "Just a little banged up, is all."

"The marks from that time on Mona Street are barely gone," Katie said, not sure if she was trying to joke or if she were feeling sorry for herself. "I've got bruises on my bruises."

Tower nodded, seemingly at a loss for words. Finally, he said, "Once word gets out that you can have visitors, you know there's going to be a parade of cops coming up here."

Katie shook her head. "Can you tell Radio that they want me to sleep or something? I don't want to see a bunch of people right now."

And I don't want to be seen looking like this. Like a victim.

"Sure," Tower said. "I'll take care of it."

"Thanks."

"Finch and Elias are going to want to talk to you, though."

"I know."

"But, uh, that can probably wait a few days."

"Good."

The two officers fell silent. Avery stood quietly next to Tower, saying nothing. Katie glanced at the woman, taking in her open expression and warm features. Empathy seemed to radiate from her. Katie imagined that made her very good at her job.

Avery caught her looking and smiled.

Katie cleared her throat and turned her gaze to Tower. "Can you tell me something?"

"Sure." He leaned forward expectantly.

"Did he die? Did I kill him?"

Tower looked at her for a moment, then shook his head slightly. "No," he said in a low voice. "He's at a different hospital. Sacred Heart, I think."

Katie nodded. She felt tears sting her eyes. Ashamed, she looked away.

"Are you all right?" Tower asked.

Katie let out a shuddering breath and wiped her tears away with her unbandaged hand. Confusing thoughts swirled through her head.

I don't know if I'm crying because I shot him or because I didn't kill him or because I wish I had.

"I'm fine," she said.

"Sorry," Tower muttered. "That was a stupid question."

Katie didn't answer. Another long silence ensued, this one more awkward. Eventually, Tower said, "Well, I just wanted to check in on you. If you need anything, give me a call."

"Okay."

Tower removed a business card from his jacket pocket and scrawled something on the back. He placed the card on the nightstand next to her bed. "That's my home phone on the back," he said. "Call anytime."

"Thanks," Katie whispered, her voice husky with tears. She desperately wanted to stop crying, but the goddamn tears just kept welling up in her eyes. Instead of wiping them from her cheeks, she avoided his gaze.

"I'll let Radio know about no visitors," Tower said. He turned to go.

Avery slid a card from her jeans pocket and placed it next to Tower's. "If you ever need to talk," she said quietly.

Katie didn't respond.

"I hope you feel better soon," Avery added. Then she turned to leave with Tower.

Katie lay still, listening to their departing footsteps. When the pair reached the door, Katie turned her head.

"Wait."

Tower looked over his shoulder at her, but it was Avery's gaze that she met. Katie took a shallow, wavering breath.

"Can...can you stay a while?" she asked Avery.

Avery nodded. "Of course." She returned to Katie's bedside.

Tower watched for a moment, then said, "I'll wait out here."

"Thanks," Avery said, without turning toward him.

Tower gave Katie a nod and left, closing the door behind him.

Avery stood next to Katie's bed. To Katie, she seemed patient, as if she were willing to wait a year for Katie to speak.

Katie licked her lips, wondering where to begin. The two women remained silent for a long minute while the monitor next to her bed beeped.

"There's something I want to tell you about," she finally said.

"Okay," Avery said.

"Not this," she said, motioning toward her bandages. "Something else. From a long time ago."

Avery reached out and touched Katie lightly on her hand. "We can talk about whatever you want," she said with a light squeeze.

Katie swallowed. She looked up into Julie Avery's warm eyes and nodded. "All right," she said. "All right."

2145 hours
Graveyard Shift

Connor O'Sullivan drove in silence while Battaglia looked out the window. The pair had been uncharacteristically quiet during the early part of the shift. Sully wondered if Battaglia was having issues at home or if, like himself, he was concerned about MacLeod.

"The El-Tee said she was going to be fine," he finally ventured.

"Huh?"

"MacLeod. Saylor said she'd be all right."

Battaglia nodded without turning from the window. "Good."

"Yeah," Sully echoed. "Good."

They drove a few more blocks in silence. Then Sully said, "I guess she nailed the guy four or five times. Probably crippled him."

"Good."

"She's a good shot."

"Yeah."

"Blasted the guy all around the groin area."

"That fits." Battaglia was silent for a moment, then added, "Sounds like she ten-ringed him like that rat under bridge."

Sully smiled. "Exactly."

Battaglia turned away from the window, a dark grin already fading from his face. "She's the bomb," he said. "MacLeod, I mean."

Sully nodded in agreement.

"Guy attacks her in her own house. In her bathrobe, for Christ's sake. But she still wins." Battaglia shook his head. "I guess you just never know when it's going to happen."

"When what's going to happen?" Sully asked, though he knew what his partner meant.

Battaglia stared out through the windshield, uncharacteristically deep in thought. "You never know what moment on this job will turn into *the* moment."

Sully raised his eyebrows, marveling at Battaglia's serious side. It didn't come out very often. Most of the time, he wondered if the man even had one.

"Adam-122?" the radio chirped.

Battaglia picked up the mike. "Go ahead."

"Disorderly person at 2114 E. Wellesley," the dispatcher recited. *"Refusing to leave the Tacos Plus restaurant."*

"See?" Battaglia said. "This could be the big one right here. You never know."

"Also," the dispatcher continued, *"the suspect is apparently wearing a clown suit."*

Sully and Battaglia looked at each other. A slow smile spread over each man's face.

"Or maybe not," Sully said.

Battaglia pushed the button on the mike. "Copy on the clown," he said.

"This call is a joke," Sully deadpanned.

Battaglia chuckled. He motioned toward the light controls. "We should run lights and siren."

"Oh, Lieutenant Hart would love that."

"Hell," Battaglia said, "it probably *is* Lieutenant Hart. This is probably his off duty hobby. Getting drunk, dressing in a clown suit and raising hell."

Sully let out a loud laugh.

"Oh, man," Battaglia said, shaking his head, "We were born to take this call."

Saturday, May 10th, 1996
0913 hours

Lieutenant Alan Hart sat at his desk. It being a Saturday, he was dressed casually in a pair of jeans and a neatly pressed collared shirt. The silence of his office was the same as it was every other day of the week, no change in his lonely existence.

He'd told his wife, Marianne, that he'd needed to run a couple of errands. That was true, he supposed, but he still ended up seated at his desk, whether by design or happenstance. He stared at the far wall, which was adorned with photographs of all River City police officers. Everyone was there, from the Chief of Police to the newest recruit in the Academy.

And I'm here to watch over them.

It's not like anyone else would. He saw the summary judgment that the Patrol Captain filed on Officer MacLeod's so-called accidental discharge. A cop lets a bullet fly in a public park, and all she gets is a written reprimand? All Hart saw there was a continuation of the century-old code of silence that has permeated and corrupted law enforcement for far too long. It was that same warped sense of loyalty that no doubt motivated the Chief to issue oral reprimands for O'Sullivan and Battaglia. Worse yet, he didn't even give that light punishment to Chisolm for his violations.

Clearly, the cops in River City believed they were above the law.

"They aren't," Hart muttered, turning a heavy, gold pen over in his hands.

And it was his job to watch over them, to make sure that they paid for their mistakes. The public deserved it. Justice demanded it.

He knew the cost. Ridicule. Hatred. Ostracism. It was a small price to pay to do the right thing.

The *River City Herald* lay open on his desk. The front page headline blared RAINY DAY RAPIST CAUGHT! He'd read the article. Normally critical of the police department, the editors allowed this story to positively praise the stalwart bravery of Officer Katie MacLeod. The only negative element of the story was a subtle jab at Detective John Tower for failing to identify the suspect before the attack. The close resemblance between the police sketch and the suspect's photograph made that failure seem like a particularly inept one.

Hart wasn't concerned so much with that. There had been other mistakes. He was sure of it. Those mistakes needed to be answered for. Not just with an oral or written reprimand, either. With suspensions. Maybe badges.

How high did the mistakes go? He knew the only way to find out was to investigate thoroughly.

Lieutenant Alan Hart fired up his computer. He opened his word processor program and began drafting a memorandum to send to the Chief.

He planned on getting to the bottom of things.

1113 hours

Chisolm set aside the newspaper after reading the article about Katie for a third time. The reporter rightfully made Katie out to be a hero, but he didn't like the dig against Tower. He knew the detective did the best job he could. Hell, if anyone was at fault, it was Chisolm.

Once again, he'd failed to be where he was needed.

Just like Mai. The image of the young prostitute was burned into his mind. Despite stopping two assaults on her, he couldn't save her in the end.

Hell, Bobby Ramirez, too. When a sniper took his best friend's life, had he done anything to prevent it?

No. He'd failed.

And, of course, there was Officer Karl Winter. He was a good man who died alone on the dark asphalt of a River City street. No help from Chisolm.

Other faces danced in front of his eyes. That kid he and Ramirez had teased mercilessly from the day he arrived in the unit until the day he hit a trip wire in the jungle. A young mother and her baby, on the run from an insane husband. That husband eventually hurt that little baby, didn't he?

Sylvia's knowing eyes came next. The image hovered before him, growing even more vivid when he closed his eyes against it.

All my ghosts are here today.

Thomas Chisolm clutched at his coffee cup, squeezing the porcelain in an effort to avoid going to the fridge for a drink.

1222 hours

Crawford turned onto Reott's street. He drove to the front of the captain's house, easing the car to a stop.

"Thanks for lunch," Reott said.

"My turn to buy," Crawford replied easily.

"So it was. But thanks, anyway."

"You're welcome."

Reott reached for the door.

"They're releasing MacLeod today," Crawford told him.

Reott paused. "Good. She's all right?"

Crawford shrugged. "A few good cuts. Some hard knocks. But I think she'll be fine."

"Good."

"Our rapist won't be out for another month. Maybe two," Crawford continued. "Tower already has his affidavit to the prosecutor. Hinote said he is going to charge him with all four rapes, plus the attacks on MacLeod. He doesn't believe he can win them all, but he figures he'll win enough of them to send the guy up for life, or close to it. And if he decides to plea instead, then he has plenty of charges to bargain away."

"Good," Reott repeated.

Crawford's eyes narrowed with concern. "You okay, Mike?"

Reott nodded. "I'm fine. Where are you headed from here?"

Crawford scowled. "Oh, the wife has us going out searching for antiques or some such shit." He eyed Reott more closely. "You sure you're okay?"

"Yeah," Reott answered. He slapped Crawford on the knee. "Thanks for lunch. And good work on this case."

Crawford snorted. "Good work? Hell, we got luckier than a falling drunk on this one."

Reott clenched his jaw, his penetrating gaze burning into Crawford's eyes. "You think that's luck? Him attacking one of our officers like that?"

Crawford returned his stare without faltering. "I don't think what happened to MacLeod was lucky at all," he said quietly. "All I'm saying is that we didn't do anything to catch him. We got lucky."

Reott took a deep breath and sighed. "Maybe so," he said. Then he opened the door and got out of the car. "See you Monday," he told Crawford as he closed the passenger door.

Crawford gave him a wave as he pulled away from the curb.

Reott made his way up his sidewalk, unlocked the door and went into the house. The slam of the door echoed throughout the emptiness of the home. Tossing his keys on the table, he walked directly into the kitchen and swung open a cupboard. Inside, two fancy bottles of seventeen year old Glengoyne single malt Scotch whisky stood waiting for him. He wrapped his fingers around the neck of one bottle and pulled it from the cupboard.

At the table, he poured himself a glass, neat. He stared down at the amber liquid for a while, then raised it to his lips and sipped. The burning smoothness coated his mouth and his throat, before emanating outward from his belly.

Lucky.

Crawford's words burned in his ears. He didn't believe in luck. He believed in choices. And it was a series of choices that brought things to a head. A series of choices that put one of his officers in the hospital.

His choices.

Captain Michael Reott took another sip of the whisky.

"Damn fine scotch," he said aloud. He allowed himself a wry chuckle, remembering Crawford's theories on pay scale.

Maybe the lieutenant had been right about that.

But lucky?

Reott was pretty sure that wasn't a word he'd use.

1658 hours

Katie MacLeod glanced to her left. Kyle, the large, bespectacled man in the driver's seat remained focused through the windshield wipers and the rain upon the road ahead.

"Thanks again for the ride," she said, her voice still a little groggy.

"No problem," the hospital security officer said. "It's an honor."

Katie looked away. She remembered what Stef had gone through after his gun battle with the Scarface robber. There'd been a mixture of hero worship and contempt from the different members of the department. She wasn't entirely sure which he'd been more uncomfortable with, but she knew that he'd struggled with both. She didn't particularly want to go through that.

I only did what I had to do.

An image of her gun sight trained on the back of the rapist's head flashed through her mind.

"Is this it?" Kyle asked her, pointing as they rolled up the street.

Katie followed his gesture toward her familiar brick house. Somehow, in the windy, rainy darkness of the night, it didn't seem as welcoming as it once had. Yellow crime scene tape still hung from the screen door, flapping in the wind.

Kyle put the car into park. "Here we are."

Katie paused. Suddenly, she didn't want to go inside. She knew that he wasn't there. Neither was Phil, for that matter. Those demons might not be vanquished, but after talking with Julie Avery, she felt like maybe they would be eventually.

But not yet.

In the meantime, she wasn't so sure she wanted to be alone. A strange need swept over her and she thought about calling Kopriva. Maybe he would understand.

"Are you okay?" Kyle asked.

Katie turned toward him. "Yes," she answered. Then, "No. Not really."

Kyle gave her a confused look.

"Can you take me to a pay phone?" Katie asked. "I think I want to go somewhere else instead."

1704 hours

Stefan Kopriva sat at his kitchen table, staring down at his hands. His knuckles pressed against the cool bottle of beer in front of him. A small black and white television flickered on the table. The mindless jingle about car insurance did little to keep his attention.

He glanced up and around at the small downtown apartment. The already narrow walls seemed to close in on him. His tiny kitchen lay only a few feet from the living room, which doubled as a bedroom when he remembered to unfold the bed inside the couch. Right now, a twisted pile of blankets lay in the corner of the ratty couch. Empty beer bottles were strewn across the rickety, stained coffee table.

Brave, dead soldiers, he thought mockingly. *They served their city well.*

"Better than I did," he muttered, and lifted the bottle of beer to his lips.

He wondered in passing if he ought to consider taking up smoking. A few cigarettes might prove an interesting way to make the time pass. But he rejected the idea. He had precious little in the way of money as it was, and he much preferred the beer. And, of course, the pills that the nice doctor at the free clinic gave him for his arm and his knee.

"Too bad he can't prescribe something for my heart," Kopriva told the woman on television who was hawking insurance in a bright red dress.

Sadness awash in self-pity flooded through him, coupled with some shame. The idea of sitting around his tiny apartment smoking cigarettes all day made him think of convicts in prison. The irony that he used to be the instrument that put men behind those walls was not lost upon him

He took another drink. An image of a child's still body in a half-empty body bag flashed through his mind.

"Fuck," he muttered. He took another drink and glanced at the cheap Casio watch on the table next to him. One hour and eleven minutes. He had one hour and eleven minutes before he was supposed to take another pain pill.

The commercial dropped off suddenly. In the pause between the advertisement and the broadcast show, the TV screen went black. Kopriva saw his own disheveled image on the dark glass.

"You look like shit," he said, raising the beer in mock salute, then draining the bottle.

The screen lit up with the station's logo, accompanied by intro music for the news. Kopriva rose and went to the small brown fridge that he was pretty sure the landlord had bought from a Motel 6 going-out-of-business sale. Inside, three more bottles of beer stood tall and ready.

"We need some reinforcements," he said. "And we might just have to move to cans." He removed one bottle and twisted off the cap. "But what the hell. Not everyone can be a Marine. Not everyone can be a hero."

Especially me.

He stumbled back to the kitchen table and settled into the chair just as the music faded and the news anchor affected a serious expression.

"A reign of terror is over tonight in River City," he said. "Police have the Rainy Day Rapist in custody. For more, we go to Shawna Matheson, live at Sacred Heart Medical Center. Shawna?"

The screen cut to the perfectly coifed Shawna Matheson. Kopriva's lip curled at the sight of her. She'd been on the forefront of reporting the Amy Dugger story last year. Chronicling his mistake and the tragedy that followed.

"You bitch," he muttered at the reporter.

"Thank you, Jack," Shawna said in polished tones. "I'm here at Sacred Heart Hospital, where accused rapist Jeffrey Allen

Goodkind is being treated for gunshot wounds he received yesterday during his apprehension."

A small gust of wind pushed Shawna's hair into her face. Without missing a beat, she raised her hand and brushed it aside, continuing. "Apparently police believe Mr. Goodkind is responsible for the recent spree of violent rapes to rock River City's north side. Dubbed 'The Rainy Day Rapist' by this reporter over three weeks ago, this suspect is responsible for attacking four different women since March of this year. Now, he is in custody."

The camera switched to a photograph of a police sketch.

"This is a sketch police released of the suspect," Shawna said, "and this is Mr. Goodkind."

The camera cut to a professional photograph of a man that closely resembled the sketch. Kopriva immediately knew the man was guilty, simply by the way the face in the picture bore a forced smile.

"Instincts are still good," he mumbled, a little rueful.

"What's most interesting about this story," Shawna continued, "is how Mr. Goodkind was apprehended. Police almost caught him during a sting operation in April, but he was able to escape. Instead, he was captured tonight at the residence of the very same police decoy that he attacked during that sting operation."

A picture of Katie MacLeod filled the screen.

Kopriva's eyes flew open in surprise. He leaned forward, turning up the volume of the tiny television.

"Officer Kathleen MacLeod, a five year veteran of the River City Police department, was attacked in her home, allegedly by Mr. Goodkind. She was injured, though police sources say she is recovering from her wounds at a different hospital. Officer MacLeod shot the intruder several times before police arrived to take him into custody."

"Jesus," Kopriva breathed.

The broadcast returned to a very serious Shawna Matheson. "It is unclear what Mr. Goodkind's intentions were when he allegedly assaulted Officer MacLeod. What is clear is that people in River City can rest a little easier tonight." She paused a beat, then finished gravely, "For Channel 5 Action News, I'm Shawna Matheson."

Kopriva leaned back in his chair and looked at the ceiling. He felt tears well up in his eyes and roll down his temples while he stared up at the low ceiling.

"I'm sorry, Katie," he whispered huskily. "I'm a selfish bastard, and I'm sorry."

He continued to stare up at the ceiling for a long while, his hand wrapped firmly around the cold bottle on the table in front of him.

1712 hours

Thomas Chisolm sat in his dark living room, staring at the photographs on the wall. He'd surrendered to his ghosts, letting them run free throughout his consciousness. They battered through his feeble defenses, trampling down any mild excuses he might have been working up that even he didn't believe.

His first beer of the evening sat on the coffee table, half full.

Who would it be tonight?

Mai?... Bobby?... Karl?... Sylvia?

Or would someone else step up to remind him where and how he'd failed to save them? It wasn't like the list wasn't long enough.

As if on cue, his telephone rang. He considered not answering it, but the shrill tones annoyed him enough to pluck the receiver off the cradle and bark a hello into the mouthpiece.

"Tom?" a female voice came over the line, with vehicle traffic in the background.

"Yeah?" he answered.

"It's Katie."

Chisolm clenched his jaw and nodded. This was fitting. It was right. She should let him have it for not being there when she needed him.

"Tom?"

"I'm here," he said evenly.

"Oh." She paused. "Listen, I'm out of the hospital and...well, I really don't want to go home just yet. I was wondering if I could come by your place?"

It was Chisolm's turn to pause. Then he answered, "Of course."

"Thanks," Katie said, relief plain in her voice.

Chisolm gave her the address.

"All right," she said. "I'm about five minutes away."

Chisolm hung up the phone. He moved around the house, turning on several lights. Then he pulled some bedding from the hall closet and plopped it down on the couch. He stripped his own bed and re-made it with clean sheets. He was just tucking the top blanket into the foot of the mattress when he heard the knock at his front door.

Katie smiled tiredly at him when he swung open the door.

"Come on in," he said.

"Thanks," Katie said, stepping inside. She slid off her jacket and handed it to him. He noticed she moved a little woodenly, as if her entire body were sore and not just her direct wounds. In addition to the smell of rain, the unmistakable antiseptic odor of a hospital still clung to her, filling his nostrils as she passed by him.

"Please," he said, motioning toward the couch, "have a seat."

Katie lowered herself gratefully onto the cushion, letting out a sigh as she did so. "It feels so good to be out of the hospital."

"I'll bet." Chisolm hung her coat and cleared his throat. "You want something to drink? A beer or...?"

"Some water would be great."

Chisolm retrieved a few ice cubes from the freezer and filled a glass with tap water. In the living room, he set it in front of Katie. He sat down in the chair across from her. She smiled her gratitude, raised the glass and took a sip.

The two sat in silence for a few moments. Katie leaned back on the couch with another sigh. "I'm so tired," she croaked in a drowsy tone, suppressing a yawn. "I feel like I've been up for a month of graveyard shifts."

"You can have my bed," Chisolm said, motioning toward the bedroom. "I changed the sheets for you."

Katie reached out and took hold of one of the blankets on the couch with her hand. "Oh, this'll be fine, Tom. Really."

"You sure?"

Katie nodded tiredly, pulling the blanket toward her and kicking off her shoes.

Chisolm rose from his seat. He picked up one of the pillows and tucked it in the corner of the couch.

Katie smiled at him as she nestled her head into the pillow. "Mmmmm, thanks."

Chisolm helped spread the blanket over the top of her. Once she was covered, he kissed her lightly on the top of her head.

"You did damn good, Katie," his whispered into her ear.

"Thanks," she replied, her voice already thick with sleep.

A lump rose in Chisolm's throat. "I'm sorry I wasn't there for you."

Katie took in a deep breath and let out a peaceful sigh. "You're here for me now, right?"

"Yeah."

"That's all I need, Tom. I just need you..." she yawned into her shoulder, then finished, "...I just need you to be a friend."

Chisolm smiled slightly. "I can do that."

"Then that's all I need."

He rose and turned off the living room lamp for her. Then he sat down in the chair across from her in the dim light of the living room. Outside, the heavy rain battered the windows of his house. He picked up his bottle of beer and took a sip, looking at her curled form on his couch. She wasn't asking to be saved. Just for him to be her friend. To watch over her tonight.

I can do that.

Also by Frank Zafiro

UNDER A RAGING MOON

HEROES OFTEN FAIL

Coming March 2011

Sample The Next
River City Crime Novel!

AND EVERY MAN
HAS TO DIE

Russian gangs are taking over the River City underworld. The men and women of the police department are the last line of defense against these former Soviet bloc criminals. Both groups will soon learn how far the other will go to win this battle. They'll learn that the price of victory can be high. They'll learn that sometimes blood flows... *And Every Man Has to Die.*

ONE

Friday July 11th, 1998
2214 Hours
Graveyard Shift

"*Adam-122, on scene*," chirped Officer Katie MacLeod's radio.

Adam-122 was the call sign for Officers Battaglia and O'Sullivan. Despite the joking demeanor both of them always seemed to put on display, Katie was glad they were responding with her. The call came in as a violent domestic dispute in apartment #7 of the Delilah Apartments. The neighbor who called it in reported crashing noises and screaming from inside the apartment. If there was a scrap going on, it'd be nice to have Sully and Batts at her side.

Katie guided the patrol cruiser along the curb, gliding to a stop. She allowed herself a quick look at the small four-inch by four-inch computer display in the console area. The devices were fairly new to the River City Police Department, though she knew they'd been in cars down in L.A. for almost a decade. The amber screen was so small that she had to page down twice to read the entire description of the call, including which apartment the witness lived in. Then she reached for her own microphone.

"Adam-116, on scene."

"*Copy, Adam-116.*"

Katie glanced around and didn't see another cruiser. Then she remembered that the Delilah Apartments had a rear entry, too. Battaglia and O'Sullivan probably parked behind.

Katie grabbed her PR-24 side-handle baton and stepped out of the vehicle. Out of habit, she closed the door silently, easing it shut instead of slamming it. She slid the heavy metal baton into the ring on her belt and made her way to the front door. The heavy sway and solid tap of the baton against her side gave her confidence. Most smaller officers seemed to prefer the straight wooden baton, but Katie stuck with the larger side-handle. While some complained that it was unwieldy, she found that she liked the heft. More than that, it got the job done.

The front entrance to the apartment complex was supposed to be secure, but someone had used a softball-sized rock to prop the door open. Probably Sully. He was more thoughtful than Batts. Grateful, Katie pushed the door open further and stepped inside. A large, steep staircase awaited her on the left. On the right was a narrow hallway. A sign indicated that apartments one through five were on the ground floor. Six through ten resided upstairs on the second floor. The third floor was home to eleven through fifteen.

Katie started up the stairs toward number seven.

"Adam-122, start medics." The slight elevation in Battaglia's voice came through, even over the radio. *"I've got a conscious female, suffering from blows to the head."*

"Copy. Is she breathing?"

"I just said she's conscious, didn't I!"

"Copy, but Medics need to know—"

The harsh buzz of multiple radio transmissions interrupted her.

"Other unit?" the dispatcher asked.

"-22," O'Sullivan said quickly, *"the neighbor says the suspect is probably still in the building. He just left less than thirty seconds ago."*

Katie quickened her steps as she neared the top of the steep staircase.

"Description?"

"He's a white male," O'Sullivan answered, *"large build, wearing a white tank top."*

Katie reached the top of the stairs. She started to turn the corner to her left when a mountain in a sleeveless, white tank top barreled toward her. As soon as his chest brushed up against her, he immediately stopped short.

The man gave Katie an appraising look. She stared back at him resolutely. "Police," she said in a firm voice, pointing at the top stair. "You need to have a seat right there."

He didn't comply. Instead, he stood staring at her with dark, flat eyes. Katie could see the gears working inside his mind and immediately sensed she didn't have much time. Wrapping her left hand on her side-handle, she depressed her radio mike with her right.

"Adam-116, I've got him here on the stairs. He's –"

The man burst forward. He barreled into Katie, driving her backward. Panic flared in her stomach as she lost her balance, falling to the rear. The man's huge hands clutched at her shoulders and upper arms, pulling her to the ground with him. The two tumbled down the narrow stairs in a heap. As they bounced and jostled awkwardly, Katie's equipment on her belt dug into her sides, caught on the railing, twisted on her belt. Her baton momentarily caught in the fold of her knee, causing a twinge of pain.

Suddenly, a shot of piercing pain blazed through Katie's left ankle. She imagined a piece of the banister must have shattered and been jabbed through the leather of her boot and into her flesh. She tried to suppress a cry, but could only dampen it to a painful grunt.

The disorienting roll down the stairs ended as the pair flopped into the entryway. Katie landed on her back with his weight on top of her. The bullet-resistant vest softened the sharpness of her landing, but did nothing to blunt the force. Her breath whooshed out as her lungs collapsed. Frantically, she struggled for breath, her mind whirring.

Where's backup?

What's my next move?

Why can't I breathe?

The large man let out a long, ragged grunt and pushed himself up. The release of weight from her chest provided some relief, but she still gasped and labored to fill her lungs. The sickening feeling of being unable to breathe began to fade as sweet oxygen trickled in.

The man got his knees under him and started to rise. His head turned left and right, searching for an escape. Katie's hand flashed out, clutching his wrist.

"You're under arrest!" she tried to say, but could only wheeze out the final syllable.

His gaze snapped back to Katie. He stared at her a moment, his flat countenance revealing nothing. Katie took advantage of his hesitation to draw a shallow breath. Then she repeated, "You're under arrest. Stop resisting."

She felt a momentary sense of the ridiculous, uttering those words while lying on her back beneath his powerful frame. An image of the defiant mouse firing a middle finger at the descending eagle flashed through her mind.

"*Nyet*," the man grunted. He jerked his arm, breaking Katie's grasp on his wrist.

Katie drove her left knee upward with as much force as she could muster, slamming into his groin. His eyes bulged in surprised pain. The collision sent throbbing waves of pain down her leg to her injured ankle. She did her best to ignore it.

Reaching up, Katie cupped his chin in her right palm. With her other hand, she tried to find a grip on the hair at the back of his head. The short military haircut allowed her no purchase, so she settled for pressing her palm against the rear of his skull and corkscrewing. This forced the man's head down toward the floor beside Katie. His large form twisted slowly, then fell like a giant redwood. Katie imagined the entire move took almost an hour, though she knew that it had been perhaps a second.

That single second seemed to be enough time for the massive man to recover his senses after the blow to his groin. He drew back his left hand and threw a ham-sized fist at Katie's head. Instinctively, she tucked her chin and pulled up her shoulder. The blow land square on her shoulder joint. Pain reverberated through her arm and chest. She let out a small cry of pain and anger.

He smiled and drew back his arm again.

Tucking her shoulder had caused her to lose her position of modest control on his chin, so she abandoned that grappling move altogether. Instead, she pulled back both arms to defend against the punch. She took the blow on the meaty part of her forearm.

Katie bit back a yelp. Without hesitating, she rolled away from the man, giving herself some distance. The roll was awkward as she bumped and clumped over the gear on her belt. As soon as she was facing him again, she pushed up to her knees.

He stood, rising up like a grizzly bear in front. Cold anger flashed in his eyes. He muttered something in guttural Russian. She didn't know what the words meant, but she understood the sentiment.

Katie dropped her hand onto her radio. Her thumb sought out the small, depressed red button that would tell every cop in the city she needed immediate help. Before she could find it, he took a step forward.

Katie rose to her feet to meet him. As soon as she put weight on her left foot, a flood of pain thundered up her leg. She shifted her weight and struggled to remain standing.

A cruel smile formed on his lips as he moved toward her. His fists hung at his sides, clenched into massive, tight balls.

Katie felt strangely calm. She knew what she had to do. This guy was a wife-beater. He was a big man who thought he was indestructible. He was double her size and strength. She was going to have to shoot him. Or at least demonstrate that she was willing to do so.

She reached for her pistol, but her hand clutched at nothing. Her fingers searched wildly for a moment before she realized that her holster was empty.

Panic flared in the pit of her stomach. Before she could piece together what might have happened to her gun, the man was upon her. Instead of punching her, he barked out a short laugh and said something derisive in Russian. His palms exploded toward her, catching her full in the chest. The force of the push drove her backward into a row of metal mailboxes along the wall. Something clipped her on the back of the head. She felt a trickle hot blood ooze out of the cut.

No gun.

What now?

He started toward her again, that same expression of cold anger and utter arrogance beaming out at her. She could read his thoughts in his icy eyes. He thought she was nothing more than something to toy with now. Someone to express his dominance over, just like he'd probably been doing with whatever woman was upstairs for however many years. The same kind of guy who didn't think she could do her job because she was a woman.

Katie set her jaw.

"Fuck you," she whispered, sliding her baton out of its holder and pulling it into a ready position.

He paused for a moment, watching as she brandished the metal tube. The smile on his lips spread, exposing his square, yellow teeth. "Fuck me?" he asked, his accent thick. He pointed at the baton. "I fuck you with that, *suka*."

"You're under arrest," Katie repeated grimly.

He let out another short, barking laugh and started toward her again. He offered no caution, no defense. Arrogant confidence accentuated his every motion.

Katie loaded her weight on her good leg, blading her body slightly. She held the baton by the side handle with her right hand, wrapping her left hand around the shaft and cocking it near her body. She drew in a deep breath and waited.

When he was within range, he lashed out suddenly with a hard right. Katie was prepared, though. She launched straight forward, putting every ounce of strength into her attack in an all-or-nothing gambit. She propelled forward, driving the tip of the baton directly toward his solar plexus, every bit of her weight behind the blow. His huge fist grazed past her ear as she slipped inside his range.

A moment later, the baton struck. All of her energy combined with his forward motion to seemingly impale him upon the baton. He let out a cry of pain, surprise and anger. His sour, harsh breath washed over her as both of them toppled to the ground.

This time, Katie landed on top. Immediately, she scrambled up his body until she knelt straddling his chest. She slammed the tip of the baton into the floor next to his throat, then lowered the baton across his throat. She stopped short of applying anything more than token pressure. Her eyes blazed into his.

"You make one more move and I will crush your throat," she growled at him. "You'll choke to death on your own blood. You hear me?"

He stared back at her, saying nothing.

She nudged his throat slightly, causing him to wince. "Do you understand?" she said, raising her voice.

He gave her a short nod.

"Good," she said. "Now put your hands straight out to the side. Slowly."

The man moved his arms in a slow motion until they were in position.

"Turn your palms to the ground," Katie ordered, staring into his eyes, but watching his hands in her peripheral vision.

Slowly, deliberately, he rolled his wrists until his palms were on floor.

"Good," Katie said again. "Now just lay there and don't move."

As if on cue, Katie heard the thundering sound of heavy boots on the stairway.

"MacLeod!" a male voice called out.

"Down here!" Katie yelled back.

The tramping boots came closer. A moment later, Sully reached the landing. He pulled up short for a moment, taking in the scene.

"Jesus," he whispered, then stepped forward and immobilized one of the suspect's arms at the elbow and wrist, using his knee and one hand.

A moment later, Battaglia appeared at the bottom of the stairs. He took one look at the scene, whispered, "Jesus," and then moved quickly to the other arm. "You cuff," he told Sully.

Katie kept her baton in place as Sully retrieved his cuffs from his belt, even though she knew that if the man chose to fight now, she would never use such a desperate technique. Not with Sully and Batts here. But, before, when she'd been alone...

The metallic sound of ratcheting cuffs broke into her thoughts. "Got him, Katie," Sully said as he secured the suspect's wrist. "You can move."

Katie released her dominant position, then slid off the suspect to her own right side. The adrenaline that had sustained her just thirty seconds ago was already beginning to fade. She could feel the warm sticky blood in her hair. Her shoulder and arm throbbed with each pulsing beat of her heart. But it was the cold, cutting pain that lanced upward from her ankle worried her the most.

She slid backward until she backed into the wall, this time below the mailboxes. Dimly aware of a second set of ratcheting sounds while the other two officers took her attacker into custody, she set her baton on the floor, reached down and pulled up her uniform pant leg. She fully expected to see a ragged cut, but was surprised that the boot remained intact. No cut.

Katie stared for a moment, then realized that if the cutting hadn't occurred *out*side the boot, then the injury was all *in*side the boot. Which meant –

"You all right?" Sully's voice pierced her realization.

Katie glanced up at him. "What?"

"I said, are you all right?" Sully repeated, his face darkening with concern.

Katie swallowed and nodded. "I'm fine."

Sully gave her an appraising look, his eyes taking her condition in more completely. He opened his mouth to speak, but Katie cut him off.

"Just stuff him," she said, her voice sharp. "We'll talk after."

Sully's eyes widened slightly at her tone, but then he nodded in understanding.

"Let's go, asshole," Battaglia said, standing the suspect up. Sully took his other arm and together, they escorted him down the narrow hallway and out the rear door.

Katie let out a long sigh and looked down at her trembling hands. She knew that they'd have to walk him to the car in the rear, search him and put him in the back seat. That gave her about two minutes. Two minutes to get her act together.

She forced herself to her feet, leaning heavily on her right leg. She half-hopped, half-shuffled toward the stairs, her eyes scanning the dimly lit landing. When she didn't see anything, she moved to the bottom of the stairs and peered upward. Her eyes scanned each step, but she saw nothing.

Katie pulled her small backup flashlight from her belt and flicked it on. She bathed every step with the wavering light, but there was still no sign of her gun. She turned and swept the light beam slowly around the landing. Her heart began to pound again, a different brand of fear growing in the pit of her stomach.

Any cop that loses her gun –

Then she saw it, tucked into the corner of the landing. It must have been torn from her holster as the two of them were tumbling down the stairs, then skittered across the landing into the corner.

Katie limped heavily to the corner, reached down and retrieved the pistol. A quick examination revealed no damage. She slid into her holster with relief, then shuffled back to the foot of the stairs. The throbbing in her ankle now dwarfed the pain in her shoulder. She eased herself onto the third stair from the bottom and straightened her injured leg.

Waiting, Katie took several deep breaths to calm herself. Even so, her hands still trembled with the after-wash of adrenaline. She felt like she wanted to cry. She wanted to scream in anger. Sink into a warm bath. Instead, she sat and waited.

A short time later, Sully appeared again. "He's in the back of our patrol car," he reported. "Now, are you okay?"

Katie swallowed. "I'm a little hurt. Did you get probable cause to arrest him up there at the apartment?"

Sully shrugged. "Close enough. I'll need to finish my interview with the neighbor. The wife has a shiner and a split lip, but she's not saying anything."

"Well," Katie said, "you can add assault on a law enforcement officer to whatever other charges you end up with."

Sully's eyebrows went up. "He hurt you?"

Katie nodded.

"Bad?"

She shrugged. The motion caused her to wince in pain from her shoulder. "Bad enough," she said, trying to keep it together. "I probably need to see a doctor, anyway."

"What happened?"

"I think I broke my ankle when we fell down the stairs."

Sully looked up at the steep, narrow staircase and whistled. "I can see that happening easily enough. What else? Do you need anything?"

Katie took another deep breath. "I could use a ride to the hospital," she half-joked.

"I'll call an ambulance," Sully said.

"I don't know if that's necess—"

Sully raised his radio to his mouth. "Adam-122, I need an RA here for an injured officer. Conscious and breathing. Possible broken ankle."

"Copy."

"And start me a supervisor," Sully added.

"Copy."

Katie scowled. "Thanks, Sully. Now the whole world knows."

He shrugged. "Everyone on the job is going to find out that you kicked the shit out of a guy three times your size anyway, MacLeod. So what's the big deal?"

"The big deal is, I'm hurt. I don't want everyone to know that."

"Why?"

She didn't answer the question. He wouldn't understand, anyway. Instead, she said, "It's not just cops, bonehead. Everyone with a scanner knows, too."

Sully shrugged. "I still don't see—"

"The asshole in the back of your car knows, too." Tears rose in her eyes. She used the back of her hand to brush them away with annoyance. "I don't want him knowing he hurt me, all right?"

"Okay," Sully said.

"I mean, I know he's going to find out eventually, once we charge him and everything," Katie said, her words tumbling out. "He'll see the report and we'll go to court and all that. But I don't want him to know *now*. I don't want him to know how close –"

Sully reached out and rested his hand on her left shoulder. "It's okay. I understand."

Katie looked up and met his gaze. "Do you?"

Sully grinned and shrugged. "Kinda. But not really."

Katie smiled through her tears. "You're an asshole, Sully."

"Aye, lass," he whispered in his faux brogue. "But don't worry about it. The dude in our car isn't listening to anything except country music right now." Laughter glinted in his eyes. "Cranked up country music, actually, since he looked like the heavy metal type."

Katie let out a small chuckle. "All right. Good enough."

Sully squeezed her shoulder gently. Then he raised his radio to his mouth again. "Adam-122 to Officer Battaglia."

"Go ahead," replied Battaglia. Katie heard a snatch of a twanging guitar in the background.

"Go ahead and transport to jail," Sully transmitted. "I'll stay here and finish up."

"Copy."

Sully slid his radio back onto his belt. "He'll be long gone before the ambulance gets here," he told her.

"Thanks," Katie said. Slight nausea crept into her stomach as the adrenaline faded further. She swallowed heavily.

Sully chuckled and shook his head. "Katie MacLeod, I've gotta hand it to ya. You are the bomb, lass."

Katie managed a weak smile, but said nothing.

Together, they waited for the Sergeant Shen and the ambulance.

2217 hours

Valeriy Alexandrovich Romanov stood in the enclosed bus stop, smoking. He watched what he thought of as something akin to a street opera performance at the apartment complex across the street...

Read the rest of *And Every Man Has To Die*!

About the Author

Frank became a police officer in 1993. During his career, he has served as a patrol officer, corporal, detective (his favorite job), sergeant, lieutenant, and captain. He has written and taught courses in Report Writing and Sexual Assault Investigation at the Basic Law Enforcement Academy. He has also written several college courses in police subject matter.

Many of Frank's stories take place in the fictional setting of River City, a mid-sized city in Eastern Washington, with recurring characters. His first River City novel, *Under A Raging Moon*, was originally published in 2006. The second, *Heroes Often Fail*, was originally published in 2007.

Over fifty of his short stories have been published in ten different anthologies, as well as print and online magazines. His story "Good Shepherd" was a finalist for the 2006 Derringer Award. In 2007, his story "The Worst Door" was a finalist for this same award. Most recently, his story "Dead Even" was a finalist for the 2009 Derringer Award.

In addition to writing, Frank is an avid hockey player and a tortured guitarist. His wife, Kristi, and his three children are about the only folks who will watch him do either activity.